ERIC GOEBELBECKER

SHADOWS

OF THE

PAST

THE GREAT WAR OF THE
WORLDS BOOK #1

Trick of the Tale LLC

25 Veterans Plaza #5279

Bergenfield, NJ 07621-9998

For Nanasdaddy

FOREWORD

The Great War of the Worlds stories are set in a universe where H.G. Wells's War of the Worlds happened.

In 1894, aliens crashed to Earth in spacecraft that operated like meteorites. They attacked us with fearsome weapons like Black Smoke, a chemical weapon and heat rays that can melt steel in a few seconds. Then, they built processing centers and used humans for food.

But the attack ended quickly because the Martians, if that was where they really came from, weren't prepared to deal with Earth's microbes and died from disease.

What happened after the attack? What did humanity do with the technology the Martians left behind?

If you are unable to find the truth right where you are,
where else do you expect to find it?

DOGEN

1

Emil launched himself out of the trench and over the parapet. His heart pounded as he hurled himself down-range toward danger. *Find the enemy gunners and kill them.* Those were his orders. *Kill the other men who don't want to be here any more than you do.*

One hundred fifteen . . . one hundred fourteen . . . one hundred thirteen . . .

He stayed low as he scanned for cover. Fritz Seith pulled away as he ran to Emil's left. Fritz always outran Emil, a natural forward to Emil's midfielder back in their school days. Knots of barbed wire forced both men into a serpentine path. There were still blotches of vegetation scattered between the wire, and less erosion than one would expect considering the rain of the past two days.

This place had been someone's livelihood. A few weeks ago, it had fed a family. Soon, it would be an abattoir. And for the third time in a couple of weeks, Emil was leading an advance through hastily abandoned Belgian positions.

One hundred ten . . . one hundred nine . . . one hundred eight . . .

He threw himself to the ground and low-crawled behind a

small berm sitting near an X-shaped barbed wire entanglement. The pounding in his ears slowed as he caught his breath, and he remembered to keep his head down to hide. Ahead, Fritz hurled himself to the ground, face down, almost as if he had read Emil's mind.

Rotting asparagus stalks jutted out from one side of the berm. Its leaves drooped, as if mourning the loss of their home. Emil held his breath, raised his head, and looked for a place to go next.

Ninety-four . . . ninety-three . . . ninety-two . . .

In ninety seconds, the rest of the company would charge. Emil and Fritz needed to get as close as they could to the Belgian trench and kill their machine gunners before they could fire on the Third Company.

Unteroffizier Oberacker always chose Emil and Fritz for this job because they were the smallest and fastest, and because they worked best together. But that didn't mean Emil had ever gotten used to it.

The count took over. It was something for Emil to focus on, instead of what he had to do.

Eighty-six . . . eighty-seven . . . eighty-five . . .

Emil rolled to his right, jumped up to his feet, and ran to another berm, this one barely tall enough to conceal him. Fritz found another one 200 meters away.

Eighty . . . seventy-nine . . . seventy-eight . . .

The sun was high enough to hang behind the enemy positions to the east, interfering with visibility. The German Army was attacking into the rising sun—a bold move. But they were rolling over the Belgians so easily that the officers didn't think they would lose.

The sun cut through the morning chill, but no-man's-land remained a cold and muddy shambles. Emil's knees sank into the ground as he peered over the berm and spotted the glint of a machine gunner's weapon. Either no one had shown him how to dull the metal with mud and oil, or he was as sloppy as this field. Emil scowled and brought himself back to the count.

Seventy-six . . . seventy-five . . .

It was a safe bet that the gunner was barely eighteen, his life dominated by schoolwork and schoolgirls a few months ago.

Emil scanned the line to either side of the shining enemy gun. There must have been at least two more gunners to the south.

He rolled to his left and stopped. No response. Staying in a crouch, he advanced to a thick entanglement of wire twenty-five meters downrange. Fritz appeared and started toward the next bit of cover in front of him.

Seventy-three . . . seventy-two . . .

The whistle blew.

They were sending the rest of the regiment in early? But Emil and Fritz hadn't taken out any gunners yet. The Belgians would cut their men to pieces.

The enemy gunners sprang to life. Emil dove back behind the wire, took a deep breath, poked his head around, and saw Fritz lying face down in the mud. Bile rose in Emil's throat. Fritz hadn't expected the early whistle, either, so he hadn't been behind cover. Emil jumped up, sighted the muzzle flash, fired, and dropped to his stomach. Behind him, the rest of the platoon advanced. Rounds flew over his head from both sides.

Fritz shifted, struggled to his hands and knees, and scooted forward to the nearest berm. Emil breathed a sigh of relief.

He jumped up again and fired another round toward the enemy's position. No response. He could still hear the other gunners firing, but the advancing men kept them busy. Maybe the gunner was already dead or had fled. Emil ran in a crouch and reached Fritz at a full trot, nearly landing on his face as he reached him.

"Are you okay?" Emil gasped, wiping mud from his chin.

"Yeah, got lucky," Fritz said, smiling. He held up a fold of fabric in his trousers, showing two perfectly aligned holes, and laughed. "Through and through!"

Emil dropped his head down toward the mud again, sighing in relief. He'd known Fritz since they'd been kids, playing soccer back in Euleheim. Losing his best friend here, in a field in Belgium, was unthinkable.

"I guess we might as well get this guy together?" Fritz asked.

"He's quiet now. I might have got him, or maybe he ran," Emil said. "The rest of the platoon is about to charge, anyway. If I didn't stop him, Fluse's early start will."

"So he sent them early? Idiot. I thought I lost count."

"No, he did. Maybe he thought he'd earn a promotion if he took that hole in the ground a minute earl—"

The whistle blew again, three sharp blasts this time.

"Gas?" Fritz said, his eyes huge.

Emil took his mask from its pouch and slid it on in one practiced motion. But no matter how many times he'd done that before, the thought of gas was always terrifying. The hairs on the back of his neck stood up as he looked toward the German position, expecting to see a cloud of yellow-brown mustard gas.

Instead, a massive, roiling black cloud swelled across the field, moving from behind the German trench toward them.

Black Smoke.

The Martians were back? A weight dropped in Emil's stomach. He gasped for air as the mask closed in to smother him.

Breathe in. Breathe out. He worked the drills he learned years ago in basic training.

But were the Martians actually back? They'd dropped dead nearly twenty years ago.

Emil listened for the sound of a Wanderer's steel feet or the terrible hum of a heat ray, but no sound came. Soon, the lethal Smoke reached him and Fritz.

"Fritz, are they really here?" Emil shouted, his voice muffled. "I don't see anything, do you? Let's run for the Belgian trench. We can't get trapped like we did back home."

Fritz was lying on the ground a few meters away, his gas

mask askew. Emil's heart raced as he reached for his friend and tried to fix it.

"No! Fritz! Wake up!"

Troops ran past them, but Emil couldn't make out friend or foe through the thick haze. Somewhere downrange, a lone Belgian gunner still fired.

"Medic! Help!" Emil shouted as he struggled with Fritz's mask, trying to straighten it onto his friend's head. Sweat ran into his eyes, and he nearly dislodged his own mask while trying to wipe it with his sleeve. Fritz's mask had two holes in it, one on each cheek. Bullet holes. Fritz's mask pouch was lying on the ground next to him, with the same two holes.

Through and through.

Fritz was dead. Killed by a bullet that had never touched him. He'd survived that day on the soccer field, when the Martians had attacked, only to be killed by a damaged gas mask in an asparagus field.

But a bullet hadn't killed him. A career-obsessed Leutnant had.

More soldiers ran past, but Emil still didn't see any sign of attacking Martians. The men were from the 109th Reserve Regiment, though, running toward the Belgian positions. That seemed to be the safe place to head to.

Emil picked his friend up in a firefighter's carry. He wouldn't leave Fritz for the aliens. Waves of Smoke nearly blinded him, and he stepped carefully, afraid to get stuck in the clots of barbed wire.

The miasma sank then, an ebony pall draping itself over a dying field. As it settled, it left a pitch-black residue, and the rising sun lit a very real hell.

The outlines of the machine gunner's nest loomed 100 meters to the east. Emil headed for it, picking up his pace as he listened for a Wanderer or a heat ray.

He nearly walked into the black mass of a barrel and a large patch of overgrown asparagus. The alien powder had scorched the plant's leaves. A dead soldier was sprawled across the barrel, black dust still settling on his helmet and back as if he had fallen asleep next to a coal scuttle. Three more men lay near him, one of them tangled in barbed wire and not quite covered with dust yet.

Emil reached the gunner's nest and craned his neck to look inside. The gunner was only a boy. His right hand gripped the stock of a still-shiny gun, and his left the trigger. A single bullet hole between his eyes.

Emil's stomach heaved. Had he made that shot?

No. It must have been someone else.

He found a ladder and climbed down, struggling under Fritz's weight. German voices rose as he descended into the gloom.

"Who's that?" thundered Ludwig Oberacker's deep voice, recognizable as it strained to overcome his gas mask. Ludwig was Unteroffizier of Third Platoon, Third Company, and a man born for the role. He was tall, with broad shoulders and a pot belly. He was one of the eight men from Euleheim in Third Company, Fifteenth Reserve Jaeger Battalion, but a few years older than Emil and far too dedicated to the kaiser's army for Emil to think of him as a friend from home.

Emil hoisted Fritz off his shoulder and laid him on the floor of the trench, wiping the black powder off his dead friend. He looked around then. No Belgian casualties. The boy had been guarding an empty trench.

"Who's there?" Ludwig repeated as he stomped over to intercept Emil.

"It's Zimmerman," Emil said, then pointed at his friend's body. "And Fritz Seith."

Ludwig stopped and stared at Emil, then looked at the body. "You carried him here?"

"He couldn't make it on his own."

Ludwig faced the body. Fritz's mask was hanging off his

head to one side, and his arms and legs were arranged in an unnatural pose. Ludwig turned back to Emil, eyeing him through fogged lenses. Before he could reply, shouting rose a few meters down the trench.

"All clear! All clear!"

The Black Smoke had settled in the trench, leaving a black pall that drained the light from its walls.

"What happened?" Ludwig asked. "And why did you bring him here? We have crews to recover the dead."

"I didn't want to leave him for the Martians," Emil said. The stench of black tar and Benzin filled his nostrils as he lifted off his mask.

"Martians?" Ludwig tilted his head and eyed Emil up and down.

"Yes, the Martians. This is their Smoke, isn't it?" Emil pointed to the dust on the ground.

Ludwig sighed, and his shoulders fell in a half-shrug. "No. That's German Black Smoke. The Martians have been dead for a long time, Emil," he said, folding his mask.

German? "We used Black Smoke to take an empty trench?" Emil asked, struggling to keep his voice down.

"Yes, we did. Apparently, the Pioneers got their signals crossed and thought we needed the support."

So Fritz had been killed by friendly fire. By the German version of a weapon the Martians had used to kill humans before they'd succumbed to Terran microbes.

Nearly a year ago, Bosnian terrorists had celebrated New Year's Day by killing Archduke Franz Ferdinand, younger brother to the Emperor of Austria-Hungary, and his family in their castle. They had used Black Smoke to do the job. The kaiser's righteous indignation over their use of such a "barbaric weapon" was one of the many reasons he'd started this war.

"So they decided we needed support and deployed the same weapon that started this war?" Emil shouted.

"Calm down, Emil," Ludwig said, lowering his voice as he held out his hands. "We've talked about this. You're going to get yourself in trouble. Why don't you tell me what happened to Seith?"

The pounding in Emil's ears threatened to drown Ludwig out. Emil took a deep breath that was more about preparing to speak than calming down. "His mask had a bullet hole from when that idiot Leutnant sent you out too soon. A gunner opened up on us and got him before he found cover."

Ludwig grimaced. "Look, Emil—"

"So Fluse sent you out too fast, and the Pioneers released this poison. He got Fritz shot and then gassed with German Black Smoke. He can count that body twice." Emil took a step forward, his fists clenched.

Ludwig frowned again but didn't step back. He tilted his head to lock eyes with Emil, who stood at least a foot shorter than he did.

Before either man could speak, Leutnant Fluse appeared, pushing a hapless corporal out of his way to join their conversation. Somehow, the tall, thin man with a weak chin had a spotless uniform.

"Unteroffizier, gather up your men," he said. "We're moving to the next position. This one's too primitive—what the hell is that doing here?" Fluse's face grew red as he pointed at Fritz as if he were a messy bunk or a pair of poorly shined boots.

"His name is Fritz Seith," Emil said.

"What is it doing here?" Fluse screamed, his voice gaining an octave.

"*He* is the man you got killed, idiot!" Emil shouted. His vision clouded as adrenaline surged through his body.

"What did you call me?" the Leutnant shrieked.

Ludwig stood between the two men, looking back and forth at them like a line judge at a tennis match between two madmen.

"I called you an idiot," Emil said, trying to push his way past

Ludwig to get to the officer. He clenched his fists and wound up to throw a punch.

Only Ludwig placing himself between them stopped Emil from killing Fluse.

2

The car lurched forward, and James's stomach heaved with it a half-second after he struck the seat back. He'd spent little time riding in automobiles and never driven one, but he didn't think it was necessary for the corn-fed marine sergeant to treat the clutch and the accelerator like a wayward recruit in need of discipline.

The Cadillac was bigger than the Ford that James had ridden in last time, but the government didn't drive Fords anymore. It was beautifully appointed, with stylish wood panels, leather details, and a hard top that muffled much of the road noise. So it was more of a luxury carriage than a military vehicle. It wasn't a car for transporting a radio engineer, but a limousine modified for a general.

Sergeant Christensen of the United States Marines, First Advanced Base Brigade, struggled with keeping the sedan moving in the Brooklyn traffic, as if he had more experience driving tractors on farms and empty country roads. "You're from around here, right?" he asked, turning left onto Fulton Street and under the El. He smiled at James in the rearview mirror.

"No, I'm not from Brooklyn," James said, turning his gaze

out the window, hoping a curt response and lack of eye contact might ward off more questions. The less he said, the better, and neither Long Island nor Brooklyn were home.

Two hours earlier, a pair of marines had picked James up at home, back in West Orange, New Jersey. They said the radios at Sayville weren't working, and he needed to go to Long Island immediately. They insisted the problem couldn't wait, even though James had taken a train in the past.

Was it because of the situation in Europe? Were they going to war? The marines didn't have answers, just orders. They drove him north and escorted him by train to the Hudson Terminal, where Sergeant Christensen had been waiting with the Cadillac.

The military had commandeered the Sayville station nearly two years ago, after President William Jennings Bryan's reelection in 1912. But they still didn't have any idea how to manage it. Taking James from his home and escorting him to the site on New Year's Eve was a new low. Why did they take the systems away from Edison Labs if they couldn't keep them running?

Was Edison headed in the same direction as Ford? Maybe tonight was part of making that happen, and James would help them hammer the final nail into Edison's coffin.

A policeman signaled the car to stop, then changed his mind, making the car lurch again. James's stomach caught up, and they jerked in unison this time.

James checked his watch. He'd be out here all night. It was afternoon, and the shadows were getting long, but Brooklyn was bustling with activity. People were crowding Fulton Street, darting in and out of shops, presumably getting in some shopping before heading home for a holiday meal. It would be quieter and less crowded in Menlo Park right now, where James would miss a New Year's dinner and play with his fiancée. But in both towns, everyone else got on with their lives. They weren't sitting in a car, heading to fix radios far from home.

The tools and parts James had hastily grabbed from the lab

were threatening to fall off the bench seat in the back of the car. The marines couldn't describe the issue, so he'd carried a full complement of germanium diodes and triodes, a new transformer, and his tool bag. He now pulled the box back onto the seat.

"Well, ya know, you're from around here. New York." Christensen's bright smile faded with a touch of disappointment. "Your security file said you were born in Manhattan."

Security file? "Yes, I was born in Manhattan," James said, sitting up straight. It made sense that the Security Police had a file on him, since he worked for Edison. The marines must have requested it after they'd taken over operating Sayville. But why had his driver reviewed his file?

"Yeah, around here." Christensen's smile returned.

"We moved to New Jersey when I was young, after the fire," James clarified. It wasn't worth trying to explain that being born in Brooklyn and not Manhattan made a difference to people from around here. James had been a boy when Brooklyn became a part of New York City, and he still remembered people fretting about how it would lose its unique flavor when it became a borough. He didn't know how different the two cities were then. But today, Fulton was no different from any busy street in Manhattan. So Christensen had a point.

"Your family moved to New Jersey after the Martians attacked? I thought they hit New Jersey harder than New York."

"No, we moved after the Tesla fire a few years later."

"The big fire? That happened near where people lived?" Christensen's brow furrowed in the rearview mirror.

The Tesla fire had been across town from where James had lived, and where his dad had worked as a cop. James sighed, and a tear welled up in one eye before he caught himself. His family had moved to New Jersey so the fire's aftermath could kill Dad out of sight and out of mind. Christensen knew little about the Tesla fire, but James knew that was by design. The government went to great lengths to make sure nobody did.

"Yes, it did," James said, scanning the traffic again. He would miss the play, and since the marines had picked him up at home without warning, he couldn't tell Susan. Even worse, his mom was home alone for New Year's Eve. Hopefully, when he didn't pick Susan up on time, she'd head to his house and spend some time with Mom.

Christensen swerved to dodge a cart pulled by a horse that seemed old enough to have carried George Washington. The sedan fell into line behind about a dozen cars under the Atlantic Avenue railroad.

Pushcarts laden with goods lined the streets of East New York. The aroma of freshly baked bread floated through an open window, providing James some relief from the perfume of cigars and sweat embedded in the car's leather upholstery. The yeasty fragrance made weathering the cold winter air worth it. A man in sandwich boards advertised the best suit a man could buy.

"Busy out here today, isn't it, Jimmy? It's okay if I call you Jimmy, right?"

It wasn't okay, but James had already made Christensen feel bad about being from around here.

"Captain Reynolds is keen to get you out to Sayville as soon as possible," Christensen went on, smiling again. "With the war heating up in Europe, we need to know what's going on."

So Germany was the difference. Or, at least that was the story. James shifted the box of repair parts again.

"So, you're good with these radios, huh? They just stopped working, Jimmy! Both of 'em!" Christensen smiled into the mirror again. "They're making this awful humming noise. Sometimes it sounds like someone is talking on the other end, but the operators can't make anything out."

Edison Laboratories had installed the transceivers at Sayville as part of a joint venture with Deutsche Telefunken and Marconi's Wireless Telegraphy Company. James had designed the US-based systems and supervised the installation. He had visited them every few months until the military had commandeered the site.

Now, James didn't miss leaving his mom and traveling out there to see them, but he missed the station itself. At least back then, he'd ridden in a steady train instead of a rumbling, jerking car.

Christensen attacked the clutch again, then jammed down the gas. The car lurched forward, and James's stomach tried to reach the back of the sedan.

"It sounds like a bad ground," James said after catching his breath. The ground connection for the transceivers in Sayville had been an issue before. James had added heavier cabling and deeper ground stakes the last time.

"They checked that," Christensen replied.

The chimney stacks of the Ridgewood Water Works loomed straight ahead, growing larger as the car crawled down the avenue. Christensen stopped for a large crowd of people leaving the stairs of the Warwick Street Station and let them cross the road. James shifted in his seat again. They would never reach Sayville at this rate.

"Who did?" James asked. "The regular operators? Or the soldiers?" The marines had had problems with the systems before. They had fired all the skilled operators Edison had hired, and they had taken good care of the units. But radios weren't guns. Or Cadillacs.

But what if the radios were broken now, and James couldn't fix them? Would the War Department replace Edison with Westinghouse?

Christensen turned to look at James, one eyebrow raised. His chiseled features and close-cropped blond hair made him look like the drawing you'd find in a dictionary entry for "marine sergeant." James sat up straight again.

"I see what you're trying to say, Jimmy," Christensen said, raising his voice a little. "But we know how important it is for the systems to have a good ground. Any radio a civilian can handle, a marine operator can, too. Besides, a few of your civilian guys are still there. The ones who passed the security checks, anyway."

Christensen turned to face the front of the car again. The crowd had cleared, and he attacked the clutch again. James looked at the back of the sergeant's head. He'd offended him. Would an apology help? Or should he keep his mouth shut before he made things worse?

James didn't dare speak as they reached the waterworks and turned right to head toward Queens and Long Island. Getting out of traffic was a relief, but the stillness made the feeling short-lived.

Finally, Christensen broke the silence. "My unit arrived at the station last month, but like I said, civilians still help. We're there for additional security, but Captain Reynolds is the ranking officer, so he's taken command."

"Well, maybe I can get it back on the air right away," James said. Making the marines angry wouldn't help if this was some kind of test.

The streets thinned out and gave way to open fields and a new asphalt road. Christensen opened the throttle, and the Cadillac purred.

A sign welcoming them to Ramblersville flew past, and they were out of Brooklyn and East New York and well on their way to Long Island. James tried to calculate how quickly he could get home after looking at the radios.

"We're going to need those radios if we send troops to Europe," Christensen said, raising his voice again to be heard over the engine.

"Do you really think we'll be sending troops there?" James asked, hoping small talk was a sign that the big man wasn't too offended.

"The Krauts need to be stopped. You've heard the news, haven't you?"

"So you think there's truth to those stories? They're using Martian technology? Like Black Smoke?"

"The papers wouldn't say it if it wasn't true, would they? I'd believe anything about them anyway, especially after what I saw in Mexico." Christensen's brow furrowed.

"You were in Mexico?"

"Yeah. They're animals, Jimmy. You don't want to mess with the Germans." Christensen looked at James in the rearview mirror again. His tone had made it clear he didn't have more to say.

The car fell silent again as it rumbled east along the island. The ocean peeked out from behind some trees to the south, then receded again. Soon, the Sayville radio station's twin antennas appeared on the horizon like two fingers pointing to the sky. At first, it was too far away to see the guy wires holding them up, but after a few minutes, the thicker ones came into view. They were giant aerials, each anchored on concrete foundations and held upright by steel wires. The operators could raise and lower them from ball joints in the foundations, but the antennas stayed raised often enough that Mr. Edison had talked about replacing them with steel towers.

One aerial would have sufficed, but the Bryan administration had insisted on two: one for the Planetary Warning System, and another for direct overseas communications. The White House had refused to believe that one antenna was enough for two systems.

The sun was high in the sky as the car motored into the northern part of the village. On the far side of town, Christensen stopped the car at a guard shack and gate James hadn't seen before. The entrance controlled access to a fenced-in area extending on both sides as far as he could see.

"What's this?" James asked.

"Security, Jimmy," Christensen said. "Can't be too sure."

"They've fenced in the area around the towers?"

"Wouldn't make sense to only cover part of it."

The radio station was a military compound now, and Christensen was escorting James in like a prisoner.

Christensen spoke to the guards and eased the wide sedan inside. He brought it to a halt at the door, next to two more Cadillacs.

The station was a squat, windowless, single-story brick building at the base of the two antennas. The door opened into an office, where the radio operators processed the constant streams of numbers making up the incoming and outgoing messages. Spoken words weren't safe enough for President Bryan's War Department.

The operators would then relay the decrypted messages to couriers or use an aging telegraph to forward them to Washington. The station's other room was the "closet," which contained the radio equipment.

Three years ago, James had practically lived in this building while helping to upgrade the station from one tower with an arc transmitter to two towers with heterodyne transceivers. He'd taken the train home whenever he could, but he'd still spent more time here than he'd liked. He was proud of the radios and the work he'd done to design and build them, though he'd hated being away from his mom so much. The units were like old friends who'd moved too far away for him to visit.

Now, as James entered the building, the place was alien. Occupied territory. A fence surrounded the building, and it was full of marines. The control room that the civilian operators had once decorated with notes and transcriptions was now sparse and spotless, and reeked of cigar and cigarette smoke.

James hated smoke and the memories it stirred.

He approached a man seated in the corner, wearing a captain's bars. He seemed young for a captain, probably not much older than James himself. He wore a neatly pressed uniform and was the only marine not holding a cigar or cigarette.

The captain made a ceremony of remaining seated by crossing one leg over the other. "You must be Brogan," he said.

James nodded.

"Captain Reynolds," the officer said, introducing himself. "I expect a report within the hour. We need communications with Germany and the Planetary Warning System ASAP."

3

mil's mask still reeked of Benzin and black tar. A quick wipedown with a damp rag was usually enough to clean a Gummimaske, even after exposure to something as rank as mustard gas. But after tearing it off, cleaning it twice, and trying two new filters, Emil's still stank of Black Smoke. He reached for his canteen to try again, but it was empty.

This Black Smoke smelled different from the stuff the Martians had used when they'd attacked years ago. Emil and Fritz had been playing soccer when the aliens had arrived in Euleheim, and they'd both escaped that day. They'd fled the field so Fritz could be killed in a German uniform by his own army's imitation gas two decades later.

Emil headed toward the water tanks. The aroma of scrambled eggs and sausage wafted over from a group of men eating nearby. Breakfast pushed away the stench of gasoline and tar, leaving faint reminders of home. Emil's stomach rumbled, but he was too busy for breakfast. The men were laughing and celebrating a hot, tasty meal on a cold winter morning, but he frowned as he went back to work on his mask. All it took was a plate of warm eggs and sausage for the fools to forget where they were.

Emil lathered up the mask with hand soap and water from his refilled canteen. He rinsed it and shook it dry. The sickly sweet perfume of Benzin still lingered, and now his wet hands were cold.

Fritz had still been on the field when Emil had fled to find his sister, Hermine, in Euleheim. After a harrowing trip through the village, he'd made it home in time to see the Martians destroy it—with her inside.

Emil looked down at his mask. A freshly worn spot in the rubber stared back at him. He poured more water and soap onto it.

After his home had been obliterated, he'd found himself at Fritz's house, relieved to see that his friend had survived.

Emil's hands now ached from scrubbing, and the water had wrinkled his fingertips.

The real Martian Black Smoke had smelled of blood and scorched iron in the summer sun. His parents had found him the day after the invasion. They'd taken a room at the Wirtschaft zum Ochsen while Father rebuilt the house. Mother had made him bathe in the restaurant kitchen's steel tub. The bathwater's tang had made Emil think of Herr Schleicher's barn, where he'd repaired tools over an anvil and hot coal fire.

Tools! If he had the right tools, Emil could take the mask's filter housing apart and remove whatever was trapped inside.

This stuff—the German Smoke—was different. It had a harsh, caustic stench. Benzin and black tar. The Germans had taken a Martian weapon and somehow made it worse.

Emil shook out his hands before pouring more water into the mask. He grasped a cheek flap in each hand and rubbed them together so the friction warmed his hands. Then he stopped and sniffed again. The tar stink still lingered. He'd taste it during the next gas attack. He'd taste it for the rest of his life.

Emil swore out loud and raised the accursed thing over his head.

"Whoa, Emil. Wait until there's an enemy near enough to hit

before you throw that." Ludwig stepped up, blocking the sun from Emil's view—and making it harder for him to work on his mask. "Why are you over here, playing with that thing again? It's a holiday! We're having a special breakfast this morning. We've got eggs, cheese, bread, and real coffee without any of that verdammt chicory in it. We even have cigars! But you're over here, alone again."

"Holiday?" Emil asked, shaking the mask out before looking up. The platoon had only been awake for a couple of hours, so Emil was hard-pressed to think of anything he'd done to deserve a lecture.

Ludwig leaned back against the trench's western wall. He shaded his eyes with one hand and held a steaming cup of coffee in the other. His omnipresent unlit cigar was clenched between his tobacco-stained teeth.

He crouched down, grunting now that the sun was out of his eyes, and fished a match out of his coat pocket before looking Emil in the eye. "Neujahrstag, Emil," he said. "We start a new year today. But you're too angry over the Black Smoke to remember, I guess."

It was going to be the "bad attitude" lecture again. Emil rolled his eyes. "The Black Smoke? Yes, that's not a bad guess. Not to mention how Fluse got Fritz killed. Then again, it's been made clear to me that I can't say that. So forget that I brought it up."

"Accusing officers of getting their men killed is never allowed. It's nearly as bad as attacking them." Ludwig lit his cigar and exhaled a long plume of smoke to the side. "You did both."

"That's me, the overachiever. Now I'm trying to clean my mask like a good soldier." Emil pulled a filter out of his pocket—the third one he'd tried since the attack two days ago—and attached it to the mask. Before it reached his face, tendrils of Benzin and tar reached his nose. He fought back a wave of nausea. It was time for a new mask.

"Soon we'll break through the Belgian lines, and before you know it, we'll be drinking champagne in Paris," Ludwig said. "No lying in the mud. Or the ice. Or the icy mud."

Champagne in Paris? Celebrating? Emil glowered at the men talking and laughing over their fresh eggs and coffee further down the trench. Heat rose to his face, and once again he considered throwing the mask. "And what about Fritz?" he asked. "Where's his eggs and cheese? Who'll drink his bubbly wine? Who got his share of that fine, chicory-free coffee this morning?"

"Seith's death was a tragedy, but this is war, Emil. He's not the first to be killed. And he won't be the last."

"Is he the first one killed by German Black Smoke?"

"There you go again. Forbidden Black Smoke. I'm tired of hearing about that. Does it matter what weapon we use? This is war. We should use whatever is better for *us*." With that last word, Ludwig pointed his cigar at himself and then at Emil.

"I'm sorry. Does the army killing its own troops bore you? I can't talk about Fluse getting Fritz shot, and now the Black Smoke is off-limits, too. Not to mention the thousands of Belgians and French they must have killed with it already." Emil shook his head. If the men couldn't talk about it, it would go away like it had never happened.

"You're going to get yourself in trouble with this talk, Emil. It's borderline treason, and an apology won't save you like last time."

Ludwig flourished his cigar at Emil, making him want to grab it and toss it into the nearest puddle. But he didn't. "I still regret letting you talk me into apologizing to him," Emil snarled.

"Really? You regret doing what you had to do to avoid a court-martial?" Ludwig's face was red. "Do you understand how serious it is to assault a superior officer? What would that have cost you?"

Emil crossed his arms and turned away.

"Answer me."

How serious was it to attack a superior officer? What did

Ludwig want him to say? He wanted to hear that it was dire, of course. He wanted Emil to say he could have been executed or shipped off to prison for life. The real problem was, Emil hadn't actually hit the man.

"I didn't attack a superior officer," Emil said. "I attacked an inferior officer. An inferior officer who got one of his men killed."

"Cute. That could get you hanged, but cute." Ludwig took another sip of coffee, grimaced, and poured the rest onto the trench floor. "Look, the war will be over soon, like I said. Just give the officers what they want, and they'll leave you alone."

"You think we'll reach Paris, and the French will hand us a croissant and the keys to the city? Then they'll welcome the kaiser's benevolent rule? We're invaders. We invaded Belgium because some Serbs killed a cousin the kaiser barely knew he had. On our way through, we attacked civilians with one of the weapons the Martians used to slaughter and eat us." Emil caught himself before throwing down his mask. Instead, he folded it and searched for its case, deciding to put it away before he risked losing it.

A soldier seated a few meters away glanced at Emil, then turned away to avoid his gaze.

"How does this end?" Emil continued, lowering his voice. "Does the rest of the world sit by while we invade France? Does the kaiser have a Martian death ray he can use to wrap things up in a few days?"

"That's enough," Ludwig warned.

"No. How does this end? Will we be gassed by the Pioneers during the next advance? Or cut down by one of those infernal Sturmpanzerwagens? Maybe we'll be lucky and be part of a successful invasion of two countries. If we're quick, they'll send us over to Russia next!"

Before Ludwig could retort, a young soldier approached. "Excuse me, Herr Oberacker. I have a message from the Hauptmann. He wants Herr Zimmerman sent to the command post immediately. There's a problem with the phones."

Ludwig nodded. The soldier scurried away.

Ludwig shrugged. "Get over to the command post, Emil. And keep your mouth shut. Like I said, an apology won't save your neck next time."

A trip to the command post would mean spending time near the Hauptmann and his staff. There wouldn't be time to worry about military etiquette, clean uniforms, and the rest of the army's games in the trenches. In the command post, that was all there was.

Of course, Fluse would be in the command post, too. Nothing good would come of seeing that fool again. Just being near him might bait Emil into another attack, and Ludwig was right. An apology wouldn't work next time.

"Didn't we talk about making Frenz work on the phones?" Emil offered. Better to send the new kid to the wolves.

"The Hauptmann asked for *you*," Ludwig said.

"I think this is a great time to give Frenz a chance to work under pressure—"

"What happened to the man who only wanted to get back to Telefunken to work on the Planetary Warning System?"

"He heard Fluse was nearby and left."

"Well, I heard Fluse is putting together a detail for covering the Belgian latrines and digging better ones. Would you prefer that to fixing the phones?"

"No, he isn't!" Emil said. Fluse would never lower himself to getting within ten meters of that kind of duty, let alone supervising it.

"Maybe he just hasn't thought of it yet." Ludwig crossed his arms and gave Emil a toothy, yellow smile.

Then again, given the proper motivation, Fluse might enjoy that duty. Emil slumped his shoulders in defeat.

"Go. Now. And keep your mouth shut." Ludwig pointed his cigar toward the command post.

Emil stuffed his mask inside its case. Then he picked up his pack and slung it over his shoulder. Even though the regiment seemed settled in, they might be ordered to move with only a moment's notice. It was never a good idea to stray too far from your gear.

His stomach rumbling again, Emil set off for the command post. He didn't want to risk keeping the Hauptmann waiting. When he wasn't risking death at the hands of an incompetent lieutenant, his job was maintaining the phones that connected Third Company to itself and to headquarters. If he was being summoned in a hurry, it was probably because the Hauptmann was having problems talking to command. He might be out of wine or caviar.

As Emil made the first turn out of Third Platoon's area, he nearly stumbled. The formerly narrow passageway that separated Third from Fourth Platoon had a new step that hadn't been there the day before. It was wider now, too, and nearly half a meter deeper. Even the turn from the empty byway to where the men stayed seemed sharper.

Emil continued toward the command post, hoping Fluse had stepped on a mine or gotten lost on the way there.

4

James opened his mouth to ask Captain Reynolds a question, but the officer's fixed gaze made him choke on his words. He collected himself and walked past the marines into the equipment room, shutting the door behind him. It was a relief to leave the cigarette and cigar smoke behind.

The radios' comforting hum was a faint reminder of Edison Labs in West Orange. And even with the fans pulling out the heat generated by the germanium tubes, the room was sweltering. But James preferred to not open the door and let in smoke and the marine captain's prying eyes. He shrugged off his jacket and hung it carefully over the room's only chair. The oddly soothing notes of formaldehyde from warm Bakelite filled his nose, replacing the cigars and sweat from the control room.

James gave the systems a quick once-over but couldn't find any immediate issues. Other than a light coating of dust—the marines probably hadn't cleaned since they took over—they looked fine. He turned up the volume on the Planetary Warning unit, and the continuous hum Christensen had described came over the speaker, clear as a bell. It was too stable to be random noise from a bad power supply, and the frequency sounded high for a ground fault.

He turned up the volume on the German unit then and listened. The sound from the German system merged with the other into a single tone. Both radios were producing the same frequency.

He took the covers off the units, expecting to find another, heavier coat of dust. But the units were perfectly clean. Score one for the marines.

The Planetary Warning and German systems were completely discrete. The only thing they shared was a connection to the Edison power station down the road. Even though two aerials were overkill, James had designed them this way to avoid this very problem. They were crucial, and having one out for an extended period was unacceptable. Having both radios out was a critical failure. Less than two years of military control, and the unthinkable had already happened.

James bit his bottom lip.

The two systems were identical, however, and had interchangeable parts. James had kept enough spare parts on-site to build a third transceiver and then some. Between that and the gear he'd brought, he was ready for any problem.

He swapped the power supply in the Planetary Warning unit with the spare. No change. He swapped the amplifier. The hum continued. He sat down and bit his lip again. This wasn't a typical problem.

He wired in one of the spare tuners. The hum was louder and more distinct, as if the new tuner made it easier for the interference to make it through.

Interference?

A terrible thought formed in the back of James's mind. What if the signal wasn't coming from the equipment? He bit his lip again as he picked a pair of pliers out of his tools.

"Well, what do you see?"

Captain Reynolds's voice made him jump. How had he opened the door without James hearing him?

James took a deep breath. "Has it been an hour already, Captain?" He fidgeted with his pliers, waiting for an answer.

"It looks like you're just swapping parts. We already did that."

"I wasn't aware your soldiers had already tried. If you had told—"

"Marines. Not soldiers, marines." The captain crossed his arms and eyed James for an uncomfortably long time. "You didn't serve."

There it was, the subject James hated more than any other, more than "So when are you two getting married?" or "You still live with your mother?" Every man of a certain age was expected to have "served" since President Bryan instituted the draft in 1902. But James had gotten a waiver because of how important his work on Edison's radios was. At least that was the reason the waiver had been offered. The real reason—the promise he'd made to Dad on his deathbed—wasn't something he wanted to explain.

"No, I got a waiver—" he began.

"I know the story. I reviewed your security file before I allowed you onto my site. It's not up to me to judge why men might want to evade their duty, but while you're here, you'll do what's expected of you. Get my radios back on the air." The captain maintained eye contact as he closed the door.

A knot grew in James's stomach. He needed to fix this problem as fast as possible and bring these systems back on the air.

James powered up the German system and adjusted the volume so the "hum" was almost too loud to tolerate. He disconnected the coaxial connection to the antenna. The volume dropped, but the sound remained.

He repeated the process with the Planetary Warning unit. Same result, except the noise was louder with the new tuner.

James shivered despite the heat coming off the radios. The hum was a problem with either both radios—which was unlikely—or Edison's power. Or it was coming from over the air. Was someone broadcasting that noise?

Christensen's words echoed in his mind. *They're animals, Jimmy.*

James opened the door and called for Captain Reynolds.

"What?" the officer snapped.

James beckoned him into the equipment room and showed him what he'd done.

"So it's not the antennas," Reynolds said. "You thought it was?"

James ignored the question. "I want to kill the power and cut over to the backup batteries. Have your men been checking the electrolyte levels?"

"Of course they have!"

"Tell me when you're ready," James said, hoping that ignoring the captain's tone would make him go away. He turned off both units, walked to the fuse box in the corner, and picked up the lantern that sat on top of it.

The captain herded his men outside and signaled with a whistle. James flipped the switch. The room went dark, the lantern casting a long shadow from the two radio chassis. He switched the radios on and watched them come back to life. Both speakers hummed with the mysterious noise. James's stomach rolled as he turned the radios off and switched the station back to regular power.

The sound was coming over the air. But the droning was too steady—too perfect—to be a fluke or natural phenomenon. It had to be man-made. Intentional.

You don't want to mess with the Germans.

This is something they would do before an attack—and James was stuck on Long Island, more than a hundred miles from home.

He sat down in the room's only chair.

The German system was primarily for diplomatic communications, but the Planetary Warning System served several purposes. Edison and its partners around the world had built it in response to the Martian Attack to give the world time to prepare if something approached Earth again. But it also served as a general warning system, too, playing a part in the Mexican War.

Were German spies or soldiers close enough to interfere with the radios? If they were, they were probably right off the coast.

James needed to be sure before he voiced his suspicions. He stared at the floor and bit his lip again, fighting the urge to run out of the room and demand a ride home.

"So?" Captain Reynolds asked as he reentered the room.

James looked down for a few seconds longer, then raised his eyes to meet the captain's. "I saw a few cars parked in front of the building. I need one of their batteries."

"But you already tested battery power."

"Yes, but I need a separate battery for another test. Removing a backup would take too long."

"What's going on? What do you think this is?"

"I need to run one more test, then we can talk," James said, hoping the captain didn't hear his voice waver.

The captain opened his mouth but said nothing. He turned and left the room.

Christensen entered a few minutes later with a car battery. He heaved it onto the table and turned to face James. "What's going on?" he asked. "The captain seems upset."

"I'm not sure yet," James said. "Is he upset because I haven't found the problem? Or because I asked for the battery?"

"Probably both." Christensen grinned.

If James was wrong, he'd be accusing a foreign power of starting a war. But if he was right, he'd be in the middle of something he wanted no part of.

"Lighten up, Jimmy," Christensen said, clapping him on the back. "You'll figure it out," he added on his way out of the room.

James connected a speaker to one of the spare amplifiers. He coiled a few meters of copper wire around some pencils and soldered the makeshift device to the amplifier's input. Then he used heavy cables to connect the car battery.

As soon as he switched the amplifier on, the hum enveloped the room. It sounded muddier than before, with no tuner to sharpen it, but the system still picked it up.

James's mind raced. This was an act of war, and if he was the one to reveal it, he'd be putting himself right in the middle of it. What if he showed this to Captain Reynolds and went home? *Here's your evidence of sabotage, Captain. We'll send the bill to the War Department.*

James sat down and stared at the floor again. His lip was starting to hurt. A few minutes later, he called the captain in.

"Yes?" the captain said, his mouth fixed in a straight line.

James turned on the amplifier, let the humming run for a moment, and shut it off.

"You built another broken radio?" Reynolds asked.

How could James explain this? What words would convey what was going on and get him on his way home?

"It's not a radio," he said eventually. "It's the car battery powering an amplifier with a coil connected to the input. No tuner. No discriminator. Just a rough antenna. But it's still picking up the frequency and playing it for us."

"Picking it up? What does that mean?"

"It means the hum is being broadcast from somewhere nearby, and it's so strong that any electronic device will pick it up. The radios aren't broken."

"I don't understand. Someone is sending out that . . . noise? Why?"

"So we can't talk to Germany or Planetary Warning?" James said. How could the captain not understand? He wanted to scream, "We're under attack, you fool!" Instead, he sighed.

He'd found the problem, and it wasn't the radios. He'd done his job. It was time for him to leave.

"Like sabotage?" The captain's eyes grew large.

"Yes, exactly. Like sabotage." James took a breath and wiped his brow. "That's one reason. Another is someone might be trying to build a transmitter. But that would be illegal without clearance from the federal government." He checked his watch. He'd missed the show, but that wasn't important now. The Germans were on US shores and waging an attack.

"How would someone do this? What would they use? Where are they?" the captain asked, pacing across the small room.

This didn't help James feel any calmer. If he told Captain Reynolds his suspicions, he'd stay involved. But he wanted to go home. War was coming. He needed to take his mom and Susan away from the city.

"I don't know," James said.

"What do you mean, you don't know?" Captain Reynolds stopped pacing and raised his voice. "You're the expert."

"This isn't about technology. It's about tactics. Maybe the Security Police already have an idea of where the Germans have spies or sympathizers. It's not up to me just because they're using radios."

"Not up to you? Why? Because you never served? Because you're a civilian?"

"Of course I served. I built these radios. You wouldn't even be here if it wasn't for me—" James stopped when he realized he was helping make Reynolds's point.

"We need to find out who's doing this and stop them." The captain crossed his arms.

"There's no way a signal this strong is coming from more than a few miles from here. Will Sergeant Christensen be involved with the search? Or can he drive me back? If you need him, I can find my way home from Brooklyn."

"What?" Reynolds's jaw dropped.

"Can I at least get a ride to the Sayville station? If there's a late Sunday train—"

"You're helping us find these saboteurs."

"I'm not a soldier—"

"Clearly. But 'serving at Edison' means supporting these

radios—and according to you, someone is sabotaging them right now. Don't worry, you won't get your hands dirty."

James's stomach lurched again. Finding the saboteurs could take all night, if not days. And what if the attack started while he was out here?

"Isn't that what your boss would say? Do I need to have some men bring him here, too?" The captain stepped toward James.

"No," James said. Mr. Johnson, who had gotten him the waiver from the draft, would have said it was his responsibility. So James couldn't force his way out of here, and he couldn't refuse to help, either. This was his job, and if he managed to get out, there was no guarantee they wouldn't send him right back if the radios were still out tomorrow.

James nodded. "I guess you're right."

"So if you were going to interfere with a German radio, what would you do?" Captain Reynolds asked, crossing his arms again.

"Well, I'd need a transmitter with a lot of power. I'm sure the Security Police can find whoever it is. They could round up the usual suspects, couldn't they?" The Security Police didn't need an engineer to find German spies.

"Nice try. How would they know which frequencies to block?"

"Either inside information or by scanning the airwaves for a few days. We really can't conceal what frequencies we use." If the US Marines couldn't figure that much out, they'd need James after all.

The captain tilted his head. "But we're scrambling strategic traffic."

James suppressed a sigh. The government had given this man James's radio station, but he didn't know anything about how it worked. "Yes, and they probably can't decode that stream of numbers. Otherwise, they might just let us talk. But since they can't listen in, they're making sure we can't communicate at all."

"So, then, where are they?"

Finally, a good question. James thought for a moment. They were near the ocean to send messages to Europe. If someone wanted to block the signal, getting between the two transmitters would be a decent step. It would be easier to hide on the water, wouldn't it? "Well, we're near Long Island Sound. If I have to guess, they're doing it from a ship."

The captain raised an eyebrow.

"It's a good way to position yourself between this station and the other receivers," James said. "They don't have to worry about being seen, and they could outfit the ship with enough power to block us from a few miles away. I think the first step is to contact the navy and have them send some boats over here to have a look."

"But we need to stop these people," the captain said. "Now."

"Do you have a boat?"

"No, but I have a car. We can scan the coastline."

"We?"

"You already outfitted that device with a battery. Can't we use it to locate where the signal is coming from?"

James had to admit it wasn't a bad idea. "A meter would be better than a speaker, but I don't understand. What will we do? Attack it?"

"That's my problem. Get to work."

5

Emil rounded a corner and entered Fourth Platoon's section of the trench, where the men shared Ludwig's New Year's spirit. The sun was still rising, and they greeted him with shot glasses of warm schnaps.

A chessboard sat on a purloined cable spool; two soldiers, chins resting on their hands, were playing for a small crowd. Even if Emil hadn't been on his way to the command post, this was no time for drinking and celebrations. He shook his head and pushed past the onlookers.

The path between Fourth and Fifth Platoons was longer and took him through a tight passageway with crumbling walls, a crooked wooden frame, and an uneven, muddy floor. The frame stood at dissonant angles, with rotting wood that had no coat of creosote or varnish—no evidence of pride in the workmanship. Just a long hole in the ground. Clearly, the Belgians lacked the German zest for war.

The 109th had taken a similar trench from the Belgians a few weeks back, somewhere near Huy or Liège. Fritz had been appalled by the handiwork there. He'd fixed a pair of crossbeams himself, despite his insistence he'd never be a carpenter like his father. These trenches would have had him outraged.

In the next passage, Emil's boots stuck in the muck with a sickening sound. The mud forced him to brace himself against the wall and pull his way through, grunting with effort and cursing under his breath. But that wasn't what made bile rise in his throat. It was the evidence of how the Germans had taken these positions. Jet black powder dusted the crevices between the lopsided framing and the walls. The stink of gasoline and tar reminded Emil of where he was and how he'd gotten there.

A bend in the trench led him to Fifth Platoon. This group had two different card games going. Sounds of joy and laughter vied for attention with the stench of gasoline and tar. The celebrations made the already narrow trenches more challenging to navigate. No one wanted to deal with pedestrians; and Emil had to beg, plead, cajole, and threaten to make his way through.

"You're Zimmerman, right?" a tall man asked as he reached through a group of men passing a soccer ball back and forth across a rare wide stretch of trench. The soldier seemed vaguely familiar, with dark hair and a neatly trimmed mustache.

"Yes?"

"I saw you play for Euleheim. I'm Beckenbauer, from Leimersheim. You and that other guy . . . Schultz? You tore us to shreds the last time we played, just before we were called up."

"Seith."

Beckenbauer cocked his head.

"Seith," Emil repeated. "His name was Fritz Seith."

"We're setting up a game this afternoon against Second Company. We need you for our side. Bring Seith, too, if he's around."

"You're planning soccer?" Emil's nostrils flared. They were going to leave the trench and play a game? One of the mass graves would make an outstanding goal.

"Ja," Beckenbauer said, grinning. "Our Unteroffizier says we deserve the break."

Emil shook his head and continued walking.

At the last corner of Third Company's trenches, the entrance to the command post came into view. A canvas tent protected it from the elements, with wire-framed screen doors at both ends. As Emil approached the door, someone shouted. He jumped back as a piece of timber nearly brained him, crashing onto the dirt floor. A jolt of fear shot through him as he steadied himself.

"Sorry!" two sheepish-looking men shouted, waving from the top of the trench. They stood between the beginnings of a wooden frame, one holding a hammer and the other a saw. Emil took a deep breath as the shock of adrenaline washed through him. Grunting, he stepped over the two-meter piece of pine that had nearly put him out of his misery.

The men literally slept in holes, but a canvas tent wasn't good enough for the officers. They had troops building a new command post, while some trenches were still muddy quagmires.

Two men with perfectly clean, neatly pressed uniforms guarded the door to the command post. Even their boots were spotless. The distance from Emil's platoon's trench to the command post was less than 100 meters but spanned two worlds.

Emil nodded to the guards and let himself in. Hauptmann Degenscheide stood at a table in the middle of the command post, looking over a colorful map. He squinted in concentration as he absentmindedly drummed his fingers on the table. The Hauptmann was almost as heavy as Ludwig, but more fit. He had a tailored uniform, the obligatory sculpted mustache, and stylish riding boots, though he'd probably never been within two meters of a horse that wasn't harnessed to a coach. He didn't look like a military man, but like most men in the kaiser's Germany, Degenscheide had no choice but to serve. At least he had a better position than most draftees.

Emil's stomach sank when he saw Leutnant Fluse huddled near a small stove in the corner. He flexed his icy fingers as he put down his pack, but approaching that martinet of a platoon leader so he could warm up was out of the question.

Fluse was speaking with two men Emil didn't recognize. One wore goggles around his neck, initially making Emil think he was the other man's driver. But then the two pips on his shoulders came into view. He was a Hauptmann, likely a Sturmpanzerwagen officer. The other still wore his leather coat, though he was the closest to the stove. The three officers stopped talking and stared at Emil as if he were a servant approaching with the wrong drink order.

"I'm here for the phones, sir," Emil said, bringing his feet together.

"What took you so long, soldier?" Leutnant Fluse demanded from across the room. The man in the coat sneered.

Emil snapped the rest of the way to attention. "I got here as fast as I could, Herr Leutnant."

"Stop interfering, Fluse, and let the man get to work," Degenscheide said. "None of the phones are working, soldier. There's only noise."

"Noise, sir?" Emil approached the table and picked up a handset. A steady hum was all he heard.

"You don't believe the Hauptmann?" Fluse asked. "You had to check?"

"Leutnant, I said let the man work," Degenscheide ordered.

Emil suppressed a smile. Maybe the Hauptmann would help him through this without him getting into more trouble. He took off his coat. The tent was warmer, the warmest place since . . . well, since the last time he'd been called there.

He started examining the equipment, hoping that focusing on the problem would help him blend into the background. These phones were newer units, with germanium-based amplifiers and modulators that were supposed to improve their range. But they were sensitive to wiring problems, and the German Army believed that "more complicated" was the same as better.

"You drove one of those Sturmpanzers here?" Fluse said. "You two are insane." He chuckled and turned back to one of the other officers.

The Hauptmann wearing the goggles smiled back. "It's dead out there," he said. "Silent. The enemy is hiding in their holes. If I don't make up a reason to drive it, I might never have a chance."

"Hiding?" Degenscheide asked, arching an eyebrow. "You think there are still Belgian troops alive out there?

"Oh!" Fluse raised his voice and gestured toward Degenscheide. "Let me introduce you to my company commander. Hauptmann Degenscheide, this is Hauptmann Thurman. We were at university and the Academy together."

Of course they'd gone to the same school. This wasn't a war for them. It was a social event. Emil disconnected the phone to check the connections.

"First Armored, sir," said Thurman. "It looks like the war is over. The Belgians have all but left the field, and the French are cowering around Paris."

Thurman was a shorter, stockier version of Fluse. His uniform wasn't as spotless; there were traces of oil on his boots, and his nails weren't perfectly clean. The man might have worked for a living in the past. His take on the war was possibly worth listening to. Of course, it wasn't hard to believe the enemy was on the run when the Germans were using Black Smoke.

"So are you familiar with what led to the decision to have the Pioneers deploy the Martian Smoke?" Degenscheide asked. "I thought that, with your Sturmpanzerwagens, we didn't need to use chemical weapons anymore. The Black Smoke caught my unit by surprise." He set his jaw in a way that said he didn't approve of the Smoke any more than Emil did.

"I can't say I was involved in the decision, sir," Thurman said. "General Falkenhayn was unhappy with our progress. He was also upset with how the mustard gas was injuring our men, despite masks and gear. The Black Smoke is less of a danger to our own forces and allowed us to remain on the offensive, as I am sure you know, sir."

Emil snorted before he caught himself.

"Do you have something to say, soldier?" Fluse asked.

"No, Herr Leutnant," Emil said. He picked up a phone and tried to shift his focus back to his work, hoping Fluse would leave him be.

Fluse left the stove and approached Emil. "No, I think you do."

"Leutnant," Degenscheide interjected.

Even though Emil had tried to attack Fluse two days earlier, he examined the man closely for the first time. He was taller, but Emil had a few pounds on him. Fluse was thin and pale. His hair was light blond, nearly white. Everything about him oozed callowness.

Fluse bared his teeth and took another step toward Emil. "Herr Hauptmann, this soldier was disrespectful. I want to hear what he has to say before I punish him."

Emil looked at the Hauptmann, then back at Fluse. Heat rose in his body, and he was conscious of the sweat soaking through his uniform.

Degenscheide opened his mouth to speak, then closed it.

"What is it, soldier?" Fluse asked.

Degenscheide stepped away from the table and approached the two men. His brow was knitted as he looked at Emil, waiting for an answer.

"I'm not sure how the Black Smoke is any better than mustard gas," Emil said. "I watched it kill one of the men in my platoon."

"Yes, you mentioned that soldier's death after our victory, didn't you?" Fluse replied. "You nearly assaulted me, but I let you off with an apology."

That soldier? "Seith," Emil said, and set his jaw.

"What?"

"Seith. His name was Fritz Seith."

"You don't know when to stop."

Emil stuck out his chin and crossed his arms. Stop talking when it comes to putting names on dead bodies. Of course.

"Stop? The weapon that started this war killed one of our men. His mask was damaged when you sent the platoon in before we cleared out the enemy machine gunners. But I should stop?"

"Soldier," the Hauptmann warned.

"Say his name, Fluse," Emil said, unfolding his arms and pointing a finger at Fluse's chest. "Seith. Seith! At least say the name of the man you got killed. Or is it hard to keep track? How many others are dead because of you?"

The Hauptmann sighed and shook his head.

"Guards!" Fluse stepped toward the entrance to the command post. "Take this man into custody."

"Leutnant!" Degenscheide ordered.

"Yes, sir?"

"Let him fix the phones first."

6

The car hit a bump, and James found himself thrown into the lap of the marine seated to his right. He ducked his head to avoid the man's cigar, gagging from the acrid stench. James mumbled an apology and checked his makeshift signal strength meter. The level had fallen again.

When they'd left Sayville, Captain Reynolds had insisted that "the commanding officer rides up front," placing James in the back. So the signal meter sat on his legs, making the ride more uncomfortable. The device gave off some welcome heat, but three normal-sized men would have found fitting into the back of the sedan difficult, and the captain had wedged him between the two largest marines in the radio station, if not all of North America.

Reynolds had wasted no time on introductions, so name tags were all James had to go by. The marines' read Greenwood and Reeves. He was called "Brogan."

Greenwood shifted his position, pushing him into Reeves on the other side. James's right leg burned with pins and needles. After a minute, Greenwood moved enough to let his blood flow back in.

The meter continued dropping. James slipped a hand down

to the amplifier. It was still warm, so it wasn't dropping because the car's generator was too weak. It shouldn't have been a problem with the Cadillac. It had plenty of power to spare, even with the headlights on. The overpowered, overappointed car had its advantages.

So they were moving away from the signal. Instead of getting closer to finding the rogue transmitter, they were leaving it behind. James needed to be home, not driving in circles on Long Island.

"Captain," he shouted over the sound of the car's engine, "I think we need to head west."

"West? We need to head west?" Reynolds arched an eyebrow. "Stop the car, Christensen."

The car stopped, and all the eyes of the four marines fell on James. Now it was his mission, and finding the saboteurs was on him. Besides being uncomfortable, he was under pressure to finish a job he didn't want. Was that what he'd missed when Mr. Johnson had gotten him a waiver from the draft?

James cleared his throat and fixated on the meter to avoid the marines' gazes. Being on the water in a large ship would have given whoever was blocking the signals a clear line of sight, a self-contained power supply, and a comfortable means of escape. With a powerful enough transmitter, sitting in international waters was a possibility. But as the car was moving east along the shore, the signal was getting weaker. Whoever was broadcasting this signal wasn't on the water.

"Well, the signal strength is dropping," James said, searching for an answer as he stalled for time.

Reynolds reached back and tapped the device with an impatient index finger. "Are you sure that thing is working?" he growled. "Turn the car around, Christensen. And you better be right, Brogan."

James stared at the meter, willing it to rise again. He hoped he was right. If he wasn't, he didn't know what to do or how to end this search and go home.

Christensen executed a three-point turn and hit the gas, slamming James into the seat while Reeves, the larger of the two marines, fell into him. They hurtled down the road back toward Sayville, the Cadillac's transmission whining.

They turned off the shore road and back onto the parkway, which had a smooth, fresh coat of gravel—part of the War Department's preparations for battle. Talk of conflict with Germany had been continuous since Bryan's reelection, and James had seen parallel efforts in New Jersey.

They passed the turn for a village called Patchogue, and the needle on the meter pointed higher. James sighed with relief. They were headed in the right direction again. If only there were a way the car could keep going right to the Hudson Tubes and a train home.

"The meter is going back up," said Reynolds. "I guess turning around did it, but where are we headed now? I thought you said the signal was from a ship?"

James racked his brain, desperate to come up with an answer that would point to the transmitter and a way home. He'd never said he was sure it was coming from a ship. But if it wasn't coming from one, where was it coming from?

"Yeah, so where are the Krauts hiding, Jimmy?" Christensen asked.

"Focus on driving, Sergeant," Reynolds said, then turned back to James. "So, where?"

"A place with power and a structure high enough to broadcast a signal over a broad area," James said, hoping that thinking out loud might make an idea spring to life. He leaned over the front seat to view the meter as they passed the turn for Sayville and headed farther inland toward Brooklyn and Queens. He spied a star he'd never seen before, sitting on the horizon.

"Power. That's the tricky part, huh, Jimmy?" Christensen smiled in the rearview mirror. "They'd need a generator that could power a lot of lights. Like a million of 'em."

"Sergeant, watch the road and let him think," Reynolds chided.

A million lights. James searched the dark sky for the star. It was too low. It was . . . Dreamland's Beacon Tower? Lit in the middle of winter? The Coney Island parks should have been closed for the season.

Of course.

James was an idiot for not thinking of it sooner. With more power than most neighborhoods in the city and some very tall towers, Coney Island was an excellent place to put a rogue radio transmitter. But it was at least fifty miles from Sayville. That would require special equipment. How did they build it in the tower without being noticed? No portable transmitter could generate a signal with enough noise to knock his radios off the air from fifty miles away. And, Coney Island would be a terrible place to search for spies. If they were willing to interfere with the transatlantic radios, they'd be ready to attack anyone who tried to interfere with them.

"Coney Island," James said, only half-aware he was speaking out loud.

"What?" Reynolds said. "Coney Island? Isn't that an amusement park?"

If James told the captain about his theory, they would head to the amusement park. If he didn't, the soldiers would either figure it out themselves or drive until they were out of fuel. Which one would get him home sooner? He wasn't sure, but he couldn't maintain a lie for long. So he explained his theory to Captain Reynolds.

"Let's go, Sergeant," Reynolds said. "As fast as you can. And you better be right, Brogan."

Even though he'd avoided the draft, James had had ample experience with military men. Mr. Edison himself was involved with decoding the hardware the Martians had left behind after their invasion. That project had blossomed into several contracts with the War Department. One of them was the radios James was trying to get back on the air right now.

Not that he disliked the military, either. Dad had been a veteran of the War of the Rebellion before settling in New York City as a police officer. James's final promise to his dad—to protect his mom—was driven by the same sense of purpose and service Dad had lived by.

But the military was far from perfect. Edison's first and last military liaison, Colonel Fleming, was one of the most difficult men James had ever worked with, and he'd made Susan's life a living hell when she'd started at Edison. Later, the Security Police had caught Fleming selling Martian hardware out of Edison's warehouse.

And now, instead of letting him go home, Captain Reynolds was insisting that James help him do his job.

"I'm doing my best, Captain," James said. "But isn't this a job for the Security Police? Aren't spies their purview?"

"No, absolutely not," Reynolds said.

James slumped back in his seat and tried to cross his arms. He couldn't, because of the two marines on either side, so he let out a frustrated sigh instead.

Why didn't the captain want to talk to the SPs? Not that anyone ever wanted to talk to President Bryan's federal cops, but this was literally a matter of national security. Maybe Captain Reynolds and Colonel Fleming had something in common. Could James trust this man? Was he sharing this car with another rogue officer?

As they sped west, the captain asked how the saboteurs could run a transmitter in the parks. Most of James's knowledge of the parks was secondhand, since he hadn't visited there since the early 1890s, before the Martian Attack and his dad's fatal injury in the Tesla fire.

Edison supplied the power to the parks, and James worked with the men in Menlo Park, who had built the power stations and helped wire both Luna Park with its 250,000 lights and its rival, Dreamland, with more than a million colorful bulbs. Both parks had enough power to drive a transmitter, but the 100,000 burning lights of the Beacon Tower were a bright, shining hint. The parks shut them off between Labor Day and Memorial Day.

"Wouldn't that mean someone in the park is working with the Krauts?" asked Christensen.

The captain shot him a look.

"Or someone smuggled in the equipment. Coney Island is nearly deserted this time of year. The Security Police probably left for the season back in September," James said. Christensen had a point.

"Why would they abandon the park?" Reynolds asked.

"No one is there off-season except a few locals," James said. "The bigger question is why the tower is lit. Why would they advertise that they're there? Unless it's a trap?"

"Pretty obvious for a trap. It could be a signal. Either way, we need to go there. Check your weapons," the captain told his soldiers. They nodded, and Reeves reached into his holster to check his pistol.

James cleared his throat. Was the captain going to get him killed? He was dragging him to a siege with no weapon, not to mention no training.

As the Cadillac barreled down the road, the fields and farmhouses James had passed with Christensen earlier that day loomed in the setting sun's weakening light. He'd never spent this much time in a car before, and he hoped he never would again.

Reeves opened his window, letting a blast of freezing air into the car. He lit a cigarette and pulled out a rag to wipe down his pistol. Tobacco mingled with gun oil and sweat, taking James back to Manhattan and the tiny apartment he'd grown up in. Dad would sit in the kitchen and clean his pistol at least once a week. The only thing missing today was a bottle of Irish whiskey. Dad had let James try the whiskey once when Mom wasn't looking, but he'd never let him near the gun. "Stay away from guns, James," he'd said. "No good ever comes of 'em."

They drove for another hour. The meter read full strength twice, forcing James to adjust the scale.

"Jimmy's from around here, did you know that?" Christensen asked no one in particular as they entered Brooklyn.

"Focus on driving, Sergeant."

"There. That's the Iron Tower." James pointed at it as they approached the parks on Ocean Parkway.

"It's sure big enough," Christensen said.

"No. Look at that," Reynolds said, indicating the gleaming Beacon Tower. "That's the one."

"Unless they lit that one to throw us off?" James offered. "The Iron Tower would make an excellent antenna, and it was the tallest building in New York until the Beacon was built."

Reynolds grunted.

The Beacon Tower at Dreamland loomed ahead, wiping the closer, unlit structure from the skyline. It dominated the horizon with its thousands of bulbs. The men shaded their eyes as they adjusted to its light.

Ocean Parkway ended near the water. On the right, the empty beach stretched out to the bay. The shadowy profiles of dogs wandered on the sand in the setting sun's long shadows.

Christensen guided the car onto Surf Avenue's broad expanse. James took a deep breath as the Cadillac passed a peeling sign that read Galveston Flood and entered Coney Island.

7

Fritz's pass connected perfectly with Emil's foot, as if guided by the soccer gods. Emil feinted to his left, then darted right, leaving the tall Leimersheim defender behind.

"Wake up, Zimmerman!" someone shouted from the sidelines.

Emil glided across freshly cut grass that was still a little wet from the morning dew, but his new shoes kept him from slipping. The goal loomed ahead, but Fritz flew by, closing the gap.

"I said wake up, soldier!"

Should he give the shot to his friend? Or put it away himself? Emil poured on the speed and passed Fritz. Leimersheim's goal lay ahead, a fat, wide target.

"I'm going to come in there if you don't come out!"

Emil tripped and fell. He woke before hitting the ground, wrapped in a musty blanket.

"Last chance, Zimmerman. Wake up!"

This was the Somme, not Euleheim. Fritz had died a few days ago playing soldier, not soccer.

Emil lay in one of the crevices First Platoon had cut into the walls at the northern end of the trench. It had served as his detention area since Fluse had him arrested two days earlier. Since then, Emil had been waiting here for a court-martial. His mouth felt dry, and a lump had settled in his stomach. Sleep was his only escape, and now someone took that away, too.

"Soldier, you'd better wake up."

"Why are you threatening me if you think I'm asleep?" Emil said, raising his voice so he could be heard from inside the trench wall's cut-out. The guard stood in front of the berth, and only the perfect crease of his trousers was visible. Three different men had guarded him since he'd been confined here. This Gefreiter was the worst so far.

"Who do you think you're talking to?" the guard said.

"Watch it, I'm coming out," Emil said, sliding out and planting a muddy boot on the guard's trousers.

"Hey! You're getting mud on my—" The guard stepped back, bumping into the far wall of the trench while trying to brush off the mud, more concerned with his uniform than with his "prisoner."

"You didn't answer my question. Why were you threatening me if you thought I was asleep?"

"Shut up and start marching." the guard said. He was tall, with perfect blond hair and bright blue eyes. His uniform was spotless—or had been, until it had met Emil's left foot.

"That's not an answer. Talking to people when you think they're asleep isn't normal." The guard reminded Emil of Fluse, but unlike the Leutnant, this man barely outranked him. He didn't face execution or prison, either, but that didn't mean Emil had to put up with him.

"I said shut up!" The guard set his jaw and took a step forward.

"Is it hard work?" Emil asked, refusing to move.

"Huh?" The guard's brow crinkled.

"Keeping a uniform that clean while there's a war on," Emil said, making a show of slowly rolling up his blanket. "You're aware there's a war on, right?" He tilted his head toward the guard and affected a stage whisper.

"You'd better watch it, Zimmerman."

"Why? Are you going to take me into custody again? Will you have your buddy Fluse bring me up on more charges? Like insubordination and ruining a pair of pants? You can't threaten to beat me. You might crease your jacket." Emil swept the dust off his uniform and started south, toward headquarters.

"Hey! Where are you going?"

"That way." Emil pointed south. "Or do you want to head away from command? You won't get any argument from me."

"You need to be escorted," the guard said. "The Leutnant wants to see you."

Fluse? What did *he* want? The last two days of waiting had been excruciating, but Emil didn't want to see him. Better to go ahead with the court-martial or head back to face charges in Germany.

Emil dodged the guard and held out a hand to stop him. "I don't need to be escorted. I know the way there. I know these trenches better than you. I ran the phone lines. I guess you missed that. Maybe you were at the laundry?"

"This way!" the guard snarled, grabbing Emil's shoulder and pushing him forward.

Willi, Emil's older brother, had died while serving as an infantryman in Mexico. Now Emil would end up in a letter to their mother, too, but not for the same "noble" reason.

Last night, Emil had fantasized about being called before the Hauptmann and given a stern lecture on military discipline, with a wink and a nod acknowledging that Emil was right. The Hauptmann would silently acknowledge that Fritz was dead because of Fluse and send Emil home for his trouble.

Of course, that would never happen. But maybe the Hauptmann would reduce his sentence down to that latrine duty Ludwig had threatened. Emil would have agreed to that for the kaiser's next three wars.

But he wasn't going to the Hauptmann. Would Fluse make an example of him with a firing squad? Or have him shipped to prison back home? Either way, Emil wouldn't make it home, let alone back to Telefunken to work on the radios.

They reached the first intersection at the end of First Platoon's trench. On the right was a tunnel that led underground and exited near Mametz Wood. Emil had run an extra set of cables through there as a backup for the ones that ran out to regimental headquarters. If he knocked out this peacock of a guard and fled through that tunnel, he'd get halfway to Germany before they found him. Then they'd take him home instead of making him face Fluse. But that would guarantee an execution, not avoid it. Only cowards ran. Emil was no coward. A coward would have kept his mouth shut. A coward wouldn't have been in this mess.

The trenches meandered through a set of switchbacks before the last turn at headquarters. The winding paths kept newcomers off-balance and created bottlenecks. A new tent sat on the wooden frame the carpenters had been working on two days ago. It stood at least twice as high as the old command post. A stainless-steel stovepipe, with black diesel smoke belching out from it, jutted out from one corner.

The guard jerked Emil's shoulder, guiding him toward the doorway.

"Yeah, yeah, I know!" Emil said, pushing back at the guard.

"Shut up."

Emil started to retort but cut himself short as the door opened. Fluse walked out and blocked their path. Even though a twinge of weakness shot through his legs, Emil stood his ground. He wouldn't let Fluse see he was afraid.

"Good morning, sir," Emil said. "I was just complimenting Gefreiter . . . uh, what's your name?"

"Shut up," the guard snapped.

"Yes, of course. I was complimenting Gefreiter Shut Up on his spotless uniform, sir. You should be very proud of him."

The guard's hand left Emil's shoulder, and he snapped to attention. Emil slowly brought his feet together and his hands to his side. He locked eyes with the young Leutnant but didn't lift his hand to salute. The man didn't deserve it. Besides, what could he do to Emil at that point?

He thought about Fritz. He thought about the Black Smoke. He shocked himself when he found no urge to attack Fluse. He only wanted to get away from him. To end this conversation as quietly as possible.

Fluse held Emil's gaze, waiting for his salute. His mouth curled up at one end. "You still can't show me even the most basic respect, can you?"

Was it a test? Should he salute? Apologize? No. Fritz was dead because of Fluse. Emil wouldn't give him the satisfaction of an argument—or more charges to throw at him.

"Very well," Fluse said. "Despite my input on the matter, the Hauptmann has ordered that you be released to your platoon. Gefreiter, take this man to Unteroffizier Oberacker and out of my sight." He stepped aside to let them pass.

They'd dropped the charges? Why? Emil stood still, light-headed and dumbstruck, until he felt a push from behind.

"Get moving," the guard said.

Emil started walking, but slowed his pace as soon as Fluse was out of sight. "What was that all about?" he asked.

"Shut up."

They kept walking, retracing the steps Emil had taken two days earlier. Why had he been released? What had changed?

There were no open bottles of schnaps this morning. The chessboards and card decks were gone. The men were awake, wolfing down egg biscuits and drinking water from canteens. A few of them were rolling blankets and packing up gear.

"Get off me," Emil said to the guard.

No response this time.

The men were packing and getting ready to move. That was

why he'd been released: they needed him. Fluse would find a way to get him later.

Emil stopped.

"Get moving!" the guard said, shoving Emil at his shoulder.

"I can tell you're upset," Emil said. "We're bugging out, and you'll have to leave that warm command post. So why don't you head back to command? I know the way."

"If you don't shut up and start walking . . ."

Gefreiter Shut Up was getting repetitive. Emil spun around to face him. "I think we've covered how toothless your threats are. Leave. I know my way back," He crossed his arms.

A crowd gathered around them. Emil recognized the dark-haired soccer player from Leimersheim and nodded to him.

"What's going on?" the soccer player asked.

The guard spun around to face him. "Back off, Beckenbauer. Or I'll have you up on charges, too."

"Oh, you want to threaten him now, too?" Emil asked. "Mix it up a little to hone your skills." He turned and resumed walking. "I'm heading to my platoon. It looks like they'll need my help packing."

The guard started to object, then fell in step with Emil. They rounded another corner, and his hand went back on Emil's shoulder. "I need to take you to Unteroffizier Oberacker," the guard said. "Those are my orders."

Emil brushed his hand away. "Whatever. If you want to waste your time following me, that's your problem."

They reached the muddy trench between Fifth and Fourth Platoon, and Emil braced himself against the wall. "Oh, you're going to mess up those perfect boots now," he said, smiling.

"Shut up."

"And you need to work on your vocabulary."

Emil turned the corner, with Gefreiter Shut Up trailing behind, and entered Third Platoon's trench. Like the other platoons, Third was packing up and getting ready to move out.

Were they preparing for another attack? Or getting ready to move behind the Pioneers?

Ludwig Oberacker was supervising operations down by the next turn in the trench, with one arm on his hip and the other brandishing an unlit cigar. Emil was too far away to tell if he was lecturing a young soldier on the finer points of rolling a sleeping bag or cleaning a mess kit.

The guard steered Emil toward Ludwig with one arm on his shoulder. Emil pushed back enough to let him know that if he hadn't submitted earlier, he certainly wasn't going to now. As they closed in on Ludwig and the men, the smell of egg biscuit filled Emil's nostrils and his stomach rumbled. He hadn't eaten since last night.

Ludwig was, in fact, lecturing on mess kit maintenance. He stopped and turned toward Emil.

"Well, here we are," Emil said, turning to face the guard. "I wish I could say it was fun, and I'd say I was sorry about the mud on your boots, but you didn't have to follow me. You could have been somewhere else, telling someone else to shut up."

"That's enough, Zimmerman," Ludwig growled, lumbering toward them. His trench coat was open, his helmet was missing, and a ribbon of sweat decorated his brow. He was the opposite of Emil's escort in almost every way, but still twice the soldier.

The guard exhaled and shifted to one side to engage the Unteroffizier directly. "Here he is, Herr Unteroffizier. He's all yours." Shut Up's voice dripped with contempt. He clearly wanted to say more but lacked the courage.

"Thank you, Gefreiter," Emil said, smiling. "You're dismissed."

The soldier tilted his head and opened his mouth, then shook his head and walked away.

Ludwig raised an eyebrow. He waited until the guard disappeared around the corner before speaking. "Still making friends, I see?"

"He's just a Gefreiter. Who does he think he is, trying to push me around?"

"He probably thinks he's one of the men who had to stand watch over you the last two nights because you got yourself arrested."

"True. He'll have to stay up late again to make up for lost time ironing uniforms."

"That's enough," Ludwig repeated. He put the cigar in his mouth and reached down to close his coat.

Were there really not going to be consequences for Emil going after an officer twice? Why had he been let go over Fluse's objections?

"So, why am I here?" he asked. "Other than to help you move out."

"Why are you here? As opposed to being marched east to a prison camp? Or tried and shot over at headquarters? That's a good question." Ludwig took the cigar out of his mouth and produced a knife to cut off the end.

Emil crossed his arms, anticipating a lecture.

Ludwig turned and glanced at the rest of the platoon. "Let's take a walk down here," he said, guiding Emil toward where he'd entered the trench with the guard. Whatever Ludwig had to say, he didn't want to broadcast it to the rest of the men. That could be good—or bad. When they were out of earshot, Ludwig turned back toward Emil with a sigh.

Emil crossed his arms again. Would this be the standard "be a better soldier" lecture? He tapped the fingers of his right hand on his left elbow.

"You're here for two reasons," Ludwig said, lighting his cigar. "One, because Hauptmann Degenscheide has taken pity on you."

"Pity!" Emil spat.

"Yes, pity. And you would do well to appreciate it. After he learned how close you were to Seith and how it drove you to flagrant, pointless, and stupid insubordination not once but twice, he decided to let you go with a warning."

The image of Fritz lying on the trench floor came rushing back to Emil, and with it came a flood of anger. Fluse had gotten a man killed, but Emil was the one to get off with a warning. Military justice.

"A warning that I will deliver now," Ludwig went on. "Shut. Up."

"I've been hearing that a lot, but I doubt Degenscheide said that," Emil said.

"Well, whether you believe that Hauptmann Degenscheide used those exact words, take it to heart. The war's nearly over. Shut up. You'll make it home, and you can go back to your wireless."

"I guess it was you who told him about Fritz." Had Ludwig talked with the Hauptmann about poor Emil, who'd been so upset over his buddy, and they'd agreed to give him a break?

"He knew about Seith," Ludwig said. "Our company commander knows when his troops are killed, and he knows where they're from."

Emil frowned and crossed his arms again. How would Degenscheide have known? Or cared?

"He's a lawyer back in Karlsruhe, you know," Ludwig said.

"So?"

"He's one of you. A reserve soldier. A civilian. He doesn't want to be here any more than you do, and he's not your enemy."

"So you say."

Ludwig smiled wryly. "He could have gone along with Fluse on a court-martial. He could have sent you back home to a prison. He could have pulled his sidearm and shot you himself. But he didn't."

"Because you intervened. I didn't ask you to do that." Emil's face warmed.

Ludwig took a long drag on his cigar and puffed out a few

smoke rings. "No, of course you didn't. Your instinct for self-preservation never was that good."

"Shouldn't we start packing now?"

"You have an unusual way of saying thank you, Emil. Tell me, what do you want?"

Emil cocked his head. Was this his punishment? More of Ludwig's philosophy and tips on how to be a good soldier? Career advice in the trench? Prison seemed better.

"It's not a hard question, is it?" Ludwig asked, and blew three perfect smoke rings. Philosophy and a floor show.

Emil shook his head. He had no answer. No answer that a career soldier like Ludwig would accept. Get out of the trench. Go home. Get away from men like Fluse. Those answers would only lead to a longer lecture with advice on how to succeed in the army, not get away from it.

"You want out," Ludwig continued. "You attacked Fluse twice. Once physically. What were you trying to do? It wasn't revenge. You carry a loaded gun. If you wanted revenge, you would have shot him."

"Well, maybe I will." Emil reflexively looked down at his side for his weapon and remembered that his tools, gun, and mask were still back at headquarters.

"No, you won't. I wouldn't have intervened if I thought you would."

Emil exhaled in frustration and stared at the ground.

"You want to make things better," Ludwig went on. "You see the stupidity. You see puffed-up peacocks like Fluse, and you want to fix them."

"No. I just want to go home." Emil wasn't trying to fix this war, just get away from it.

"Sure, even a lifer like me doesn't want to be on the battlefield." Ludwig took another drag on his cigar and held it for a moment before exhaling. "But you still want things to be better here. Men like Fluse piss you off."

Emil nodded. He still didn't know why he hadn't gone for Fluse again back at the tent.

"It won't get better if you fight the system. I told you before, you need to fall in line and do the right thing."

Emil shook his head. "I'll never fall in line."

"Well, that may be true. But class is over. 'Thank you, Ludwig, for saving me from prison, or even execution.' You're welcome, Emil," Ludwig said, mimicking Emil with a higher-pitched voice before returning to his own.

The warmth spread to Emil's ears. Ludwig was right; Emil should at least thank him. But the words wouldn't come.

Before he could decide if—or how—to respond, shouts rang out nearby.

Emil and Ludwig looked at each other, then for the source of the noise.

The shouting grew louder before two soldiers jumped into the trench from the east, screaming and pointing back behind the lines.

Emil ran to the frame on the trench's eastern wall. He scrambled up and looked where the men were pointing. About a half kilometer away, a cloud of Black Smoke was filtering between a cluster of trees.

Black Smoke? Again?

Emil's chest tightened, and his heart started to race. There was no fighting nearby, and even if there were, why would they have deployed the Smoke behind German lines? Was it an accident? Or were they under attack?

The Smoke reached a group of men on Emil's side of the trees, and they fell to their knees. Emil jumped off the scaffolding. "Gas! Gas!" he shouted, reaching for his mask—

But he didn't have his mask. Fluse had taken all of his gear away when they'd taken him into custody. He hadn't picked it up after his stand-off in front of headquarters with the Leutnant. Had Ludwig saved him from a court-martial so the army could kill him with Black Smoke, like they had with Fritz?

8

The Beacon Tower cast a wide shadow across Surf Avenue, which was littered with colorful flyers, crumpled newspapers, and shattered glass. The sudden shade made it feel as if the car was driving directly under the tall structure, despite it standing hundreds of feet away.

On one side of the street, a thirty-foot-tall Martian Tripod loomed on three stilt-like legs. Its chrome sparkled in the Beacon Tower's light, guarding a sign declaring Dreamland the brightest park in the world. Its single red eye scrutinized the Cadillac as Christensen guided it onto West 8th Street. He parked the car about a block down the street, across from the local police station.

"What was that?" he asked as everyone climbed out of the sedan.

James stood slowly, wincing as his legs stung with pins and needles. He braced himself against a fender, taking deep breaths of cold air free of cigar smoke and gun oil. After a moment, he realized the big marine was talking to him.

"That silver thing we passed," Christensen said. "It looked like a fancy water tank."

"That's Dreamland's idea of a Martian Tripod," James said.

"Oh. I never saw one before."

"You still haven't," James said.

The New York City Police precinct's lights were on, and people were moving behind the glass doors and big, street-level windows. The shuttered Security Police station was next door. Both buildings sat in the long shadow of the hotel on Surf Avenue.

"You were right, Brogan," Captain Reynolds said, shaking his head. "No Security Police."

"We can talk to the local cops instead," James said. They might tell the captain to send him, the civilian, home.

"No. This is national business."

James's dad had come home angry from his beat one night, a few months before the Tesla fire. The Security Police had intervened in a labor demonstration, killing fifteen people and putting more than twenty in the hospital. "National business" rarely went well.

"I didn't see anyone as we drove in," Reynolds continued. "So if the saboteurs are here, either they haven't posted guards, or they're well concealed. How do we get to that tower, Brogan?"

"We cross the avenue." James pointed and cleared his throat. "How do we know we're not walking into a trap?"

"We don't. Stay in between us, and keep quiet."

Captain Reynolds led them down West 8th Street back to Surf Avenue. Greenwood walked on one side of James, a fresh cigar hanging out of his mouth, pistol raised in his right hand. Reeves was on the other side, his weapon hanging more casually at his side. Christensen took up the rear, his gun still holstered.

As the group reached Surf Avenue, the silence grew heavier, blanketing the street. A chill ran down James's spine. He'd never seen Coney Island so desolate before. Weather-worn signs hawked gaudy attractions, fried foods, and cheap trinkets. The silent avenue put the Beacon Tower's bright lights in stark, unsettling relief. The tang of salt water mingled with dust, horse manure, and what was either a lingering hint of kettle corn or the distant memory of it.

Was it always this quiet here in the winter? Where were the locals? Were people scared off by the tower being lit out of season?

"It doesn't look real," Christensen said, tapping James on the shoulder.

James followed the marine's gaze to the chrome Walker down the block. "No. Real Walkers are taller. They're not chrome, and the legs aren't rigid stilts. I've never seen one with a big red eye, either."

Christensen's jaw dropped. "You've seen more than one? How old were you when they attacked?"

Greenwood glowered at Christensen and shook his head.

"I didn't see any during the Attack," James answered. "I was young, and we still lived in Manhattan. They didn't make it to the city." His mind wandered back to the pictures of the wreckage in the newspapers. That was the first time his parents had talked about leaving the coast, but it took the Tesla fire and Dad's injuries to force them out of the city a few years later. "We have the remains of a few at Edison," he continued. "But I'm no expert."

"Shhhh," the captain hissed.

The hotel's exterior door creaked open. Two locals, a tattooed man and a man of short stature, walked outside.

"He couldn't hear me," the shorter man said. "The telephones are still busted."

"Still? Boss ain't gonna like that." The tattooed man stopped and glared at James's group. "Whaddya lookin' at, rube?" he snarled, singling out Christensen with a colorful finger. "You got a problem?" He laughed.

Before Christensen could answer, the tattooed man climbed into a carriage as the shorter man untied the horse and jumped in next to him. He grabbed the reins and spurred the horse down the avenue.

"Try to avoid staring at the locals, Sergeant," Reynolds said.

"Sorry, sir. I never saw anyone like that, not even at the state fair."

"Me neither, but we're here about the radios, not crowd control. But it's good to see that someone was still around. If the saboteurs are here, they haven't taken over the area."

So the interference was strong enough to affect the telephones. The signal was originating here, then.

"The locals aren't dressed in marine uniforms, either," James said.

"What are you trying to say, Brogan?" Reynolds sneered.

"There's a difference between a couple of locals living out the winter and four marines carrying pistols."

"Let me worry about that." Reynolds started across the avenue and into the shadow of an enormous building that curved away from the street corner with faux Grecian columns and lintels. From a distance, the building appeared to be sculpted from marble, but it was formed from wooden cladding and plaster painted white with gold highlights.

James and the others followed the curve of the garish arena down West 8th Street and stopped at a grand entrance. Its sign shouted in bright letters "BOSTOCK THE ANIMAL KING. TRAINED LIONS, TIGERS, BEARS, PANTHERS, WOLVES, ELEPHANTS, HYENAS, ETC." A rope hung across the gate with another sign: "TOURING EUROPE. PLEASE COME AGAIN."

"A zoo?" Christensen asked.

"Circus," James said.

"Enough with the chatter," Reynolds growled. "What's that? I hear engines running."

"That's the power station. Across from the walkway to the tower."

"This park has its own electricity?"

James had mentioned the generators in the car. But even if he hadn't, how did the captain not understand? He was in over his head—and pulling them all down with him.

"Well, yes," James said. "Like I said, they have more than a million lights. But I'm not sure it should be running with the park closed. Unless Dreamland is supplying power to the other businesses around here. Edison has a station for Luna Park, but he needed to add another one to handle the additional load." He pointed to Surf Avenue and gestured in Luna Park's direction, where the primary station stood.

Dreamland's owners used the power station as an attraction, making the wheezing and sputtering of the engines audible from a few hundred feet away. But why were they running at full capacity, even with the park shut down? Someone had been there—or was still there. Were they watching James and the others?

"The transmitter is here," James said.

"What?" Reynolds asked.

"The generators are working too hard. Something is drawing extra power."

"Well, the tower is lit." The captain stepped out of the shadow of Bostock's, pointing at the illuminated structure.

"Edison designed this power station for the tower and the rest of Dreamland," James said, a chill running down his spine. What were they using? What could draw enough current to strain the generators?

"So you're saying something else is using the power? Like a transmitter?"

"Yes, I think so," James answered. The captain was still having a hard time grasping the situation.

"You think so? You're supposed to be the expert. Should we go to it?"

Something was up there. Would Reynolds force him to go with them to find out?

"Well?" the captain asked.

"Yes, let's go."

The five of them left the shadow of the circus building and entered an open area, where a ring of boat-shaped "airships" hung from steel arms, waiting for summer. They were still in the gray evening light, casting shadows in the tower's light that rose hundreds of feet behind them.

Christensen whistled. "I definitely saw nothing like that in Iowa."

"Wait here, out of sight," Reynolds said, then glared at Christensen. "And keep your voices down." He walked around the airships, staying in the structure's shadow, and disappeared around the corner.

"Did you come here as a kid, Jimmy?" Christensen asked.

"No," James said. "My dad didn't like it here. He said it was full of criminals and freaks."

"Oh. I thought you knew the place."

"Only from talking to the men at Edison who helped set up the generators. Even if I had, Dreamland has only been here since '04. I was already in West Orange by then."

"The tower entrance is on a bridge that straddles a pool," Reynolds said as he reappeared. "I see access ramps on two sides. Christensen, take Reeves and head around that way to the other side. Stay in the shadows as long as you can."

Christensen and Reeves left, and the captain led James and Greenwood in the other direction. They walked under the airships, then veered right before stepping back into the light near the Dreamland Power Station. A walkway led away from the station to the base of the tower.

Reynolds sent Greenwood up the ramp, covering him from one side. The marine made the run with no sign of trouble.

"Your turn, Brogan," the captain said in a stage whisper. "You have two men covering you now."

"You want me to run?" James asked.

Reynolds grinned. "Well, you can walk if you like, but I'd recommend keeping low and moving as fast as you can."

"That's very helpful."

The ramp was short, barely a few feet long. No one had shot at Greenwood, so it was probably safe. Unless Greenwood had only alerted the saboteurs, and now they were waiting for a second runner to shoot.

"Sometime tonight, Brogan," Reynolds said.

James took off with his heart in his throat. He barreled up the ramp as fast as he could and nearly knocked over Greenwood when he got to the tower's base. Christensen and Reeves were already there.

"Well done, Jimmy!" Christensen whispered, smiling. "We'll make a marine out of you yet."

James smiled despite himself as he caught his breath.

"Well, either no one's watching, or they're waiting for us at the top," Reynolds said as he arrived at the top of the ramp. His breathing was normal, even though he'd covered the distance in half the time James had.

The Beacon Tower straddled a moat full of stagnant seawater and rotting trash. A rat skittered by as James and the others walked up a ramp.

The tower continued the Greek theme established at Bostock's, with four freestanding pillars at each corner that did nothing but ostentatiously occupy space. Planters on either side of the doorway overflowed with cigar and cigarette butts, doing little to enhance the attempt at an ancient ambiance, but they matched the patina of dust and smoke covering the painted cladding.

The top narrowed into a gaudy light bulb-encrusted steeple with enough room for one person and equipment at the top. One sign blared, "50-MILE VIEW," next to another that proclaimed, "ONLY 10 CENTS!" Both halves of a chain hung from either side of the elevator, and a broken link was lying on the ramp. The door was open, beckoning people to climb on board. James gaped at the damaged chain, then at the top of the tower. Was whoever had done that still here?

"Someone wanted to use this elevator badly enough to cut the chain," Reynolds said, his voice still low. "But if they're still around, this will turn into a trap very quickly."

"Sir, there's a door and stairs over here," Christensen said from around one side of the tower.

"Won't they hear someone taking the stairs?" James asked.

"If someone's up there, they already know we're here," Reynolds said. "But even if they don't, we can defend ourselves or retreat by the stairs."

"We?"

"I'll go, sir," Christensen said, nodding at James. "There's no reason for Jimmy to be in the first group."

Reynolds appraised James for a moment, then said, "Fine. The three of you go first. Me and Brogan will wait down here for your signal."

James sighed, making a note to thank Christensen later.

"If you see anything, leave it alone," the captain said to his men. "Come right down. Brogan can go up once we know the coast is clear."

If the coast was clear, James could see the transmitter that blocked the radio signal in Sayville from fifty miles away.

Christensen, Greenwood, and Reeves entered the tower, their weapons out. Captain Reynolds stepped away from the door and back onto the ramp, looking over to where he and James had entered. Another plaster and plywood structure sat next to the power station, bathed in the tower's light. It was a castle with a leering Satan looming over its battlements. One of Satan's elbows perched jauntily over a forbidding entrance. For just ten cents, you could take a boat ride through Hell.

"Hell Gate?" Reynolds asked.

"Popular attraction," James said. "In the summer, there's always a line to get in."

"I guess city folk find going to Hell funny."

No. People who survived the Martian Attack and the Tesla fire found the concept of Hell funny.

James looked up at the tower and wiped his brow. He was sweating despite the cold.

"You really don't want to be here, do you?" Reynolds asked.

His uniform was still neatly creased under his unbuttoned parka, even after an hours-long car ride and exploring the park.

"I think I made that clear."

"I didn't need to read your file to tell that you never served," Reynolds snapped.

"Wh—I served. I'm serving right now. I'm the only reason you found this tower." James's cheeks burned as his voice cracked on the word *only*.

"Serving? You've been trying to get out of doing your part since you arrived at my station."

It was hard to tell what hurt more: that the captain was right, or that it was "his" station.

"I have a mom at home," James said. "I should be taking care of her before this turns into a war. This is sabotage. The Germans are pulling us into their conflict."

"You're right. This'll give Bryan his reason to go to war." Reynolds shook his head.

James stopped walking. The captain wasn't eager to fight, either?

Before he could reply, a blast filled the air, slamming James to the ground. Wood splintered and groaned in protest as burning cinders fell onto the nearby ramp.

James struggled to his feet and looked up. The top of the Beacon Tower was engulfed in flames. As he turned toward the airships, a second explosion knocked him onto his side. Acrid smoke from burning pitch filled his lungs, and he could only get to his knees as he choked.

Hell Gate was on fire.

Was it a bomb? Or a trap? Had the Germans attacked? The war had started, and James was kneeling ten feet from burning Hell instead of home, where he belonged.

Reynolds was hidden somewhere in the thick smoke. James squinted, trying to use the airships as a landmark to find the tower. As he stumbled to his feet and away from the smoke, he heard Reynolds screaming the names of his men. James changed direction, following the sound of the captain's cries before stumbling at the end of the ramp.

He found Reynolds in a break in the smoke. The marine was standing at the foot of the remaining corner of the tower, heaving pieces of smoldering plywood in the air. "Greenwood! Christensen! Reeves!" he screamed.

James froze as he heard wood splinter again. A dark shape hurtled toward him, but before he could duck, the world went black.

9

Emil ran as fast as he could. Beckenbauer had been right; he'd been one of the best midfielders in Baden. Few men were faster than him, and one had died for lack of a mask. Now Emil dodged and leaped, sprinting for his life through the trenches. The sick feeling in his stomach receded as he found his rhythm, and his heart rate evened out.

Men cheered and jeered as he flew by. Some shouted, asking which Offizier he was running from. Another joked about the latrine. But then the whistles blew, and they were too focused on getting their masks and rifles to pay him any mind.

Only when Emil was about halfway to headquarters did he look back. Two soldiers from Third Platoon turned the corner and came into view. Neither were wearing their masks. What were they doing? Emil turned and poured on the speed.

He reached the command post as Fluse burst out the door. The Leutnant certainly spent a lot of time by that door. "Zimmerman!" he yelled. "What the hell are you doing back here? Who blew those whistles?"

Not him. And not now. Emil needed to retrieve his gear before the Smoke reached them. He pushed his way past the Leutnant and into the tent. Fluse hit the ground hard, and Emil allowed himself a moment of satisfaction as he scanned the tent for his gear.

"Zimmerman! I'll have you shot! Hanged! Beheaded!"

Emil's pack was sitting in the corner, where Shut Up had thrown it two days earlier.

The door creaked open. Emil braced himself for the Leutnant as he picked up his mask. Footsteps echoed off the trench walls outside as the rest of the men arrived.

"Who are you? What's happening here?" Fluse's voice was almost a screech.

"Smoke, sir," Beckenbauer answered. "Black Smoke."

"What the hell are you talking about?" Fluse shouted.

Hauptmann Degenscheide emerged from a doorway at the other end of the command post, brandishing a mess kit piled high with eggs and pork sausage. The room-temperature egg biscuits the other men had had that morning apparently weren't good enough for the kaiser's officers.

"What's all the shouting in here, Leutnant?" Degenscheide asked. With no helmet and his uniform jacket hung half open, he came across more like the lawyer Ludwig had said he was than a company commander.

A group was still collecting outside the tent. Ludwig pushed his way to the front. "We're under attack," he gasped, then managed to choke out "Martians" before leaning forward and resting his hands on his knees. His breath sounded like a pipe organ in desperate need of repair.

Emil spun to face him. Ludwig had mocked Emil for thinking the Smoke had come from Martians when Fritz had been killed.

"These men are playing a prank, sir," Fluse said. "Now they claim—"

A deafening howl cut him off.

The tent fell silent. Degenscheide's gourmet mess kit hit the plywood floor of the command post with the muffled jangling of fine silver. A chill settled in the pit of Emil's stomach, spreading to the rest of his body as the sound rose again.

A Martian howl.

It was the electronic wailing noise the Martians made as they attacked in their walking machines. The same sound Emil had heard for the first time fifteen years ago, on a soccer field with Fritz.

Panic broke out in the command post as German discipline dissipated. Men struggled to enter the command post, as if a piece of canvas and a flimsy wood frame could shield them. Fluse ordered everyone to calm down, but a bystander would have been forgiven for thinking he was only trying to pacify himself.

Emil pushed the images of home away. He and his comrades needed to get out of the tent and away from the Smoke. He reached for his mask, and the Hauptmann made eye contact with him.

"Silence!" Degenscheide shouted. "Zimmerman's right. Get your masks on!" Once everyone in their platoon had lowered their masks, he asked, "Which way are they coming from?"

"South and east, sir," Ludwig replied.

"West!" Beckenbauer bellowed. "The Wanderers were on the west side of the trench."

Degenscheide stood there, arms at his side. Even with the mask on, he was a lawyer who'd lost his briefs.

Another howl rose outside the tent, this time from the west. The soldiers were surrounded on at least two sides.

Degenscheide's eyes grew into saucers. "Clear the doorway! We need to get out of here and on the move."

"You heard the Hauptmann!" Ludwig bellowed. "Clear the way!" His shouts shocked the men out of their panic, and a pathway appeared. Degenscheide went through first, heading north. Fluse was behind him, Emil next, then Ludwig, followed by the rest of the group.

More howls sounded behind them, followed by the deep, throbbing hum of a heat ray. It was the sound of his friends being incinerated on the soccer field, of his house bursting into flames with Hermine inside. Emil's stomach heaved, and he stumbled, falling onto his hands.

The soldiers hurtled through the trenches, somehow managing to avoid colliding with one another, even as they ran into more men who joined the desperate run. Finally, the Hauptmann took the left passageway that would take them to regimental headquarters.

Emil slowed. If the Martians had already attacked Third Company, wouldn't they attack the regiment, too? Degenscheide was taking them toward another military position. First Platoon's trench lay to the right, with the underground passage to Mametz Woods a few hundred meters past it. They'd have a better chance at avoiding the Martians underground and looking for cover in the woods.

"What's wrong?" Ludwig asked.

Emil shook his head and started moving again. It wasn't his decision. Degenscheide was in charge.

They moved more rapidly than before, since the trenches between the company and regimental headquarters were empty. But there were more switchbacks and false passageways. It looked like Degenscheide knew the way, though.

They neared regimental headquarters, and Degenscheide led them around a sharp turn and stopped short. Fluse ran directly into him, forcing the Hauptmann to the ground. Emil avoided the same fate by vaulting over both men and landing on his back.

When he looked up, he was facing a Martian Wanderer.

It was different from the ones he'd seen in Euleheim. This one had a larger, irregularly shaped, muddy brown body adorned with patches of green, not the unfinished metal he'd seen before. Camouflage! The Martians had learned from the last attack. It still lacked a front or back, so Emil couldn't tell where it pointed as its arms snaked in every direction. The Wanderer loomed over the soldiers, a malevolent tower casting a long shadow.

Emil was close enough to touch one of the steely, snakelike

tentacles that ended in razor-sharp pincers. This wasn't the first time he'd been this close to a Wanderer. One had tried to catch him back in Euleheim during the first attack, right after he'd fled the soccer field.

The deep, throbbing hum of the Wanderer's heat ray yanked Emil back to the present. He turned back toward the corner of the trench. The hum sounded again, and his feet turned to lead.

Ludwig waved his arms, gesturing to Emil and two other officers. Fluse and Degenscheide backtracked around the sharp bend.

Emil couldn't move. He stared over his shoulder at the Wanderer and waited for the sound that had destroyed his home in Euleheim, killing Hermine.

Ludwig grabbed Emil and pulled him away from the Wanderer.

"We're trapped!" Fluse said. He had a firm grasp on the obvious.

"I can take us back to the company," Degenscheide said. "But is it even still there?"

"You didn't want to come this way, did you?" Ludwig asked, locking eyes with Emil.

The tunnel at the end of First Platoon's trench was nearby. Emil could lead them through it to Mametz Woods, but the tunnel might be a terrible place to find yourself with Martians attacking and Black Smoke in the air.

Why should he take charge—and responsibility—for the soldiers? The officers who'd been ready to send him to prison should have known what to do.

Ludwig's hand fell onto his shoulder. "Which way, Emil? You know these trenches better than any of us."

10

The chemical bouquet of Lysol greeted James as he regained consciousness. Bleach's caustic bite followed, working its way like smelling salts through dizziness and a dull ache in the back of his skull. He scrunched up his eyes to make it go away. He was in a hospital—and he'd spent too much time in hospitals, watching his dad waste away.

He'd been on Coney Island with Captain Reynolds. Christensen had been at the top of the Beacon Tower. And then it had burned and collapsed.

James opened one eye, but the glare from bright lights and white walls forced it closed. He lifted a hand to check himself for injuries, but the room started spinning before he could raise it far enough to reach. Something had hit him hard.

Something? Or someone?

Germans.

Memories flooded back to James, and his heart raced. The Germans had blocked the radios and attacked the marines at Coney Island.

And they might have killed Christensen.

They're animals, Jimmy.

Who was next? Mom? Susan? Lysol and bleach fought for his

attention, and a wave of nausea pushed his headache into the background. A swell of dizziness stymied him when he tried to sit up. Another, more severe bout of nausea came, and he fell back onto the bed with a groan.

"He's awake, sir."

A nurse's head appeared, seemingly suspended in the air from around a doorframe. James blinked at her. The rest of her stepped into the room, followed by a tall figure. "James! It's a relief to see you with your eyes open," the figure said.

After a few seconds, James's vision cleared, and he recognized Ben Johnson, his boss at Edison Laboratories.

Mr. Johnson ran a hand through his dark, unkempt hair, which contrasted the uncharacteristic salt-and-pepper stubble on his cheeks. James gaped at his casual slacks and winter jacket. He couldn't remember ever seeing his boss in anything but a suit.

"What am I doing here?" James asked. "Help me up. I need to go home." His throat hurt with each word; and when he tried to sit up, a new surge of dizziness made him slump back onto the bed.

"Whoa. Take it easy, James. You're not going anywhere until a doctor releases you." Mr. Johnson offered a crooked smile. "You've been through a lot. You're in a hospital in Brooklyn. I know you're not happy here, so I'll make sure you're released as soon as possible."

Mr. Johnson had been around when Dad had died. They'd met in the hospital, and he knew all too well how much James hated being in one. He'd been involved in an investigation into how Tesla had gotten the power supply that had quickly burned downtown Manhattan before slowly killing Dad.

The nurse edged past Mr. Johnson, poured a glass of water, and helped James sit up enough to take a sip. His head swam as she pulled him into place with gentle, surprisingly strong hands, but the cool water helped.

"You need to stay here, young man," the nurse said as she

locked eyes with James. "I'll fetch the doctor, Mr. Johnson." She then turned and left the room.

"Have they attacked yet?" James asked.

"Attacked?" Mr. Johnson answered. "Who?"

"The Germans."

"Germans? You saw German soldiers?" Mr. Johnson's eyes widened, and he took a step back.

"No," James said, freezing for a moment. What had happened after the explosion? Had Captain Reynolds made it out alive? His heart sped up again as he fumbled with the water. "But it must have been the Germans who set up the transmitter. There was a transmitter at the Beacon Tower. It was blocking the signals at Sayville, and over the whole area. Some marines went up to see . . ." His throat was hurting again.

"I know what happened at Dreamland, James. I spoke to Captain Reynolds."

So the captain was alive. James breathed a sigh of relief. But what were the Germans doing now? Why would they block the radios if it wasn't a prelude to war? It was time to go home and take his mom away from the city. Away from the coast.

James groped for the water glass and took another drink. "I want to go home. I need to get Mom away from here before they attack." He sat up a little further, fighting the dull aching in his head.

"There's no attack," Mr. Johnson said, shaking his head, "But you may be right about it being Germans." He raised an eyebrow, stepped in closer, and lowered his voice. "I need you to examine the wreckage. Seward recovered the debris and is taking it to the lab."

James thought about the signal they'd followed from east of Sayville back to Coney Island. What had the Germans been using? Had they developed technology they hadn't shared with Edison? What else were they hiding?

He didn't have time for that.

"What if the Germans are going to—"

"James, the Germans can't get ships or troops here without getting past our navy." Mr. Johnson shook his head again and held out his hands. "And there's no way here from Mexico without crossing half the country. Slow down, and tell me what happened. I spoke to the captain, but he's injured and couldn't say much. Why don't you tell me while we're waiting for a doctor to release you?"

James rubbed his face with one hand. The room tilted, then righted itself after a moment. Through the haze of pain and dizziness, he tried to remember what had happened. The events at Coney Island wouldn't make any sense if he didn't explain what he'd found at Sayville first. So he started with how he'd figured out the signal was coming from over the air.

"Good job, James!" Mr. Johnson said, smiling. "I wouldn't have thought about connecting an antenna right to the amp."

"What happened to Christensen?" James asked. Maybe he'd survived.

"Who?"

"Sergeant Christensen. The marine who drove me from Manhattan to Sayville, and then drove the car to Coney Island."

"Captain Reynolds was the only other survivor, James. I'm sorry."

Nausea returned, even though James was still. So Christensen hadn't made it. He'd volunteered to go before Reynolds had had a chance to send James, and he'd gotten himself killed. The papers would call Christensen a hero, just as they'd done with Dad—and he'd ended up dead, just like Dad, too.

"Captain Reynolds will be okay," Mr. Johnson continued. "He was trapped under the debris that struck you and took the brunt of it. Tell me what you saw at the station."

"Can we do this tomorrow?" James asked. "I want to go home."

Mr. Johnson frowned. "You can't go until the doctor releases you, James. And I want you to go to the lab and examine the wreckage."

"Today?" No. James didn't care what Mr. Johnson said. He looked at the ceiling again, his eyes open. The room shifted again and seemed to stay tilted to the left.

Mr. Johnson pursed his lips. "Can you tell me how you got to Coney Island?"

If James appeared too injured, the doctor might keep him in the hospital. He needed Mr. Johnson to vouch for him. So he braced himself against the dizziness and spoke about building the tracking device and how it had taken them to Coney Island.

"You should be proud," Mr. Johnson said, smiling again. "It might have taken days for the marines to find that transmitter without you."

James grimaced at the compliment. Leading those men to their deaths was nothing to be proud of. For the second time in a few minutes, he thought about how much better it might have been if he hadn't helped them find the transmitter. He'd nearly been killed. Where would that have left Mom?

James pushed the guilt down and explained what had happened after they'd gotten to Dreamland and the Beacon Tower.

"So it appears that whoever set up that transmitter set a trap, too," Mr. Johnson said before sighing.

"I was worried that they'd be waiting for us," James said.

"Probably what the captain expected, too."

Captain Reynolds had been so sure he was doing the right thing, and he'd walked them right into a trap.

"Why take that risk?" James asked.

"It was his job," Mr. Johnson answered, "and the right thing to do. We needed those radios back on the air."

"But he got his men killed."

"If he had done nothing, the radios would still be down. Sometimes you have to take action, James, even if you know it's dangerous."

That sounded like something Dad would have said. It might have been what he'd been thinking when running into the Tesla fire and getting himself killed. Was "taking action" worth leaving his family behind? James shivered.

"Well, the wreckage is at the lab by now," Mr. Johnson continued, raising his eyebrows. "Seward said he had found some parts that looked curious."

"Curious?"

"That's what he said." Mr. Johnson brought his hands together with a muffled clap.

What had Seward meant by that? He'd spent more time working on telephones than radios, so it might have been circuitry he'd never seen before.

"Well, let's take a look at Mr. Brogan here," said a doctor as he walked in behind the nurse. He began examining James, and when he reached his eyes, the doctor said, "You've got a little scrape on the side of your head, but we only had to clean it. Can you stand up?"

"Yes," James said. "I'm fine. I'd like to go home now."

He was still weak and a little dizzy, but cooperating with the doctor seemed like the best way to free himself. When he got up, the room spun for a moment, then stopped.

The doctor took him by the arm. "Walk over to the door with me."

James took one step, then another. He was wobbly, but he made it to the door without leaning on the doctor.

"What's today's date?" the doctor asked.

"Well, it was New Year's Eve when we got to Coney Island. So now it's January first?" James could walk. Wasn't that enough?

"Good, good. What year is it?"

"Nineteen fifteen." If James could remember the date, why wouldn't he know the year? His head ached a little, but he suppressed the urge to bring up his hand and give the doctor something else to ask about.

"Very good. Who's the president of the United States?"

"William Jennings Bryan." Who could forget that? He'd been the president for most of James's life.

"Okay. One last thing. What does this say?" The doctor handed James his clipboard and pointed to the top of the page.

"My name?"

"Read it to me."

"James Brogan."

"Perfect. Normally, I would keep you overnight. But take it slow, and Mr. Johnson here promised that someone would be keeping an eye on you."

A wave of relief washed over James, but it subsided when he thought about looking at the wreckage. He could head home right away, but only after making it clear that he wasn't going to see Seward's "curious" radio parts today.

The doctor left, and the nurse brought James his clothes.

"There's a car waiting for us," Mr. Johnson said.

He led James through a labyrinth of hallways. The glasses of water climbed back up James's throat as they walked past rooms that reeked of Lysol and bleach. Finally, they reached the stairs; and James took them one at a time, fighting dizziness and a dull pounding that came and went with each precarious step. They stepped out of a stairwell into a brightly lit lobby.

"Mr. Johnson? Mr. Johnson!" A disheveled man in wrinkled tan slacks and a linen jacket that was far too light for winter nearly knocked James over. He held a small notebook in one hand and a lightly chewed pencil in the other. "Carl Urich from *The Spectator*. Do you have a moment to talk about the attack last night? Who set off that bomb in Coney Island? What do the radios at Sayville have to do with it?"

Mr. Johnson's eyes flew up to meet Urich's. He opened his mouth to say something, but closed it and quickly turned away.

Who had set off the bomb? Why would the reporter have asked that? Wasn't it obvious?

Urich was blocking the doorway, shifting left and right in

perfect time with Mr. Johnson. James grew dizzy just watching them and placed one hand on the wall to keep his balance.

"No comment, Mr. Urich," Mr. Johnson said, his irritation evident in his voice. "Please let me take this man home."

"He needs to go home? Is he hurt?" The reporter turned to face James. "What happened to you? Who are you, sir? Who did you see at Coney Island? Were they wearing uniforms?"

James's nausea returned. He hadn't seen anyone, but he didn't want to answer. He tried to turn away, but inadvertently made eye contact with Urich instead. The reporter raised his eyebrows and nodded to James.

Mr. Johnson muscled his way past the reporter then, dragging James behind him by his shoulder. The doorway spun as James passed through it, struggling to keep his balance as they hurried down the front steps to a car. It was another Cadillac, similar to the one James had ridden in with the marines yesterday. This time, there was an army private behind the wheel, separated from the back seat by a pane of glass.

James got in and slid over to the far side to let Mr. Johnson in. The back seat had a lot more room with just two normal-sized men in it and was more pleasant without the stench of cigars and gun oil. But James's head still ached, and he wanted the trip to end before it started.

"Take us to the ferry," Mr. Johnson said as soon as he closed the door. Then, quietly, he asked, "How did he know about the radios?" He was looking down, as if asking himself out loud.

It took a second for James to realize Mr. Johnson was talking about the reporter. That was a great question. How did he know about the radios, but not who was responsible? Why didn't he think it was the Germans?

"Why did he ask you who did it?" James asked.

"Huh? What do you mean?" Mr. Johnson's forehead furrowed.

"He asked you who set the bomb. He asked me if I saw any uniforms. Why? He doesn't think it's the Germans?"

"Oh, that's just Urich. He always has some ludicrous theory, especially when it comes to Edison. Ever since he broke that story about pow—uh, about equipment thefts, he thinks he's going to catch us doing something wrong." Mr. Johnson shifted in his seat and stared out the window as if he didn't want to talk about Urich anymore.

"So you *do* think it's the Germans. They're going to attack!"

"I'm not sure who else would try to block the radios, James," Mr. Johnson said without looking at him. "They've been doing stuff like that since the war in Mexico. But there's a big difference between German sympathizers setting off a bomb and a military attack. We're not going to war."

But this *would* give Bryan his reason to go to war. That was the last thing Captain Reynolds had said before the explosion. Was he right? Would the US be the one to start the war? What a strange thing for a military man to say. Did Reynolds dislike President Bryan? Or was he a marine who didn't want to fight a war?

The driver turned into an unmarked gate.

"Where are we?" James asked.

"This is the War Department's new terminal," Mr. Johnson said. "It was easier for the marines to take you through the tubes yesterday. This one moves heavy equipment and men in and out of the city. We'll take a supply ferry to Hoboken."

The car drove onto the ferry, and the driver turned and opened the window between the two seats. "I'll ride with the pilot, sir. You'll be more comfortable here."

Mr. Johnson nodded, then turned to James. "About going home: Before I take you there, we'll stop at the lab so you can look at those parts Seward recovered from the fire."

James's mouth dropped open. The last thing he wanted to do was spend time with a pile of burned transmitter parts. "But I want to go home. I need to get my mom away from here."

Mr. Johnson raised an eyebrow. "What? Away from here? You're going to run away?"

"We already know it's the Germans, and they're going to attack. I need to get her away from the city." James's head pounded as his heart rate rose.

"James, there's no attack coming." Mr. Johnson put a hand on his shoulder, "Not yet, at least, and I'm sure the War Department is ready. The best thing you can do right now is help me verify the Germans did it."

"Verify? You just said it was ludicrous to think otherwise!" James smacked his hand against the car door. His head really hurt, and he regretted the sound as soon as he made it.

"Yes, but a report analyzing the remains of their equipment that ties it to them will help the government deal with their embassy."

This didn't make any sense. Was Mr. Johnson sure it was the Germans, or not? Why did he need James to confirm anything? And why did it have to be right away?

"I want to go home," James demanded. "Now."

"You're upset. I would be, too." Mr. Johnson kept his voice low and even. "You were almost killed last night, and three of the men you were working with were."

James looked away, studying a piece of equipment that might have been an armored tractor.

"You want to go home," his boss continued. "You're worried about your mother. But if you're really worried about her, you'll help me prove who did this so the government can protect us."

There it was again. Prove who did this. Was Mr. Johnson hiding something?

"I know how much you care about her, but you're overreacting here. She's fine, and the best thing you can do right now is—"

"Forget about her and go to work for you, right?" James hadn't talked to Mr. Johnson this way in a long time, not since he'd tried to make James go to college in Boston.

The ferry lurched and started to move across the river. Mr.

Johnson stroked the stubble on his chin. He set his brow and took a deep breath. "That's not fair, James."

James didn't answer. Instead, he turned his attention back to the tractor. It had gigantic steel wheels in the back and wooden wheels in the front that were reinforced with metal treads. He couldn't tell how they supported the massive vehicle. Mr. Johnson said something else, but James had stopped listening by then.

As they approached the New Jersey shore, two soldiers arrived at the tractor. One climbed onto the seat while the other grabbed a crank and started it. The tractor left the ferry before the car. Mr. Johnson told the driver something, and James shifted his gaze away from his boss to avoid eye contact.

When the car finally reached Menlo Park, Mr. Johnson spoke again, this time with a frown. "I can hold off the War Department until tomorrow, James. But you're not making this easy for me."

James slammed the door after getting out of the car.

11

The Martian Wanderer howled behind the soldiers. Another answered from somewhere out of sight. Emil's legs quaked, pleading him to run. But there was nowhere to go.

"Emil, can you hear me?" Ludwig said, apparently no longer worried about the Wanderer hearing him as he shouted through his gas mask. "Which way do we go?"

Emil didn't want to take charge. He didn't want to lead a squad, a platoon, a company, or a latrine detail. Especially not one comprised of soldiers who'd considered court-martialing him yesterday. But he had no choice. He had to lead them out of here, or run and leave them to die. Even Fluse wouldn't have done that.

First Platoon's trench lay back the way they'd come and had the tunnel to Mametz Woods. Even if there were Martians ahead, the tunnel might take them out of the trenches where they had room to run, instead of into the trenches where they were rabbits trapped in a warren.

"Follow me," Emil said, pushing past the other soldiers. The words felt strange on his lips.

He ran hard, gasping for air through his mask and reaching the branch for First Platoon in less than a minute. The rest of the men fell behind him, but as soon as a soldier came into sight, Emil made the turn and ran ahead. The entrance was about twenty-five meters beyond the turn, partially hidden at the base of the wall.

Emil followed the path around a long curve and nearly ran in front of another Wanderer. It loomed a few meters past the tunnel entrance, its brown-and-green cylindrical body blotting out the morning sun. Black Smoke poured from a tube in one of its octopus arms, while the aiming mirror of a heat ray shone in another.

The Wanderer took a step toward Emil. He backed around the end of the trench again, holding out one hand to stop the men.

"What's going on?" Degenscheide asked, pushing through the group to reach Emil.

Emil pointed at the Wanderer.

"Can we make it?"

"No," Emil said. "It's too close to the passageway." His mind raced. Maybe the Wanderer would move? But what if it came this way? Could it see them? He felt sweat pooling inside his mask. He'd led the men here, into the tentacled arms of another Martian.

"I'll draw it down the trench and away from the opening," Degenscheide said. "Zimmerman, you lead the way to the tunnel." He reached into his open overcoat and pulled out a grenade. It was one of the new models, a Stielhandgranate, with a more reliable fuse than the older models and a wooden handle that made it easier to throw.

Degenscheide was ready to risk his life to protect his men.

"Sir, you can't do that," Ludwig said, putting one hand on the Hauptmann's shoulder and reaching for the grenade with the other. "Let me go instead."

"No, the men will need you after you escape, and they need Zimmerman for that." Degenscheide pulled the grenade back. "I have two more of these. I'll throw them past the Wanderer and distract it long enough so I can follow you."

"But, sir," Ludwig replied.

The only other option would be to try to scale the trench wall and approach the tunnel opening from above. But the Wanderer was tall, and that would make them easier to spot.

"That's an order, Oberacker. Zimmerman, watch for my signal." Degenscheide pushed past Emil without waiting for an answer.

Emil peered around the corner. The Hauptmann was already advancing toward the Martian craft. He didn't look like a lawyer anymore. He was a soldier.

Degenscheide set the fuse on the first grenade and threw it. It arced to one side of the Wanderer and landed on the trench wall, close to the Martian craft's water tower body, hitting the ground in a cloud of dirt. The Hauptmann had a good arm.

The grenade exploded, showering the Wanderer with soil and stones. Its heat ray tentacle swung to where the explosion had originated, and the silver targeting mirror flashed green. Emil's ears filled with a familiar deep hum as the arm raked the area to its side with the ray. His heart raced, even though the ray wasn't pointed at him. He nearly missed Degenscheide's signal to start the run to the tunnel.

"Let's go!" Emil shouted, then ran to the tunnel entrance. He threw the wooden door propped on the entrance to one side. If he hopped in then, he'd be in the woods in a few minutes.

Degenscheide stood his ground a few meters away. The Wanderer's aiming mirror swung over from where the last grenade had landed and was almost pointed at them when the Hauptmann threw the second grenade. It exploded on the far side of the trench in a shower of soil and splinters.

Someone jostled Emil from behind and brought his mind back to the tunnel entrance. He stepped aside and pointed at the hole. The men dove in, one after another, some of them skipping the ladder altogether. Ludwig was the last man in line. He frowned in Degenscheide's direction as he hefted himself onto the ladder.

Emil turned back to the Hauptmann, but he was gone. Then he found Degenscheide on the Wanderer's far side. He must have run underneath it!

Emil froze. He thought about running over to help Degenscheide when something grabbed his foot. It was Ludwig, pulling him into the hole. Emil stepped onto the ladder instead of diving in. He turned and looked out of the entrance to the tunnel in time to see Degenscheide's final throw. The grenade landed on their side of the Wanderer this time, covering Emil's helmet with debris.

The Wanderer didn't fall for it. The mirror swung around and pointed at Degenscheide. The Hauptmann froze as the ray's deep drone filled the trench.

"Move!" Emil shouted to him.

The Hauptmann burst into flames, just like Emil's family's house in Euleheim.

Emil was still staring out of the tunnel entrance when Ludwig grabbed his arm. He allowed himself to be pulled off the ladder, still dazed, and peered into the anteroom where three tunnels met. Somehow, despite the chaos outside, the trench lights had remained lit, and all eyes were on him.

The anteroom was nearly big enough to hold the soldiers, but a few had been pushed into the tunnels that branched off in several directions. All eighteen men were waiting for Emil to make a move. He walked to the passageway that led to the woods—and, hopefully, safety. As he reached the tunnel, a plume of Black Smoke streamed into the anteroom.

The Wanderer knew they were in here.

Chaos broke out. Men screamed, pushing one another in every direction. One flew into Emil at the tunnel's opening. Emil and Ludwig locked eyes before the Smoke filled the room, and

Ludwig signaled for Emil to lead the way into the tunnel. Emil turned and headed in, hoping that between the panic and the Smoke, Ludwig could lead the men into the right passage.

The tunnel was nearly tall enough for Emil to stand, but he had to walk in a crouch. If he remembered correctly, the tunnel was 350 meters long. At an aggressive pace, he should cross it in just over ten minutes. The other men couldn't move as fast, but it was a straight run to the woods. He didn't need to wait. His best bet was to get through and out of their way as quickly as possible.

With no breeze to carry the Smoke into the tunnel, it was easy to navigate. Emil started counting.

One . . . two . . . three . . . four . . .

With the count keeping him focused, Emil was running point again. Alone this time. Fritz would have had something to say about it.

Thirty . . . thirty-one . . . thirty-two . . . thirty-three . . .

The lights went out. A crash thundered from behind, followed by screams. One was clear and unmuffled, as if the man wasn't wearing a mask. The unmistakable hum of the Martian heat ray rose again.

One . . . two . . . three . . . four . . . five . . .

Emil started over as he reached each minute, but quickly lost track of which minute he was at. He panted under his mask as he forced himself to move through the dark.

Fifty-five . . . fifty-six . . . fifty-seven . . . fifty-eight . . .

The ground shifted under his feet. Emil stumbled and fell face-first into the dirt. Something ran across his mask, then two somethings ran across his back. Rats. The ground hadn't moved. Rats had. They were fleeing the Smoke and the noise, and now they were running over him.

The screaming started again. Was the Wanderer following them? Could it dig? Emil scrambled to his feet and flailed until he realized that knocking the mask free was more dangerous than the rats.

One . . . two . . . three . . . four . . . five . . .

The screaming stopped. Or had Emil been screaming when the rats had been on him? The rodents' squeaking and scrabbling filled his ears now as they ran past him. He stepped carefully, not because he cared about the vermin, but because he didn't want to fall and be overwhelmed again.

Seventy-six . . . seventy-seven . . . seventy-eight . . . seventy-nine . . .

Emil had forgotten to start over at sixty. But light came into view then. He blinked, though it wasn't bright enough yet for him to squint. He picked up the pace as the stream of rats thinned, and he regained his footing.

The tunnel opened onto a ramp ending in a stand of trees. The trees offered good cover, so Emil could safely survey the area. The rats disappeared into the woods. He pulled off his mask, let out a long sigh, and drank in the mid-morning sun in the quiet woods.

He shook black dust off the mask and folded it as he waited. Where were the rest of the men? Had they fallen that far behind?

Minutes felt like hours, then the sound of boots hitting the hard ground and mumbling rose from the tunnel entrance. He ran to the end of the ramp and gestured for the soldiers to be quiet. They slowed down, stared at Emil, and slowly pulled off their masks. They were terrified, with wide eyes and sagging jaws. Another group arrived, including Ludwig, who joined Emil at the top of the ramp.

"You're the eighth man," Emil told him. "There were eighteen at the trench. There's still men behind you?"

"I don't think so." Ludwig grimaced. "The Wanderer got a few before we made it out. You counted?"

"Didn't you?"

"Of course, but I'm an Unteroffizier. You're the mutineer."

"I didn't lead the men out because I'm a soldier," Emil snapped. He'd done what anyone else would have done.

"What happened to Degenscheide?" Ludwig asked.

"The last grenade didn't stop the Wanderer. The heat ray got him." The Hauptmann must have known he wouldn't survive, yet he'd still done it. And just a few hours ago, Ludwig had said the man didn't belong in the army any more than Emil did.

More boots hit the ground. Gefreiter Shut Up stumbled out, with Fluse close behind. Emil didn't recognize the Leutnant at first. He was hunched over, his uniform covered with mud and black dust. Fluse ripped off his mask, fell to his knees, and vomited into the mud.

A lump formed in Emil's throat. Fluse didn't belong here, either. He just didn't know it yet.

The Leutnant wiped his mouth with his sleeve. He glared at the soldiers as he jumped to his feet. "What are you men staring at?" he shouted. "Unsling those weapons! Set up a perimeter!"

"Shut up, you idiot!" Emil hissed as he approached Fluse. "Do you want to bring the Martians over here?"

"Who do you think you're talking to, soldier?" Fluse screeched.

"A fool I'll shoot right where he's standing if he doesn't pipe down," Emil said, pulling his rifle off his shoulder.

"Wait!" Ludwig said. "Let's not do the Martians' work for them. Leutnant, I'm afraid he's right. We need to be quiet. And Zimmerman, calm down. We're all upset."

"I'm in charge here, Unteroffizier," Fluse said, crossing his arms. "I'll say who's wrong and who's right. Men, grab Zimmerman and take him into custody."

Only Shut Up moved. Most of the other men looked at Emil, as if waiting for him to respond. A few others turned away.

"We need to work together, sir," Ludwig said to Fluse.

"I said—"

"Everyone heard what you said, and they don't care," Emil snapped, then walked away. He didn't have time to argue. The Martians had ended the war, and it was time to figure out how to get home. He found a tree stump and sat next to it.

A few moments later, Ludwig walked over to him. "What next, Emil?"

"You're asking me?" Emil said. "I got us away from the Martians. I didn't take command."

Ludwig pointed over Emil's shoulder. The men were standing in a huddle, looking back at him. "Explain that to them."

12

"I cooked your favorite breakfast, James. Wheat cakes!" Mom held an iron skillet, her face enveloped by the steam rising from it. She was dressed as if she was going to work at the university library, though she'd retired nearly two years ago. "Have a seat," she added, gesturing toward the kitchen table. James's place was already set, with a jar of honey and a stick of butter patiently waiting.

James sat down as Mom put the wheat cake in front of him, its perfectly browned edges hanging over the side of the plate.

"How's your head?" she asked. "You were out of it last night. All of that nonsense about leaving Edison and Mr. Johnson."

James took a deep breath. His head wasn't much better than it had been last night, and he didn't want to resume last night's argument. "I'm fine." Then he spread butter on the wheat cake and poured honey over it, starting at the center and moving the jar in a spiral, careful to space out the lines evenly.

Mom put a cup of coffee in front of him. "The paper should be here," she told him as she left the kitchen.

She returned with the newspaper, poured herself a cup of coffee, and sat across from James as he took his first bite of wheat cake. It was perfect. Heavenly. The headache receded a tiny bit, and James's shoulders relaxed. He felt well enough to head to the lab.

"Well, it looks like your adventure made the news." Mom held the paper up so that the front page faced him: "GERMANS BOMB CONEY ISLAND, THREE MARINES KILLED."

"Can I see that?" James asked, reaching for the broadsheet. It read:

Coney Island locals were in for a shock last night when German agents ignited an explosive at the top of Dreamland's Beacon Tower. The resulting fire consumed the entire park and took parts of neighboring Luna Park with it.

United States Marines were inside the tower during a routine inspection when it ignited, killing all three soldiers. Firefighters from four stations were called . . .

James's wheat cake turned to honey-coated cardboard. He choked it down as he finished reading the short article. There was no mention of Christensen or Captain Reynolds, much less the radios at Sayville. Instead, the article quoted an "eyewitness" claiming they saw the marines enter the tower. But a "routine inspection"? That was an outright lie. Where had they gotten their story? Had someone fed them false information? Mr. Johnson had seemed upset that Urich had known anything at all. Did he have a hand in planting this story with another paper?

"So they say the Germans did it, too," said James. There wasn't any reason to share his misgivings with his mom.

"Well, of course. Who else?" Mom's eyes grew wide. "Did you see someone else? Are you allowed to talk about it?"

"No! I mean, no, I didn't see anyone. This reporter at the hospital asked us who did it."

"That's a dumb question." She took the paper back from James and shook it to stress her point.

"Yeah, he said he was from a paper called *The Spectator*," James said, taking another forkful of wheat cake. "Have you ever heard of it?"

Mom nearly dropped her cup, spilling some coffee on the table.

"Are you okay, Mom?"

She stared at James for a moment, then sprung to her feet, saving the paper from being submerged in the hot liquid and lunging to the sink to pick up a dishrag. "I'm okay, just a little tired," she grumbled as she wiped the coffee from the table. "*The Spectator*, huh? I'm surprised that rag is still in business."

"You know that paper?" James asked, holding his plate in mid-air.

"One of their reporters stopped here while your father was still alive. He wanted to talk to him. Couldn't give me a straight answer when I asked him why he couldn't go through Edison like any other reporter."

"I'm sure it was just about the fire."

"No. He wanted to prove that Edison was involved in something shady."

Mr. Johnson had said something about Urich and ludicrous theories in the car. Had it been about powder? Or maybe power? Could Urich have been the one who was investigating the story?

"Enough about the past and the press," Mom continued. "Are you okay, James? Waking up in the hospital must have been tough. I wish Ben had brought me out there."

Mom was already upset, and she'd said she was tired. It was best to let the subject of Urich drop. "Well, all he cared about was me getting back to work," James said with a sigh.

"Don't start that again. He wouldn't have asked you to do that if it wasn't necessary, and after all he's done for us, you can at least work for a few hours for him." It was the same thing Mom had said last night.

James tried another piece of wheat cake, but it was inedible. How could she take his boss's side? Didn't she see how close he'd come to ending up like Dad?

He pushed his plate away and picked up the coffee mug. "But—"

"But nothing. Finish your wheat cake, and get to work."

13

"This is ridiculous, Ludwig," Emil said. "I hold the lowest rank in the kaiser's army, and that army has been overrun by Martians. It's not too much of a leap to assume that what's happened to the 109th has been happening all over France and Belgium, if not the rest of the world."

"So you won't lead us because of your rank, and because there's no army? You're not making any sense, Emil," Ludwig replied, blowing a smoke ring and raising an eyebrow before grinning. "At least pick one excuse and stick with it."

"You know what I mean. I'm no leader." The image of Degenscheide bursting into flames came back as Emil said the word *leader*. The Hauptmann had taken on a Wanderer by himself. Every one of the fourteen men who'd made it out owed their lives to him.

Emil had frozen when faced with the same Wanderer, though.

"I'm heading east," he said. "I want to see if the aliens attacked back home."

"Did you say you wanted to go home?" Beckenbauer asked, approaching Emil and Ludwig with a few other soldiers in tow. The rest were standing near the tunnel opening with Fluse.

Emil nodded, hoping Beckenbauer and the others might want to go home, too. Maybe they would support him, rather than watching.

"And what if they haven't attacked Germany? What if, by the time you're home, the nonexistent army has someone waiting to put you on trial for desertion?" Ludwig asked.

"I guess I'm ready to—"

"What are you doing, Unteroffizier?" Fluse said, stepping into the middle of the group. "Get these men in order and ready to march."

"Adults are talking," Emil said, moving to stand between Fluse and Ludwig. Fluse was one of the reasons he wanted to head home. He didn't want to put up with his madness anymore.

The Leutnant turned his familiar shade of red as he glowered at Emil. "I'm the company commander now!" he nearly screamed. "I'll make sure you're shot when we return to command this time."

"If you don't stop screaming loud enough for the Martians to find us, I'll do the shooting, and I won't wait until I can find someone to give me permission," Emil said, struggling to keep his voice down. "There's no army. There's no chain of command. There's no Hautpmann to change your diapers for you. If you think you can find one, go right ahead. I'm not interested."

"I'm not going to put up with this!" Fluse said, his tone noticeably lower despite his declaration. Gefreiter Shut Up was standing behind him, his arms crossed as he frowned.

"You shouldn't," Emil said. "Head west. I'll go the other way."

"Wait, Emil," Ludwig said, concern knitting his brow. "Let's talk about this."

"Talk about what? The Martians are back. Either they landed again and we were too busy trying to kill one another to notice, or they never really left. Let's go home." Emil looked first at Ludwig, then at the rest of the men.

"We're with Zimmerman," Beckenbauer said. The men standing with him nodded in agreement. Good, they were going to chime in, too.

"So this is a democracy now?" Fluse said.

"No, it's a bunch of men stranded in the woods, and they need to find somewhere that isn't here," Emil said. "We have no supplies and no water." He hoped Ludwig would interject, but the Unteroffizier was looking at the ground, puffing on his cigar.

"I'm not so sure that we're free to just walk home, Emil," Ludwig eventually said, shaking his head. "But I agree. If we stay here on the front and look for the rest of the German Army, we might find more Martians."

"This is unbelievable," Fluse said. "He's infected you, too."

"We need to go, Ludwig," Emil said. "Are you with me?"

Ludwig scratched his chin and looked back and forth between Emil and Fluse. He'd never seemed this confused or unsure before. He was a soldier, and he was having problems coping without the safety of the chain of command.

"What if we head southeast?" Emil asked.

Ludwig blinked.

"We can head southeast and see what we find," Emil continued. "Maybe the Seventh Army is still there, intact. If they are, we can join them." He didn't think that would be the case, but Ludwig needed a little push. With Fritz gone, Ludwig was the closest Emil had to a friend. He would rather travel with him than without him.

"I guess that works," Ludwig said.

"Does that work, Beckenbauer?" Emil asked.

"Whatever you say, sir."

The image of Degenscheide charging the Wanderer returned to Emil then. "Emil. Not 'sir.' I'd love to have a group to go with, but I'm not your new commander."

Beckenbauer's head tilted to one side as Emil started walking east.

The woods were silent as the soldiers hiked. They should have set up a formation, but Emil didn't want to start giving orders, especially after shutting down Beckenbauer like that. Soon, they reached a road that led southeast, and all eyes were on him again. Instead of acknowledging the implicit question, Emil turned and headed in the right direction.

The soldiers walked in silence, with Fluse and Shut Up bringing up the rear. The sun was high in the sky by the time they set out, so they stuck to the shade whenever they could. A stream ran alongside the pockmarked road at a few points, with a dark foam—likely from Black Smoke, from somewhere upstream—frothing on it.

Emil and Ludwig led the group side by side, but in solitude. Degenscheide bursting in flames that morning, his own home bursting into flames years ago—the images wouldn't leave Emil, and he didn't want to talk about them. Ludwig walked with his head down, clearly not wanting to engage, either.

Finally, the outlines of a small village appeared down the road. As the soldiers drew closer, shadows from buildings straddling a crossroad came into view. Emil hadn't eaten since last night, and his stomach rumbled as they neared the crossing.

The deep hum of a Martian heat ray filled the air then.

The sound resonated in Emil's gut. He dove between a church that stood at the intersection and a smaller house, probably the parsonage next door. The rest of the soldiers followed him.

"There's the Wanderer," Beckenbauer said, pointing across the intersection to a barely visible brown shape behind a building.

The ray sounded again. Someone screamed, and then . . . someone laughed?

The hum sounded, and Emil's entire body vibrated with it. Laughter followed again.

"Is someone laughing?" Ludwig asked.

"Yes," Emil responded. "And that Wanderer hasn't moved, has it?"

Ludwig shook his head.

They needed food and water, and Emil had no idea how far the next village would be. The German-Belgian border was days from here, and they needed supplies before continuing toward it. Emil was the best person to find out what was going on, since he normally acted as a scout.

He raised an eyebrow toward Ludwig. "What should we do?"

Ludwig shrugged.

"I'll take a look," Emil suggested.

"Sounds good," Ludwig said. "Be careful."

Emil considered Ludwig for a long moment before launching himself across the road to another building. He could worry about whatever the Unteroffizier's problem was after they ate. Hugging the building, he moved closer to the intersection. The yeasty fragrance of fresh bread filled his nose as he moved, and his stomach rumbled again. Hunger was taking its toll.

The ray sounded once again, followed by more laughter. Biting, grating, nasty laughter. The sound brought up bile in Emil's throat, eclipsing the essence of baked bread. Emil had heard that kind of laugh during his first few weeks in Belgium, usually the night after they'd taken a village. It was the laugh of a cruel man treating people like playthings.

When the 109th had arrived in Belgium, they'd been attached to a regiment from Preussen. This regiment consisted of "professional" soldiers who had been serving in Poland when the kaiser had split the country in half with the Russian tsar. They'd brought that laugh back with them.

Emil dropped to the ground and crawled the last few feet to the corner, then peered around. The village was small, what he would have called a Dorf back home. Three or four buildings were on each side of the narrow main street. Gashes of black and brown painted a picture of a recent Martian attack.

The lone Wanderer was propped up against a tall barn across the road. Only one of its legs was touching the ground, as if it would fall off at the first sign of a breeze. A German soldier, his uniform torn and covered with mud, guided the heat ray, still attached to the Wanderer's arm, in two hands. Even from forty meters away, the glint of madness was visible in his eyes.

The man laughed again and fired the ray. A woman screamed, and a cloud of smoke rose from down the street, on the same side as Emil. He crawled forward on his elbows. The smoke was coming from a bakery, where the woman must have been trapped.

Emil stared up at the German soldier on the Wanderer, frozen in shock.

"Hahahaha!" the soldier shouted, spotting Emil. "Another one!"

The hum resumed, spurring Emil to launch himself backward. The corner of the building where he'd just been burst into flames. He jumped to his feet and ran back to the church.

"What happened?" Ludwig asked, clenching his teeth so tightly that he nearly bit his cigar in two.

Emil leaned forward, hands on his knees, and caught his breath. His heart pounded as he pictured himself bursting into flames like Degenscheide. That had been close. Could he and his men get what they needed here without getting killed? If they didn't, where would they find food and water?

"There's a disabled Wanderer leaning against a barn," he said. "Some madman figured out how to operate the heat ray and has at least one person trapped. He took a shot at me as soon as he saw me."

Emil looked behind the men and the church. If they circled the tall structure, they'd cross the village without the madman seeing them. His stomach rumbled again, and almost as if on cue, the ray sounded and the woman screamed. Could he and the soldiers just run away when that madman was ready to burn the village to the ground?

"We can't leave him here with that weapon," Beckenbauer said. "The only reason he hasn't burned down the entire village is because he's having fun torturing the locals. At some point, he'll get bored."

"Yeah, and we need supplies," Emil said, "Let's work out a plan."

14

James eased his bicycle around the corner and coasted to a halt at the entrance of Edison Labs. The morning air was cold, but it took his mind off the dull headache, the cardboard wheat cakes, and his argument with Mom.

The turn that offered an extra mile of riding had beckoned to James, but he'd opted for the direct route. He wanted nothing to do with the possibility of war but needed to look at the wreckage that had Mr. Johnson so concerned. It might answer the questions the reporter had raised at the hospital.

Mr. Edison had founded the "radio team" soon after the Martian Attack, in a room here in the West Orange facility. Since then, the facility had grown into a sprawling campus covering nearly three square miles. Mr. Johnson's group occupied an entire building.

It was early, so the receptionist wasn't in yet, and the door was still locked. James briefly considered locking it behind him, but grabbed the paper from the mail slot instead and eased through the inner door and straight to his desk.

Mom liked the local New Jersey broadsheet, while Mr. Johnson read a paper from New York City. James usually arrived before anyone else, so he'd check the city paper over coffee before putting it back by the door. After starting a pot, he took a seat at a table in the break room and scanned the headlines:

THREE MARINES KILLED AS GERMANS BOMB CONEY ISLAND

Coney Island, N.Y.—German spies set off an explosive device at Dreamland's Beacon Tower early Saturday morning. The attack was a response to a routine inspection by a local marine detachment. The resulting fire engulfed Dreamland and set parts of neighboring Luna Park alight, too. . . .

So they were reporting the same story as the Jersey paper. The wording was eerily familiar, including the quote from the alleged eyewitness. Someone was lying about what had happened.

James scanned the rest of the paper, looking for something to distract him while the coffee brewed:

GERMANS RESORT TO MARTIAN SMOKE IN ATTACK ON FRANCE

Fruges, France—According to eyewitnesses, the German Army unleashed Black Smoke on French and Belgian soldiers, as well as civilians, during their relentless march to Paris. . . .

James's palms started sweating as he read the story. Were the Germans on their way here? Would they turn Martian weapons on the United States? He put the paper down and stared at the coffeepot until it finished.

With a fresh cup of coffee, James went to his desk. He'd need a pad and paper for notes as he inspected the wreckage Seward had recovered from Dreamland.

The notes from his work on a new power supply caught his eye. James fought back the urge to sit down and continue working on that instead. Maybe if he ignored the wreckage in the other room and the Black Smoke in France, it would all go away. Maybe he'd wake up in bed with a headache from overindulging on New Year's Eve.

Power supplies. He'd been trying to make a smaller power supply that was capable of handling more power. The device in the Beacon Tower had saturated the receivers in Sayville, more than fifty miles away. James had been able to follow it without a tuner. What had they been using? They had Dreamland's generator station, but something still had to harness that power and channel it into a usable signal. How?

He took a pencil and paper, and headed to the small workshop. The larger one was already in use for another military project, so the smaller workshop was the logical spot to find Seward's "curious" parts.

The "smaller" workshop was big enough to park two of the army's new Cadillacs. The door opened in the center of one of the long walls, with workbenches covering the length of each end. The benches were outfitted with hand tools, soldering irons, electronic instruments, and—at one end—an oscillograph. Four pieces of plywood, each straddling a pair of sawhorses, sat in the center of the room.

James circled the improvised tables, taking time to examine the debris. The headache receded as curiosity took over. The tables might hold evidence of how the transmitter worked. There might even be something pointing to why Mr. Johnson had been so evasive after they'd spoken to Urich.

Most of the remains were charred wood and crumbling plaster. One table bore pieces of singed piping that might have been an antenna mast. On another table, a coil of copper cable. James pulled on a pair of gloves and lifted a loop of cable. It was heavy stuff, nearly as thick as the clothesline Mom had strung up on the back porch.

A piece of burned planking concealed something on the next sheet of plywood. A blackened lump with square corners poked out from a pile of ash. James picked it up and dusted it off with a gloved hand.

A steel chassis.

James smiled and carried it to one of the workbenches. He'd been looking for stray components, but he'd struck gold with a complete chassis.

At first glance, it looked like the charred remains of a typical radio set, smaller than the systems Edison built. A large coaxial connector, likely the antenna connection, protruded from one side. The cable had been ripped off, leaving a frayed head behind. It was larger than the connectors for the radios at Sayville—surprising for a system that only needed to cover 100 square miles or so to do its job. Had the Germans overengineered the system on purpose? Were they just working with what they'd scrounged up in a hurry?

Either the input connections for a microphone or telegraph had been burned off in the fire, or the chassis had never had one. Since it could have been a device designed purely for generating interference, there was no way of knowing without a cleaning and closer examination. James grabbed a boar bristle brush and gingerly cleaned soot off the chassis until he found what appeared to be a power connector.

It was huge. He blinked and leaned in for a closer look. The connector was large enough to accommodate eight- or even six-gauge wire. James went back to the table and picked up the copper cable. Was it the power line? It looked like it might have handled fifty amperes of power or more. They must have tapped directly into the feeds for the lights at the top of the tower.

The generators at Coney Island had been working hard. Was it for this one tiny chassis? How was that possible? James's heart skipped a beat. How could such a small chassis handle so much power?

He wiped the sweat from his brow, ignoring what felt like

soot smearing across his forehead. Then he brushed more ash from the unit and regarded it closely. His eyes fell onto the components near the power connector. James shook his head in disbelief and picked up a magnifying glass. The components looked like a diode bridge, right where he'd expect it, especially if there was no separate power supply chassis. But the components were small, and different from any diodes he'd seen before. They were attached directly to the chassis with no heat sinks.

James rubbed his eyes and grabbed the magnifying glass again. He raised the glass and stared at the mysterious components for a full minute. This chassis was unlike anything he'd ever seen before. Curiosity wrestled with fear. This equipment was fascinating, but where had it come from? What else did the Germans have? Did Mr. Johnson know they had this technology? Was he trying to cover it up?

Picking up a rag, James sponged his brow. This was years ahead of Edison.

Next to the diode bridge was a quartz crystal and a set of resistors and capacitors that likely made up the signal generator that had produced the noise he'd heard in Sayville. The components appeared normal, if a little small. James let out a long breath. At least some of these parts were recognizable.

But leading out to the antenna connection was a power amplifier from another world. There were no glass tubes. In their place were flat metal discs. James lifted the chassis and looked underneath to see how they were connected. Each of them had three connections—triodes. The bodies of these mystery triodes looked like they were designed to dissipate the heat. Still, compared to what Edison had to do to cool a germanium tube, it seemed inadequate. What had kept these circuits from burning themselves out? The interference had lasted for hours. That power amplifier had transmitted a signal powerful enough to disable radios nearly sixty miles away. Heat like that, if left unchecked, could destroy germanium circuits.

How had this chassis worked? How far ahead of Edison were the Germans? James bit his lip. They were using a new type of component. The Martian tech had been made with silica, which dissipated heat better than germanium, but no one had figured out how to refine it.

Unless the Germans had. If this technology was as advanced as James thought, the US was in trouble.

A chill ran down his spine. Edison was working on portable radios for the military. With technology like this, the Germans could disable them with a stroke. Were they about to attack with it?

It wasn't safe to power up the chassis after being exposed to fire and soot, so James set about dismantling it. He removed the boards that held the components and was using alcohol to clean the board with the power amplifier when a shout reverberated in the hall outside.

"I'm from the SPs, and I'm taking that wreckage now!"

15

At Emil's suggestion, the soldiers had scouted the area around the barn and confirmed what he'd suspected: balancing on the steep roof while wielding the heavy Martian arm as a weapon limited the madman to a tight arc directly in front of the building.

They'd agreed that flanking him made the most sense. At least Emil thought they'd agreed. Ludwig had gone silent partway through the discussion, and Fluse repeatedly interrupted with a worthless plan of his own.

Now, despite the presence of an Unteroffizier and a Leutnant, Emil was the man sending troops into battle against a lunatic armed with one of the deadliest weapons known to humanity. Why? Because the Leutnant lacked the skills to manage a beer tent, and the Unteroffizier was gazing at his shoes.

So you won't lead us because of your rank, and because there's no army?

Emil stepped into the center of the group and made eye contact with each soldier. His hands went to his hips; and he stood up straight, despite wanting nothing more than to find a nice corner and curl up for a nap. "It's time to go," he said. "I'll take seven men behind the bakery and to the northwestern side of the barn. Ludwig, you'll lead the rest?"

Ludwig grunted, picking his head up enough that it was probably a nod.

The soldiers still had their rifles and at least a few rounds, but if someone took a shot and missed, the madman might panic and raze the village to the ground. Beckenbauer would take the first shot since, based on all accounts, he was the best shooter in the group. If he missed, Emil would try from the other direction. If that failed, they'd open fire like a bunch of third-week draftees.

They split into two groups and headed in opposite directions. This wasn't the first time the soldiers had faced combat twice in one day, on an empty stomach, after marching for miles with no water. But it was the first time they were defending a village instead of shooting it up on their way through.

Emil took a deep breath and led his squad across the road. They pushed their way through the hedges between the road and the cemetery that sat behind the bakery. He checked his rifle for the third or fourth time since they'd talked about this mission. Instead of throwing the weapon in the middle of this field and walking away, he was playing sniper. The Martian return had ended the war. The killing—at least the killing of humans by humans—should have ended with it.

A row of new graves lay at the edge of the cemetery. Markers named four men who had died within the past year, none of them older than twenty. Each headstone had a reference to the war or a battlefield. Emil pictured the dead boy in the machine gunner's nest back in the trenches a few days earlier. He'd been a child, dragged into a conflict he'd known nothing about. Would Emil have to kill another man today? This one was terrorizing an entire village. He was no innocent draftee, but they should have been worrying about Martians, not other men.

The sharp odor of burnt wood and smoking varnish reached Emil as they left the cemetery and crossed behind another building, but the yeasty fragrance of baking bread vied for his attention. It reminded him of the Kleins' bakery in Euleheim when the Martians had attacked the first time. Emil had frantically searched the bakery for Hermine before heading home; he'd left her there before heading to the soccer match.

But now wasn't the time to think about that. Emil pushed the memory away and surveyed the area.

The buildings stood close enough together to conceal the group as they moved. One of the buildings must have held a restaurant or Gasthaus, since the aroma of fresh soup was wafting from the rear entrance. Emil forced thoughts of food out of his mind, scanned for a break in the buildings, and led the soldiers across the road.

The barn opened into a yard large enough for chickens and gathering crops. An old wagon sat near the back, with a ragged canvas cover sprawled over it and an enormous split near the top of its yoke.

The rest of the lot had few spots for cover. But the late afternoon sun was behind Emil and the other soldiers, giving them an edge. They gathered stones to throw at the madman and found vantage points along a short stone wall that separated the farmyard from the wooded lot next door.

The wagon sat far enough away that it made a perfect sniper's nest. Emil crawled under the tarp and set his rifle up on one of the wagon rails, sighting his weapon through a hole in the canvas. The sun shone through a slit behind him, warming the back of his head as he removed his helmet.

The Wanderer stood five or six meters from the wagon. As close as the one Emil had nearly run into that morning, half the distance from the one that had killed Degenscheide a few minutes later, and closer than the one that had chased him through Euleheim after burning the Kleins' bakery.

Emil shook off the memories again. He put the madman in his gun sights and took a deep breath.

The heat ray arm sagged behind the soldier, threatening to

pull him off the roof. If only Emil and his comrades could wait for him to run out of strength. But how much more damage would he do?

As if reading Emil's thoughts, the man hefted the weapon and fired at the bakery. Bile rose in Emil's throat as he waited under the canvas for one of his soldiers to start the distraction, unable to move in case he needed to take his shot. A rock sailed through the air and struck the side of the Wanderer. Two more sailed toward the barn, falling short of the man and striking the roof with loud thumps.

The man whirled around to where the sound of the stones had come from, the heat ray arm following him partway before stopping. "Who's there?" he shouted, trying to twist the rest of the way, but the heavy tentacle wouldn't let him. Emil struggled to keep his weapon trained on the madman as he flailed.

A shot rang out. The madman dropped to his knees and—in defiance of gravity—clung to the weapon and the roof. Emil kept him in his sights as he screamed and fired the ray uselessly into the air. As he flailed about, the ray hit a tree and threatened to set the nearby Gasthaus alight. The weapon continued to fire, arcing through the air, searching for something else to destroy.

Emil watched in horror through his rifle sight. He squeezed off a shot, striking the man in the back of the head. The ray switched off, and the man fell to the ground like a sack of potatoes. Training took over, and Emil's gun sight followed the man to the ground. The Martian arm swung like a pendulum alongside the barn.

The soldiers cheered as they climbed over the wall and ran into the barnyard. More voices rose in celebration from the street, and townspeople came into view. A crowd gathered around the man's body, but even from a distance, it was clear that Emil's shot had killed him.

Emil let out a long sigh and lifted his eye from the rifle sights. He did it. He was the one to end the threat—and kill another man.

He put on his helmet and came out from under the tarp. The men from Ludwig's group approached from the other side of the barn, a few of them clapping Emil on the back and cheering. He smiled back weakly, trying to make it clear that he didn't want to celebrate without insulting them.

Dark stripes from the heat ray adorned the bakery storefront, and parts of the picture window were lying scattered over someone's new wedding cake. Inside, a woman was kneeling next to a little girl, sobbing as she held the child to her shoulder. Emil had been here for her, but he hadn't been there for Hermine.

"Great shot, Zimmerman!" a voice said behind Emil. He turned to find Beckenbauer. "He moved, and I only got him in the shoulder."

Emil accepted his congratulations and arranged for the soldiers to have some food and water.

Finally, with their men taken care of, Emil approached Ludwig.

"So, you did it," the Unteroffizier said.

Emil gaped at him. That was all Ludwig had to say? The military was filled to the brim with fragile egos and erstwhile leaders. Emil wanted a loaf of bread, a stein of beer, and a map home to Baden. He didn't want Ludwig's job.

"I did it?" he said. "We all did it. No thanks to you."

Ludwig looked up and opened his mouth.

"Unteroffizier! Over here!" It was Fluse, standing next to the barn.

Emil let out another sigh. What was it now? What did Fluse want?

The soldiers walked over to the barn. Fluse stood next to the dangling robot arm, pointing at it. "We need to figure out how to detach this heat ray!" he said, then pointed to Emil's sniper's nest. "And find a horse for that cart!"

Heat flushed over Emil. After all the destruction today—first by the Martians, and then by one of their own—Fluse wanted to take the weapon for himself? That wasn't why Emil had taken responsibility for disarming the madman, much less made the shot that had killed him.

"We are not taking that," Emil said. "We'll destroy it."

"Who do you think you're talking to?" Fluse sputtered.

"Someone who survived what we went through this morning and still wants to take one of these things. A fool."

"I'm not going to listen to this."

"Then like I said before, Fluse, goodbye!"

"You need to show him some respect, Zimmerman," Gefreiter Shut Up said from behind Emil.

Emil spun around and looked Shut Up right in the eye. "We're in the real world now. Respect is earned, not given. Degenscheide earned my respect when he took the lead to save us from the Martians. Where was this weakling?"

Ludwig stood to one side of Shut Up, his face blank. All the soldiers were standing nearby, watching the confrontation. Didn't they have anything to say? At least Shut Up had the courage to argue with Emil.

"We're taking this," Fluse said, "and we're commandeering that cart. We'll confiscate supplies from this village and head south. That was your one good idea."

A few men nodded, most noticeably Shut Up. But most of them shook their heads or crossed their arms as Fluse spoke.

Ludwig still stood there, stone-faced.

"No," Emil responded. "We're going to destroy this weapon. I already asked the villagers if they can spare some supplies for us. We'll share what they have and find a place to rest tonight."

"For a man who insists he doesn't want to be a soldier, you're eager to take command, Zimmerman," Fluse said.

Emil stepped back and shook his head. "I'm not trying to take command."

The faintest hint of a smile flickered across Ludwig's face.

"You're telling me—us—what we're going to do," Shut Up said. "That sounds like a man taking charge."

Heat rose in Emil's cheeks again. This was a game—a game military men played. Someone had to be in charge.

"What's your name?" he asked, looking at Shut Up.

"Huh?"

"Your name. You have one, right? Something other than Fluse's biggest admirer? What do I call you?"

"Miller."

"Good. So, Miller, we saw what happened when the wrong person got his hands on this weapon. Who's to say it won't happen again?" Emil pointed at Fluse. "What if that 'wrong man' is young Kaiser Fluse? He hasn't shown me any reason to trust him, and neither have you."

Ludwig stood there watching the exchange, expressionless.

A wave of fatigue and hunger swept over Emil. He just wanted to eat. "And even if we did try to take it, without the power supply up there, the ray is worthless." He pointed to the Wanderer's body, still leaning against the barn. "You've heard what happened when Tesla got his hands on one of those in New York? He nearly burned the city down."

All eyes were on Emil. He wiped his brow and looked at each soldier, hoping someone would break the silence.

Finally, Beckenbauer said, "Tell us what to do."

A few other soldiers mumbled in agreement. They had to play the game, too. It was all they knew. The men couldn't work together; they needed a leader.

Emil looked to Ludwig again.

"I need a moment. Ludwig, can we talk?"

Ludwig shrugged. Emil led him over to the cart.

"What do we do?" Emil asked.

"What do *we* do?" Ludwig repeated. "You're the one making proclamations."

"Is that the problem? You think I'm taking charge? You're the Unteroffizier." Emil held his hands out.

"And if I say we're going to follow the Leutnant's orders?"

"What?! No."

"I thought you just wanted to go home, Emil. Now you suddenly want to make sure we do the right thing. You haven't made sense since we left the trench. What's it going to be? Are you making sure we don't take this weapon? Or are you heading home?"

So that was it. Emil would have to play their game to keep Fluse from taking this weapon. "Fine," he said. "If that's what it takes. Can I count on you to help? Or are you going to just stand around and mope?"

"Are you saying you'd hate to have someone with an attitude problem in your platoon?" Ludwig asked with a small grin.

Emil was too tired to argue with him. He'd play along, at least until they got to the border. Or maybe they'd get lucky, and Fluse and his sycophants would find a unit to join up with. "Okay, fine. Let's disable that ray and get the men some supplies. I'll start with the mirror."

Ludwig smiled again and relit his cigar.

16

The door to the workshop flew open. In walked Colonel Fleming, flanked by six uniformed officers of the Security Police. What was the colonel doing here? He'd resigned from Edison in disgrace years ago. Now he was leading a squad of SPs?

Without thinking, James shoved the power amplifier board back onto the workbench and threw a rag over it.

"Brogan. There you are." Fleming smiled. "You've got some schmutz on your forehead." He stepped over and extended a hand to James, who shook it. Or, rather, Fleming shook his hand while he stood there, attached to the other end.

Susan came in behind the SPs. Her hazel eyes grew with shock as she watched the two men shaking hands, then narrowed into an expression James had only seen a few times before. The last time had been when he'd forgotten they'd had tickets for a play in the city. He wiped his forehead while trying to keep one eye on Fleming and the other on Susan.

Fleming reached into an inside pocket of his trench coat and produced a piece of paper. Even though he'd been forced to resign from the army, he was clearly comfortable in the black leather of an SP officer. "This is a security letter, signed by the

President of the United States," Fleming said, smiling. "Edison Laboratories is to turn over all material salvaged from the incident at Coney Island."

"We're examining this equipment for the War Department," Susan said, struggling to keep her voice level.

"This is a matter for the Security Police. We have three dead marines and thousands of dollars of property damage."

That didn't make any sense to James. Even if the death of three marines was an SP matter and not one for the War Department, the Security Police didn't have anyone as qualified as Edison's radio team to examine the wreckage.

"You're not touching this debris before we talk to Ben Johnson," Susan said, stepping in front of the officers. Most of them jumped back, but one officer—a burly man with a bushy beard—pushed her out of the way. Susan stumbled and fell.

James froze, his mouth falling open.

The rest of the officers stepped around Susan and started shoving the wreckage into burlap sacks. The sound shocked James to his senses. He rushed over to help Susan and led her back to the workbench once she was back on her feet.

"Animal!" she hissed at the bearded officer, who never looked up from the debris.

"Adams?" Fleming said to the agent. "Get her out of here. I need Brogan, though," he added, fixing his smile on James.

Adams took a step toward Susan with an outstretched hand.

"Stay away from me!" she said, baring her teeth.

Adams stepped back as if he'd been scalded.

James shifted, putting himself between Adams and Susan. He locked eyes with the agent, and for a moment there, a flash of regret crossed the other man's face.

"Fine," Fleming growled. "Just make sure she stays out of the way."

James needed to get the SPs out of there before someone was hurt—and before they found the board stashed under the rag.

"What the hell is going on here?" Mr. Johnson said as he

entered the room, cleanly shaven and back in his business suit. His eyes widened at the sight of the colonel. "What are you doing here, Fleming? Get out. Now!"

"Colonel Fleming of the Security Police," Fleming answered. "Hand over everything you have from Coney Island."

"Tell your bosses to send over someone with a little more authority," Mr. Johnson said, his voice dripping with contempt.

Fleming flushed and stared at Mr. Johnson. James knew that the two men had met during the Martian Attack, then worked side by side at Edison for a long time. But before he'd joined the lab, something had driven a wedge between them. By the time Fleming had left, he and Mr. Johnson hadn't spoken to each other for years.

"You don't have a choice," Fleming said. "Whatever the Germans left behind is a government affair now. It's a new world, Ben."

"A government affair? Edison works for the government, too."

"I have orders, and you're close to sedition. Pick a side, Ben. You're either with us or against us." Fleming nodded to Adams. "Check that workbench."

"Don't give me that SP bull, Fleming. Give me that letter." Mr. Johnson snatched it so sharply that it nearly tore.

Adams set down a full sack and picked up an empty one. He walked over to Susan and James, gesturing for them to move away from the workbench.

"Stay the hell away from me," Susan growled, clenching her fists and taking a step toward the officer. They froze, toe-to-toe. Susan must have been oblivious to the fact that Adams was twice her size.

If James didn't do something, Susan would get herself hurt. Or worse.

"Wait," he said, grabbing the rag with the board inside it. "This is all I have over here."

Adams took the board and nodded.

Susan whipped around to face James and opened her mouth, but Mr. Johnson interrupted. "This seems legitimate, but you still have to leave," he said, handing the letter back to Fleming. "I need to talk to a few people before we release this material."

Susan stared at James, her lip curled. Did she think he should have hidden it? He hadn't really had a choice. And if Mr. Johnson won the argument, they'd get the board back anyway.

"Three marines are dead, Ben," Fleming said. "There's no time to wait. We need to verify that it was the Germans and take action."

"We're already working on that. James was here early today, getting started on that. We'd be happy to send a report. Tell your men to put that material down." Mr. Johnson pointed at the sacks they were carrying. He could be frightening when he was angry.

But Fleming was unfazed by him. "Not good enough," he said. "You might not be taking the Germans seriously, but the SPs are."

Mr. Johnson stepped toward the officers, his fists clenched. For a moment, James thought he was going to grab one of them.

Fleming held up a hand. "Don't make me arrest you."

Mr. Johnson let out a long sigh. Susan started to speak, but Mr. Johnson turned and shook his head at her. It was over, his expression read.

"I can show myself out," Fleming said.

He did, and his men followed, carrying the sacks of debris. The chassis was in one of those sacks—and with it was James's chance of unlocking whatever secrets its new components held. But Susan was safe.

Once they were gone, Mr. Johnson faced James, his fists still clenched. "James, did you at least have time to figure anything out?"

"Well, it was definitely diff—"

"I hope now you can see why I needed you to look at it

yesterday," Mr. Johnson snapped. "I need to get a car to Washington. I'll be back tomorrow." Then he stormed out of the room.

James leaned back against the workbench as if he'd been struck. His face started to burn; and with all of the commotion gone, his headache started to take over.

"What was that?" Susan growled at him, her face red. "You're greeting Fleming with a handshake, then handing over the equipment with a smile? To the guy who knocked me over? You could have at least kept that piece in the rag."

James couldn't remember ever seeing her this angry. "No, I—"

"Don't you dare say you did that to protect me. I don't need protection like you think your mother does. She spends more time shielding you, anyway." Susan stamped her foot to emphasize that last word.

James leaned back further on the bench. A bead of sweat fell into one eye, carrying soot with it. He wiped his face with his sleeve as he struggled to come up with a response.

"And what was that with Ben?" Susan asked, nearly bowling him over as she stepped toward him. "Did you two have some kind of argument yesterday?"

"I . . . He wanted me to come here from the hospital, but . . ." The room tilted a little, and James's head started to throb.

"Let me guess. You wanted to go home to your mom. Well, I hate to be the one to say it, but Ben was right. You should have been here."

Susan turned and left the room.

James rubbed his eyes, unable to speak as Susan receded down the hall. Why didn't she understand that keeping the chassis might have gotten her hurt?

17

Emil and the other soldiers reached a tiny village named La Bièvre, nestled between farmland and a river. The place was so decimated that even the sign bearing its name was missing. Two days earlier, the group had crossed the Somme at Saint-Quentin, a smoking ruin of a city. From there, the carnage had only increased. They'd passed through six or seven similar settlements since then, and each one had born evidence of a Martian attack.

The soldiers had covered a lot of ground since breaking camp that morning in Vendeuil, a village that had nothing to offer but moldy bread and rancid meat. They needed food, sleep, and cover from the Martian Wanderers that filled each night with their howls and heat rays. But this tiny Dorf had been devastated, with only a few buildings still standing.

"Over there," Ludwig said, pointing to the southeast.

Emil followed his gaze to a building standing twenty meters or so from the main road. It appeared incongruous amid the carnage, but Emil wasn't going to look a gift horse in the mouth. "Four walls and a roof," he said. "At least we can sleep inside tonight. Let's see if there's any food or fresh water."

"We haven't seen a living soul, but it's still possible someone unfriendly is waiting for us," Ludwig warned.

"It looks perfectly abandoned to me, and we've been lucky so far. We could storm the place. Fluse and Miller would love it."

Fluse and his sidekick had been sulking since leaving Belgium, walking at the back of the group and eating by themselves. Emil had been hoping he'd wake one morning to find them gone, but no such luck.

He turned and faced the rest of the soldiers, who'd gathered nearby. "Let's head over there. If it's safe, we can try to scout up some food and stay the night. We'll go slow. There's no need to spook any squatters."

"The German Army doesn't worry about 'spooking' civilians," Fluse sneered.

Emil rolled his eyes and nodded to Ludwig, who gestured that he'd stay back and ensure Fluse and Miller didn't make any trouble.

The sign over the door read La Terrasse, which hopefully meant they'd blundered their way into an inn that had food and beds. Emil shrugged, checked his weapon, pulled out a torch, and nodded to Beckenbauer. They entered the building together.

"Hello? Is anyone here?" Emil called out, wishing for the twentieth time that one of the soldiers spoke French. "We're just looking for a place to stay tonight."

He shined the light around the dark room. Tables, benches, and a bar. It *was* a restaurant! This was the soldiers' lucky day.

Emil moved deeper into the room, using the torch to illuminate a massive brick fireplace ringed by more benches.

Something moved then.

"Hello?" Emil asked. "Who's there?"

A shadow crossed in front of the hearth, followed by a clattering and a groan of pain. Emil moved toward the noise, and his torch found the source: a young woman, sprawled in front of a bench, her chest heaving and eyes bulging in terror.

"It's okay," Emil said. "We're not here to hurt you. Let me help you up."

He held out his hand. She scrambled back to avoid it, slamming her back into the bench, and looked nervously at the fireplace. Emil instinctively followed her gaze, shining the light in its direction. A small girl, maybe six or seven years old, was trying to conceal herself behind a stack of firewood. Emil's jaw dropped.

A sudden burst of brightness blinded him before he could collect himself. Beckenbauer had lit a gas light in the center of the room. He gasped as he spotted the young girl. The woman sprang to her feet, jostling Emil as she dashed to the girl, placing her body between the child and the men.

"A woman?" Miller asked from the doorway. "Make her tell us where we can find food and water."

Emil ignored him, hoping Ludwig would have the sense to shut him up. He handed his weapon and torch to Beckenbauer, then turned to the woman with his hands outstretched, palms facing her. She couldn't have been much older than twenty-one, if that. There was an equal chance that the little girl was her daughter or her sister.

"Do you understand German?" Emil asked.

She remained frozen for a moment, then mumbled, "Please . . . not hurt."

"We don't want to hurt you," Emil said, keeping his hands visible. "We need a place to stay tonight. What is your name?" He spoke a little bit of French he remembered from school.

"Gabrielle," she said. "This . . . my sister, Juliette." She took a half step to her left.

Juliette had the same auburn hair and brown eyes as her older sister. Gabrielle's hair was held back by a kerchief, similar to how Emil's mother kept her long hair out of the way when she worked in the kitchen. Juliette's hung freely, down to her waist. They both wore floral-patterned dresses, soiled with ash and dust. A few days ago, Gabrielle had probably been helping her mother in the kitchen—maybe even this one—while Juliette had been playing with the stuffed animal she now clutched under one arm.

Emil's eye fell on the stuffed animal. It was an anthropomorphized rabbit, stylized to stand on its hind legs. It was wearing a green felt apron and bore the distinctive metal Steiff tag in its right ear. Hermine had carried the same rabbit for a year when she was five years old.

"That's a very nice rabbit you have there, Juliette," Emil managed to say, his throat constricting.

Juliette smiled, and Gabrielle relaxed the slightest bit.

Emil turned to the men. "We should go. They found this place first, and we're only going to terrify them by staying here."

Ludwig opened his mouth to speak, but Fluse pushed his way to the front of the group. "We're not leaving here. The German Army—"

"The German Army does a lot of things, according to you," Emil said. "If you want to participate, go find them. We're leaving."

An uneasy silence fell across the room until another soldier broke it. "Zimmerman, there's food in the kitchen, and fresh water."

A lump formed in Emil's stomach. No good ever came of playing army games. This might be the best place they'd found since leaving the trenches, but he'd already ordered that they leave. If he reversed it now, it would leave an opening for Fluse and Miller.

"We could stay tonight, and take the girl and her sister to safety tomorrow," Beckenbauer said.

Ludwig nodded in agreement. They were giving Emil a way out. If Ludwig was willing to question him, they weren't really playing army games, were they?

"What, are we babysitters now?" Fluse asked.

"No, we're refugees from the Martian attack, just like they are," Beckenbauer said.

"That's an excellent point," Emil said. "As I already said, we're not the German Army. We're refugees."

He turned to Gabrielle and squatted down to be at eye level with her. "Did you understand that? We can stay here tonight, and then you can come with us. We're headed to Reims."

"Reims," she said with a small smile. "Yes. That would be good."

18

The paper was already on the kitchen table when James came downstairs for breakfast the next morning. He picked it up and scanned the front page. The war in Europe was back in its place there, with the Coney Island incident nowhere to be seen. Like the wreckage from the fire, the story had been spirited away.

"Good morning," Mom said, placing a soft-boiled egg and two slices of cinnamon toast at James's place on the table. The egg's narrow top was cut off with surgical precision, and the toast gleamed golden brown. Cinnamon and sugar wafted up from the plate. Mom's carefully styled hair and dress meant she was headed out for grocery shopping or a visit to the library later.

"Good morning," James said, taking his seat and picking up his spoon. "Are you still angry?"

"I wasn't angry, James. I said so last night. I'm just surprised you would take that terrible man Fleming's side over Ben's."

"I'm not taking sides, Mom!"

"You said you think Ben's hiding something and he should have been more willing to give in to that . . . that . . . man," she struggled, clearly wanting to use a different word for Fleming but refusing to say it out loud.

James took a bite of his toast, hoping the discussion would never start if he didn't answer her.

"And after everything Ben's done for us, you think he's hiding something from you?" Mom continued. "Even if he is, how do you know it's not to protect you? And why haven't you discussed it with him?"

"I will, I promise. I'll talk to him today."

"I met that man Fleming once."

"You told me last night."

"Well, I'll tell you again. There's something wrong with that man. He visited the hospital while your father was there. Never said a word about how he was doing. Not a single comment about how he saved all those people. Nothing. All he cared about was whether your father had spoken to the Serbian lunatic." Mom picked up her coffee cup, took a sip, and grimaced. She poured it out into the sink as if the thought of Fleming—or maybe Tesla—had made it go rancid.

James didn't know Colonel Fleming well. He'd left Edison only a year or so after James had joined, and they hadn't had a reason to work together. Fleming and Mr. Johnson had had some kind of falling-out; and Susan disliked the man, too, for some reason.

Mr. Johnson and Dad had connected at the hospital because Mr. Johnson's father had served in War of the Rebellion, just like Dad. Colonel Fleming, it seemed, didn't feel any connection, even though he was a military man, too. Did that make him a bad person? Or was he just all business?

"I don't have to tell you everything Ben did for us," Mom added.

No, she didn't. Not again. Besides, Colonel Fleming hadn't acted like he'd had anything to hide. The SPs wanted the wreckage from Coney Island for an investigation. It was their turf, after all. But Mr. Johnson was hiding something. He hadn't answered James's questions in the car, and he had been furious when the SPs had come to Edison to do their job.

James nodded and finished his egg. It was time to go to Edison and talk to Susan. She hadn't so much as looked at him yesterday after Fleming had left. James still didn't understand why, but he wanted to make peace with her one way or another.

The ride to Edison was short, a quick three-and-a-half miles over predominately flat, quiet streets. The ride to and from the office was usually James's alone time, for planning the new day or mulling over the events of the one coming to an end. Today, he was trying to figure out how to approach Susan after what happened at the lab yesterday.

His deliberations were interrupted about two blocks before the office, when Carl Urich appeared in the street.

James steered his bike to one side to avoid hitting the reporter. He briefly considered not stopping at all. But then Urich's questions at the hospital replayed in his head.

Who set off the bomb in Coney Island? What do the radios at Sayville have to do with it?

James turned the bicycle around and stopped in front of the reporter. He was relieved to learn Urich owned an overcoat, even if it was a color he'd never seen before. Was that what Mom had meant when she'd said "taupe"? It looked like what taupe sounded like, but the coat might have been a different color when he'd purchased it.

The reporter had shaved at some point in the past couple of days, but gray stubble dotted his chin, and part of his gray shirt that the open coat exposed was stained with ketchup and coffee. "Good morning, Mr. Brogan," Urich said, smiling.

He'd found James and Mr. Johnson at the hospital. He'd figured out the explosion was linked to the radios in Sayville. Now he'd found out who James was?

"Where are you getting your information from? A fink at Edison?"

"Fink?" Urich laughed. "That's a strong word, isn't it, James? Can I call you James?"

"How do you know my name?"

"That I can tell you. You made the local papers a few years ago, and they printed a photo. I found it in the archives. Took some searching, but by starting with stories in this part of Jersey and searching for links to Edison, it wasn't hard."

James's brow furrowed. He'd been expecting Urich to evade the question or reveal some dark secret, not come back with a completely reasonable explanation. "How did you learn about the link to radios in Sayville?" he asked.

"Is that a confirmation that the bomb is connected to them?" Urich grinned.

James frowned.

"Don't worry, I already knew. The three marines killed at Dreamland were assigned to the unit guarding the towers. I've been investigating another story about the radios."

"Another story?"

"Yeah, but I want to talk about Coney Island."

James blinked. Despite knowing this was why Urich had tracked him down, he was completely unprepared. Should he tell Urich anything? What could he tell him? Why didn't the reporter assume it was the Germans, like everyone else had?

"I don't know what I can tell you," James said.

"You don't know what you're allowed to tell me? Or you don't know anything? You were there. You saw something. And, Edison took the wreckage from the Beacon Tower back to your office."

"Oh, the wreckage isn't there anymore. The SPs took it all away yesterday." The corners of James's mouth went up in relief. There was nothing to tell.

"What? They took it away? They don't want Edison to help

with the investigation?" Urich pulled a notepad out of his coat and scribbled something on it.

James sighed and looked in Edison's direction. "I guess not. Maybe they think Colonel Fleming can help them examine it, although I'm not sure what's going to be left for them to see after they hauled it away in sacks like—"

"Colonel Fleming? Sean Fleming? He's with the SPs? And they assigned him to this?"

"You know who he is?" James asked, staring at the reporter.

"Oh yes, I've spoken to him before. It's surprising to hear he's with the SPs now, considering his involvement with the Tesla fire."

The ground shifted under James, and he leaned onto his bike. The headache, which had receded overnight, came back. Fleming was involved with something suspicious regarding the fire? But he'd been investigating it alongside Mr. Johnson. How could it have anything to do with him leaving?

"You didn't know? But you were at Edison when he left. I guess they did a good job of covering it up."

James blinked. He looked around for a place to sit, but couldn't find anything.

"Are you okay?" Urich asked. "How bad were you hurt at Coney Island? Should you be out here?"

"I'm okay. I just didn't know . . ."

"Wait. Brogan. Your name is Brogan. How did I miss that? Your father, wasn't it? He was the hero cop. And now you work at Edison." Urich stared at his notepad, then back at James. "I'm sorry. That was thoughtless of me. You didn't know Fleming was involved, did you?"

"What . . . what are you talking about?" James choked out. "He was involved in the investigation, but . . ."

"Colonel Fleming left Edison under questionable circumstances. He was involved in the fire that killed your father, James. I'm sorry you had to find this out this way." Urich reached out to touch James's shoulder, but James pulled away.

"No, that can't be," James said. "They would have told me. They would have told my mom."

"The SPs shut that story down. If they don't want people to know, they don't. They might not have had a choice." Urich shrugged.

"I gotta go," James said. Fighting dizziness, he jumped back onto the bike and left Urich standing there, notepad in hand.

At Edison, James stared at the prototype on his desk, unable to form any thoughts that didn't involve Dad, Fleming, or Mr. Johnson. Was Urich lying? Why would he have made up such a hurtful story?

"James, are you okay?" Susan asked from behind him.

James jumped and dropped a screwdriver.

Susan pursed her lips and leaned over him to look at the scratch on the side of his head. "I didn't see this before. It looks terrible. Maybe you should have stayed home for the rest of the week."

"I need coffee," he said. "Let's talk in the kitchen."

Earlier that morning, James had wondered why Susan had reacted so violently to Fleming. Now, after talking to Urich, he suspected there was a good reason. But did that mean she was hiding things from him, too? Or was Urich full of ludicrous theories, like Mr. Johnson had said? What did "involved" mean, anyway?

"James, what's going on?" Susan asked after they sat down in the kitchen. "I'm worried about you."

He sat at the table and held his head in his hands. "I'm okay. Just distracted."

"I'm sorry." A tear welled up in one of Susan's eyes. She didn't cry often, and it shocked James out of his funk. He reached out and took one of her hands. She sat down, still holding his hand. "When Fleming came here, I lost my temper," she continued. "Too many bad memories. You'd almost been killed, and I completely forgot that when he arrived. To see him here trying to benefit from what happened to you . . . it was too much for me."

Too many bad memories? Of what?

"I understand," James said. "And I'm sorry, too. I should have stood up to him. And maybe I could have come here Saturday to inspect the wreckage. I might have found something . . ." He started to tell her about the chassis, but if she found out he'd given that up, she'd get angry again. And, she might get Mr. Johnson involved.

"No, you were right to stay home. But either way, I shouldn't have said that about you and your mother. I'm sorry." Susan squeezed his hand and looked him in the eye.

James bit his lip. It felt good to put yesterday behind him—but what had Urich been talking about? Could James trust Mr. Johnson? "What do you mean, Fleming was here to benefit from Coney Island?" he asked.

"Well, you know, he was pushed out after they caught him selling those Martian Smoke generators." Susan's eyes narrowed in anger.

"He was selling Martian technology?" James's heart sped up. Edison had access to a warehouse full of Martian equipment from the attack. The War Department had collected it after the aliens had succumbed to Terran microbes. It was under close guard, and James had only been allowed to visit it a few times. So Fleming had been smuggling gear out and selling it? Had he sold the reactor to Tesla? "Do you think Fleming had anything to do with the Tesla fire?" he asked.

"What? You mean, could he have been involved in your father's . . . Where did you get that idea? He didn't start stealing the Smoke generators until his mother got sick, well after the fire."

James shrugged. "It's just that after seeing him leading a couple of SPs, I'm ready to believe anything, I guess."

"If he'd been involved in that fire, he'd be in prison. There's no way he'd be walking the streets, let alone working for the SPs."

"Of course." James squeezed Susan's hand. "It was shocking to see him back here, wasn't it?"

"Yeah. Everything they say about the Security Police must be true. They're more crooked than the criminals." Susan shook her head.

James nodded and chuckled. That was what people said about the SPs.

"So, what was that chassis you gave to them?" Susan asked, getting up to pour coffee. "Why had you set it aside?"

"Oh. It was nothing."

19

At least five centimeters of snow had fallen overnight, with scattered flurries in the air as the men filed out of the restaurant. But even that, combined with a sharp chill, couldn't dampen Emil's spirits. He, his men, Gabrielle, and Juliette had slept inside, with a warm fire, a hot meal, and mugs of mulled wine filling their bellies.

As the group struck out southeast toward Reims, Emil half expected them to break into song. And Ludwig did, once he started carrying little Juliette. The snow and cold proved too much for her after a few kilometers, so the men let her ride on their shoulders. Ludwig scooped her up after Emil's turn and sang "Hoppe, hoppe Reiter" with a voice that belied his gruff tone and ever-present cigar.

"You can sing?" Emil asked between performances.

"Sounds that way, doesn't it?" Ludwig said with a wink.

They passed through a few villages during the morning, and the evidence of Martian attacks grew sparser with each one. When they reached the fifth village, Hermonville, just after noon, it was intact. Not a brick was out of place, with stores and houses lining a wide road feeding into the town center.

Before the group reached the first storefront, Emil saw

something they hadn't seen all day: another person, apart from themselves. An older man was walking toward them, a loaf of bread under one arm and a bottle of wine clutched in the other hand. He nodded to Emil as he approached. "Good morning," he said.

"Good morning?" Emil said, surprised enough that the words sounded more like a question than a greeting.

"Sorry. Good afternoon. I didn't expect to see any German soldiers today."

"You've seen soldiers here? Recently?"

"Yes, of course. But our day is Saturday."

"Saturday?" Emil looked around. Was a garrison near here? How much of a presence did the Germans have in this region? The war had been fought in the north.

Ludwig cocked his head, looking just as confused as Emil did.

While the rest of the group looked around, Emil noticed a woman exiting the butcher shop. Even though she seemed less thrilled than the old man to have the army in town, she continued on her way as if it were any other day.

"Yes, that's when we usually see a patrol," the old man answered.

"Do you know where they come from?"

"Don't you? They usually come from the southeast. That's all I can tell you."

Emil frowned. No need to attract attention by asking too many questions. "Thank you," he said.

The old man smiled and continued on his way.

"Why don't we head over to that Gasthaus?" Ludwig asked. "Maybe the girl and her sister can stay there, and we can get a warm meal and a beer."

"We have provisions from last night," Emil said. "And we don't have any francs."

Ludwig frowned.

"We're not going to start begging or looting," Emil added.

"But bringing Gabrielle and Juliette to the Gasthaus is an excellent idea."

"What did the old man say to you?" Beckenbauer asked as he approached.

"He was surprised to see us. Their day is Saturday."

"What? Their day?"

"Yeah."

They found a small clearing next to a barn. Beckenbauer and Roth, a soldier from Beckenbauer's platoon, handed out provisions; and the men found spots to eat.

"Do you want to stay here?" Emil asked Gabrielle. "They have a Gasthaus—an inn—over there." He pointed across Hermonville's main street.

"Yes, I will stay there," Gabrielle said with a smile.

Emil nodded to Ludwig and headed across the street with Gabrielle and Juliette. It would be a relief to find a safe place for the girls, and he could focus on getting home.

The old man had said that soldiers came often, and on a schedule. That meant patrols, and patrols meant a permanent camp of some kind nearby. Reims—or somewhere near Reims— seemed likely. They were only a few hours away on foot, and it was a big enough town to support a garrison.

But what kind of unit was making regular patrols? And what were they doing here? The German Army hadn't come through this part of France. The attack had been a race to the sea, by way of Belgium and the Somme Valley. That was where Emil and his regiment had been when the Martians had attacked. Regular patrols weren't something an attacking army did, not to mention an army trying to survive an alien invasion. Who had the time for patrols so regular that "Saturday was their day"? What German unit was running routine checks—and not running for their lives from Martians?

When they reached the inn, Emil held the door open to let Gabrielle and Juliette in first. Gabrielle seemed more relaxed than she'd been in the morning. She smiled at Emil as she walked through the door, and his heart skipped a beat. She reminded him so much of Hermine.

The doorway led to a well-appointed, wood-paneled dining room. A handful of tables were occupied by couples, small families, and a few loners.

The innkeeper—a middle-aged woman wearing a white apron—greeted the group. As she spoke with Gabrielle in French, Gabrielle started to cry. The older woman reached out and hugged her. Eventually, Gabrielle turned and spoke to Emil. "I can stay here. Thank you for seeing me here safely. I . . . I don't know how to repay you."

Repay him? Emil shook his head. "I don't need anything. I just wanted to be sure you were safe."

The innkeeper said something in French.

"Do you want some bread?" Gabrielle interpreted. "Some wine? For your men?"

The innkeeper's expression told Emil that the only answer was yes. He left with several loaves of bread and four bottles of wine in a basket.

"No beer, Ludwig, but we have some wine," Emil said, smiling when he got back to the clearing. He handed out the bread and wine, keeping a piece of bread for himself.

Before Emil could join the men's conversation, Fluse came over. "Where is that from?" he asked, pointing toward the bread and wine.

"The Gasthaus," Emil said, taking a bite of bread. "I took Gabrielle and Juliette there. They were grateful."

"That's all you took?"

"I didn't take anything. It was offered."

"We're the German Army. We don't wait for things to be offered."

"We're not the German Army. We're refugees on our way home."

Fluse stiffened, but Emil continued before he could speak. "Until an hour or so ago, I wasn't sure if the German Army still existed, but it seems it does. The old man we met on our way in told me that patrols pass through here regularly."

"Patrols?" Fluse wrinkled his brow.

"Yes. Patrols." The more Emil thought about this, the more worried he became. An army that did this was confident in their position, playing war games instead of fighting a war. Was their group about to run into a unit ready to prosecute them for desertion?

Fluse crossed his arms. "Then we should wait here for them and occupy that Gasthaus."

"We're not an occupying force. We're not even part of an army. And when we were, we slept in trenches and ate our own food. We didn't commandeer beds and restaurants, and I'm not about to start."

Fluse scoffed.

"You think that's a good idea?" Emil responded. "Fine. Leave. Find your own way to . . . wherever you're going. But you're going without us—and without your weapons."

"What?"

"I think I was clear. Hand over your weapons—you, too, Miller—and go."

"You can't do this," Fluse said, his voice growing louder and his eyes growing larger.

"I think I can," Emil said. "Go demand that the Gasthaus feed you. Storm it and take over one of their beds. I won't get in the way, but my men won't help you, and I'm not letting you do it with weapons."

He held out his hands expectantly—and saw three men on horseback approaching from the south.

A hollow knot formed in Emil's stomach, and he started to sweat. The men were wearing uniforms—clean ones—and their horses looked healthy and well-fed. The man in the lead wore glistening Hauptmann's pips that were visible from twenty-five meters. These must have been the soldiers the old man had mentioned earlier; and they looked like they were still part of the army, not another group of strays.

Emil put his hands down to hide their shaking. He'd hoped for a chance to figure out how to deal with meeting these soldiers, if at all.

"Emil, soldiers coming on horseback," Ludwig said.

"I see them."

"What? From there, too?" Ludwig asked, turning to face Emil.

Emil turned. Three more men were riding from the north. The group was surrounded.

The trio on Emil's side reached them first. The men formed a loose line and came to attention. The Hauptmann kept his sword sheathed, and he wore the kind of hat one expected to see in a ceremonial parade. He was dressed like a true believer—not the kind of officer Emil had had luck dealing with.

"I'm Hauptmann Ritter from the Third Royal Saxon Hussars," the Hauptmann spoke as the rest of his soldiers held their weapons across their bodies. "Identify yourselves."

Hussars! That explained the uniform.

"I'm Leutnant Fluse, acting commander of Third Company, Fifteenth Reserve Jäger Battalion," Fluse said, snapping to attention and saluting.

Emil clenched his fists. Fluse hadn't wasted any time declaring himself the leader. Now, if Emil tried to establish himself as the leader, he'd have to explain how a lowly Soldat had ended up leading them.

Ritter assessed the rest of Emil's group. Would he identify them as deserters? Emil had led them most of the way across France and right into the arms of a regular army unit run by a career officer. Did their next step involve being folded back into a unit? Or a court-martial and execution? How would Emil get home now? He clenched his fists so hard that his fingernails cut into his palms. Then he took a deep breath to force himself to relax.

"At ease, all of you," Ritter said. The men on horses slowly let go of their weapons after Ritter returned their salute. "All the Badische reserve regiments came through Belgium, didn't they? It appears to me that your group has wandered a good way south."

This officer knew too much to just be the leader of another orphaned group. The next few minutes might be the difference between life and death, let alone home or back to the battlefield. Fluse's quickness to speak up and identify himself as the commander might have saved their lives, since Ritter seemed ready to treat them as deserters. So Fluse had gotten exactly what he'd wanted. He was their company's commander now, and Emil was as far from home as he'd been in the trench.

"Yes, sir. We were overrun by the alien invaders and have been searching for a command." Fluse eyed Emil as he finished speaking.

Ritter tugged at his carefully sculpted mustache. Would Emil's group be shot for desertion? Or would they be led to their deaths fighting Martians now? Either way, Emil knew they didn't have a choice.

"We got word that the troops in the Somme Valley were decimated," Ritter said. "Well, you found your command, Leutnant . . . ?"

"Fluse, sir."

"Leutnant Fluse. General Wegener has been assembling troops outside Reims. Come with me, and we'll see where you fit in."

20

James knocked quietly on Mr. Johnson's door and let himself in, like he had a thousand times before. This office was a familiar place, where James had learned about radios, first laid hands on salvaged Martian technology, and trained on countless other things under Mr. Johnson's guidance. He wasn't sure that would make this conversation easier or more difficult, though.

He closed the door—and turned to find Colonel Fleming sitting behind Mr. Johnson's large oak desk.

James's jaw dropped. The back of his neck began tingling.

"James!" Fleming said. "Are you a mind reader as well as the radio team's best engineer? I was about to send for you!" He stood and held his hands up like he was presenting James to a theater audience. Then he gestured to a chair in front of the desk. "Please, take a seat."

James's feet seemed to be glued to the floor.

"I guess you're surprised to see me. Ben Johnson has been relieved of his position. Since I have experience here and there's a security investigation underway, the War Department decided I was the most logical person to fill in until a permanent replacement is found. Please. Sit." The last two words came out firmly.

So Mr. Johnson was gone. Relieved of his position. That sounded serious. But were the SPs still looking at Edison Labs? Was James in danger of losing his job, too? And what about Susan? They'd just been talking about how much she disliked the Colonel. Now, James needed to find out what Fleming's plans were and—if it was safe—learn if Urich had been right about him. He started sweating as he forced his feet to carry him to the chair.

"You look nervous, James," Fleming said, his smile broadening but not quite reaching his eyes. "You have nothing to fear. I only want to discuss what happened at Coney Island on Sunday. Captain Reynolds said you'd be a big help."

"I see," James said, sighing with relief. If Fleming only wanted to talk about Coney Island, this wouldn't be so bad after all. And, he'd already spoken to Captain Reynolds.

"It must have been tough for you," Fleming continued. "You're not a marine. You're an engineer. You're not prepared to face German saboteurs, nor should you be." He fished a cigarette out of his jacket pocket and offered it to James, then lit it and took a long drag after James demurred.

"So you think it was Germans?" James asked.

"Of course. Who else would it be?" Fleming held his hands up. "Did anyone tell you it was someone else? Was Ben telling stories?" His voice rose with that last sentence, pushing James back in his seat.

"Uh, no, of course not," James said. Telling stories? What did that mean? He forced the question down, afraid of Fleming's reaction.

"Captain Reynolds said you fashioned some sort of tracking device to find the transmitter. That was outstanding work." Fleming's smile returned to his face.

"Thank you."

"How did it work? You can follow the signal's direction somehow?" Fleming raised an eyebrow as he leaned onto the desk.

"Well, no, not direction," James said. "Strength. It was so strong, I could figure out where it was coming from by watching the amplitude of the signal go up or down based on were we headed." Colonel Fleming didn't understand technology as much as Mr. Johnson did, but he was trying.

"I see. Then what happened when you got to Dreamland? How did you know it was the Beacon Tower?" Fleming asked.

James sat back and collected his thoughts. His eyes fell on a photograph on the wall behind Colonel Fleming. It was a portrait of Mr. Johnson and Mr. Edison. Next to it was a portrait of Senator Mather, who Mr. Johnson had saved from the Martians during the attack. Where would those photos go?

Would Mr. Johnson ever come back? What would Mom say? Or Susan? What did Mr. Edison have to say?

"Are you okay, James?" Fleming asked, his brow furrowed.

"Sorry. I was just woolgathering." James cleared his throat. "I had to adjust the meter a few times by the time we got to Coney Island, but the signal was too strong to follow right to the source. I knew Dreamland had its own power generation right next to the tower, since Edison had built it. And I remembered how it was so tall that they had to remove lights from the top because it was confusing shipping traffic. So we started there . . ." James trailed off, his pride in guessing the right tower colliding with his guilt over Christensen and the other marines getting killed by his lucky guess.

"That was outstanding work, James," Fleming said, repeating himself like the military man he was.

Outstanding work? But it had led three men to their deaths.

"So you were here early yesterday, weren't you?" Fleming continued. "You had a good chance to examine the wreckage? I'm sure Ben was in a hurry to have you look at it." He took another puff of his cigarette and sat back in his—Mr. Johnson's—chair.

Sweat trickled down the back of James's neck as his heart rate picked up. Did the Colonel recognize the chassis James had handed over to the officer? Did he know what it was? Did he know about it at all?

"No, not really. Other than a few pieces of cable, it was all burnt," James said. Lying was getting easier and easier.

"That's what I thought. I had it all sent right to the incinerator. We know everything we need from Coney Island. The Germans are planning an attack, and we need to get to them first, right?" Fleming smiled again.

"Uh, right." Had James just passed some kind of test?

"You're worried about Ben, aren't you? You've always been very loyal to him. That's usually an admirable trait, James. But you need to be a bit more pragmatic."

James lifted an eyebrow.

"Ben wasn't willing to work with us, the Security Police. And that's never the right choice. We're all working together to keep the country safe. Right, James?"

"Yes. Yes, of course."

About six months before the Tesla fire, Dad had come home with a bottle of whiskey wrapped in a paper bag. As he'd walked in the door, he was already reeking of liquor. But Dad hadn't been a drinker. He'd always said he'd "drank his share" during the War of the Rebellion.

But he'd been drunk that night, and Mom had sent James to bed early with a stern warning not to leave his room. But while she'd send him to his room, she couldn't make James sleep. So he'd laid in bed for hours, listening.

Dad had caught a man attacking a young girl. James hadn't understood what that had meant back then, but as the story resurfaced now, he did. His dad had taken the man to the precinct, charged him, locked him up, and gone back to his beat. Later that night, when Dad had finished his shift, the man had disappeared.

The Security Police had intervened. Some "bastard wrapped in the flag" had said releasing the man was necessary to "keep the country safe."

Keep the country safe. Those words now reverberated in James's ears.

"So we're starting a new era for Edison and the radio team, James. Can I count on you?" Fleming asked.

James opened his mouth to answer. Before he could get a word out, the door crashed open, and he nearly fell out of his chair.

"You're pledging your loyalty to him?" Susan asked. Her voice was level, but she'd flung the door open so hard that it caromed off the wall and nearly struck her in the face.

James spun around in his chair. Susan's eyes were glowing with fury, but her voice had been perfectly steady.

"Well . . ." he began.

"Pull a chair over for her, James," Fleming said, standing to face Susan. "We can discuss this together."

"I'll stand, thank you." Susan closed the door and crossed her arms. She pursed her lips and held a square stance, as if daring either man to try to leave the room. "So, why was Ben Johnson relieved?"

"You've been eavesdropping? Maybe you're the spy who's leaked information to the press." Fleming stared at Susan as if he'd forgotten James was in the room.

"Yes! Yes, that's it, Sean," Susan snapped. "I'm a spy. I have special training in listening in on private conversations and then interrupting them to announce myself. Is that what passes for detective work in the Security Police? No wonder they snatched you up after you left Edison in disgrace."

Fleming's face reddened ever so slightly. He sighed and came around from behind his desk.

"Are you going to answer my question, Sean?" Susan pressed. "Why was Ben Johnson relieved? Or will you hide behind the SP's skirts?"

"I can't tell you," Fleming said, carefully enunciating each word in what sounded like an effort to control his temper. "But I'll thank you for addressing me by my rank."

James's dad had spent nearly a year in the hospital before finally succumbing to the cancer Tesla's fire had given him—a year that had been a blur to James. Every day, he'd woken up dazed. And every afternoon, he'd come home from school to an empty apartment, make himself a sandwich, do his homework, and read while waiting for Mom to come home from the hospital, half expecting her to tell him Dad had died.

But there was one day that still stuck out in James's mind. The day Mom transformed from Mrs. Brogan, timid wife of an NYC cop, to Siobhan Brogan, a woman who stood up for herself.

It was a Saturday, the one day each week when James could see Dad. He and Mom would visit him early in the morning, when his dad had more energy, and James would recount the events of his week in school.

A doctor came that day—a doctor Mom clearly didn't like. He asked to speak to her in the hallway, and an argument broke out moments after they left the room. James watched from the doorway, positioned behind Mom so she couldn't see him and the doctor couldn't, either. Or didn't care to see him.

The doctor wanted to move Dad out of the hospital to a "home." He talked about wasted beds and inevitable outcomes. He spoke to Mom like she was a child, telling her she "didn't understand."

Mom had shaken with rage during that conversation, fists clenched at her side. But her tone had stayed even, just as Susan's did now. Very clearly and firmly, Mom had told the doctor that she did understand. She'd said she understood the doctor was more worried about money than patients—that he wanted to give up on a hero and send him off to die.

Susan had never been what James would call timid, but he couldn't help but think that the woman he'd left in the break room had stormed into this meeting as a different person. She was on the attack, risking her job and freedom by directing her attack on her new boss—a boss who was also a colonel in the Security Police.

James wiped sweat off his brow. The atmosphere in the office had become oppressive. He hoped Colonel Fleming wouldn't light another cigarette. The room might burst into flames like the Beacon Tower had.

"Can't? Or won't?" Susan asked. "Are you worried the truth might make James recant his oath of loyalty to you?"

James jumped at the mention of his name. Susan was staring at him, her eyes threatening to make him combust without the help of a lit cigarette.

"Are you angry with James feeling more loyal to Edison than you?" Fleming asked.

James blinked. He was more loyal to Edison than to Susan? What did that mean?

Susan raised an eyebrow and titled her head.

"I mean, more loyal to Edison than you are, of course," Fleming said with a slight smile.

"Of course," Susan said. "You'd never try to exploit a personal relationship for your advantage. At least, not again."

Fleming turned a darker shade of red this time, and he ground his teeth.

James needed to get Susan out of there before things got out of control. She was going to lose her job—or worse, end up in trouble with the Security Police.

"Let's go, Susan," he said, approaching her with a hand outstretched.

She took a step back, glaring at James with even more intensity, before stepping around him to regain eye contact with Fleming. "You showed up here yesterday and impounded the wreckage from Coney Island," she said, her voice remaining level. "Now Ben is gone, and you're bragging about having it destroyed. What are you hiding? And you"—she turned to James—"you're going along with this?"

James jumped again. This was escalating too quickly. He needed to end this meeting and get Susan out of this office—maybe even the building.

"I'm not hiding anything," Fleming said before James could react. "Ben Johnson has become, regrettably, a threat to national security. I can't share any details with you, but I can tell you this: Things are going to change at Edison. Perhaps even the name over the door." He shrugged, then looked at James. "We're done for now. Feel free to come to me with any questions. I'll talk to Susan now. It's clear she's hysterical and needs help calming down."

"I'm hysterical?" Susan said. "I'm not the one turning beet red, Colonel."

"This is getting out of hand," James said. "Let's go, Susan. We can take a break and work things out later—"

Susan pushed his hand away.

"You just burst into my office after eavesdropping on a private conversation," Fleming said, ignoring James. "You've questioned James's decision to remain loyal and accused me of hiding something. How else would you categorize your behavior, young lady?"

"Don't 'young lady' me," Susan said. "That might have worked a few years ago, but not anymore. I know why you were fired from Edison, even if James doesn't."

She faced James again, looking him in the eye. "If I wasn't clear earlier, James, this man is a thief. He stole Martian technology and sold it to rival companies and—as far as we know—other nations. Staying here with him in charge is a mistake."

Had Fleming sold the reactor that had killed Dad to Tesla? Was Urich right?

"Now, see here, young lady," Fleming said.

"I told you not to call me that," Susan said before looking back at James. "I'll leave with you now, but we're going right out the door."

James blinked.

"I'm quitting. And you should, too." Susan was shaking now, just like Mom had been that day in the hospital.

James suspected Fleming was hiding something, just like Mr.

Johnson was. There was no reason to doubt Susan that Fleming had been pushed out of Edison for stealing equipment, and Urich's story was more believable now than it had been this morning. But why had Mr. Johnson covered it up?

But could James quit? How would he support Mom? How would he help Susan if she quit and lost her income? And, how would he find out what had really happened to Dad?

21

War was bad.

That was self-evident. Saying that war was bad was like saying that water was wet—or that officers were clueless. It wasted breath to belabor the obvious.

But war wasn't the worst part of being a soldier. War focused one's attention. When an army was at war, it didn't have a lot of time to worry about anything else. But an army at rest? That was trouble, because an army without a war was an army searching for something else to worry about.

An army at rest was bored—and it would find uncreative ways to fill the time.

Emil gazed into the pot and saw himself gaze back. Hopefully, the pot was clean enough for the tyrant running the kitchen.

"That'll have to be good enough for now, Zimmerman," the mess Unteroffizier bellowed, though he was standing less than a meter from Emil's left ear. "You can pick up where you left off after the assembly."

Emil pulled off his apron, hung it on a hook near the door, and hustled in the direction of his tent. He walked past the large entrance gate that controlled entrance to—and exit from—the perimeter. It was the only way in and out of the fenced-in compound, as far as he knew. It was where he'd arrived with Hauptmann Ritter and the soldiers from the 109th four days ago. Six men guarded it, as they had every other time Emil had passed by it.

"There you are," said the country bumpkin who shared a tent with Emil and six other soldiers. He was a big bumpkin—taller than Ludwig, but with the muscles of a young man who'd grown up harvesting crops and chasing sheep. "I thought I was going to have to send out a search party for you."

The army had separated Emil from his men so that none of them shared the same tent or platoon. They did this without comment and—based on what little Emil had managed to learn so far—were following standard procedure.

Bumpkin came from some Bavarian unit and was fascinated with French cheese. But at least he was social. The other soldiers had barely grunted three words between them, annoyed that Emil had dared to take the extra bunk.

"Just managed to get myself out of the kitchen," Emil said, changing into clean boots and grabbing a clean uniform jacket. He and his men had all been issued new uniforms. This was a pleasant surprise, and having three square meals a day was a welcome change. But both were signs of a peacetime unit playing army out in the woods.

Except they weren't in the woods. They were camped out in groomed fields near Reims, one of the largest cities between Paris and Karlsruhe.

What were they doing here? Where did these supplies come from? And how could Emil escape and head home?

He and Bumpkin left the tent and joined the stream of soldiers heading to an open field in the compound's northeast corner. The eight-foot-high fence was visible at the field's northern end, but woods stood to the south, with nothing visible but a tall radio mast extending from somewhere out of sight. Was it part of this operation? Or the Planetary Warning

System? Reims was a large enough city to have a node in the network.

Emil looked around as he and Bumpkin found their platoon and took their places, and did some quick math. At least 200 men were jockeying for position in the field. They sported clean uniforms and carefully shined boots, as if they were lining up for a parade or some anonymous Hauptmann's retirement ceremony.

As the soldiers fell into ranks, Emil noticed how some of them scanned around as subtly as they could, nodding to familiar faces. Even as they lined up in rows, each man was alone.

The ranks faced east, toward a platform with a podium at one end and gallows at the other. Three nooses hung from heavy frames built from fresh wood, gleaming white in the midday sun and still clean and straight, as if they'd yet to see a drop of rain.

Three men stood under nooses, with armed guards flanking them. Burlap sacks covered their faces, and their arms were tied behind their backs. Emil's stomach lurched.

The fence was clearly visible at the field's northern end.

Ludwig was standing in another group nearby. Before Emil could decide whether it was worth getting his attention, a Stabsfeldwebel in full dress walked in front of the ranks, bringing an uneasy silence with him. Based on his rank, uniform, and ostentatious bearing, he was the highest-ranking noncommissioned officer in Wegener's organization.

The Stabsfeldwebel proceeded to earn the respect of every solider on that field with a call for attention that sprang from an impressive set of lungs. Then he spun and faced the platform with the precision of a ballerina on her hundredth performance of *The Nutcracker*.

General Wegener, who commanded this division, appeared behind the podium. His helmet gleamed in the mid-morning sun, its reflection racing through the ranks of men. The General didn't look much older than Emil, but his tunic boasted the array of ribbons, crosses, and medals you'd expect from a seasoned veteran. He lacked the elaborate mustaches Emil had thought were required for his rank, and was clean-shaven instead.

"Men, we're here today to mete out a solemn duty," Wegener spoke. "Last night, three of you decided that you weren't part of this army. Those men were wrong: we belong to one another. Indeed, we were born for one another, and therefore we must always hold firmly together, whether God ordains peace or storm. You have taken the oath of allegiance and obedience, and the eyes of your ancestors are looking down upon you. One day, you shall have to render an account of your actions to them. For those three men, that day is today."

He nodded to the guards. They fixed a noose over a prisoner's mask, then guided him over a hatch in the floor. The prisoners remained eerily still during this process, almost as if they'd been drugged.

But why wasn't someone reading out the formal list of charges? Had these soldiers been court-martialed? Where was the panel who convicted them? Soldiers could be executed for offenses like desertion and insubordination, but there was a process.

The specter of execution hung over the head of every German soldier during the war. Despite Fluse's constant threats to Emil in the trench, they weren't common. While the difference between civilian law and military law was made clear to every soldier on the first day they reported for duty and was frequently reinforced, there were laws and strict procedures for enforcing them.

The guards returned to their places, unshouldered their weapons, and came to attention.

Wegener gestured again.

The prisoners dropped about two meters through the floor. The sickening cracks of breaking necks reverberated across the field, startling Emil. His breakfast climbed into his throat, but he pushed it back down. A few other soldiers shifted position and exhaled sharply.

Wegener waited a moment before speaking again. "These are indeed days of trial and affliction. But Providence and God's will have placed me at the head of this army. We are entering a new era. The war between Germany and its aggressors has ended, and now we must repel invaders. It will be a thankless job. Some of you will never make it home, but your sacrifice will live on in the shape of a newer, better, larger Germany."

He paused, then called out, "Stabsfeldwebel."

The Stabsfeldwebel called the men to attention and dismissed them, instructing them to be on time for dinner.

Providence and God's will. That was the kind of language the kaiser used when he claimed his right to rule the country. Generals spoke about the trust the kaiser placed in them, not the trust of God. Wegener was either a madman, an opportunist, or both. Emil needed to find a way out of there as soon as he could.

Wegener descended the stairs on the back of the platform, where he was met by a group of men, most of whom were in similar dress uniforms. Emil recognized Ritter but couldn't make out any of the others. Was Fluse with them? Emil hadn't seen him since their group had been split up, but this would be an opportunity for Fluse to kiss some ass.

"We haven't had an afternoon off since I got here," Bumpkin said.

Emil tore his gaze away from Wegener. They'd attended a public hanging, and Bumpkin was now celebrating an afternoon off? "They usually make you go back to work after an execution?" he asked.

"What? No," Bumpkin answered. "This is the first one I've seen. Hey, I wonder what they really did. Just tried to desert?"

He was right. Wegener hadn't said what the three men had done.

Fluse was over there with Wegener now. The general was

holding court with eight different officers. He was gesturing toward the gallows, then the field, then the soldiers. His audience was enraptured.

"There you are, Emil." It was Ludwig.

Emil shook his hand. It was odd, shaking the hand of someone he'd spent most of the war and a week-long odyssey with. But the four days apart had felt longer. "I saw you before the . . . execution, but there was no chance to say anything," he said.

"Yes, they've done a good job of keeping us distracted, haven't they?"

"I think they want us to spend some more time out here near the gallows." Emil gave a wry smile.

Ludwig shook his head, but not in disagreement.

The Stabsfeldwebel had made it to the back of the platform. Now he, Wegener, and the other officers were laughing about something. Was it the sound one man's neck had made when it had snapped? Or how stunned the soldiers had looked when they'd been dismissed for the afternoon?

Beckenbauer arrived with a few more men from the 109th in tow. Soon Emil was surrounded. All eyes were on him again.

"So, what did you think?" Beckenbauer asked.

Emil looked back at Wegener again, then turned to the men. His men. Were they still his men? They leaned in, waiting for his answer.

Bumpkin wandered off to find his unit.

"You know," Beckenbauer continued. "The execution. And the general's speech."

They'd just seen a summary execution and heard a speech by a madman who'd said God had placed him at the head of this army. Emil knew what he wanted to say, but it was too risky to speak his mind. He might endanger himself and the others. They couldn't be his men anymore.

"Well, we're back in the army now, I guess," he finally said. "We'll have to see what they expect from us next."

Beckenbauer frowned. Ludwig raised an eyebrow.

Emil looked back at the platform. Wegener was looking right back at him.

22

Three-and-a-half miles wasn't far enough. The bicycle ride to and from work had been James's only chance to think—his only time alone for the past two weeks. He could only do so much to drag the time out, so he rode as slowly as possible and took a few long cuts. But the ride was still too short.

While he was on his bicycle, James had the peace and quiet he needed to figure out what he'd say to Susan. They hadn't spoken since the day she'd stormed out of Colonel Fleming's office and Edison Labs—and, as of now, James's life. He didn't have a plan, or the courage, to talk to her yet. Not until he figured out what to say.

At home, Mom wouldn't give him a moment's peace. She was angry he hadn't quit as soon as Mr. Johnson had been fired. She was angry he hadn't backed Susan. She was just angry.

At work, Colonel Fleming would speak to James at least four times a day. He was nice—maybe too nice. He kept asking the same questions about James's work, often straying into transparent attempts to get more information about what James had seen at Coney Island. He'd also ask about Mom, and even Susan once. James wanted him to go away so he could lose himself in his latest design and pretend everything was the way it had been before the explosion at the Beacon Tower.

He'd told himself he'd only taken Fleming's "pledge of loyalty" as a means to learn more about the Tesla fire. He wasn't going to learn anything by hiding from the colonel. Last night, while trying to avoid Mom's harangues, James had realized Seward had been at Edison when the fire had struck downtown New York City. He'd know something about the investigation, even if it was only enough to tell James where to start looking.

Now, James rounded a corner about two blocks from the office. Standing on the right side of the street, almost exactly where Urich had been two weeks earlier, was a new obstruction.

James squinted. It was a person. A person who looked suspiciously like Susan.

"Are you okay?" the obstruction asked. "Why are you riding so slow?"

It was Susan.

"Just taking my time," James said, coasting to a stop. "Am I really that predictable?"

"What?" Susan was standing with her arms crossed and an expression that was neither a smile nor a frown.

James's heart jumped in his chest. Here she was. What should he say?

"I . . ." he began. Two weeks of rehearsals for this conversation slipped away, never to be heard from again.

Susan's nonsmile turned into a frown.

What could James say? That he was sorry? Sorry she was angry? Sorry she'd left Edison? He wasn't sorry he'd stayed there. He needed the job, and he wanted to find out more about how his dad had been killed.

"If you insist on working for that criminal, you can at least make yourself useful," Susan said.

"I'm not—"

"I don't want to hear it. I ran into Seward yesterday, and

something suspicious is going on in Sayville. Have you heard anything?"

"No. But I—"

"I figured you were doing your best to hide behind your desk and pretend that nothing happened." Susan frowned again.

James winced. "Susan, I just want to say . . ." He paused, waiting to be cut off again, then continued when he wasn't. "Will you go to dinner with me tonight? So we can talk?"

She bit her lip and turned away. "I don't know if that's a good idea."

"But . . . I'm sorry. I can't quit. I have to support Mom. And if I leave Edison, I'll never find out how Tesla got that reactor."

Susan looked back at him. Her eyes were moist, but her jaw was set. "I'll consider it . . . if you'll do something for me."

"What?" James's heart jumped. He would have done anything for her.

She reached into her handbag and produced a key. "This is a key for Ben's office. I need you to take a look at what Fleming is hiding."

Anything for Susan, except that. "You want me to sneak into Fleming's office? When he's not there?"

"Well, it'll probably be easier that way." She gave a wry smile.

"What do you think he's hiding?"

Susan sighed. "Do you really have to ask?"

James shrugged. "I'm not sure what I'd be looking for."

She threw up her hands. "James, wake up. Look around you. Whatever's Fleming's up to, he's not working alone. Someone got him into the SPs with his full rank. He didn't do that alone. There's a chance he got your father killed. Don't you want to know more?"

She was right, as usual. But breaking into the office of a colonel in the Security Police? James would be risking jail at worst, unemployment at best. But Susan really wanted him to do this, and it was the fastest way—probably the only way—back into her good graces. What if he took the key and told her he didn't find anything?

James took the key. "Tonight? I'll pick you up around seven?"

"You're going to do this? Today?" Susan looked him in the eye.

"Yes. He takes a lunch. I'll do it then."

But James was lying again. It was getting easier every time.

23

"Zimmerman? There you are."

Emil looked up from the pot he'd been scrubbing and came face-to-face with Hauptmann Ritter. What was he doing in the mess? "Yes, sir. Here I am."

"General Wegener wants to speak to you. Come with me."

Emil swore his stomach dropped to somewhere around his knees. The man who'd led a hanging yesterday wanted to speak to him.

"Let's go," Ritter said. "We can't keep him waiting."

Emil disposed of his apron and followed the Hauptmann out of the mess tent. "What does the general want with me?" he croaked. Out of the frying pan and into the fire, as his mother used to say.

"It's not my place to say." Ritter looked at Emil and read the concern on his face. "It's nothing to worry about, Soldat. Quite the opposite."

What did that mean? If Emil wasn't headed to the gallows, what could Wegener want from him?

The general's office was a heavy canvas tent with a heavy wood frame, not unlike the one that had been nearly completed for Degenscheide when the Martians had arrived in Mametz.

Wegener was seated at an oak desk that was the size of Emil's bunk. It was a beautiful piece of furniture, with gold inlays and delicate scrollwork circling the top. At the other end of the room sat a table so large that Emil assumed the tent must have been assembled around it. It was adorned with a lace tablecloth, a silver coffeepot, a tray of porcelain mugs, and a map of Europe. There were no chairs; Wegener's officers must have done their planning on their feet.

Fine furniture. Silver coffee service. While the office seemed temporary, Wegener had made himself at home—exactly the way a general would have. Would a waiter take their lunch order?

Wegener glanced up from his mammoth desk and flashed Emil and Ritter a huge smile. "Zimmerman! Great to finally meet you. Take a seat." He gestured to a chair in front of the desk. "Thank you, Ritter. We'll talk later."

Emil approached the desk and the offered chair, which was upholstered with red leather. He unshouldered his rifle and sat with it across his knees. He kept his hands on his lap to conceal their shaking. Wegener knew him by sight. How much harder would it be to get out of here now?

Wegener closed the book he'd been reading and looked at Emil for a moment. Up close, he appeared younger than he had at the assembly. Was he clean-shaven by choice? Or because he couldn't grow the customary Junker mustache?

"I couldn't figure out how that moron Fluse managed to lead fifteen men from Mametz to Reims," Wegener said, smiling conspiratorially.

Emil sat up straight. What had Fluse told him? Did he know why they'd been heading to Reims? Were they going to be the next soldiers sent to Wegener's gallows?

"I already knew what happened to your regiment. It was wiped off the face of the earth." Wegener made a sweeping motion with one hand. "I'm surprised five of you made it out alive, let alone an entire squad. A reserve regiment run by lawyers and shopkeepers! It's a wonder the Belgians couldn't beat you with rocks and sticks, let alone with help from the Anglische." He shook his head.

Lawyers and shopkeepers? Who the hell was this man? He'd been sitting behind his precious desk while Degenscheide had faced down the Martians and saved their lives. Emil clenched his fists, relieved for the second time in as many minutes that Wegener couldn't see them.

"Fluse struck me as the kind of weakling who would have immediately fled north or east, looking for another unit to latch himself onto," Wegener continued. "At first, I thought that Unteroffizier must have been the one who saved your lives. But then I saw those men run to you after the assembly."

Emil started to sweat. Wegener had figured out he'd been in charge. What if he figured out why they'd been heading toward Germany?

"It's clear to me you got those men here, and they see you as their leader," Wegener added. "I need men like you, Zimmerman."

Emil frowned. "I'm just a Soldat, sir. I'm trained to work on field phones and radios."

"And you think you have to stay a Soldat, don't you? I can respect that. I'm sure you were taught that a farmer like you had to stay an enlisted man. But I need you. Germany needs you."

Emil blinked. Wegener had called him here to offer him a promotion? He relaxed his fists but kept his hands out of sight. He wasn't facing execution—but this was worse. Wegener wanted to make him everything he hated. How would Emil escape if the general was going to make him more visible?

"I admire your humility, Emil. May I call you Emil? But I don't need humility. I need leaders, and it's clear that's what you are." Wegener smiled again, and for a moment he was almost believable. But this was the monster who'd hanged three soldiers to put on a show. "You're a natural leader. You're not one of those pathetic reservists you served under. But you're not one of those entitled Junkers, either. They had everything handed to them, and they still weren't ready to make the right decision. . . ."

He looked away from Emil briefly. "But I'm getting ahead of myself. Let's talk about your place on this team. I'd like to start you out as a Leutnant."

Emil tensed. A field promotion to Leutnant? Not Unteroffizier? Everything he'd fought against since he'd been drafted? Absolutely not.

He opened his mouth to object, but Wegener cut him off with another one of his smiles. "You'll run the squads that have been recovering hardware in the west," the general added. "You'll be replacing Fluse."

Emil's grip on his gun loosened. Salvage duty? In the west? That would get him out of the compound—but he'd be headed in the wrong direction. Then again, with a leadership position, it might be easier for him to slip away and go unnoticed long enough to put some distance between him and this lunatic. Was it worth it? And why was he replacing Fluse? Had he been promoted, too?

"You're still thinking about it?" Wegener asked. "Emil, you're a born leader. What is there to agonize over? A lion doesn't wonder what he's going to do in the morning. He gets up and hunts." He shrugged matter-of-factly.

Was there really a choice? What would be the penalty for saying no? Wegener might not punish Emil outright, but he'd have him watched. Emil had to agree to this—and then try to use whatever came next to his advantage.

"You're right, sir," he answered. "This is a unique opportunity and I would be a fool to turn it down. I'd love to get started right away."

Wegener smiled. "That's what I wanted to hear. Let's talk to Ritter and get you started."

24

James was the first person to arrive at Edison that morning. He brought in the paper, turned on the lights, and started coffee.

He felt for Susan's key in his pocket. It would be at least a half hour before Fleming arrived. Enough time for James to open his office, check the desk, and tell Susan tonight that he hadn't found anything. He wouldn't have been lying.

But what if someone showed up? What would James say? He sat and listlessly shuffled the newspaper while the coffee brewed, running through the different scenarios that all ended with him being arrested for treason.

By the time Seward arrived, James was at his own desk, picturing several ways the security police would catch him.

"Good morning!" Seward chirped. With thick glasses, a neatly trimmed beard, and a cherrywood pipe, he belonged at the head of a lecture hall, not in a lab wielding a soldering iron and a pair of wire cutters.

"Good morning!" James said, picking up his cup and approaching the older man, hoping to follow him into the kitchen and get him talking about the Tesla fire.

"So, I guess you'll get a lot done today, eh?" Seward asked, pouring himself some coffee.

"Huh?" James tilted his head.

"The boss is out at Sayville today. He didn't mention it yesterday?"

Sayville? The colonel had gone to Sayville and hadn't told James? That was his station. He built it—and had nearly been killed getting it back online. James reached into his pocket again and fondled the key. "Uh, no. Must have slipped his mind. Any idea why?"

"Nope. Must have been a business issue if he didn't need you." Seward shrugged.

"Yeah. I guess so," James replied, filling his cup with coffee.

A half hour later, he realized he'd forgotten to ask Seward about the fire.

Lunchtime came and went. The key sat like a boat anchor in James's pocket. He didn't want to lie to Susan, but he didn't want to risk getting caught in Fleming's office. Seward had referred to the colonel as "the boss." Could James trust Seward?

By 4:30 p.m., James was already thinking about heading home to clean up for his date when a courier arrived.

"I have a letter for a Colonel Fleming?" The courier, a young man, was wearing a uniform so crisp that it might have come out of a box that morning.

"He's not here," Seward said, his hat and jacket already on. "He'll be in tomorrow."

"I can't come back tomorrow," the courier said. "I need to drop this off today, or my boss will kill me."

"I'll take care of it," James offered.

"Thanks," Seward said. "I need to run."

James took the envelope. "Do you need a signature?"

"Huh?" The courier's brow wrinkled.

"Never mind. Thanks."

James returned to his desk and put the envelope down. The key was warm in his pocket. He could let himself in and put the mail on Fleming's desk. But then he'd know James had a key.

He picked up the envelope and inspected it. The return address was in New York City but lacked a name. That was odd. Most of the correspondence to the radio lab was from the government and other Edison offices. Come to think of it, the government used the Postal Service, and Edison had its own intra-office delivery system. Who would use a private courier?

Had someone delivered what Susan was looking for?

James looked at the exit door, then back at the hallway to Fleming's office. If he took the letter, no one would know. It might take days for Fleming to miss it, and by then Seward would have forgotten about the delivery. James hadn't signed for it, either.

He went to the kitchen, turned on the stove, and put on a pot of water. After a few minutes, there was enough steam for James to open the envelope without tearing it.

The letter read:

Fleming,

We'd rather convey this message in person, but after the mess in Brooklyn, we need to stay out of sight. There's word that Mather is asking questions about the radios being down.

It's critical they stay that way, whatever the cost. We don't care how you do it. They better stay offline, and quietly this time. No more theatrics.

James dropped the letter, nearly dousing it in the pot of boiling water. He picked it up, put it back in the envelope, and leaned against the stove, taking a deep breath.

25

The heavy canvas tent where Emil had met Wegener the day before was now outfitted with windows and the beginning of a frame. Emil caught his reflection in one of the glass panes and needed a moment to recognize the man with the thinning hair and Leutnant's pips on his uniform.

The promotion had been all but a secret; Emil could lose it as quickly as he'd gotten it. The day before, Wegener had produced three sets of Leutnant's pips from a desk drawer—two for field uniforms, one for dress—and handed them to Emil. Then he'd called for Ritter, who arranged for Emil's gear to be moved to an officer's tent on the other side of the compound. Ritter had then escorted Emil to his new home and made it clear he shouldn't visit his old quarters.

Now, Emil stood outside Wegener's headquarters, a favorite spot for officers to assemble their details. It never hurt to make sure the boss saw you doing something resembling work at least once a day. He was facing Hauptmann Ritter, who wore a uniform so colorful that Emil considered asking him where to find the circus tent and if it, too, had windows. But the grimacing soldier accompanying Ritter dampened the mood.

"I'm sending you out with Unteroffizier Schmidt for your first run," Ritter said. "He'll show you the ropes."

Show him the ropes? What a polite way to describe acting as a babysitter and prison guard. Emil already knew his promotion was probationary. Now he'd need to build up some trust before using it to escape Wegener's clutches.

Or, he might flee the first chance he had during this run.

There had been no opportunities to see Ludwig or Beckenbauer since Wegener's "assembly," but Emil had been clear since leaving the trenches that he was going home. If he found a way to escape, they'd need to find their own way out.

"We're heading to Épernay," Schmidt said. "It's one of our collection points. We'll take four carts. There's at least that much to be picked up and brought here."

Unteroffizier Schmidt was a lighter, meaner-looking version of Ludwig. A tinge of gray accented his hair and long sideburns, but not an ounce of fat showed on his lean frame. He spoke with an odd accent. Perhaps German wasn't his first language. He crossed his arms and looked over Emil's shoulder instead of making eye contact, as if studying something in the distance. Maybe Paris. Maybe the rising sun.

"Where does the salvaged equipment go?" Emil asked.

"To the salvaged equipment yard." Schmidt still refused to look at him. He turned and walked to the stables, fast enough that Emil struggled a few steps before giving up trying to catch him.

The carts were lined up in front of the stables, harnessed to four draft horses each. Six soldiers with clean uniforms, shiny boots, and polished weapons milled around the first cart. With a total of eight men, Emil might find a way to lose himself in the crowd before slipping into the forest. Especially if Unteroffizier Friendly continued to ignore him.

Schmidt arrived at the carts and pulled the soldiers into a huddle. They spoke in whispers as he gestured for Emil to climb into the lead cart. Emil approached the group instead, hoping to catch a word.

The Unteroffizier stopped speaking then, and the group broke up and headed to their carts. Schmidt climbed onto the lead cart and waited for Emil to follow. Then he steered it out of the stable entrance and south toward Épernay, with the other three carts in tow.

"How long a ride is it?" Emil asked.

"Couple of hours," Schmidt said. "Just relax."

Emil flushed with anger. Probation was one thing. Being saddled with an antisocial jerk was another. Even if he intended to leave as fast as possible, he wouldn't put up with being treated like a doormat. "Is there a problem, Schmidt?"

Schmidt's jerked his head so quickly to make eye contact that it must have strained his neck. "Excuse me?"

"You barely said two words to me this morning, and you made sure I didn't hear you brief the men. Is your problem with outsiders? Officers? Me?"

"Uh, well . . ."

Emil kept his gaze on Schmidt and raised his eyebrows.

"You're the third Leutnant to be assigned to this detail in a few weeks," Schmidt said, returning eye contact for the first time, but with a wavering voice. "There's no reason to believe you'll be any better than the others. Wegener loves to pick his favorites."

"Wegener mentioned that Fluse had this job before me."

"Yeah."

Emil chuckled. "Well, I promise I'll do better than him."

"You knew him?" Schmidt said, his mouth hanging open.

Was Schmidt surprised by the coincidence? Maybe Emil had a chance to win this guy over now. If he couldn't skip out today, getting this guy on his side might come in handy later. "Yeah, real jerk," Emil said, smiling.

Schmidt sighed and sat back in his seat. "We'll be there in

about three hours. I don't want to strain the horses. We have to haul a lot of gear back on this trip."

"Thanks. Where are you from?"

"Spandau."

"Near Berlin?"

Schmidt grinned. "Yes, that's it. We're a factory town. The center of Germany's weapons production."

"Ah. I see why Wegener put you on this detail."

Schmidt nodded. "Exactly! He asked where we were from and picked me because I worked in the factories."

They followed the road into woods that grew thicker as they progressed south. Emil and Schmidt talked about home, what they did before the army (Schmidt was a lifer, of course), and how they missed home. Emil held off on pumping him for information about Wegener's plans. While the background might point to a way to escape, jumping right into questions about that might make Schmidt clam up again.

They were debating the finer point of bread dumplings when a howl sounded somewhere south of them. A Martian howl.

Emil picked up his weapon, hoping he'd misheard. "What was that?"

"Martian," Schmidt said without missing a beat.

So the invaders had made it this far south. Why had they skipped Reims? Had they landed near here? Or were they wandering around France, attacking whatever they happened to come across? Had they landed all over Europe?

"We need to get out of sight. Find an opening to hide the cart." Emil turned to signal to the other carts, but Schmidt grabbed his shoulder and turned him around.

"Quiet down, and put your weapon away. They won't bother us."

"What? How can you possibly know that?"

"We've been using this path for weeks, and they leave us alone, just like Ritter said." Schmidt turned back to face the road.

"Ritter knew they were here? How long have you been doing this?"

"Almost two months."

Wegener's men had been in Reims that long? Before the Martians had shown up in the Somme Valley? And they had some kind of peaceful coexistence with them? How? Hermonville and other villages near Reims had all been intact, too. What was so special about this area?

Trees cracked off to one side of the cart, pulling Emil back to the present. A Wanderer poked up between the thick rows of spruce and oak. Emil jumped and brought the rifle up to his shoulder, even though it was worthless.

Schmidt reached up and pushed the barrel of Emil's rifle down. "It's fine, honest. They're just passing through." He chuckled. "The last thing we need is you drawing their attention with gunfire."

The Wanderer disappeared into the trees behind them with a desultory howl. An afterimage of Degenscheide being vaporized played behind it. Emil swallowed.

"You were in Fluse's unit, right?" Schmidt asked. "You were overrun by the Martians?"

"Yes." Overrun, and it had taken the sacrifice of Emil's commanding officer to get them out of there. But this guy was laughing at the aliens.

"Ah, that explains why you're afraid. Fluse nearly wet his pants. Well, they're not a problem for us."

Emil's eyes remained wide. "Not a problem? I don't understand. I mean . . . don't you remember them from before?"

"Actually, they never made it to Spandau. Or to Berlin."

"But . . . you have to know they'll come for us eventually."

"Maybe. Maybe not. Wegener has a plan. The best we can do in the meantime is get ready, right? What would be the point of attacking them only to be wiped out?"

Schmidt had a point. But how were they getting ready? Was

Wegener planning on living with the Martians somehow? Madness!

"We're almost there," Schmidt said. "You can stow your weapon."

Emil nodded and put his rifle back down. Fluse might have been an insufferable jerk, but he couldn't be blamed for panicking when finding himself face-to-face with another Wanderer. But it was weird that Schmidt wasn't worried about them at all. "You didn't see Martians on the front?" Emil asked.

"No." Schmidt shifted in his seat. "We were on our way to Paris when Wegener took us to Reims instead. New orders."

Interesting. Wegener's unit wasn't completely made up of units that had been attacked by the Martians. At least one unit—Schmidt's—had made it to Reims without seeing them. But how? Why were they now sitting in the city, and not trying to help the units on the front? Was Wegener still reporting to the kaiser? Or running a rogue operation?

Light broke at the end of the path, interrupting Emil's reverie. Schmidt angled their cart into a clearing; and the others followed, bringing their horses to a stop.

The clearing was a salvage yard. Parts dotted forty or fifty square meters of gravel and yellowing grass. Thick scraps of metal—some massive, others insubstantial—concealed the terrain. Rather than stacking them into piles and sorting them by shape or purpose, whoever had delivered the parts had spread them out, like butter on toast.

Trees bordered two sides of the yard, but the others were open. If Emil could get clear of Schmidt and the other men, he might have a chance to sneak off into the woods. If he moved quickly, he might even give himself a half-hour head start. He scanned the timberline, looking for the densest cluster of trees.

After a moment of scanning back and forth, Emil's eyes focused on the parts.

Martian parts.

Martian power supplies. Martian heat rays. Martian gas

guns. Arms and legs from Wanderers. Some of the wreckage bore the camouflage he'd seen in Mametz. Others had the plain metallic finish he remembered from the first attack. Some of the pieces were corroded and crusted with soil. Was it a mix of refuse from both wars?

"This is Martian tech," Emil said, not fully aware he'd said it out loud.

"Yes, of course," Schmidt said. "They didn't tell you what we're here for?"

Emil shook his head. A chill ran from the back of his neck down his spine. What was Wegener up to? First, they rode right past a pair of Wanderers, and now they were gathering up the spare parts?

"This is what we're taking to the salvage yard," Schmidt said.

"Do you know what they're using it for?"

Schmidt shrugged.

They were salvaging Martian technology. Wegener was doing what Emil had stopped Fluse from doing after they'd stopped the madman back in the village in Belgium. And not only was he stockpiling Martian technology, but he was also peacefully coexisting with the aliens.

Was Wegener collaborating with the Martians? It was almost unthinkable.

Emil needed to escape. Now. If he told Schmidt he wanted to take a look around, he could create some distance between him and the other soldiers. He opened his mouth to say something, but his eyes focused on a Martian arm. The same kind of arm that had nearly captured him in Euleheim. The same type of tentacle he'd landed near in that trench in Mametz.

Just before Degenscheide had sacrificed himself to save his soldiers.

Could Emil walk away from this? Could he leave Ludwig, Beckenbauer, and the rest of their men to whatever Wegener was planning?

Schmidt was watching Emil, his head tilted to one side. "Are you okay?" he asked.

"Yeah. Just . . . surprised to see this much hardware in one place."

"Oh, Wegener's got people all over Europe collecting it. Pretty strange that we've never run into them, though. I guess they need to keep tight schedules."

"Yeah. I guess. Well, let's get loaded up and go."

Schmidt nodded.

Emil had come here hoping for a way to escape Wegener. Now he needed to use his new position to free his soldiers instead.

26

"Did you find something?" Susan whispered as James entered Mrs. Prendick's boarding house. The home was beautiful, with nineteenth-century woodwork decorating the door frames, chair rails, and a fireplace in the sitting room. That sitting room was as much of the house as James had ever seen. Women were strictly proscribed from entertaining men in their rooms, as Mrs. Prendick was fond of reminding him when she wasn't dropping hints about how he should make an honest woman of Susan—who was nearly as fond of reminding Mrs. Prendick that she didn't need help being honest, since she already was.

James nodded. "Let's talk at the Inn."

They left Mrs. Prendick's and turned in the direction of downtown and the Inn. It was about a ten-minute walk; and the cool air was refreshing after the long, stressful day at Edison. But James was flushed with excitement, sweating in the fresh shirt he'd thrown on before running to their date. The mysterious letter was a gift from heaven. It would help him reconcile with Susan and expose Fleming's involvement in the bombing in Coney Island without risking his or his mom's safety. He'd hand it over to Urich and let the newspapers take care of the colonel.

He smiled as he and Susan crossed Bayard Lane.

"You seem happy," Susan said. "I wasn't sure you'd really sneak into his office. Whatever you found must have been good."

"Actually, I didn't have to go into his office at all. What we needed came to me." James grinned again. No reason to tell her he never would have done what she'd asked.

"Came to you? It's not some rumor, is it? We need something solid. Something tangible."

"I'll show you at the Inn." The letter was neatly folded in James's pocket, and he didn't want to risk damaging it or losing it outside. He needed to deliver it to Urich safely.

"So you have something to show me? I hope I didn't come with you for nothing."

James stopped in his tracks. For nothing? Was seeing her contingent on his capability to gather intelligence on Colonel Fleming? What if she still didn't want to see him afterward? The joy seeped out of him.

Susan turned to him. "What?"

James stared at his shoes, debating what to say.

"Oh, that's not what I meant, and you know it."

"You only agreed to meet with me if I broke into his office. As a matter of fact, you didn't think dinner was a 'good idea.' What if I hadn't found anything?"

Susan crossed her arms. "James, I'm disappointed with you for staying at Edison, with that man in charge."

"One of us has to work. I have to support my mom. And what about you? How are you going to pay for your room?" James raised his hands in frustration, working to keep his voice down.

"We can both find jobs, James. Let's not argue out here on the street." She offered him her hand. After a moment, he took it, and they made the turn onto Nassau Street.

The Inn was a regular dinner spot for many West Orange residents, as well as a popular spot for people visiting Edison

Labs. James and Susan had dinner there at least once a month, and it wasn't uncommon for them to see Mr. Johnson, Seward, and even Mr. Edison when he was up from Florida, where he spent most of his time.

"James! Susan!" said Stefan, the maître d'. "Nice to see you."

"Hi, Stefan," Susan said.

Stefan took their coats, then took them to their table. James considered asking him whether he'd seen Mr. Johnson, but he didn't want to start a conversation he couldn't finish.

Other than the addition of electric lights—courtesy of Edison, of course—the dining room was largely unchanged from when the neighborhood had been part of Llewellyn Haskell's planned community. The walls were painted a simple white, and dark green curtains decorated the tall windows on one side of the room. A huge fireplace took up a third of the wall farthest from the door, where a small fire was burning. Stefan always sat James and Susan close to that wall, since Susan liked the warmth.

"So, what's the deep dark secret?" Susan said after Stefan left, slightly smiling.

James instinctively looked around, then realized they'd sat at this table and gone over papers from work many times before. If he acted like they had something to hide, he'd raise more suspicion than usual.

He pulled the letter out of his jacket pocket and handed it to Susan. She unfolded it, then exhaled as she read it. "Wow. Someone handed this to you?"

"A private courier showed up at the office looking for the colonel."

"So you took it?" Susan held the letter up, her brow furrowed.

"Seward was on his way out the door. No one else was around." James shrugged.

"Huh. Who uses a private courier?"

"Someone with something to hide? Someone who needs to send a message quickly? He didn't even ask for a signature."

"So, other than Seward, no one knows you have this."

"Yes. If the colonel misses it and Seward remembers, it's easy enough to say I left it under his door." James shrugged again. Was he downplaying the risk? It was worth it, if all he had to do to protect Mom and Susan was lie about a missing letter.

"Mather," Susan said, reading the letter again. "They must be talking about Senator Mather, Ben's friend."

James drew in a breath. In his excitement, he hadn't realized the Mather in the letter might have been Mr. Johnson's friend and ally in the Senate. Mr. Johnson had saved Mather's life when they'd encountered the Martians down in Grovers Mill during the first attack. If there was a conspiracy to disable the radios, getting Johnson and Mather out of the way made sense.

But why would someone want to do that? The radios were the fastest way for the US to talk to Germany. But what about the telegraphs? They were slow and less reliable, but they still existed. Had they been attacked, too?

"So those marines died for nothing," Susan said.

James set his jaw. "Yes."

"The colonel's got to be working with the Germans. But why? Why would he betray his country? And why would they want to take the radios off the air?" Susan tilted her head and raised an eyebrow.

She was probably right. The power supply James had found in the wreckage was advanced technology that Edison didn't have. Which meant it had to be German technology, since no other country was more advanced. But telling Susan about it would risk her safety, too.

"Who knows?" he answered. "Mr. Johnson told me that blocking the radios wouldn't help the Germans with a surprise attack. I suppose he's right, since the navy is watching the Atlantic. Maybe they don't want us to talk to Planetary Warning? Why?"

"But why would Fleming work with the Germans? What does he get out of it?"

"Money? Revenge for getting fired? Why would he steal technology and sell it in the first place? It doesn't matter. He's going to prison as soon as the newspapers break this story." James grimaced. "Do you think he was involved in the Tesla fire? Did he really have something to do with my dad getting killed?"

"I don't know, James. Either way, there's no reason for you to stay at Edison. You can get away from all of this. We could head to the city and see if AT&T has any openings at their new office. They don't have a radio program or any government contracts. You could get a position helping them compete with Edison." Susan smiled.

James shifted in his seat. Leave West Orange and Mom to be an executive in the city? That sounded too risky. Would they have to move there? What if it didn't work out?

"Are you two ready to order?" It was Mary, their usual waitress.

"Uh, I'll take my usual," James said quickly.

"What's the special tonight?" Susan asked.

Mary gave them a big smile. "We've got shepherd's pie tonight, Susan. It's fantastic."

"Oh, I'd love that. Are you sure you won't try shepherd's pie, James? Something different for a change?" Susan arched an eyebrow as she looked at him from across the table.

"Uh, no thanks. I'll stick with the pot roast."

Susan sighed.

"The usual drinks?" Mary asked, still smiling.

"Yes, please," Susan said. "Unless you want to try something different there, James?"

Mary giggled and left without waiting for an answer.

"Great timing, huh?" Susan said without a smile.

"Huh?" James asked.

"Just as your head was about to explode from the idea of changing jobs, you had the added pressure of changing meals."

"It's not like that, Susan."

"It's not? Then what is it like?"

"Well . . ."

"It's about your mother, right? You're terrified of the idea of spending time away from home. We'd have to spend a lot of time on the train or—heaven forfend!—talk about getting married and moving there."

Mary approached with their drinks then. James waited for her to finish serving them.

Instead of fixing all of his problems, the letter had stirred an old one up. Susan was tired of living alone at Mrs. Prendick's, and she had a reason to feel that way. They'd been serious for a long time, and most couples would have at least announced an engagement by now.

James wiped his brow with his napkin before putting it on his lap. Getting married would mean moving out and leaving Mom. He couldn't do that. But he couldn't leave Susan hanging forever, either. "We've talked about this before," he said.

"We've never actually come to any kind of agreement," Susan said.

James set his jaw. "I can't leave my mom alone."

"Why not? I know she's asked you when you're going to propose. She's joked about it in front of me! She's retired, and with a pension. She has friends. She's more independent than you are, James."

Susan was right. But she didn't know he'd made a promise to his dad. He couldn't leave Mom. The last time James had seen his dad was on a Sunday. He and Mom would visit him in the hospital every Sunday after church. Mom would tell him what the priest's homily had been about, and James would have a chance to recount what had happened in school that week. Mr. Johnson was usually there, too. By this time, his investigation into the Tesla fire for Edison had drawn to a close, but he'd still visit Dad as a friend. What had that investigation found? Would James ever learn the truth?

Dad had seemed to know it would be the last time they'd see each other. He'd pulled James close to his bed before they'd left. "You're the man of the house now," he'd said. "I need you to take care of your mother. I can't be there. It's your job now. Things are going to change, and you need to be strong for her."

Dad's actions during the Tesla fire had made him a hero. But they'd also taken him away from his family. Once he'd died, protecting the family had become James's job, and he wasn't going to make the same mistake.

He'd never told anyone what his dad had said. Not his mom, and not Susan. Heroes might brag about their missions, but men did what was needed.

But now, with Mr. Johnson missing, Fleming backing a mysterious conspiracy, and the Germans threatening to attack, Susan wanted James to find a new job in the city and move there. This wasn't the time to spend more time away from his mom. It was time to stay close to home.

"You don't understand . . ." James began.

"I don't understand?" Susan asked. "Or I don't agree? They're not the same thing."

"I . . ." James started to explain, but this wasn't the time. Not until this was over. When he had time and space to breathe. "We don't need to go to the city or AT&T. Fleming is going to jail, and Mr. Johnson will be back. We only have to wait."

"Are you sure?"

James blinked. "Of course. You said that the letter proved he's a spy. How can he not end up in trouble?"

Susan took a drink and looked down at the table. "So everything just goes back to normal, right?"

James began to agree but caught himself. Susan's head stayed down, but he could tell she was biting her lip. She didn't want things to go back to normal, and she'd been waiting for a long time for their relationship to move on to an engagement or marriage. But quit Edison? Commute to New York City? Leave

West Orange? While the madness with the Germans and Fleming was going on? That was too much.

So what could James offer her?

"What if . . . I stay at Edison for now?" he suggested.

Susan sighed.

"Wait. Let me finish. If I'm right, you could be back there in a couple of weeks. Then we can talk about getting married and moving in together. If Fleming isn't arrested or at least fired, then I need to stay close enough to figure out what it will take to get him out and the radios back online." James held up his hands. "No?"

"That makes sense," Susan said, looking up again. Her jaw was set, and she was playing with her drink. She might have thought James's idea made sense, but she wasn't happy with it.

"I understand. You want things to be different. I promise you, once we're past this, we'll make plans. For us."

But they wouldn't include the city.

27

Emil shivered as he reached Wegener's tent. No, Wegener's *cottage*. It wasn't a tent anymore. It was the kind of cottage that a man interested in comfort and displaying power would build for himself.

Even though it was a crisp morning with barely a cloud in the sky, Emil stamped his feet and hugged himself for a moment to warm up. It would be warmer in an hour or so, and wearing a coat would have meant worrying about where to stow it later.

This would be his fourth trip to the Martian salvage yard. He was still curious about what Wegener was doing with the equipment but hadn't been able to follow it to its final destination. A crew would meet his group when they returned to the stables each day, then take the carts into an area concealed by a covered fence.

As perplexing as that was, the more pressing problem was getting Emil's men added to this detail. That was the clearest path to getting them to safety. So he needed to focus on making Ritter happy and keeping Schmidt on his side.

So far, the latter had been easy, since Schmidt was easy to please. He was still a Wegener loyalist, but that was a problem Emil would deal with once he got a few of his soldiers on the team. Ritter, on the other hand, was inscrutable. He was capable of swinging from unbearable martinet to affable aristocrat in the space of a few words.

Right on cue, Ritter emerged from Wegener's cottage. His uniform was perfect, with each crease in its place and boots gleaming in the morning sun. Today's footwear had white piping, and his parade hat was brushed to a shine. It was the uniform of a man who didn't have to worry about doing real work. He returned Emil's salute with the air of a man who thought he had something better to do.

"Where's Schmidt?" Ritter asked, looking around.

Emil was an officer now. He was in charge of the salvage detail, and asking for his sergeant was disrespectful at best. But Schmidt had accompanied Emil to these meetings for the past two days, so Ritter was probably expecting to see him. "He's already at the stables, getting the carts ready, sir," Emil answered.

"I want you to take seven carts today," Ritter said, without missing a beat.

"Seven carts, sir?"

"Yes. So you'll need six more men. Tell Schmidt to pull them from combat training. Quickly." Ritter was in martinet mode today.

"I can round up a few, sir, while Schmidt gets the extra carts ready." Time to bring over two or three of his men. No reason to overdo it.

"No, Schmidt knows where to find troops. We don't have time to spare."

"What's planned that we need so much salvage?" If Emil couldn't use his men, he could at least learn what the Martian parts were for.

"That's not your concern. Get as much salvage up here as you can today. You've done a great job so far. I know I can count on you." Ritter looked Emil in the eye then.

"Yes, sir," Emil replied. Ritter could count on him, but the

Hauptmann still had to deliver a lecture?

Emil turned and headed for the stables, his sweat accentuating the morning chill. Nearly twice as much Martian equipment in a single day. What was Wegener up to? He had to get his men out of there quickly.

He let himself through the stable gate and took a deep breath as he closed it behind him. The stables were always a relief after his morning meetings with Ritter. Emil had spent much of his youth trying to find a way off the family farm, but this was the closest thing to a home he'd seen since the Gasthaus where they'd found Gabrielle and Juliette. If someone had told sixteen-year-old Emil he'd one day welcome the smells of hay, horse, and manure, he would have laughed. But young Emil had never lived in a compound that reeked of unwashed men and gunpowder—or found himself in the service of a madman building a cache of Martian weapons.

Schmidt was already standing next to the first cart, his arms crossed.

"Change in plans, from Ritter," Emil said.

Schmidt raised an eyebrow.

"We need to take seven carts. Ritter said to commandeer more men from combat training."

Schmidt's arms fell to his sides, and he made a face. "They tell us this now?"

Emil gave a wry smile. "It's the army, Schmidt. You get the men, I'll get the carts."

Schmidt nodded and took off.

Within a half hour, seven carts were lined up in front of the stables, the convoy reaching all the way to the stable gate. The men were lined up in a perfect row, with six faces Emil was just starting to recognize and six he'd never seen before.

Where were these men from? Salvaging Martian equipment wasn't something Wegener advertised, so it was safe to assume the men chosen for this detail stayed on it.

"Do they know what we're doing?" Emil asked Schmidt. "Do

they know the Martians are wandering around the woods we'll be riding through? We can't have them panicking if they hear a howl or see a Wanderer."

So far, they'd encountered Martians every day. Emil still had problems believing it was safe and could only imagine how these six men might react.

"I can brief them for you, sir," Schmidt said.

Emil nodded, more than ready to let Schmidt take charge.

Thirty minutes later, the convoy was well on its way, deep in the woods between Wegener's compound and the salvage yard. Schmidt had broken up the crews, so each cart had one experienced man and one new one.

"So there's an operation planned soon?" Schmidt asked.

"Seems that way," Emil said. "Ritter wouldn't give me any details, though."

"Makes sense. Operational security."

Almost on cue, a Wanderer howled. A loud rustling and the sound of tree limbs cracking then rose from the east. Some of the soldiers started chattering behind Emil and Schmidt. Emil thought about hushing them but stopped himself. Adding to the noise would only make matters worse. The men settled down after a few minutes.

"You were smart to split the men up so they could learn from one another," Emil said. It was a chance to chat Schmidt up a bit.

"Thanks," Schmidt said with a broad smile. Amazing how far a simple compliment could go. "Seemed like a good idea,

"So there hasn't been a real operation in a long time, right?"

"Nope. Maybe it's finally time to rejoin the war."

The war? Did Schmidt mean the war the Martians had ended when they'd showed up? Or a war with the Martians? "You don't think the return of the Martians ended that?" Emil asked, sitting back and trying to look relaxed.

"End it? No. Their arrival doesn't change the fact that we

needed to show the rest of Europe they can't ignore a unified Germany. France and Russia still have a lesson to learn." Schmidt almost growled that last sentence.

What lesson? Don't kill the kaiser's cousins? The war had started after a group of Serbian revolutionaries had infiltrated Artstetten Castle in Austria with Black Smoke canisters, killing Archduke Ferdinand, his family, and all of his servants. The kaiser had been furious—no, outraged. One of his most important allies, an ally he hadn't spoken to for years, had been slain with Martian weapons. And now, the kaiser himself was probably using those weapons.

Of course, that lie wasn't the real reason for the war. The recently unified Germany, galvanized by the alien attack, had been longing for a way to expand its borders after its humiliation in Mexico at the hands of President Bryan's American army.

"Well, yes," Emil said. "We still have work to do in Europe. But the Martians are back now, too." He kept his voice level as he parroted the kaiser's nationalistic line.

"One doesn't preclude the other. That's why Wegener took . . ." Schmidt looked away from Emil then.

"Took?" Emil asked. Took what? A right turn on the way to Paris? A break on the way to the war?

"Took over our units," Schmidt finished.

Emil's jaw dropped. Took over? So Wegener was a mutineer. That explained a lot. "I suspected that was the case," he said, hoping Schmidt would believe he was already on board with whatever Wegener was up to.

"Yeah. They're not exactly forthcoming with information, since we've had issues with a few people trying to report us to command."

The hanging. That was why Wegener was so vindictive toward deserters. "How did Wegener manage to take over part of—"

"The Third Army," Schmidt answered Emil's question before he could finish it. "General von Hausen was out ahead of us with most of his army. They'd pushed the French back to within thirty kilometers of Paris. He'd decided to leave a few battalions back in reserve in case some of them managed to flank him."

He took a deep breath. "Then the Martians showed up. They wiped out the Third Army."

Emil raised an eyebrow. "I thought you said you hadn't seen them?"

"I hadn't. I was back with the reserves. We heard some of the howls and even the sound of some of those heat rays. Some men broke ranks and fled. They wanted to run home."

This was amazing. Astounding, even. Not just that all of this had happened, but that Schmidt had also decided to trust Emil with it. They'd gotten along over the past few days, but it was as if Emil had poked a hole in an overfilled water sack.

"Von Hausen left a Hauptmann behind," Schmidt continued. "Müller. He commanded the Hussars before Ritter did. He had the men who fled captured and shot while we were still under attack. He was executing 'deserters.'" His face flushed, and the beginning of a tear pooled in one eye. He gritted his teeth before adding, "Then the bastard told us to form up to prepare for an attack. It was obvious the Martians were wiping us out at the front. The only question was why it was taking them so long. But he wanted to advance."

So Müller was the complete opposite of Degenscheide. Rather than figure out how to take his troops to safety, he executed the ones who tried to leave and ordered the rest to deaths that made no sense whatsoever.

"What happened?" Emil asked, struggling to keep his voice down.

"Wegener. He shot him."

Emil nearly fell off the cart. "He what?"

"Wegener shot him. He shouldered his rifle, took aim, and put one between Müller's eyes."

"Wegener was one of the Hussars?"

"No. He used to run the stables. He was an Unteroffizier."

Emil stifled a laugh. An Unteroffizier had assassinated a senior officer, appointed himself commander, and then taken his army to Reims. There was nothing funny about it, but it was hilarious. "And no one from the Third Army ever made it back from Paris?" he asked.

"Not a soul."

"I guess that's why he's so tough on deserters," Emil said, finally daring to speak the words out loud.

"Yeah. A few got away, but it seems like they fled home or the Martians got them." Schmidt gave a wry smile.

"How did they escape?" Emil asked. Might be useful information to have, if Schmidt knew.

"How?" Schmidt asked. "That's what you're worried about? How they escaped?"

"I . . . uh . . ." Emil stuttered, afraid he'd gone too far and betrayed his plans.

Before he could choke out a defense, the salvage yard came into view.

"We're here," Schmidt said icily.

The sun was high in the sky, so it was time to load the carts quickly to avoid riding home with the winter sunset. Wanderer parts gleamed in the bright light, looking more like a jewelry display than a trash heap. The soldiers left their carts and lined up without being asked. The combat training drove some of the new men; others fell prey to peer pressure. Schmidt looked at Emil warily, refusing to take charge this time.

Emil stepped in front of the group and cleared his throat. "Spread the carts out and load them up," he shouted. "Stay in the teams Unteroffizier Schmidt put you in, so the experienced men can show you how we select the gear and how to safely load the carts."

Schmidt led their cart over to a pile of Martian scrap metal and started loading it. Emil helped, hoping Schmidt might start talking again. But he didn't.

"No!" someone shouted from another part of the yard. "Knock it off! You'll kill us!"

Before Emil could react, the deep hum of a heat ray sounded, and someone screamed.

Emil dashed across the yard, outrunning Schmidt and passing two other soldiers. He rounded a stack of Wanderer bodies and came to a halt. One of the men was standing alone in a clearing, his arms wrapped around a Martian tentacle. The alien arm was tipped with the unmistakable mirror and emitter of a heat ray.

"Put it down," Emil said, keeping his voice level. The soldier had a death grip on the tentacle and seemed to be triggering it without knowing how. If he dropped it, they'd be fine.

"I can't," the soldier said, tears streaming down his face as his body shook. "I can't turn it off. It won't stop."

Emil winced each time the soldier quivered, expecting the ray to fire. "That's fine. I can turn it off. Just turn it away from us and put it down first." He held a hand out and gestured with his palm.

"Just put it down, Groenig," another soldier said, straining to keep his voice as level as Emil's. "It'll be fine."

Groenig turned toward the voice. The motion triggered the heat ray, and it made its terrible hum. The man who'd spoken only had time to widen his eyes before he burst into flames. He disappeared in a tempest of vapor and screaming, leaving a scorched circle where he stood.

Bile rose in Emil's throat. For the second time in two days, the memory of Degenscheide dying the same way replayed in his mind.

And now this, a waking nightmare come true.

"My God!" Groenig screamed. "Dieter! I killed him. I can't stop it!"

He turned toward Emil, the ray still firing. Emil slammed

himself to the ground, letting the ray stream over his head and in between two of the carts, startling the horses.

The humming grew louder, and panic rose in Emil's chest. This was it. This was exactly what he'd feared when he'd learned Wegener was hoarding Martian hardware. The stuff was deadly. No one should have it.

Emil unshouldered his rifle and brought the sight up to his eye. What would shooting the man do? Would it stop the ray?

Groenig screamed again, and the ray stopped. Emil squeezed off a shot.

The mirror shattered. Groenig screamed once more, dropped the Martian arm, and fainted.

Emil scrambled to his feet and ran to the power supply the arm was connected to, praying that if the ray still fired, it would be unfocused without a mirror. His bayonet was out of his sheath before he reached the device, and he jammed it into the panel to pry it open. The panel held a collection of thick cables. He used the bayonet to cut one, hoping that tampering with the power supply wouldn't do to this forest what Tesla had done to New York City.

He turned then. Schmidt was standing behind him. The Unteroffizier's eyes were wider than they'd been at the cart when Emil had asked about the men who had escaped Wegener. Was he angry again?

"How did you know?" Schmidt asked.

"Know what?"

"To shoot the mirror?"

"It's not the first time I've seen one of those rays up close. I was hoping I wouldn't have to shoot him." An Anglische science fiction author had written about how mirrors were used to focus the rays, but Emil hadn't thought of that when they'd encountered the madman in the village in Belgium, and it had been harder to see him on top of the barn, anyway.

Emil's heart started to settle by then, and he was suddenly very tired. He'd dodged too many bullets like this lately.

"And the wires?" Schmidt asked.

Emil smiled sheepishly. "That was a guess."

Schmidt's shoulders sagged. "I was terrified. If you hadn't . . . he would have killed all of us."

"Well, he didn't," Emil said. Schmidt hadn't seen any combat. Had any of Wegener's most fervent supporters? Had Ritter?

"Look, I'm sorry I got so—"

"It's fine. Water under the bridge, my friend. Let's get our men settled down and back to work."

"Yes, sir."

Schmidt turned to the men then. A few were in tears. Others were shaking their heads and hugging themselves in shock. Schmidt gestured to them to restrain Groenig, who was stirring.

Emil took a deep breath. One man had been killed. Another was . . . what? Insane? Unlucky?

But Schmidt was an ally now.

28

James picked a table about halfway into Renwick's. Not too close to the door, but not so far that it looked like he had something to hide. It was a Saturday morning, and there was little chance anyone would see him—or care, if they did. Colonel Fleming didn't live nearby, and few of Edison's other workers would visit a place like 'Wicks this early in the day. If they were out for breakfast, they'd be at the Inn or a bakery.

But James couldn't be too careful.

'Wicks had been an ice cream parlor for a few years before moving a little closer to the Inn and adding breakfast and lunch menus. Urich had recommended it when James had called his office number from Mrs. Prendick's parlor. James hadn't realized they were open in January and hoped it was the same for anyone who might recognize him.

He'd only be here for a few minutes. He'd hand the reporter the letter and excuse himself.

A young girl in a neat uniform approached James with a pad and pencil in hand. "What can I get you, sir?" she asked.

"I'll have coffee. I won't be here too—"

The door opened, and James spun around to see who it was so quickly that he bumped the table, catching the waitress on her knee. She dropped her pencil.

It was Urich. He was clean-shaven and was wearing a fresh blue shirt under his coat. The coat was more gray than brown, as if it had been cleaned. "You know, Brogan, most people worry about being seen sit with their backs to the wall, not the door," he said, bending to pick up the pencil. "Did he hurt you, Penny?"

The waitress shook her head and grinned. "I'm fine, Mr. Urich."

"Carl, please. Mr. Urich was my father."

So Urich was a regular here? Of course.

"We'll both take my usual, Penny," Urich added as he shrugged off his coat, threw it over a chair, and sat in the empty one across from James. "Wait. Do you want to face the door? Or should I throw my coat over you if anyone from Edison walks in?"

James grimaced. "I'm worried that someone—"

"Might see you with me?" Urich smiled. "It's okay. I'm used to it."

"I'm not hungry—"

"Best bacon this side of the Hudson, and it's on me."

James wanted to agree. If past appearances had been any indicator, the bacon would likely end up on Urich.

"So, what's on your mind, James?"

James hadn't told Urich why he wanted to meet. He'd been nervous talking to him on the phone, and he assumed if he told Urich he had physical evidence, the reporter would have insisted on coming sooner.

"I have something for you," James whispered. "It's . . . interesting. But you have to swear it won't be traced back to me."

"Of course," Urich said.

James spun around and scanned the small restaurant.

"You're attracting attention to yourself, James."

He sighed, pulled the letter out of his jacket pocket, and handed it to Urich.

"Here's your coffee, gentlemen," Penny said as she returned.

James jumped, and Urich rolled his eyes.

"Sorry to startle you, sir." Penny placed a cup in front of each of them, followed by a small pitcher of cream and a sugar bowl.

Once Penny left, Urich perused the note and was silent for a few minutes. Longer than it should have taken him to read it. He sipped his coffee as he flipped the note over and examined the back. Finally, he raised his eyes to meet James and asked, "How did you get this?"

"A private courier delivered it. Everyone else was out, so I took it."

"You signed for it, then?" Urich's brow furrowed.

"No. The courier never asked."

Urich sipped his coffee again, then rubbed his chin. "Let me make sure I understand this. A private courier delivers an unsigned letter to a government official at Edison and doesn't ask for a signature?" His eyes narrowed as he finished the sentence.

"Yes, that's what happened," James said, sitting back in his chair.

"I believe you," Urich said, stroking his chin again, "I don't know if anyone could make this up."

"Here you go, two specials," Penny announced, placing their plates on the table. Each held two eggs over easy, home fries, crispy bacon, and a slice of rye toast cut on a diagonal. "And, of course, your tomato ketchup," she added, placing the bottle in front of Urich.

"Thank you, Penny," he said, smiling as she nodded and stepped away. Then he opened the bottle and smothered his eggs and home fries in the red sauce.

James curled his lip in disgust. "I'm not hungry," he said.

"Eat your breakfast," Urich said with a mischievous grin. "You don't have to put any ketchup on it. Leaves more for me. Besides, don't you want to hear more about Fleming and the Tesla fire?"

James did, but Urich had already proven himself too skilled at getting him to say too much.

"So, you said no one else was around when this arrived?" Urich pointed at the letter with his fork, threatening to spray ketchup on it.

"Seward was, but he was in a hurry to go home." James tried to pick up his bacon with a fork, but it disintegrated into crumbs. Mom didn't make it like that. He settled for a piece of toast, even though it was cut at the wrong angle.

"Good. And no one's missed it?"

"Not that I know of. It's all yours."

That was it, then. James had handed off the letter and explained himself—and he didn't like rye toast. "I need to go," he added.

"Johnson is completely out of the picture, and Fleming is getting messages from his benefactors," Urich said.

James titled his head.

"What? You didn't know Fleming has odd friends?" Urich dunked his toast in a pool of egg and ketchup. Tiny droplets splashed off the plate, narrowly missing his shirt.

"Completely out of the picture . . . ?" James asked.

"Sorry, kid. There I go again. Should have realized you two were close. No one has seen Johnson since he was 'relieved.' He's probably at the bottom of the Hudson or the Hackensack. Hudson would make more sense, though. Less chance of being found."

James slumped back in his chair. The room spun for a moment, and he took a deep breath to force down the toast and coffee.

Mr. Johnson was dead? James had been so rude to him . . . and now he was gone? How would Mom react to this? Could

Susan return to Edison? Either way, nothing would ever be the same again.

Urich was waiting, his brow furrowed. "You okay?"

"No." James's mind raced. He took another deep breath to try to slow things down. Maybe this meant the letter would help convict Fleming of murder? Could it tie him to Mr. Johnson's disappearance at least? "Well, this letter should help. Could it put Fleming in jail? Or stop whatever he's doing?"

"It's pretty damning," Urich said. "It's got his name on it. And it mentions Senator Mather, who's been all over Fleming about what he's done to your radio team,"

"He has?"

"Yeah, but you don't know that. I don't know it, either."

James tilted his head again. The eggs were starting to smell delicious, but he wouldn't have felt right eating them.

"There's a war on, James, even if we're not in it yet." Urich looked around this time, then lowered his voice. "But information doesn't exactly flow freely, even during peacetime. And we're always in one war or another, aren't we? No thanks to King Bryan."

James's jaw dropped. He'd seen and heard criticisms of President Bryan before, but never like that—and never in public. The Sedition Act made it illegal to say things that were "profane, disloyal, defamatory, or abusive" about the government, the president, Congress, or the military. William Randolph Hearst had been the first person jailed after the law was passed in 1905. He'd died in prison. Now here was Urich, tempting fate and any SPs within earshot with disloyal talk.

James took a nervous sip of his coffee.

"That talk makes you nervous, huh? Suffice it to say that I'm not the only person suspicious about Coney Island, the radios, and your new boss. But there's nothing we can do about it. At least not yet." Urich stabbed a piece of egg with his fork, took a bite, and left a tablespoon-sized ketchup stain on his shirt.

"Dammit," he mumbled, then dabbed at his shirt with a dry napkin.

"Are you sure it's safe for you to talk that way?" James asked.

"Of course not. But none of us are safe. There was another bombing in the city yesterday. At Penn Station. Third one since Coney Island."

"What? There haven't been any more bombings."

"Why do you say that? Because they weren't in the paper?" Urich gave a wry smile, then waved for Penny to come over and refill the coffee. "Don't worry, she's heard me say worse," he added with a wink.

"I thought you worked mostly in the city?" James tried some egg. It was tasty, and his stomach started to settle a little.

"I've been out here a lot lately. You're not my only lead, James. Someone is trying to hide something, and I'm going to find it out—" Urich cut himself off when Penny arrived with the coffeepot and topped off their cups. After she left, he added, "The radios are down again, and so are the telegraph lines. We have no idea what's going on in Europe right now."

"But . . . there are stories about the war in the paper every day!" James said.

Urich smirked and raised an eyebrow.

"They're fake," James said. Susan had said something suspicious was going on in Sayville. She'd been right.

Urich nodded.

James pushed his plate away. The papers were printing false stories and hiding the ones the government wanted them to. It was too much to take in.

But if they'd buried the story about how Dad had died and lied about where Tesla had gotten the power supply, was this so unbelievable?

"I wish I knew how they were blocking the radios again," James said. "Unless they've gotten all the personnel involved on board or replaced, they must be blocking the signal. Where would the transmitter be? Even with that power supply technology—"

He caught himself before he could finish the thought. Urich had done it again.

"What power supply technology?"

"Uh, whatever they had at Coney Island must have been powerful to block the radios in Sayville from there. So where are they blocking them from now? The water?" Hopefully, that would placate Urich.

The reporter eyed James as he took his last forkful of eggs. "I need your help, James. There's a conspiracy to help the Germans. At least that's what I think it is. Johnson is gone, and now I know for sure that a member of that conspiracy took his place. I need information. Information only you can get for me."

James shook his head. "That's it. I gave you the letter. I need to stay out of trouble. I have to take care of my mom and my girlfriend." He stared at his plate while taking another forkful of eggs.

"Will you be able to take care of them after the Germans invade?" Urich asked.

James choked on the egg and had to chase it down with some coffee, which was still hot and burned his tongue. Mr. Johnson had made fun of him for saying the explosion meant an invasion was coming. So had Mom. Now Urich was telling him he was right.

"Sorry," Urich said. "That was glib. But my point is, I'm not trying to get you to help me break a story. Especially not a story that'll get me a jail cell like Hearst. I need information to bring to Senator Mather. To the men in the SPs who I can trust. This is about our safety."

Could James trust him? Or was Urich trying to get him to tell him more? But why? He'd said he couldn't print it anyway. What was his angle?

"Tell you what," Urich said, smiling. "Go to work this week.

Do what you normally do, but keep your eyes open. We'll have breakfast again next Saturday."

That wasn't too much to ask. But what if someone saw James?

"I'll even go without ketchup," Urich added. "Just for you."

James met his eyes. Breakfast. One more time. Maybe he could learn a little more about what had happened to Dad. "Once more," he said.

29

Wegener's cottage had curtains now. Curtains and a doormat.

Emil was so distracted by the latter that he nearly banged his head on the door as he approached. He stepped back and checked his reflection before stepping inside. His uniform was straight, and while it wasn't pressed to Ritter's exacting standards, it was as pressed as it would ever be after sitting under a couple of wooden planks and a bucket of water. He brushed woodchips off his left pant leg.

Schmidt had wasted no time telling Ritter what had happened in the salvage yard. He'd told the preening peacock that Emil was a hero. The peacock had grimaced and stormed out of the stables. That night, Emil had almost gotten ready for bed when Ritter had appeared at his quarters.

"I suppose you're happy now," the Hauptmann had snarled.

"Happy, sir?" Emil had replied. "We lost a man to the heat ray, and another is hysterical. I don't know if he'll ever fight again."

"Yes. I'm sure that's what you're worried about, Zimmerman. Be at command tomorrow morning, and on time."

Ritter hadn't said what "on time" meant. Maybe the exact time was sewn into one of his fancy boots.

Emil let himself into Wegener's cottage. Instead of walking into the office like he had last time, he entered a small waiting area. So Wegener had been working on the inside of his little home, too. How long was he planning to stay in Reims? Why not just take over a building in the city?

Another Leutnant, younger than Emil and dressed in a formal uniform, was seated behind a tiny desk. "Leutnant Zimmerman?"

"Yes," Emil said, raising his hand to salute before catching himself and casually brushing imaginary dust from his jacket.

"You can go right through, sir."

Sir? This guy was kissing up to other Leutnants? Ritter must have loved him.

Emil walked through the door and was greeted with the sight of Wegener sitting behind an oak desk at least a meter wider than the first one. It had writing on one side, but Emil couldn't quite make it out. Did it read *Allianz*? Or *Aral*?

Wegener looked up from his papers and flashed Emil his wide grin. Ritter, however, stood off to one side, holding a steaming cup of coffee and scowling. His uniform creases threatened to cut anyone who got too close to him, while his boots brandished an unearthly sheen.

Emil managed to tear his eyes away from the boots and snap a salute to Wegener, who returned it with a careless swipe toward his forehead before extending a hand for Emil to shake. "Zimmerman! Emil! I can call you Emil, right?"

"Uh, yes, sir," Emil said. Did Wegener use that line every time he saw someone?

"Take a seat, please."

Ritter, still scowling, brought over a cup of coffee for Emil, who took it with a weak smile after he sat down. The coffee was good. The best he'd had since before the war.

"You remember what I told you the last time you were here,

Zimmerman?" Wegener said as he sat down. "That I needed men like you. I was right, wasn't I, Ritter?"

Ritter grunted.

Emil didn't answer. He was already trying to figure out whether to ask for more coffee or serve himself.

"What you did yesterday," Wegener continued. "It's amazing. You shot out the mirror on a heat ray?"

"Yes, sir."

"Why? What made you think of that?"

"Shooting Groenig—the soldier holding the heat ray—would have made things more dangerous, since I didn't know if the firing mechanism was stuck. But the mirror focuses the heat rays. Breaking it would at least weaken it." Emil emptied his mug, then looked at it, hoping one of the other men would take the hint.

"Ritter, pour the man some more coffee," Wegener said. "That's fascinating, Zimmerman. Well, I was right about you! Wasn't I, Ritter?"

Ritter handed Emil the coffeepot. Serving one cup must have been his limit. He nodded in a masterful display of the absolute minimum of how little a man could incline his head and still have it count as a nod.

"So, I'm promoting you to Hauptmann and giving you command over the salvage operations," Wegener said.

Emil fumbled the coffeepot, nearly spilling coffee all over his freshly pressed pants. Hauptmann? In charge of the salvage detail?

Wegener and Ritter were children playing soldiers. Emil hadn't earned this promotion by being a good soldier. It had been for saving Martian hardware, like getting team captain for keeping the game ball from falling into a stream.

"Sir!" Ritter said.

"Yes, Hauptmann Ritter?" Wegener asked, an edge in his voice.

Another field promotion—and control over the carts

retrieving the salvage. Emil could now ride out of there in a cart tomorrow. With his own men! They'd be home in days.

"We talked about this, sir," Ritter said, clearly unhappy. Was it over losing the command? Or was he suspicious of Emil? He should have been.

Emil suppressed a grin and focused on his coffee.

"You talked, and I made my decision," Wegener snapped back. "We'll be needing your cavalry soon. You need to stop modeling uniforms and whip your men back into shape."

Schmidt had said Wegener had his favorites. Had stopping the heat ray secured Emil his spot? Or was something else going on?

"But he was already trying to bring his men onto this detail yesterday!" Ritter said, holding out his hands as if begging.

"Good. We need more men like him." Wegener smiled at Emil as he stood and came around from behind his desk. Emil started to stand, but Wegener held out a hand and shook his head to stop him.

"But . . . you're giving him what he wants," Ritter said, crossing his arms. He was truly displeased. Hopefully, getting the cavalry back into shape would mean he wouldn't have time to check up on Emil.

"Why is that a problem?" Wegener asked. "He just saved a platoon of men and who knows how much equipment."

He turned and faced Ritter. They seemed to be fighting over a playground toy. But the toys were weapons—deadly weapons. Martian heat rays, Martian reactors, Black Smoke gas canisters. The general had found himself a new friend and wanted to promote him, and his old friend was jealous. Emil didn't want to play with these kids.

"But, sir—" Ritter began.

"It's settled," Wegener said, fixing Ritter with a stare.

The general reached into his desk drawer, drew out three sets of rank insignia, and reached out for Emil, who took them and snapped another salute. Wegener returned it smartly this time and said, "I already told Ritter here to have Schmidt make another run. Take the day off. Rest. You earned it. Dismissed, Hauptmann." He gave Emil one of his broad smiles.

Emil left before Ritter could kick up any more dust. He had work to do.

Emil rushed to his room, grabbed his sewing kit, and sewed the Hauptmann insignia onto his uniform. Now he had free rein of the compound. Few soldiers, especially soldiers in the thrall of Wegener, would question a Hauptmann.

Wegener with his cottage and oak desk. Ritter with his spotless uniform and shiny boots. They were children—children with an army behind them.

It was time for Emil to find his men. This was one of those situations where you asked for forgiveness, not permission. First, he'd find Ludwig. His promotion was their ticket out of this madhouse, but he'd need help getting all the men together. The seasoned Unteroffizier would be a big help.

But what would Emil do with the soldiers already on the team? Would Ritter take them? Asking might be tipping his hand.

Emil left his room and set out for the gate. The compound was eerily quiet. He was usually on a salvage run by now, so he wasn't used to being there at this time of the day.

A soldier stepped out of a tent, startling Emil.

"Sorry, sir," the Soldat said, snapping a salute.

"Uh, it's okay," Emil said, awkwardly returning the gesture. "Carry on."

Eventually, Emil reached the gate between Reims and the compound. What was the best way to find Ludwig? Should he try on his own? Or wait in the assembly area? That might be hours.

"Can I help you, sir?"

Emil looked up. Another nervous Soldat was standing in front of the closed gate, trying to hold a salute.

Emil snapped a salute back, amazed at the difference the extra pip on his collar made. "I'm looking for my men, soldier," he said.

"I can help you with that, sir," the guard said. "Who are you looking for? I'll send a courier."

A courier? Of course. The two pips. Emil smiled to himself. "Yes, of course. I'll be waiting in the mess hall."

The "mess hall" was a cluster of tents. They sat a few hundred meters from the gate to Reims, far enough for soldiers to line up before heading into the city after breakfast and dismissed from formation before dinner. The tents stayed open during the day because they acted as an informal meeting place. Most of the men remained in Reims all day for training, but the army was the army—and meetings, especially between officers, were a fact of life.

The officer's mess was the tent closest to the gate, of course. All the tents were the same height and width, but the officer's mess looked larger to Emil, and the enlisted tents had muddy paths. Maybe it was the wooden walkway. Or, maybe it was the closed doors where the enlisted tents stayed open to the cold.

Two Hauptmanns gave Emil curt nods as they left the tent, while another was talking to a Leutnant and an Unteroffizier. Emil sat at a table in a corner, far enough away from the entrance that he'd have some quiet and privacy when he spoke to Ludwig.

He jumped when a pair of soldiers entered the room carrying a vat. Steam rose from its sides as the men angled it toward a table on one wall of the tent. They set it down next to another, identical vat. "Fresh coffee, sir!" one of the men said to Emil with a big smile. He and his comrade picked up the other vat and left.

Emil took a deep breath and made an effort to calm himself.

He was a Hauptmann now, and he belonged here. If anyone asked, he was waiting to talk to an enlisted man to recruit him for a detail from the post commander. He had nothing to fear.

Of course, he was recruiting the soldier as part of an effort to leave the post and military service, but no one needed to know that.

The aroma of fresh coffee wafted over, so Emil got up and poured himself a mug. A mug. The enlisted men drank from their canteen cups and cleaned them by hand. The officers, however, got ceramic mugs that were magically washed after they were left behind.

The coffee was good. Not as good as what Wegener enjoyed in his cottage/tent, of course, but Emil didn't detect a hint of chicory. He choked back the cynicism rising in his throat and let himself enjoy it.

It wasn't long before Ludwig's head poked into the tent and looked around. His eyes fell on Emil, and he squinted in disbelief.

Emil smiled and waved to him.

Ludwig frowned, turned his head to speak to someone, and stepped through the door with Beckenbauer two steps behind him. Emil stood to greet them.

"You?" Ludwig said. "You're the Hauptmann who's looking for me? You . . . you're a Hauptmann?" His eyes were wide in disbelief as they focused on the pips on Emil's uniform. He looked at Beckenbauer, who looked back and shrugged.

"Yes," Emil said.

"What are you doing?" Ludwig hissed. "We need to get out of here before someone recognizes you."

"What? No. This is real. Wegener promoted me this morning."

Ludwig's mouth dropped open, and Beckenbauer shuffled back a step.

"Wegener promoted you?" Ludwig said. "Emil, who's going to believe—"

"Please. Sit down, and let me explain." Emil gestured to the chairs across the table from him.

Ludwig and Beckenbauer looked at each other and took their seats.

"Good to see you both, by the way," Emil added. "Are you in the same platoon? I thought they had separated everyone."

"Half of my platoon is from Third Company, and we've all seen one another every day, except for you and Fluse," Ludwig said.

Interesting. Emil had been isolated from his men, but the rest had been allowed to see one another all along. They'd even let Beckenbauer train alongside Ludwig. Was it to keep a closer watch on Emil? Or to get him away from the other soldiers?

"Well, I've been doing Fluse's job for a few weeks after he failed at it," Emil said.

"You're doing his job? Have you seen him?" Ludwig's brow furrowed.

Emil shook his head.

"But you're a Hauptmann?"

"Yes, I was pulled out of kitchen duty and put on salvage detail a couple of weeks ago—"

"Salvage detail?"

"Yes. We've been retrieving Martian hardware from a salvage yard a few hours southeast of here."

"Martian hardware?" Beckenbauer gasped, speaking for the first time. His mouth hung open.

Emil nodded. He'd taken all of this in stride, but their shock was evident. Was it because he'd been so close to Wegener and Ritter? Was their insanity rubbing off on him?

Ludwig's eyes were big. He leaned forward.

"What are they doing with it?" Beckenbauer said, holding up a hand to cut off Ludwig before he could speak.

"I don't know."

"But you're okay with this. You're a Hauptmann now." Beckenbauer's eyes flashed.

"Of course not. That's why I wanted to see Ludwig. I want to get us the hell out of here." Emil's heart sped up, and he started to sweat. What was Beckenbauer thinking? That Emil was cooperating with Wegener?

"We haven't seen you for weeks," Ludwig said. "Now you show up as a Hauptmann, talking about Martian hardware. What are we supposed to think?" His eyes were as narrow as they'd been back in the trench, when Emil had just picked another fight with Fluse.

"You're not supposed to think anything," Emil snapped. "Let me finish, then you can accuse me of being one of Wegener's men."

Two more soldiers—both Leutnants—entered the tent. Emil nodded to them as they looked at his table. He turned and finished his story as quietly as he could, hoping they weren't listening. Ludwig's eyes widened again when Emil told them how Wegener had put himself in charge. Beckenbauer set his jaw as Emil described the carnage during the last salvage run.

"So Wegener shot a senior officer and put himself in charge?" Ludwig asked. "We're not part of the German Army. We're serving under mutineers."

"Yes, they're playing soldier," Emil said. "But Wegener likes me. Schmidt told me he plays favorites. Let's use that to our advantage and get the hell out of here before we get pulled any further into his games. How quickly can you find the rest of our men?"

"No," Beckenbauer said, crossing his arms.

"No? You can't? But you said you see them every—"

"No." Beckenbauer leaned forward then and lowered his voice. "We can't leave. We can't leave these mutineers with that gear."

Emil sat back and gaped at both men. It was unbelievable. Ludwig had his head in his hands. Beckenbauer looked as if he wanted to reach across the table and grab Emil by the neck. He'd finally found a way out, but Ludwig was falling apart and Beckenbauer wanted to go to war.

"We can't leave them with it?" Emil asked. "What are we going to do? Bury it? Burn it? Give it back to the aliens? You want to take an entire battalion on?" What had they expected from him? What did they think they could do? The only safe place for them was as far from Wegener as possible. They were arguably safer in Martian tentacles.

"We need to figure something out." Beckenbauer was nearly whispering, but the anger was obvious in his expression. "*You* need to figure something out. You told us about how they've already killed their own men with that equipment. What are they going to do to Reims?"

Ludwig looked at Emil blankly.

Emil had seen what the soldiers could do with the equipment —and he knew what kind of man was in charge better than Beckenbauer or Ludwig did. Wegener was willing to kill to take over these soldiers. Beckenbauer thought the answer was to take him on, but he was wrong. They'd only get themselves killed.

"What do you think, Ludwig?" Emil asked, hoping for support.

"This isn't a club meeting," Beckenbauer growled. "We're talking about madmen with Martian weapons."

Ludwig wasn't sure. What about the rest of their men? Would they agree with Beckenbauer? This wasn't an argument he could win now. His best bet was to get the group together and show them.

"Okay," Emil said. "Fine. Let's get our men together on this detail. We need to do that either way. Then we'll figure out what to do."

"There's no 'either way,'" Beckenbauer said. "We're going to stop them."

"Yes, that's what I meant," Emil said. Whatever it took to get them on a bunch of carts headed east.

30

"What are you working on, Brogan?" Fleming growled as he stomped into the break room. "What am I paying you for?"

James stumbled into a chair next to Seward, spilling coffee on the table. He hadn't been working on much of anything since Coney Island. Getting information for Urich was the priority that day.

The portable power supply shoved over to one corner of his desk caught his eye. "The power supply for the portable radios," he said. *Portable* was the generous name the War Department had given it. Based on the latest designs, it fit into a backpack. A very heavy backpack.

"I want a report on my desk by fifteen hundred!" Fleming barked, already halfway down the hall to his office before he finished his sentence.

"He's furious about that newspaper story," Seward said with a wry smile.

Mom's broadsheet hadn't shared anything interesting this morning. Had Urich printed something in his New York paper? "Story?" James asked, gaping from behind his desk.

"In the *Jersey Bugle*. It says the radios are down again. Can you believe it? Like someone could keep that a secret!" Seward chuckled through a Taylor ham and egg sandwich.

"That's ridiculous," James said. So Seward didn't know the radios were down, even though he'd told Susan something "suspicious" was going on in Sayville. Urich had made it sound like he wouldn't be able to use the story. But it had come out anyway? Had he fed it to the *Bugle*? This might put Fleming in jail, where he belonged. Would the press uncover the conspiracy he was part of?

But . . . the *Jersey Bugle*? Mom had said she wouldn't use that paper to line a birdcage. It was a scandal sheet. A trashy tabloid from Trenton. "So, the *Bugle*?" James asked. "Didn't they say the Martians had an office in Midtown Manhattan?"

"That's it. A real rag. It's a mystery why Fleming would worry about anything they print, but he saw one of the men over at the freight door reading it and blew his stack. You could hear yelling from in here." Seward snorted and took a sip of his coffee.

So Fleming was treating the story as a threat. That was a good thing. Maybe he would make a mistake. But would this make it harder to get info for Urich? Fleming would be watching everyone more closely now. Besides, what else did Seward know?

"So what does he have you working on?" James asked him.

"Still working on the audio discriminator."

Seward had been working on that for months. James suspected he'd end up finishing it for his coworker at some point. "How's it go—"

He swallowed the rest of his question as a dark-suited giant of a man thundered into the room. Seward froze, caught with his coffee mug halfway to his lips.

A smaller man, clad in a similar dark suit, strode in after the larger man.

"Who are you two?" he asked, glowering back and forth between Seward and James.

"I'm James Brogan. I work here. Who are you?"

"I'm asking the questions, Brogan. You were at Coney Island." The smaller man pointed at James, then faced Seward and put his hands on his hips.

Seward finally lowered the coffee cup. "Stephen Seward, sir."

"Ah, yes. Seward."

Nobody spoke for a few seconds. Eventually, the smaller man grabbed a chair, brushed it off with a napkin, and sat. "So," he said, ceremoniously turning to face James. He sat on the edge of the chair, his hands perched on the table and his body leaning forward as if he'd spring on top of James if he didn't like what he heard. "Coney Island! What did you see?" Menace seemed to seep from every cell in his body.

Who was this man? Was he from the government? Was this a test? "Who are you?" James asked. "I'm not supposed to talk about what happened there. I could ask Colonel Fleming—"

"You'd better start talking now," the larger man said, closing the distance between him and James in half a step. He raised a hand that cast the table into shadow.

"No," the smaller man said, holding up a hand. "I'll handle this."

The larger man stepped back, chastened.

"I don't need permission from Fleming, James." The smaller man turned his attention to Seward, who sat back in his chair and seemed to wilt like a flower in the July sun. "And you?"

"I wasn't at Coney Island," Seward stuttered.

"You were there after the explosion," the smaller man said evenly.

That kind of information wasn't in the newspapers. Was he from the War Department? Or the Security Police?

"Right. I was."

"You picked over the wreckage from the explosion? You found parts from the device that was jamming the radios?"

Jamming. What an interesting term! Jamming the signal, like cramming the airwaves with garbage.

"I sifted through the rubble, but Brogan is the one who inspected it." Seward sighed with relief. "Didn't you find something interesting? Weren't you arguing about it with Susan?"

The blood drained from James's face. He wavered in his chair. The smaller man's eyes swung over to James, and he raised an eyebrow. What was Seward thinking, giving this guy that kind of information? Was he trying to save his neck at James's expense? Should he reveal what he found? The man had to be an SP or from the War Department. If James told him about it, it might help identify where the bomb was from. And since Fleming had destroyed it, it might get him out of Edison and locked up. But it would attract attention to James, too.

"Uh, it was only a misunderstanding," James said. "I saw what could have been some damaged components, but I handed them over to the colonel's men. I guess the SPs have that stuff now."

"So you saw something?" the smaller man asked. "Components?"

Sweat trickled down James's back. He shifted in his seat. Seward caught his eye for a second, and James glared at him, hoping the interrogator missed it. "Might have been. The fire damage was too extensive to tell. It might have even been from the lights on the tower."

The smaller man held James's gaze for a few heartbeats. "And you handed the piece over," he said.

"Yes, of course. The SPs wanted it."

"Okay. Do either of you know anything about a letter delivered here a few days ago?"

That, too? But how would the War Department know about the letter? Who were these men? Seward had been there when the courier had shown up. Was he going to point the finger at James again?

Seward shook his head.

The smaller man leaped to his feet, startling Seward so much that he fell out of his chair. He exited the break room, leading the larger man down the hall to Fleming's office.

"What was that?" Seward said, picking himself up off the floor.

"You nearly getting me arrested?" James said.

"Huh?"

Seward had no clue. Maybe he didn't remember the delivery, either.

"You didn't need to bring up the argument we had over the Coney Island wreckage. It made us look like we had something to hide."

"Sorry. I was trying to help."

Help who?

Both men went back to their desks, and James fought the urge to keep looking back for signs of activity at Fleming's door. Was he about to be arrested? Fired? Had those men sent the note to the colonel?

James stared at the power supply, unable to focus on much of anything. After thirty minutes or so, footsteps echoed from the hall by Fleming's office. The dark-suited men walked out of the building without a word or a look.

Seconds later, Fleming thundered toward James's desk. "Mail," he shouted. "Where's the mail?"

James looked to Seward first. No sign of recognition.

"Mail, sir?" Seward asked.

"Yes, mail! I missed a letter somehow. Where the hell is it?"

"The carrier brings it in via the loading dock," Seward said.

Either he'd forgotten about the courier, or he was hiding something, too. But James couldn't ask without revealing what he knew.

Fleming grunted and turned to James. "You told them you found something in the wreckage?"

Now Fleming was going to interrogate him. If he needed to ask, that meant the two men had interrogated him about it, too.

"Who were they?" James asked.

"Never you mind. What did you tell them?"

Why wouldn't Fleming tell James who they were? Refusing to identify themselves hadn't only been part of an interrogation technique. Maybe they'd been part of the conspiracy.

"I told them that what I saw looked like burnt components, and that I turned it over to your men," James said.

Fleming grunted again, then turned and left.

31

Emil strode into the stables, a mug of steaming coffee in one hand, a week-old *Frankfurter Zeitung* in the other. The coffee was fresh, the newspaper from Germany stale and grim. The Martians had focused their attacks on small villages away from the cities. Did that mean Euleheim? The paper had interviewed an unnamed "military official" who said they were massing their forces east of the Elbe. That boded ill for Berlin, but what about the rest of the country? Just like the Preussen to take care of the east and forget the rest.

Emil wedged the coffee mug between his chest and his wrist as he turned to the next page.

"Zimmerman!"

He started, and there went the precious liquid, the good stuff from the officer's club, all over his right boot.

Emil looked up from his feet. His eyes met Ritter's. The other Hauptmann, who was holding a map, looked down at Emil's boot, then looked up with a curled lip.

It had been four days since Emil's promotion and takeover of the salvage detail. Ritter was visiting the stables as often as Emil was, but the senior officer had made a point of refusing to make eye contact. Was he still watching Emil? Had Wegener told him to?

"We have a change in plans," Ritter said, brushing his uniform with his free hand.

Emil raised an eyebrow and drank his last splash of coffee like a shot of schnaps.

"The general asked me to bring you this." Ritter unfolded the map and pointed to the X drawn on it. "You're to take your men here today."

Emil stopped short of asking why Ritter was bringing him the news when he realized he hadn't visited Wegener's cottage for a few days. Sending the message with Ritter made sense, and questioning that might lead to the visits becoming mandatory.

The map Ritter was pointing to was marked with a black iron cross about fifty kilometers east of Reims.

East. Toward Germany.

Emil swallowed. "A new salvage point?"

"Yes. We're not sure about the terrain. You may want to pack provisions for overnight. It's up to you, Hauptmann." Ritter dragged out the last word like he'd found coffee on one of his boots.

Overnight! Then the group could keep going. Wegener would need two days to miss them. But Emil didn't have all of his men on the detail yet, though he had more than he'd expected to by this point.

Ritter had been avoiding Emil, but that didn't mean he didn't still hold him in contempt. To make Emil's life more difficult, Ritter had helped solve his biggest problem by taking Schmidt and most of his team for the Hussar unit, leaving ten spots for Emil to fill right away. Emil had no idea what more than ten former salvage workers had to offer a cavalry company, but that was up to Ritter.

"Thank you," Emil said.

"Whatever I can do to speed your hanging for incompetence," Ritter said.

Moments later, Emil found Ludwig already in the yard, hitching horses to a cart. "Change in plans," he said, heading toward the Unteroffizier.

"This is the army, after all," Ludwig said.

"This is a big change." Emil handed him the map.

Ludwig scratched his chin as he looked. "That's a long way. We'll need two days."

"I agree." Emil smiled. Perfect. They'd hit the road with their gear, get "lost," and do some scouting before picking up the salvage and returning.

Ten of the men who had left the trenches with Emil were on the detail now, and he only needed two more spots to get them all, not including Fluse. He hadn't decided what to do about Fluse yet. Miller was one of the men Ludwig had brought onto the detail, and he'd asked about the Leutnant every day. Emil knew he should get Fluse on the team, assuming he was still alive. But it would attract unwelcome attention, since the fool had already been removed from the detail.

As the group headed to the new salvage point, Emil steered his horse-drawn cart through a small village, the fourth they'd passed through that day.

"So are you going to tell me?" Ludwig asked. "Or are you going to wait until we're in the Saarland?"

Emil pulled at the reins but caught himself before slowing the horses. "What do you mean?"

"Come now, I know how you think. We're headed due east to a new salvage yard, and we just happen to need to stop overnight? I'm surprised you arranged this already." Ludwig raised a hand like he was shushing Emil.

"I didn't arrange this." Indignation rose in Emil's throat. How could Ludwig accuse him of lying about it?

"Right."

"No. Really. I didn't."

Ludwig's lips were pressed together hard. "Okay. I believe you. But you're not going to take advantage of it? You didn't think about it?"

Emil flushed. He should have felt guilty for thinking about it. Was he the one who was wrong here? "Of course I did. Didn't you? You want to stay here? You like it in Wegener's camp more than at home? You don't want to see what the Martians have done to Euleheim this time?"

"No. I'd love to go home. But we agreed that we'd figure out a way to keep the general from killing hundreds—if not thousands—with Martian weapons."

Emil stared straight ahead. He'd agreed to it, yes. But he'd had no intention of following through. Would he have to knock this man unconscious to get him away from here?

"It's important to Beckenbauer, you know," Ludwig said.

Emil tilted his head.

"He lost his entire family in the Attack. The Martians burned their entire farm to the ground. He only survived because his grandfather threw him into the well."

"My God." Emil's throat constricted. Beckenbauer's experience during the first Martian Attack had been worse than his. That was why he hated the Martian weapons so much more than Emil.

Besides, Wegener was collecting the same heat rays the Martians had used to kill Hermine. The same weapon they'd also used to kill Degenscheide. Why didn't that make Emil as angry as it did Beckenbauer? Was he the one who was wrong?

"Even if we're going to get the hell out of here, why not wreak some havoc first?" Ludwig suggested. "We can start today."

"Start?" Emil repeated. "The best way I can think of to slow Wegener down is to take these carts to Saarbrücken and set them on fire so he can't move any more gear."

"So you *are* planning on heading home?"

"No! We don't have all of our men yet."

Ludwig frowned. "We need to sabotage the Martian equipment. You're the only one of us who can do it."

Emil stared back at Ludwig, his eyes wide. Sabotage? How would that help? How would delivering broken equipment do anything more than get them executed?

Ludwig threw up his hands. "You know about this . . . stuff. You said Tesla started a fire with one of these power supplies. Can't you do the same thing here? Burn down Wegener's salvage yard?" He held out his hands from his sides, as if pleading.

Emil's stomach churned. Do to Reims what that Serbian had done in New York? "Are you insane?" he hissed. "Do that on purpose?"

"What? It just started a fire, right?"

"It melted buildings. It killed hundreds. It kept killing people for months afterward with radiation sickness." What would it do to Reims? Would it be close enough to do the same?

"It would destroy his camp," Ludwig said, one finger extended to make his point.

That was true. It was a way to stop Wegener and whatever he was planning. It would also be a literal Pyrrhic victory.

"It's suicide," Emil said. "I don't know what Tesla did to cause it."

"It's suicide? You couldn't figure out how to set it up with a delay?"

The power supplies generated an enormous amount of energy. Tesla might have created some kind of short circuit. Maybe Emil could create a fuse out of some kind of lead or graphite alloy. But what was he thinking? He needed to scout a way home and leave Wegener behind, not figure out a way to safely destroy a French city.

"This is madness, Ludwig. We'll destroy a city to prevent Wegener from destroying more? Are we gods now?"

"Do you have another idea?"

"No, but that doesn't make this one good."

They rode in silence for the rest of the day.

Emil decided afterward that trying to convince Ludwig to go along with scouting the area for the best way back to Germany was a bad idea. So he stuck to the map and headed for the new salvage yard.

Ritter had been right. It was late afternoon by the time Emil's group reached it. They made camp and settled down for the night. Ludwig and Beckenbauer ate together, and Emil got a taste of how Fluse must have felt when the soldiers had made their way south from the trenches.

At one point, Emil started to approach them while they were eating, but Beckenbauer's glare stopped him in his tracks. Ludwig must have told him that Emil had refused to take part in the sabotage. Emil didn't want to have that argument again.

Beckenbauer had been one of his biggest supporters when he'd left the trenches. He'd come close to begging Emil to take charge. And now he stared at Emil like he was an alien.

Their group woke up early and started loading the carts as soon as they finished breakfast and broke camp. No one wanted to spend another night outside in the cold.

Emil and Ludwig worked in silence, loading their cart with lighter parts so it would be easier to lead the caravan. They were finishing up when shouting rose from the far side of the yard. Their eyes met, and both men ran toward the racket.

They skirted stacks of cylindrical power supplies and piles of steel tentacles from the Wanderers' arms and legs. When they turned a corner, Emil had to stop short to avoid a chassis from some kind of aircraft. He reached a circle of men and pushed his way through.

Beckenbauer and one of the few men Ritter had left on the detail were facing off. Emil recognized the man; he'd tried to calm Groenig after he'd set off the heat ray. Now, both men had clenched fists. Beckenbauer's face was bright red, and sweat dotted his brow. They were moments away from a fistfight.

Emil didn't need this. He took a deep breath. "What's happening here?" he asked.

"This lunatic hit me!" Beckenbauer said.

"You broke the mirror on that heat ray!" the other man shouted.

"You hit him for breaking a mirror?" Emil asked. Was the soldier worried about seven years of bad luck?

"He did it on purpose. He's broken at least two or three of them."

Emil's blood ran cold. They were already trying to sabotage the equipment, even after Emil had refused to go along with it. He needed to stay in Wegener's good graces if he was going to get them out of here, though, and they were already stirring up trouble.

His eyes met Beckenbauer's. Beckenbauer didn't blink. It was a challenge. He expected Emil to protect him.

"On purpose?" Emil asked. "Why would anyone break this equipment on purpose?"

The soldier shrugged. Beckenbauer exhaled in relief. He thought Emil was covering for him.

"Did you break this on purpose?" Emil asked Beckenbauer.

Beckenbauer's hands relaxed. The corner of his mouth went up in a smile. "No, sir. Of course not." He was playing a game. A game that could ruin their chances of leaving, if not get them hanged.

There were at least three different broken mirrors behind Beckenbauer. "But I do see a bunch of broken mirrors," Emil said. "This equipment is worthless to us broken. You will be more careful, Soldat."

Beckenbauer's face fell before his defiant look returned.

"Everyone, back to work. I don't want to spend another night out here." Emil waved them back to the piles of salvage and returned to his cart.

A few minutes later, Beckenbauer approached. "What was that?"

"What was what?" Emil asked.

"He attacked me," Beckenbauer growled. "And you backed him. Now I can't do anything." He was shaking now. He looked like he was ready to start a fight with Emil.

A well. Beckenbauer had hidden in—no, he'd been thrown into—a well during the Attack. What had he heard from down there? What had he seen before he'd been hidden?

"Do anything? You nearly ruined everything." Emil clenched his fists again, and he took another breath. "We won't be able to do anything if Wegener doesn't trust us. Get to work."

Beckenbauer's eyes flashed with rage, but he turned and walked away.

Emil had seen his family's house go up in flames with his little sister inside. He'd seen his best friend killed by German Black Smoke. He'd seen Degenscheide vaporized by a Martian heat ray. So why didn't he feel the same way Beckenbauer did?

He pushed the question down and prepared to ride back to Reims.

32

om didn't make coffee the next morning.

James had finished washing and shaving, and the customary aroma of a freshly brewed pot was nowhere to be found. Was Mom sick? He took the stairs two at a time to the first floor.

She was sitting at the table, her nose buried in the broadsheet with the headline:

IT'S WAR

American Troops on the Way to Europe

James froze in the kitchen doorway, his eyes riveted on the headline.

"Oh, I'm sorry," Mom said. "I forgot to make coffee." She put the paper down and got out of her chair.

"War?" James asked, still stuck in place.

"Yes, war. We're sending thirty thousand men to France. They may even be gone by now." She filled the coffeepot with water. "The paper says the president had been hoping the French and British would turn things around, but he's heard enough." Mom lit the stove then.

James picked up the paper and read the lede to the headline story. Apparently, President Bryan had been "observing the situation for weeks." But the radios had been down. They'd been down since Coney Island. Mom didn't know that, of course. What had President Bryan "heard"? And from where? Urich had said the telegraph lines were down, too. Was Fleming involved in this? James had thought the colonel might be headed for jail . . . but now the biggest news of the year implied the radios had never been down?

"Eggs?" Mom asked, "Oh, that's right. You're meeting Susan. I'm so glad you two are getting on again. You better hurry so you make it to work on time. Don't give that horrible man a reason to give you any trouble."

War.

The word played through James's head over and over as he pedaled toward town. His face started to go numb from the cold air, but he couldn't slow down. He couldn't spare a minute. He needed to find Susan at the café so she could take him back to Mrs. Prendick's to call Urich.

James was so breathless when he arrived at Susan's table that he fell into his chair.

"What's wrong?" Susan said, one hand up to her chest. "How fast did you ride here? You're still early!"

"War."

"What?"

"War." James held up a hand for her to wait while he caught his breath. "Have you seen the paper?"

"No. What happened?"

"War. We sent men to France. Last night." James's breathing was returning to normal, but his heart was still pounding in his chest.

Susan's hand went up to her chest again. "We're joining the war?"

"Joined. They're gone. President Bryan said he'd heard enough about what the Germans were doing over there."

"Heard? But . . ." Susan lowered her voice then. "The radios are down, aren't they?"

"Exactly. I need to talk to Urich."

"What can he tell you?"

"I don't know, but he might have leaked the story about the radios," James whispered just loud enough for Susan to hear. "This might be a reaction to it. An attempt to bury that story with a bigger one?"

"That's a huge conspiracy, James."

"Something is going on. I told you what Urich said. No one knows what's happening in Europe. There's a conspiracy, we just don't know who's behind it or how far it goes. Maybe . . . maybe it's time for me to get involved."

The words came out before James could catch them. Could he do something without putting everyone in danger?

"Didn't you meet him at Renwick's?" Susan asked. "You said he's a regular?"

James nodded. "Let's try there first."

33

"So this is the way it's going to be?" Emil asked Ludwig after the group left the salvage point. His knuckles were white from grasping the reins. "Either I let you start damaging the equipment and we all end up hanged, or you sabotage the deliveries until I disappear like Fluse did?"

"Well, when you put it that way, yes," Ludwig said, shrugging.

"I don't think you understand the position you're putting me in."

"Oh. That's rich." Ludwig grinned.

"Huh? What's so funny?" Emil cocked an eyebrow.

"Never mind. God willing you'll live long enough to figure it out."

"Look, I know how Beckenbauer feels—"

"Do you?"

"Do I?" Emil held up a hand to his chest. "Of course I do. I lost my sister. I lost Fritz to that verdammt Smoke. I'm the one who was still outside the tunnel when they killed Degenscheide."

"Then why won't you do anything?"

There it was again. "I am doing something. I'm trying to get us the hell out of here. Away from this madness, Ludwig."

"Away from this madness." Ludwig looked straight ahead and took a deep breath. "And you're sure this madness won't follow us? That after Wegener finishes whatever he's doing, he won't follow us back to Germany? Or are you going to lead us away from this madness into someone else's lunacy?"

Emil had no idea. He couldn't know. But staying here endangered all of them and kept them from learning what had happened to their families back home. Well, those of them who still had families.

He checked behind his and Ludwig's cart. Beckenbauer's team was too far back for him to see. "You'd rather fight Wegener where he's still in control?" he asked.

"Good point." Ludwig nodded. "But I'm not the only one you have to convince, am I?"

No, he wasn't. After what had happened at the new salvage yard, all of the men were upset. But what options did Emil have? Ludwig and Beckenbauer wanted him to sabotage a Martian power supply—which might kill everyone, including them, and burn Reims to the ground. The other men, including Beckenbauer, wanted to bring nothing but worthless junk back from their supply runs. How long did they think it would take for Wegener's officers to notice?

But what if Emil could use Beckenbauer's mess to his advantage? He could go to Wegener and say the other men were causing issues, then bring the rest of the 109th onto the team. "I'll get the rest of our men with us tomorrow," he said.

"You think you can do that?" Ludwig asked, puffing on a cigar.

"Yes. Do you think it'll help convince them that we need to leave?"

Ludwig shrugged. "Can't hurt."

• • •

Ritter was walking away from Wegener's cottage as Emil approached it. Good. Talking to Wegener alone would be easier. He straightened his collar and pushed open the door.

"Hauptmann Zimmerman!" the Leutnant behind the desk said, jumping to his feet and snapping a salute.

"Is the general in?" Emil asked.

"Yes, sir. I'll announce you." The Leutnant disappeared into Wegener's office.

Announce him. Adorable.

"He'll see you right away, sir," the Leutnant said when he returned.

"Thank you."

Emil found Wegener seated behind his desk with a book open in front of him. He smiled and waved Emil to a chair, not bothering to return Emil's salute.

Emil gestured to the coffeepot. No reason to pass up the good stuff. Wegener nodded and extended a welcoming hand to it. Emil poured himself a cup, then took a seat.

"You did a great job with that new salvage yard," Wegener said with another smile. "I'm hoping you can make another trip in a few days?"

"Actually, that's why I'm here," Emil said, figuring he should get to the point. "I had a little problem. Ritter's men don't like mine for some reason. I had to break up a fight, sir."

Wegener frowned. "A fight between my men? But why?"

"Some kind of misunderstanding over handling the equipment."

The general's frown stayed in place.

"I was hoping to bring some more new men in," Emil continued. What was Wegener thinking? Was it a problem with bad news? Or an inability to make a simple decision? Emil held his breath.

"Yes, that's a good idea," Wegener said. "Send Ritter's men to him. He can find a use for them. Pick some of your own." He smiled again. Either he'd forgotten about Ritter's fear that Emil had been planning this all along, or he didn't understand the risk. Was he too trusting? Or just foolish?

"Thank you, sir," Emil said, fighting a smile. "We can make the trip tomorrow if you want." They'd be in the Saarland within a week, and Wegener's carts would make a pleasant fire on the way. He sipped his coffee, not wanting to appear too eager to leave.

"No, not tomorrow!" Wegener sprang to his feet, knocking his book—a collection of stories titled *Ausländer und Ausländisch* —to the floor. "We're having the demonstration!"

"The demonstration?"

"Haven't you heard? I guess with you being away for most of the day; you missed out. We're demonstrating the weapons you've made possible!" The general held out his arms as if he was presenting a new Sturmpanzerwagen. He grinned like a little boy at a candy store as his arms fell back to his sides.

Emil's stomach sank. The weapons he'd made possible. He didn't want to hear about this. "What kind of weapons?" he asked. "What have the men made?" Hopefully, this was just more games. More childishness.

"It's very exciting! They couldn't make the Black Smoke emitters work at all." Wegener frowned a little.

That was a relief.

"But they managed to fix the heat rays. It's not quite the same as the Martians' now, of course, but it's a fantastic weapon!" Wegener came around to the front of his desk.

Emil stood and eased toward the door. "Not the same as the Martians' . . . ?"

"Something about tuning and focusing the beam." Wegener waved away the problem like an annoying gnat. "I don't understand, but they assured me it will help us win the war!"

Emil fought back a laugh. Was it a giant night-light? Maybe they could blind someone for a few minutes? Light up the enemy in the dark? "It sounds exciting. I can't wait to see how it will help us win." He forced a grin to hide his confusion over which war Wegener was talking about.

"Me neither! It's going to get the men fired up. I can't wait!" Even though Emil couldn't manage to muster up any enthusiasm or small talk, Wegener seemed to be generating enough for both of them. "Imagine our men marching behind an array of unstoppable weapons! Well, you do what you need to do. Keep up the good work!"

"Thank you, sir," Emil said, snapping a salute.

"So you called us all together, sir," Beckenbauer asked in one of the enlisted men's tents later. "What do you want?"

Emil decided to ignore the contempt dripping off the word *sir*. Beckenbauer was upset, but Emil had news that would change that. "Excellent news! We're all together." He beamed. "The salvage detail is only us now."

"What about Fluse?" Miller asked sullenly.

Emil frowned. That was Miller's first reaction? "I don't know," he said. That was the truth. He hadn't spent any time looking for the jerk and hadn't been willing to spend any political capital asking around.

"So we leave without him?" Beckenbauer asked. "And leave Wegener with these weapons?"

"That's the good news. I spoke to Wegener today. I used the trouble you caused to get all of us together."

Beckenbauer scoffed.

Emil surveyed the room and allowed himself a quiet moment of satisfaction. All fifteen men were in the room, on the same team for the first time since they'd arrived at this compound. Emil had played Wegener and Ritter's army games and beaten them. Now it was time to go home.

He turned to Beckenbauer. "Wegener is clueless. He's having some kind of demonstration of his weapons tomorrow, and it sounds like a joke. All we need to do is make an appearance, then we can head out of here the next day. We're scheduled to go to the new lot in the east again, so it will take them at least two days to miss us." Emil nodded to make his point.

"A joke? Do you think Martian weapons are a joke?" Beckenbauer asked the rest of the men, frowning.

A few soldiers mumbled no, and others shook their heads. Ludwig shrugged. Did Beckenbauer want to lead the group? Would he break up the soldiers after Emil had finally reunited them? No.

"Wegener's a joke," Emil said. "He couldn't even tell me what his weapons do, but he did say they couldn't get the Black Smoke to work at all."

A few quiet sighs reverberated around the room.

"But the heat rays? The Wanderers?" Beckenbauer crossed his arms.

The Wanderers? Who cared about them? The Wanderer that had loomed over his home in Euleheim flashed before Emil's eyes. Could Wegener's men have . . .

No. They couldn't have gotten one of them working.

"Wegener said their heat rays don't work the same way the Martians' do," he said.

"Not the same?" Beckenbauer asked. "What does that mean?"

"I know! It's a joke."

"What do you mean? Wegener is the general, not the armorer. He doesn't have to know."

Fifteen pairs of eyes focused on Emil. The room grew warmer, and he fought the urge to wipe his brow. Wegener was a buffoon; so was Ritter, in his own way. Wegener had taken over an entire battalion of men, maybe more. But he was a child playing soldier. The return of the Martians had more to do with his hold on power than anything else.

"They're clowns, Beckenbauer," Emil said as his gaze swept the room, making eye contact with all of the soldiers. "I've been working with them. I've been playing their silly games. But you've seen them, too. Can you imagine them taking Martian equipment and making deadly weapons? The army—the real army—has working Black Smoke. It killed Fritz! But Wegener told me they couldn't even do that!"

"Not good enough," Beckenbauer said. "We have to stop them. Even if you're right today, what happens if someone does figure out how to get the weapons to work?"

"We'll be home to protect our families."

Mumbles of agreement rose from the soldiers. At least half of them wanted to leave. But Beckenbauer's eyes narrowed, and Emil remembered the story Ludwig had told him. Beckenbauer had no family to go home to.

"We need to sabotage one of those power supplies," Beckenbauer said. "Tonight. So it burns his equipment. Burns it to the ground. We found the yard. All we need is for you to show us how to do it."

"That's suicide!" Emil exclaimed. "The fire would kill us, and it might take Reims, too."

"And?" Beckenbauer asked, crossing his arms again.

"I'll go with him," Ludwig said.

"But—" Not him. Not Ludwig, too. Emil needed him to go home, and he'd thought they were starting to reach an understanding.

"But what?" Ludwig asked.

"It'll kill whoever does it. It might burn Reims to the ground, too. How many people do you want to kill because you think Wegener is a threat? Do you want those deaths on your head? Who do you think you are?" Emil scanned the room as he said the last sentence and was treated to a mix of nods and shaking heads.

"So you're saying you won't help?" Beckenbauer asked. "You're going to let Wegener go ahead with whatever he's doing?"

Emil should have come here earlier and spoken to Beckenbauer before everyone else had arrived. Now he was on the spot.

"I'm saying I don't want to risk burning a French city to the ground," he said, crossing his arms.

A few soldiers nodded. Some mumbled yes.

"We'll watch Wegener's demonstration. Then we'll leave the next morning. I think most of us want to go?"

The agreement grew a little louder.

Beckenbauer's shoulders sagged, and Ludwig looked at the floor. It was a hollow victory for Emil, but he was going home. That was what mattered, wasn't it?

"I recommend you go and get a good night's sleep," Emil said.

The group broke up, with most of the men leaving the room or heading to their bunks. Ludwig and Beckenbauer approached Emil then.

"I thought you were different," Beckenbauer said.

Emil tilted his head. Different? He'd been saying the same thing since they'd left the trenches: that he wanted to go home.

"I thought you were different from the other officers," Beckenbauer repeated.

Emil's heart skipped a beat. Of course he was different. He'd just finished planning to desert the army and take his men with him. " I became an officer so I could get us out of here. I'm the opposite of Wegener's men."

"You know what I mean. You've been in charge since we left the trenches, whether you admit it or not, and you were trying to protect us. But now—"

"I still am. I'm trying to get us home."

"You're using us to get what you want. I hope you're right about Wegener, but I know you're not."

"Using you? I could have left days ago. I could be in Euleheim right now!" Emil's face felt warm, and he clenched his fists.

Ludwig put a hand on Emil's shoulder as Beckenbauer crossed his arms. "I just hope you're right, Emil," Ludwig said.

34

Urich was seated in 'Wicks with his back to the wall, coffee in hand, and ketchup on his shirt. "James, I didn't expect to see you today," he said, smiling. "I would have ordered an extra breakfast."

James and Susan sat down in the two chairs across from the reporter.

"Well, take a seat," Urich said, raising his eyebrows in surprise.

"We need to talk," James replied, leaning forward with his elbows on the table, looking Urich straight in the eye.

"Why don't you introduce me to your friend first?" Urich nodded toward Susan.

James blushed. "Susan Wilson, this is Carl Urich, Carl Urich, this is Susan Wilson."

"Ah, so you're Miss Wilson," Urich said. "You worked for Fleming, didn't you? Before he left Edison? And now you've left after he returned?"

"Yes," Susan said with a sigh.

"I'd love to hear your thoughts about him. Off the record, of course." Urich gestured for Penny then.

"That's not why we're here," James said. Urich wasn't taking this seriously. Wasn't he worried about the men sent to Europe? Didn't he care about it all being based on a lie?

"So you said."

"Can I take your orders?" Penny asked as she arrived at the table.

James wasn't hungry, but he agreed to a breakfast plate. It was the fastest way to get back to the matter at hand.

"So what's on your mind, James?" Urich asked before taking a forkful of home-fried potatoes.

"War." James put the broadsheet on the table.

"That's certainly a popular subject today. What about it?"

How could Urich be so matter-of-fact about it? People were going to die for no reason.

"You told me a few days ago that no one knows what's happening in Europe," James lowered his voice before continuing. "The telegraphs are down. The radios are out. Now the President is sending troops after monitoring the situation 'for weeks'?"

"Well, they're not going to let us talk about that, are they? Admit we lost communications with the rest of the world? But the radios are up. They spoke to Germany. They spoke to France. They gave the press written transcripts. They weren't pretty."

"What do you mean the radios are back up?"

"They got them working yesterday."

"Not as far as I know."

"What's going on with you people at Edison?"

"You don't think there's something wrong with that?" Susan said, cutting off James.

"Wrong?" Urich asked.

James slumped back in his chair, deflated. The radios were back up? That was positive news, right? The US was talking to Europe and England. Sending the troops was the right thing to do then.

"The radios have been down for a couple of weeks, and now they come up and we're at war within hours?" Susan asked.

"The War Department has troops and ships ready faster than you can order a steak in a good restaurant?"

"That's an excellent point," Urich said, nodding. "It does seem a bit coincidental. I'm still trying to figure out what to do about that, if anything. The radios just came up, and the troops were already in place and ready to go."

James stared at Urich, his mouth agape. He thought it was suspicious, so he was trying to figure out what to do? If anything?

"What?" Urich asked James as if reading his mind. "We've all seen Bryan's program before. Martial law is coming next. What do you want me to do? You're right, though. The timing is just too much to ignore, especially considering what the captain in charge of the radios said yesterday."

"Captain Reynolds?" James asked, lifting himself from slumping in his chair. "He's okay now?"

"Yes, he's recovered and back at work. He said the radios sounded . . . how did he put it? Odd."

"Odd?" Susan and James asked in unison.

"He said the people on the other end sound different. Germany was . . . let's call it 'pugnacious.' But the Planetary Warning System has new operators, and they are acting strange, according to Reynolds. At one point, it sounded like two people were on the line, and the noise on the line was . . . too consistent?" Urich looked toward the ceiling, as if he was trying to remember Reynolds's exact words.

"Too consistent? As in, the noise didn't sound like noise?" James asked.

"Noise that isn't noise?" Urich repeated.

Yes. In radio terms, "noise" was random interference. "Too consistent" meant what they heard hadn't been noise. And two people had been on the line? That was an even bigger red flag.

James had an idea of what was happening. A terrifying idea.

"So the operators on the other end have changed, and there's some kind of consistent . . . interference." He shuddered at the contradiction in terms. "So we don't know if they're talking to Germany, do we?"

Susan and Urich gaped at James, their eyes wide with shock.

"What?" Urich said. "That's impossible."

James brow's crinkled. "No, it isn't."

Susan exhaled and put a hand to her forehead. "Of course. No, it isn't."

"They'd know!" Urich said.

"How?" James asked. "It's radio. The signal you're listening to can come from anywhere. That's the point."

Urich sat back. His eyes were unfocused as he spoke. "So what you're saying is, someone blocked the radios for a couple of weeks, then turned on their transmitter and started pretending to be Germany and Planetary Warning?"

James and Susan nodded.

Urich fell silent as he sipped his coffee. Then he stared past Susan and James as he said, "Block the radios for a few days. Turn your transmitter on. Say exactly what you need to convince Bryan to send the army out of the country and declare martial law."

They nodded again.

"That's a hell of a conspiracy," Urich said.

It was. But the more James thought about it, the more he believed it.

"I need to talk to Captain Reynolds," he said. The words left his mouth before his brain fully understood them.

Susan looked at him, her expression turning from shock to surprise, to a smile. She placed her left hand over James's right.

Urich was taken aback, too. "You what? You say we can't be sure if we're talking to London, but I'm not sure I'm talking to James Brogan. You couldn't get far enough away from trouble just a few days ago."

"No one is safe right now, Urich, and there's nowhere to run," James said. "We need to talk to Captain Reynolds and come up with a plan."

35

The assembly area remained largely the same as it had when Wegener had hanged the three men for unspecified offenses. Two hundred soldiers now stood in ranks, facing a platform with a podium at one end and a wooden frame at the other. But no nooses hung in the air this time, only the buzz of anticipation.

Wegener's army wasn't assembled for an execution this time, but a demonstration. Maybe he'd light up the sky with his modified heat ray, set some linen on fire, and boil a glass of water.

Despite the disagreement the night before, Emil and his team were in good spirits. Even Beckenbauer managed a smile as they joked with one another and waited for the assembly to begin. The other platoons were too close for them to discuss what was next, but an undercurrent of anticipation ran through the group. They'd attend the silly demonstration, celebrate at Wegener's expense, and head east tomorrow morning.

What would they find at home? Did the Martians attack Euleheim again? Was Mother safe? Were Fritz's parents still alive? How would Emil explain what had happened to their son?

To distract himself, Emil scanned the area for signs of Martian weapons. Like the platform, little had changed. A pair of soccer goals stood in one corner, one drunkenly leaning on the other as if they'd spent a rough night on the town. A disused collection of empty carts was left in the other corner, their wheels overgrown with dead wildflowers and weeds. Would Wegener have his new toys carted out here? Or would he march the soldiers somewhere?

Whispers rose among the men as the Stabsfeldwebel strode out to the podium. As everyone else hustled and bustled into straight ranks, the Stabsfeldwebel tapped on something in front of him, and the noise reverberated over the field. A new public address system! Was it fashioned from Martian tech? Or had Wegener's men raided the radio system in the woods?

"Attention!" the Stabsfeldwebel called out.

The troops snapped into place.

"Platoon leaders, prepare your men to march."

A buzz rose through the crowd as Ludwig shot Emil a puzzled expression. Emil shrugged, but Wegener's men hadn't expected this, either. Did they know why Wegener had assembled them?

Either way, they were going to play soldier and march somewhere—part of their general's childish games, no doubt. Ritter's Hussars rode out front and set the pace.

They marched. For three hours.

Most of the soldiers weren't prepared for it.

Emil's team fared well; they'd only been in Wegener's compound for a few weeks after trekking across France. But most of Wegener's men had been with him for months, and they'd grown soft. They weren't prepared for a hike, while the men from the 109th still thought like soldiers. They wore dry boots and had brought their coats, while Wegener's troops wore dirty gear from training and dressed for short assembly in the sun. You can open a coat or carry it if you're too warm. But you couldn't do anything to adjust to the shade if you had nothing to close, and damp boots were trouble.

Was sending the soldiers off unprepared deliberate? A way to remind them of who was in charge? Or another sign of Wegener's incompetence? Were they abandoning the compound for a battlefield? Or starting a new invasion of France? They couldn't be. Even a peacock like Ritter knew to prepare his men for an invasion better than this. It was either a head game or more stupidity.

"What is this?" Ludwig asked while sharing sips from his canteen with Emil and Beckenbauer.

"I thought today was supposed to be a joke," Beckenbauer groused.

"It might be," Emil mused. "Moving men this far with no plans? It's certainly not something a professional soldier would do, is it?"

"Not unless he wanted to send a message," Ludwig answered. "Does he know what you're planning, Emil?"

"I've given him nothing. Have you seen how his men are doing? When was the last time they've done any real training?"

"You noticed." Ludwig smiled. "You're a natural commander, Hauptmann Zimmerman."

Emil winced, but Beckenbauer interrupted then. "Your best friend is coming."

Emil spun around to see where Beckenbauer was looking. It was Ritter. His uniform was still spotless, despite three hours of riding, but his mouth was drawn in an unreadable line. Was the peacock tense about the demonstration? Or did he resent having to speak to Emil?

"Hauptmann Zimmerman," Ritter said, lingering on the last syllable. "Bring your men to the head of the formation. The general wants you to arrive in Hermonville first."

Ludwig and Beckenbauer both frowned.

Hermonville? The village where Ritter had found them? Why would they be meeting there? Had the Martians attacked the town? And why should Emil arrive first? Was it a reward for the work he'd done picking up the equipment from the salvage yards?

"Yes. Hauptmann Ritter," Emil said. "Thank you for letting me know."

Ritter turned and walked back toward the front of the formation.

"Hermonville? Isn't that where we met him?" Beckenbauer asked. "That doesn't sound good."

"Maybe there's a field by the village for the demonstration," Ludwig offered.

"We didn't see one. I think he wants to put on a show for the civilians." Beckenbauer gritted his teeth.

Beckenbauer had already proven he expected the worst from Wegener, but that didn't mean he was reading the situation wrong. Why march the soldiers out to a tiny village like Hermonville for this demonstration? Either way, there was nothing they could do. At least not yet.

"It doesn't mean he has anything worth showing," Emil said. "Let's get the men up front before Ritter starts complaining."

Ritter stopped the formation outside of Hermonville. He turned and beckoned to Emil. "Just you," he said when Emil was within earshot. "He said your Unteroffizier can come, too."

Emil collected Ludwig and followed Ritter into town. Schmidt joined them on the way.

"How have you been?" Schmidt said, nodding to Ludwig as he spoke. "We're finally going to learn what all that work was for, huh?"

"I guess so," Emil said. "Do you know why we stopped here?"

Schmidt shook his head.

Hermonville's main street, with the Gasthaus where Emil had left Gabrielle, came into view as they walked. For a moment, Emil wondered why the young woman and her sister, along with the rest of the village, were out of sight. Then he got his answer.

An imposing gray shape loomed from the clearing. It was a Sturmpanzerwagen, but it wasn't one of the K-types Emil had seen near the trenches. That model resembled landlocked ships more than ground vehicles. This was a newer model that Emil had never seen before. It was boxier and appeared like it had the potential to move faster. A huge armored cylinder was attached to the back of the vehicle.

"What's that on the back of that Panzer?" Ludwig whispered to Emil so Schmidt wouldn't hear. "Is that a Martian power supply?"

A ring of rough, amateurish welds held the cylinder to steel plating on the back of the vehicle. The idea of a welding torch getting that close to the Martian hardware made Emil shiver. Had they welded it directly to the Panzer? Or used some kind of mounting system?

"If they welded that to a Panzer without setting half of France on fire, there's no way I could have done what you wanted," Emil said.

"Or they're lucky," Ludwig said.

Emil grunted in response.

Three soldiers stood near the vehicle. One of them wore Hauptmann's pips and held the other two in rapt attention as he spoke. They met Wegener in the center of the road, a few meters from the vehicle. A crowd of civilians had gathered nearby, but Emil's eyes stayed locked on the grotesque vehicle. A mirror attached to a long piece of steel stuck out of the front, probably where there had been some kind of large gun.

Ludwig caught his eye. Emil had never seen him so afraid before. It wasn't a comforting sight.

"Exciting, isn't it?" Wegener said, facing Emil, Ludwig, and Schmidt with his hands outstretched as if presenting a buffet or a masterpiece painting.

Emil saluted. "All I can say is it's incredible, sir."

Ludwig and Schmidt lined up in a neat row of two and held salutes.

Wegener reciprocated. "This is your Unteroffizier, then?" He held out a hand and shook Ludwig's.

Ritter approached on foot then, his horse grazing in the clearing next to Wegener's new weapon.

Emil's eyes wandered past the retrofitted Sturmpanzerwagen to the crowd. They were alternating between ogling the "exciting" weapon and mumbling to one another.

The old man Emil and his men had met on the other side of town a few weeks earlier exited a bakery and stepped toward the weapon. One of the guards rushed over to shoo him away. The old man made eye contact with Emil from across the street, frowned, and let the soldier lead him away.

"Good, we're all together," Wegener said, seemingly oblivious to the civilians.

"Yes, sir," Ritter said. "The men are waiting down the road."

"Good, good. But I wanted to let you men see the first test firing. But first you need to meet Hauptmann Grundig." Wegener gestured to the men standing near the weapon, and they came over. "Grundig, you know Ritter and Schmidt. This is Hauptmann Zimmerman and Unteroffizier . . . ?"

"Oberacker, sir," Ludwig answered.

"Right. Oberacker."

Grundig nodded to them. He shook Emil's hand with a limp grip and a clammy palm, making Emil fight the urge to wipe it on his trousers.

"Zimmerman? You're the man who stopped the heat ray in that salvage yard?" Grundig wheezed.

"Yes, that was me," Emil said, tilting his head to one side. Grundig had heard about that? Were accidents like that rare, then?

Grundig smiled. "You shot the mirror! You're a marksman and a weapons engineer?" The black splotches staining his teeth stood out against his pale gray skin, and his laugh was the rasp of a pipe organ that needed a vacation in the Baden-Baden hot springs. Wegener had said they'd had problems with the Black Smoke. Had Grundig worked on that, too?

"No. I've just seen enough heat rays in action to figure out how they're focused." Emil didn't need this man to consider him any kind of rival. Grundig might show up in his room and drink his blood tonight.

"I wish I'd had you around while we were working on this," Grundig said. "The general tells me you worked on radios? It's not weapons design, but I could mold you into an excellent engineer. Let's talk tomorrow."

Emil shivered.

"Where would you like to get started?" Grundig asked Wegener.

"We need to get these people out of here first," the general said.

Grundig gestured to the guards. They approached the crowd with their weapons off their shoulders and shouted. Some villagers ran away. Others made a show of walking slowly. They dispersed down the road and into the stores and shops, including the Gasthaus where Emil had left Gabrielle and Juliette.

Emil breathed a quiet sigh of relief. At least the soldiers were letting them find cover. But was Gabrielle gone? Had she found a home? What would she think of Emil if she saw him here with these soldiers?

"Well, we've done plenty of trees, haven't we, Grundig?" Wegener asked.

"Yes, sir."

What had they done to the trees? Wegener had made it sound like the heat ray wasn't working.

"I'd like to try a building," Grundig said, stroking his chin.

Emil's pulse quickened, and he started to sweat. A building? What would that thing do to a building? He wiped his brow and stared at the Gasthaus.

"Should we go with all wood first? How about that barn?" Wegener pointed past the Sturmpanzerwagen to a red barn.

"Something more substantial," Grundig wheezed.

What? A barn would be easy to clear out, and burning it wouldn't destroy anyone's home. Grundig was as bad as Wegener. No—worse, since he seemed to be more ghoul than goofball.

"I know! Over there." Wegener pointed in the other direction.

It was the Gasthaus.

"That's an interesting choice, sir," Grundig said. "Most of the ground floor is sandstone."

"Can you burn it without taking the entire village with it?" Wegener asked.

Burn it? As a test? A wave of anger and shame passed over Emil.

These men were animals. Ludwig and Beckenbauer had been right. He checked with Ludwig, who just barely shook his head. Emil knew what he meant, but he couldn't stop. This was too much.

"You're going to test it on a Gasthaus?" Emil asked, trying to hide the contempt in his voice. "Are you sure it's empty?"

Wegener turned to him. "You think it's too small?"

Ludwig edged closer to Emil and planted an elbow in his ribs.

"No," Emil said. "It's that you said it didn't work quite like the Martian heat ray, so I'm not sure what the test is."

Ludwig's eyes told him to stop, but he didn't.

"Are you sure it's going to work, sir? Is it safe to test it here? Should we clear the people out?" Emil spun around to look for Grundig, but he'd already left the group and was standing next to the Sturmpanzerwagen.

"You'll see," Wegener said.

Before Emil could open his mouth again, Wegener gestured to Grundig, who said something inaudible into an open hatch on the side of the vehicle.

It was a joke. It had to be a joke.

An ear-shattering hum filled the air, and the possibility of a joke dissipated with a higher pitch than the terrifying sound the Martian Wanderers made. It was angrier, like a flock of raptors descending on an unruly pack of rodents.

Emil's knees sagged, and his hands flew up to his ears. His eyes flitted back and forth between the Panzer's mirror and the Gasthaus. Schmidt and Ludwig did the same while Wegener simply smiled with his hands at his side. Ritter covered his ears but remained still.

The mirror on the Panzer glowed a sickly green, then shifted to a pale yellow, then lightened to a bright white that forced Emil to turn away. The white expanded in his peripheral vision before extending to the Gasthaus.

A tremendous explosion knocked Emil onto the main street's hard-packed surface. The shock reverberated through his body; and for a moment, he was back in the trenches, waiting out one of the failed Allied bombardments on the Somme.

When the wave subsided, the humming stopped.

The Gasthaus was all but gone.

Wegener was already cheering as he climbed to his feet. Ritter had somehow remained standing and was smiling his unpleasant smile.

Emil climbed to his feet, unable to tear his eyes away from the restaurant's ruins. It hadn't just burned. It had been transformed into a pile of timber and ash. Just like his home had during the first Martian Attack. Grundig's weapon appeared to be different, but the result was the same.

Emil jumped when a hand fell on his shoulder. It was Ludwig. His eyes were wide with shock.

"What . . . ?" Emil stuttered.

Schmidt was standing a few feet back. He looked as shocked as Emil and was shaking his head. A tear was welling in one eye.

Somewhere behind them, a woman was screaming. A man shouted angrily.

"I told you, it's great!" Wegener said as he walked up to the three men. "It takes a little bit too long to warm up, but we can fix that. Right, Grundig? We can fix that?"

"Yes, sir," Grundig said a few steps behind him. "Perhaps Zimmerman can help with that."

Wegener grinned from ear to ear. He was a child with a new toy. A new toy that liquidated buildings, but not quite quickly enough. Maybe Santa could do better next year.

"Look!" The general led the soldiers to the ruins of the Gasthaus.

Emil walked to the edge of where the basement had been. Ash overflowed where the stone foundation had met the wooden frame. Pieces of charred wood and scored stone gave the charcoal and dust texture. None of the wood fragments were more than a meter long.

Piles of debris dusted what appeared to have been the dining room. A hat covered part of a dinner plate. Half of an umbrella laid across what must have been one of the crossbeams that held up the first-floor ceiling.

A glint of something in one corner caught Emil's eye. He squinted. Somehow, something small and metallic has survived Wegener's heat ray. He squinted again.

It was a metallic tag sewn onto the ear of a stuffed rabbit.

36

CURFEW: 22:00 HOURS
PUNISHABLE BY $15 FINE AND ONE NIGHT IN JAIL
BY ORDER OF THE SECURITY POLICE

Urich had said martial law was coming, and New York City had a curfew the next morning. The sign on the lamppost wasn't more than a few hours old, but it was already torn and scribbled with profanities.

James checked his watch. It was already 4:00 p.m. He should be able to meet with Captain Reynolds and return to the ferry terminal with time to spare. If he didn't, he'd risk having to find a room to wait out the curfew, but six hours was plenty of time.

He turned left onto 46th Street and picked up his pace. According to Urich, there was a pub a few blocks west, past 10th Avenue. The captain would already be waiting there, and they could work out a plan to prove that someone was feeding false information to the government.

James didn't like being in the city.

It wasn't the danger from Tesla's fire; the wall around the

Lower East Side protected the city from the mess the Serb had left behind. It was the memories. New York was Dad's city. He'd arrived here as a child and grown tough in the streets, elevating himself from street urchin to police sergeant. Then he'd volunteered to fight in the War of the Rebellion, surviving some of its most brutal battles. When he war ended, he'd come home, rejoined the police, and started a family.

Then his beloved city, with the help of Tesla, killed him for being a hero. Would the United States have a similar reward for James if he tried to save them?

James had been ten when Edison had arranged for a house for the Brogans in West Orange, near the hospital that would care for Dad until he died. That house became a permanent home for his widow and only son. James had put his memories of the city in a box and tossed them into the Hudson years ago.

Being here brought them back to the surface.

The city was crowded, loud, and dirty. Instead of walling the neighborhood off after the fire, they should have just closed the whole island. Started the wall at the shore and told everyone to find somewhere else to live and work.

A boy who couldn't have been older than ten ran in front of James, brandishing a newspaper. "Wuxtry! Wuxtry! Bomb destroys the Stock Exchange!"

James stopped and stared at the boy. Another explosion? Was this the work of the same conspirators?

Before he could finish the thought, he was pushed from behind.

"Hey!" exclaimed a deep voice behind him. It belonged to a sailor, flanked by two women clad in gaudy dresses and more makeup on one face than James thought was possible.

"S-sorry," he managed.

The sailor gave James another shove as he stormed past. The newsboy sneered from the nearby curb.

James found the pub on the next block, took a deep breath, and pushed open the door. A cloud of stale smoke, body odor, and beer greeted him as he stepped inside. It smelled and sounded like someone had rolled the West Side docks into a carpet and unrolled it into the bar. The walls were clad with wood that was dark and dusty enough to have been petrified. The floor was cold stone, with blotches that were probably oil but might have been blood. James might have traveled fifty miles, but he'd never been further from home.

The bartender—a burly, bald man with a stunning array of tattoos—fixed James with a cold stare. He didn't want James to leave but was making it clear it could be arranged.

James scanned the room. A crew of grizzled men—either dockworkers or itinerant assassins—glared back at him. James lowered his head and turned toward the bar to break the eye contact.

A young man sat at the bar, talking to a woman. She was dressed in colorful lace, gaudy petticoats, and a loud red wig. But she appeared ready to sacrifice an arm to escape the earnest admirer.

Finally, James's eyes fell on Captain Reynolds, who was sitting at a small table about halfway into the room. It took a moment for James to recognize the officer in civilian clothes.

"You actually came," Reynolds said as James took a seat with his back to the bar.

"You didn't think I would?"

Reynolds shrugged. "Last time we met, you were determined to stay out of trouble."

"Change of heart." James scanned the pub, swallowed, and wondered about his recent choices.

"You drinkin' or what?" bellowed a voice from behind James. The bartender was leaning forward with two hands on the bar, ready to vault it on his way to James's throat.

"Well, I . . ."

"He'll take an ale, Mike," Reynolds said.

"But I don't want . . ." James started.

"Then I'll drink it." Reynolds smiled. "But if you go get it, he'll be just fine."

James paid for the ale and carried it back to the table. As he sat and slid the glass across the table, he got his first close look at Reynolds. A fresh scar snaked across one cheek, and the hand that reached for the drink was still swollen.

"You fared better than I did at Coney Island," Reynolds said, noticing James's eyes lingering on him.

"Yes," James said. "My boss took me out of the hospital before I could see you. I wanted to say I was sorry about Christensen and the other men."

"Me too. That's why I was happy to hear from you now. It's starting to look like they lost their lives for nothing."

James jumped at hearing the captain repeat the same words he'd thought a few days ago. A pang of regret followed. He should have acted sooner—and he should have thought of reaching out to the captain earlier, too. His throat was dry, but he didn't think asking for water would make him any friends in this place.

"I think so, too," he said. "So, Urich said the radios sound . . . odd?"

"That's what my operators say," Reynolds said. "I listened in and agreed. We normally hear a little bit of noise depending on what time it is and who we're talking to. But it's too regular now. It's almost like someone pressed one of Edison's cylinders with noise on it, and they're playing it over and over again."

What an idea! Recording noise and playing it back to simulate an overseas signal. Not incredibly sophisticated, but clever still. James would have built a noise generator with a crystal and some components instead. But would someone capable of creating a power supply like the one he'd seen not know how to generate real noise? Were they lazy? Overconfident?

"I thought the arrival of new operators after the radios were restored was a hell of a coincidence, too." Reynolds took a swig of ale from the new mug as James eyed it. "But then they started to slip up."

James raised an eyebrow. Slip up?

"Well, for one thing," Reynolds continued, "the British operators on Planetary Warning talked about German soldiers arriving in downtown Paris."

Huh? Why not? If they were using Black Smoke, they could roll right over the French countryside. James tilted his head and made a face.

"My mother is British," Reynolds said. "She never says 'downtown.' She says 'city center.'"

James grunted. He was ready to act based on the noise alone, but Reynolds was reaching.

"Yeah, I know. It's not much." Reynolds took another swig. "But we've leaned heavily on Planetary Warning for intelligence about what's going on in Europe. We know them and how they talk. That was enough to make me want to listen more carefully. At least one of the operators is from Boston, and he's trying to sound like he's from London. It's not working."

James sat back in his seat. He wasn't qualified to analyze regional accents, but even if he was, accusing a British radio operator of being from Beantown wasn't going to save the country from whatever the Germans had planned.

"Anyway, I was hoping I could get you to build another one of those trackers," Reynolds said.

James's eyes widened. A tracker? Did Reynolds mean to find the fake broadcast, like they had with the interference? Why hadn't he thought of that?

"You mean the receiver we used to trace the signal to the Beacon Tower?" James asked.

"Exactly. You give me a tracker, and I'll find out whoever's doing this. Nobody is going to believe us if we try to explain what's happening. But if I can kill the fake signal, the real station will break through again. Problem solved." Reynolds put the ale down to punctuate his statement.

James thought of asking how the captain planned on stopping the broadcasts. Then he looked him in the eye again and knew the answer. He was going to take it down by force. This was as much about revenge as it was about national security.

"You don't have to come," Reynolds said. "I've got some men lined up. Marines don't take well to their brothers being killed, especially by traitors."

Did it matter why Reynolds wanted to do it? It was the right thing in the long run anyway, right? Whoever was behind the plot had killed three men, injured James and Reynolds, and was likely setting the country up for some kind of coup.

All the captain wanted from James was a new tracker. He could build one in a few hours. A better one, with the portable power supply he'd been working on and better sensitivity adjustments. A child could operate it, and he'd stay out of the line of fire.

But was that enough? James had led them to Dreamland, and he'd let Christensen take his place climbing those stairs. He needed to be sure they went to the right place this time.

"No, I think I should come with you," James said.

Reynolds smiled. "You should try one of these ales, Brogan."

37

E mil emptied his mug, lowered it, and stared into the bottom. The coffee in the officer's mess was tasteless. Bland. Pointless. He set the mug down, sighed, and looked toward the entrance. The sun was getting low. His men would be back soon.

Ludwig had been managing the supply runs since Wegener's show in Hermonville three days ago. Or was it four? Certainly not five yet. Emil hadn't left his bunk until Ludwig had dragged him out of it, but he relented when it came to forcing Emil to go back to work.

Had the group taken to sabotaging the equipment at this point? Why bother? Wegener had won already. He had a weapon that destroyed buildings—and anyone inside—in moments. He'd left about half of Hermonville standing before commandeering it for a garrison. Leveling the village and killing most of its inhabitants hadn't been enough. He needed to occupy it, too.

What were his plans?

Emil shook his head. Wegener's plans didn't matter. Emil had thought the general was a fool. Maybe he was. But it didn't matter. He'd killed a senior officer, taken his men, and built a new army backed with a weapon that was more terrifying than the Martians.

What good would guessing his plans do?

Emil was going to leave. Tonight, after dinner, he would use his rank to walk out the front gate, head east, and stop when he reached Euleheim. Ludwig and Beckenbauer had planned to stop Wegener, but that would have been suicide, and all Emil had done was make things worse. Maybe he could help at home. Either way, he'd rather die there than here, under Wegener's thumb.

Emil shifted in his seat to get up and pour another cup of coffee, but settled back instead. Did he want another cup? Did it matter? He let out a long sigh.

The officer's mess was empty, save for a soldier sweeping the floor and keeping the coffee urns full. He smiled at Emil as he straightened the benches at the next table. The fool had no idea that Europe was going to be overrun by Martians and power-hungry Germans. Was the soldier a power-hungry German? An unwitting helper like Emil? Or a victim working toward his own demise?

Was Wegener working with the Martians? Was that why they hadn't attacked the supply caravans? Emil had assumed they were beneath the aliens' contempt. But was there something more to it?

He shook his head again. He had to stop. It didn't matter.

"You've actually left your room," Ludwig said, taking a seat across from Emil. "That's progress, I guess."

Emil lifted his gaze, then stared back into his empty mug.

"It's not going to refill itself, no matter how hard you try to stare it into submission." Ludwig took the mug, left, and returned with two full ones. He placed one in front of Emil. "Fine. I'll talk to myself. Don't worry, unless I start to answer."

He took a long sip from his mug, sized it up as if surprised at how good the coffee was, and set it down. "Beckenbauer and Schmidt are inseparable now," he continued. "It's almost heart-breaking to see them head off to their different details each morning. But the upside is, they can conduct parallel recruiting operations. We figure we've got at least half the compound ready."

Emil raised an eyebrow. Ready? For what?

"Yes. Ready. Some of us are taking action. Planning. But I guess you're planning, too. Were you going to leave tonight? Or wait until we head off on another run tomorrow? I've often wondered if it would be easier to desert at night or in the light of day."

Emil inspected his mug to hide his surprise. Ludwig knew him better than he did himself.

"So, tonight it is." Ludwig shook his head before taking another sip of coffee. "Well, I'm tired of trying to convince you to do the right thing. Best of luck."

Emil winced. Ludwig and Beckenbauer had both been right. Ludwig's idea to sabotage a reactor and bring this place down around Wegener's ears would have risked Reims, but not acting had cost Hermonville. Beckenbauer wanted to sabotage the gear before they brought it in from the salvage yards. It might not have saved the village, but it was something, even though it looked like it might not have worked.

"But I want you to know that I'll miss you," Ludwig added with a grin that didn't quite make it to his eyes. "Especially now that you learned how to shut up."

Ludwig was making a joke? Hermonville lay in ruins. Emil and his men had brought Gabrielle and Juliette there so they'd be safe. Then they'd helped kill the girls, and most of the village.

"You think this is funny?" Emil asked.

"No, of course not," Ludwig said. "But if I don't laugh, I'll cry."

"You're right. I failed, and the best thing I can do is leave before I do any more damage." Emil took another drink of coffee and nearly gagged. Instead of being tasteless, it offered notes of bile and guilt now.

"Damage? You really do think the world revolves around you."

Emil nearly dropped his mug. What?

"What damage did you do, Emil? You didn't do anything."

"Well, I—"

"No 'well, I.' Wegener was going to do this. All of it would have happened, whether we came here or died on the Somme. Yeah, we might have stopped him if you'd sabotaged a power supply. We might have killed ourselves and everyone on this side of the Marne, too." Ludwig craned his neck to meet Emil's gaze.

Emil stared into his mug. Ludwig was right. But that didn't mean he agreed with him.

"What's important is this," Ludwig said. "What are you going to do now? You were trying to save us. Now you're ready to go back to just saving yourself."

That hurt. But what could Emil do? It was done. Over. Time to go.

"Grundig asked you to work with him," Ludwig continued. "Imagine what you could do—"

"There you are, Zimmerman."

Ritter was standing at the far end of their table.

"Uh, yes," Emil said. "Thank you."

"The general wants to see you tomorrow," Ritter said. "He has a special assignment for your men for the campaign."

"The campaign?"

"Yes. We've been keeping it quiet, but I thought I sent word to you. My apologies. After our success in Hermonville, it's finally time to head to Paris! See you tomorrow at the general's office." Ritter clicked his heels, spun around, and disappeared out the mess tent door.

Paris. They would burn a path of destruction across the country.

Emil's stomach sank to his feet and tried to follow Ritter outside. He took a deep breath.

"Did you know about this?" he asked Ludwig.

"No."

"Are you sure?"

Ludwig locked eyes with Emil. "Am I sure that I knew whether they were heading to Paris? Or whether they're going to burn their way across two hundred kilometers of this country? Yes, I am quite sure, Emil."

How many villages would they pass through? How many dead little girls would they leave in their path? Emil shuddered as the reflection of a metal Steiff tag replayed in his mind.

"Grundig wants your help with the weapon," Ludwig said.

"So?"

"You couldn't find a better spot to sabotage their plans."

The metal tag faded from Emil's memory, replaced with Wegener's celebration after the Gasthaus had been destroyed. Ritter had stood behind him, unfazed by the destruction, his mouth twisted into that disturbing smile.

How many more times would they do that? Would Wegener celebrate the same way every time?

Emil's stomach settled as his face warmed. A trickle of sweat ran down his forehead.

Could he run? Could he leave Wegener and Grundig behind to do that again and again?

Or, could he stop them by sabotaging the new Panzer? Would that be enough?

"Half the men?" Emil asked.

Ludwig's brow furrowed.

"You said Beckenbauer and Schmidt have half the men behind them?"

"Behind you."

Emil set his mouth as he locked eyes with Ludwig.

"Behind you, Emil. You're the one who decided you were responsible for Hermonville. Everyone else is blaming Wegener and that ghoul."

Leading a mutiny might get them all killed. If Emil didn't

lead it, they'd hold it and die anyway. But with him near Grundig, they had a chance to stop or destroy Wegener's "exciting" weapon.

"That special assignment is working with Grundig," Ludwig said.

And if it didn't, Emil could arrange it within a few minutes.

"You're right," he said. "Let's get the men together after dinner. We have work to do."

38

The poster announcing the curfew was torn, its remnants augmented with a clever rhyme using language James only heard around the loading dock back at Edison. He flushed as Susan read it. She giggled.

"What? Does that kind of language worry you?" Susan asked, nudging him with her elbow. "Should I have closed my virgin eyes instead of reading it? I should have stayed in New Jersey so I wouldn't see bad words like *f*—"

"Very funny, Susan. But I still think you should have stayed home." James looked around to make sure no one was within earshot. It was a little past 8:00 p.m., so the curfew wouldn't take effect for another two hours.

James was carrying the tracker in an army backpack, which had been Susan's idea. He'd been trying to assemble a hand truck that could withstand the mix of macadam and cobblestones in the city, since he and Reynolds had decided that a car would attract too much attention during the curfew.

Susan had let herself into the lab late Friday night while James was still trying to find the right wheels. James had told her about Reynolds's plans, leaving his part out. Then he'd quickly broken down under her cross-examination, and now he was still berating himself for not working out an alibi in advance. That was when she'd told him how to carry the tracker.

So James was wearing a backpack that, to Susan's mind, proved she had the right to come along for the search for the rogue transmitter.

The idea of her coming along on this mission scared him. What if they ended up in a firefight? Or were arrested by the SPs? But this was the woman who'd been detained by the Princeton police every Election Day for the past decade. She wasn't going to take no for an answer.

The device would tell James where the danger was. The plan was to use it to find the signal, then hang back and let Reynolds and his men shut it down. That way, James could protect Susan and get her away from trouble if things got too rough.

It would have been easier to give the device to Reynolds. But he wanted—no, *needed*—to be sure the spies were found. It was the only way to make sure everyone was safe and ensure Christensen's death was avenged.

Susan was carrying the meter and a pair of antennas; one was a traditional, nondirectional "whip," and the other a directional array James had been experimenting with in the lab. He wasn't sure if the new antenna would help, with the city's tall buildings blocking line-of-sight transmissions, but it was worth a try. Both antennas were folded into a flat box under her arm.

"How far is it?" Susan asked.

"Just a few more blocks this way."

The streets weren't empty, but they were quieter than they'd been when James had visited Manhattan a couple of afternoons ago. Was everyone staying home because of the curfew? What kind of trouble was he escorting Susan into?

They reached the pub, and James stopped before the door. "Okay. This place is rough. Keep you—"

"Don't worry, I'll protect you," Susan said as she pushed past him, opened the door, and strode inside.

James rushed to keep up with her, coming close to losing the backpack as the door closed on him. The pub was packed with revelers singing along to a piano. The words to the song were impossible to figure out, although a couplet with "Bryan," "curfew," and a phrase ending in "you" were hard to miss.

Susan pushed her way past the bar, toward the tables where James had found Reynolds before. She stopped when they reached an opening. "Do you see him?" she shouted over the crowd.

The tables were full of sailors, dockworkers, and other rough-looking characters, including more women than James had seen last time. A few of them were eyeing Susan as suspiciously as the men eyed his bulky backpack. Reynolds was nowhere to be seen.

A tap on James's shoulder startled him out of his search, and he lost his balance because of the weight of the tracker and its battery. A strong hand steadied him, then spun him around, where he found himself facing the bartender. Standing in front of James instead of behind the bar, Mike loomed even larger and stank of sweat, cigars, and gin.

Mike pointed to a door at the back of the pub, then spun James in that direction.

Susan shrugged and led the way to the door.

The door opened into a room lined with shelves stocked with bottles. Beer, whiskey, rum, gin, and other spirits James had never seen before surrounded him on either side. A single naked bulb hung from a pair of frayed wires.

Under the light, Captain Reynolds sat at a long wooden table, flanked by six men. They were in uniform, and their rifles were lined up neatly on a wall behind them. The marines were peas in a pod, with matching haircuts, tanned necks, and identical expressions. They didn't need their uniforms.

"This is your man?" one of them asked Reynolds.

"Yes," Reynolds said.

"He brought a *girl* with him?" one of the others growled.

39

Ritter led Emil and his men across the assembly area to the path leading into the woods. It twisted and turned for a few hundred meters before reaching a gate at the northeastern corner of Wegener's compound. This gate controlled access to Grundig's workshop, where he transformed Martian scrap into village-razing Super Panzers.

"This is Hauptmann Zimmerman," Ritter told the guards minding the entranceway. "Add him to the access list for this area."

That was a level of security and professionalism Emil hadn't seen since he'd left the trenches.

The taller of the two soldiers walked to a tiny guard shack on one side of the gate and let himself in.

"Your rise in this army has been nothing short of astounding, Zimmerman," Ritter said. "A more cynical man might think you're just giving the general what he wants." He eyed Emil like a boot in need of a thorough shining.

"Are you accusing me of the heinous crime of following orders, Ritter?" Emil asked. Ritter's head snapped back when Emil addressed him without his rank. "I'm just doing my best for Germany and my men."

Was Emil doing his best to protect his men? Or doing his best to help them commit suicide? The plan was to use this assignment to get close to Grundig's weapon and hijack it in time to stop the attack on Paris. At the same time, Beckenbauer and Schmidt would continue their recruiting efforts. Either way, Emil didn't have time to worry about Ritter.

Wegener's army would leave in three days. So Emil and his soldiers had to enact their scheme quickly. If everything went well, the plan would be a successful overthrow of Wegener's command. If not, it was a reserved spot at the end of a rope.

Ritter sniffed, spun, and walked away without another word.

The taller guard said something from inside his booth. Walking with a limp, the other guard approached Emil, snapped to attention, and delivered a sharp salute. Emil returned it.

"You're all set, sir," the guard said. "The primary building is past those trees and the radio office. You can't miss it." He pointed to a steel structure visible past a stand of evergreens.

Emil followed the path. As he approached the primary building, the antenna mast for the Planetary Warning System grew closer. Soon, he came upon a small brick building that must have hosted a Planetary Warning transceiver. The door was chained shut.

The steel structure the guard had directed him toward loomed another few hundred meters beyond. It was gigantic—at least thirty-five meters wide—and had two doors: one for the Panzers, the other for people. Emil pulled the smaller door open and immediately jumped back. Someone had parked Wegener's weapon in front of one of the doors with the heat ray arm pointed directly where Emil stood, ready to incinerate him in his tracks.

Emil was here to figure out how to take control of that war machine, maybe even turn it against them. How did you drive that thing? Could one man drive the vehicle and operate the heat ray? Or did it require a crew? Could he bring himself to use a Martian heat ray against another person?

Twenty-four hours ago, Emil had been ready to steal away under the cover of night. Now he was back in the middle of things and couldn't afford to fail. He wiped sweat from his brow.

"I see you're admiring my masterpiece, Hauptmann Zimmerman."

Emil recognized Grundig's wheeze from behind. He spun around to face him.

"I'm glad to see you. Men with electronics experience are hard to come by." Grundig smiled a toothy, black-stained grin that didn't make it to his eyes. Emil shivered. This man resembled an officer who'd enjoy interrogating a spy far too much.

"I'm pleased to be here, too, Hauptmann Grundig," Emil said. "But after that demonstration in Hermonville, I'm not sure what I can do to help." He hoped he wasn't laying it on too thick.

Emil had two secrets to hide from Grundig. One was his plan to commandeer or destroy the Panzer before it incinerated more French villages. The other was that he was truly qualified to work in this shop. Probably more qualified than anyone else there.

Emil had been at the radio towers in Aachen for six months before being recalled by the military and sent to war. Deutsche Telefunken, the national radio company founded shortly after the first Martian Attack, had put the primary tower site for radio communications with Great Britain and the United States right next to the Belgian border.

Emil had been an apprentice, and apprentices started by building wiring harnesses. Telefunken would accept nothing less than the best, and Emil had spent many nights crying himself to sleep with burnt, sore fingers.

"Oh no, I'm sure you're more than qualified to supervise getting the third one up and running," Grundig said, then coughed into his fist.

Third one? Emil's stomach tied itself into a knot. There were more of these monstrosities? They'd already built two more weapons for Wegener's campaign? He let out a long breath.

"Yes! We've had a lot of luck with the salvage material. Follow me." Grundig gestured to Emil with another of his creepy smiles.

He led Emil past the first Panzer. Two more hulking vehicles sat beyond that one. Emil stepped ahead of Grundig so he could circle the vehicles and examine them more thoroughly than he had with the one at Hermonville.

They were of the same model as the one that had razed the village, a newer Sturmpanzerwagen that was shaped more like an armored train car on its own pair of tracks. Two machine guns were mounted on each lateral side of each Panzer, and two more were in the back. They were symmetrical, with only a mounted heat ray—in place of what had probably been a 52-millimeter gun before—to indicate the front of the vehicle.

The two new vehicles sported the same iron cross insignia as the first one, but the third was also decorated with a hand-painted death's head under the heat ray armature.

Charming.

The welds holding the Martian power supply to the closest Panzer were cleaner than the first model's, and the mirror had a concave shape. Was it designed to focus the heat ray in a tighter pattern? That might make it more powerful.

"All three are Sturmpanzerwagen Model A9Vs," Grundig said with a wry, black smile. "The next Panzer is under development in Berlin, assuming the Martians haven't destroyed the city and the weapons factory yet." He let out a phlegmy chuckle.

The ghoul thought that was funny. Or did it just fit in with their plans? If these were the last three A9Vs in existence, it would be easier to conquer Europe.

"They're powered by a single engine and have none of the weaknesses the model sevens and eights suffered from in Mexico," Grundig continued. "They need less fuel and can handle any terrain. It turns out the British are working on a similar vehicle, and one of our spies obtained a copy of the plans. Isn't it amazing how rapidly technology has moved since the aliens attacked? And now they're back. It's almost . . . exciting."

"It's as if they're providing us with evolutionary pressure," Emil said, taking Grundig's bait.

"Yes! You understand! I had hoped Wegener's faith in you wasn't misplaced. That's it exactly. They're here to show us who should live and who isn't worthy, right?"

Emil nodded while willing the bile back down to where it belonged.

"Anyway, I guess you've already spotted some of the differences from the first Panzer?" Grundig asked.

"That mirror—"

"Focusing the beam gives us more intensity and range. We're trying to fabricate another one so we can outfit all three of them. But let's take a look at yours, yes?"

Wonderful. Emil had his own evolutionary weapon. Was it an opportunity in disguise? If Grundig was willing to call the Panzer with the improved heat ray Emil's weapon, that might make it easier to use it to defeat the other two Panzers, then to destroy this workshop.

The heat ray's arm exited the chassis as if it had always been there. The new concave mirror shone like a diamond on a new wedding ring. Emil had underestimated Wegener and his men. How skilled would they be after making the fifth weapon? Or the tenth? They had to be stopped.

"Leutnant! Your new squad leader is here!" Grundig's raised voice sounded like a congested pipe organ.

"Yes, sir!" said a familiar-sounding voice from inside the third Panzer.

Fluse's head popped up from the hatch on top of the vehicle. His eyes locked on Emil's, and he frowned.

Emil's heart jumped in his chest. This was where the weasel had been? Helping them build these weapons? How would Emil take over the Panzer with him breathing down his neck?

"Leutnant Fluse, this is Hauptmann Zimmerman," Grundig wheezed, giving another of his terrifying smiles. "Come out here and greet him properly." The Hauptman didn't know they'd been in the same unit before. What would he think if they told him?

Fluse climbed out of the vehicle, jumped to the ground, and approached, holding eye contact until he was close enough to see the Hauptmann's pips on Emil's collar.

He saluted.

Emil waited just long enough for Fluse's hand to waver before returning the salute.

"Well, we don't have a lot of time, so I'll let you men get acquainted on the job," Grundig continued. "Leutnant Fluse can show you where the wiring diagram is. See if you can integrate the ray this morning, then we'll take it out to the range for testing."

The men exchanged salutes, and Grundig left.

If Fluse wasn't going to acknowledge that they knew each other, Emil wouldn't, either. Less was more when it came to what Grundig knew.

But Schmidt had said that Wegener had his favorites. Was that how Fluse had ended up on this project? But why was he still a Leutnant? Wegener promoted everyone he liked. Had Fluse been removed from salvage detail because he couldn't cope with it? Or because he was a trusted insider?

Either way, Wegener's gang of idiots was the perfect place for Fluse, and getting anything done with him around would be nearly impossible. Maybe Emil could figure out how to send him away.

"So, Hauptmann Zimmerman," Fluse said. "Amazing. I figured you'd be back in Baden by now, hiding under your bed."

"Nope. I'm here. Commanding you." Emil gave a smile he hoped was half as frightening as Grundig's.

Fluse's lip curled.

"So, where's the coffee?" Emil asked, clapping his hands as if ready to get to work.

"Over by the—"

"Black, then," Emil said, nodding. "I'll meet you in the vehicle."

He pushed his way past Fluse without looking behind him. Fluse's boots echoed off the building's walls as he stomped to wherever the pot was. No reason not to make this fun while Emil could distract Fluse long enough to look inside the Panzer.

Even with the large doors at the back of the vehicle open, the interior was cramped and stank of stale body odor, fresh leather, and incompletely burnt diesel. The driving compartment sat in a cupola near the vehicle's middle. A disconnected wiring harness protruded from the front, near a tube with a lens affixed to one end.

It was impossible to fire the weapon and drive it at the same time.

Emil put his left eye up to the tube. Two horsehairs gave him a sight that sat just above the heat ray's mirror assembly. His hands fell to a lever for moving the ray up and down, and side to side. A microphone like the one Wegener had used during the hanging hung from another cable. Did it have a public address system? For ordering troops outside the vehicle? Was this where the system at the assembly area had come from?

The weapons harness was serviceable, but it would never have passed muster in Aachen. It had no strain relief and was cut exactly to the length needed to connect to the controls instead of leaving a few centimeters so a technician could repair it without splices.

"I hope you don't think you're going to make a habit of this, Zimmerman," Fluse said as a coffee mug appeared before Emil. "We're going to return to the real army at some point,"

That was an interesting statement. Fluse bore contempt for Wegener's army? Emil hadn't seen that coming.

"Excuse me?" he asked.

"I saw you with Wegener and Ritter in Hermonville," Fluse sneered. "You may have found a bunch of traitors to take you in, but this madness has to end. Central Command will find this place, shut it down, and commandeer these weapons for the real German Army."

Emil had to catch his breath. Fluse hated Wegener? And it wasn't because he wanted to conquer Europe? Or because he'd built these monstrous weapons? Or because he'd attacked and destroyed half of a village with no sign of enemy troops, or even because he might have been collaborating with the Martians?

No. If Fluse hated Wegener, it was because he'd broken away from the German Army. How very Fluse.

Was this some kind of test? No, Fluse wasn't that smart. And if Wegener trusted him, he wouldn't be wearing the same Leutnant pips he'd left the trenches with.

Did this make Fluse a potential ally? Was he trustworthy?

Grundig expected them to work on the Panzers together; and if there were more crew assigned to the task, they were nowhere to be found. Emil looked at the driving compartment in the cupola, then back at the firing controls. Controlling this thing would be a lot easier with another man—and for better or worse, all he had was Fluse.

Making Fluse an ally would give him that man.

But Fluse was a hothead and a known bad quantity. Who knew what he might do if Emil placed his safety in his hands? Or how quickly he might crack under pressure? Even this conversation was proof that Fluse couldn't keep his mouth shut. One little push, and he was betraying his lack of loyalty.

"Traitors?" Emil asked. "Wegener would have you on the end of a rope if he heard you say that. If you think I'm one of his men, why are you talking to me this way?"

Fluse's eyes grew wide. He started to shake. A single bead of sweat ran from his brow and down his right cheek.

"I . . . um . . . I . . ."

Either Fluse had developed an uncanny sense of guilt since

they'd been separated, or he was terrified. A pang of something resembling pity stabbed at Emil's chest.

"I'm not going to turn you in, Fluse."

Fluse let out a long sigh and sagged into one of the tiny stools welded to the Panzer's floor.

This plan had had the potential for a suicide mission from the start, but Emil had thought it would have been at the end of a heat ray or a rifle. Instead, he was facing it in the hands of the worst officer in the kaiser's army.

"You know what the difference is between us, Fluse?"

Fluse shook his head.

"Well, there are a lot of differences, but here's the one in front of us right now. You didn't like it here, so you waited for something to happen. For one of your vaunted superior officers to come and save you."

Fluse looked up from the stool, his brow furrowed.

"I don't like it here, either," Emil said, lowering his voice. "So I did something, and now I need your help to do more."

40

"No, this *woman* came on her own accord," Susan growled. "No one 'brought' her."

Several marines opened their mouths in surprise, while Captain Reynolds stood up, crossed his arms, and frowned. An awkward silence fell over the room, lasting between thirty seconds and a month. Susan had forced her way into the room and immediately started trouble. Would Reynolds take the tracker and throw her and James out? Or force Susan onto a ferry back to New Jersey?

Or cede command to her?

"This is Susan," James said, remembering Urich's admonishment back in 'Wicks and hoping an introduction would break the icy impasse.

"You're in uniform? James made it sound like this was an . . . unofficial mission." Susan was clearly not as worried about formal introductions as James was. Still, she extended a perfunctory hand to the captain.

Reynolds looked at her hand. Women didn't walk into the back rooms of pubs and shake hands in his Midwestern corner of the world. After a few seconds, he took it and said, "'Unofficial' is an excellent way to put it. But the uniforms will help if we're stopped for the curfew. You brought the tracker?"

"Yes, it's here," James said, shrugging off the pack and placing it on the table under the light. Susan placed the meter and antennas next to it.

"It's in a backpack?" Reynolds asked. "I was wondering how we'd carry it. That's a fantastic idea."

James extended a hand toward Susan, being careful not to point. "A fantastic idea from Susan."

Susan smiled.

"The uniforms will make it easier for you to move around during the curfew," James continued. "But are you sure they'll work with the Security Police?"

"We're here because whoever's behind this killed Christensen, Reeves, and Greenwood," boomed one of the men who was still seated at the table.

James flinched at the mention of Christensen. Of course, that was how Reynolds got them here. Not for an official investigation, but to avenge the deaths at Coney Island.

"Goddamn the SPs, the War Department, Bryan, and whoever set that bomb and killed our brothers," the man continued. "And goddamn what they do if they find us before we find them."

The room fell quiet again. It felt like a spontaneous moment of silence for the men lost the first time they'd headed out in search of a rogue radio signal. What would happen this time?

"How does the tracker work?" Reynolds asked. "Show us, and one of us will carry it."

James turned that idea over for a moment. "No, I'll carry it. I'll need to adjust it as we approach the transmitter. It's best if I keep it with me."

"At some point, you're going to find the signal, and we're going to shut it down, Brogan. There may be another bomb. There may be armed guards."

"We know," said Susan, stepping closer to James.

"We can't guarantee your safety." Reynolds looked James in the eye before continuing. "Show us how this works, then leave the city before the curfew starts."

"No one is safe if we don't do this," James said, "I know better than anyone else how this works, and I can use it to trace the signal to a specific building. You can go inside to check it out, and we'll wait in case I'm wrong."

And wait far enough away to keep Susan safe. But James didn't say out loud.

Reynolds nodded and faced Susan.

"I already said I'm staying," she said.

James picked up the meter and the whip antenna, and attached them. He switched the device on and checked the meter. It didn't need any time to warm up because he'd tested a few theories from the German power supply he'd found in the wreckage. He didn't have access to the exotic triodes that unit had, but he'd built the tracker using germanium diodes instead of tubes. It was lighter that way, and lost less power to heat.

Even so, James was shocked to see the meter register a strong signal right away. They were already on top of the transmission? He adjusted the sensitivity, and it responded as designed. His heart sped up with a mixture of pride and apprehension. The new circuits worked as designed, but that meant they were all close to danger.

The spies were nearby. Their broadcast station was in Manhattan. James had promised himself he'd protect Susan, but they were already in danger. Would they be able to get out of the way if there was any trouble? He swallowed.

"We're close already," James said.

Reynolds grimaced, his new scar accentuating his confusion.

James held up the meter and showed it to the captain.

"They're close. Probably here in Midtown."

41

I t was still chilly, even though it was after eight o'clock, and the sun was starting to break through the woods. Emil's coffee was beginning to cool, but it was still pleasantly strong and bitter. Would he miss getting it from the officer's mess?

He surveyed the path through the trees as he and his men walked to the security gate. If everything went well, they'd have to figure out how to navigate a Panzer down this narrow passageway and across the compound to Wegener's cottage.

Emil was here with Fluse to hijack their Panzer, disable the other two, and drive to meet the rest of their men at headquarters. Schmidt and Beckenbauer would stage a mutiny during today's training in Reims, taking advantage of the groundwork they'd been laying for the past week. The troops would meet them at Wegener's headquarters after eliminating the few soldiers still loyal to Wegener.

Eliminate. Such a polite euphemism for "kill." The kind of language an officer would use. Of course, Emil was an officer now, even if he hadn't earned his Hauptmann's pips the traditional way. That didn't mean he had to fall into the trap of not valuing life, though.

But Wegener and his army were prepared to take thousands of lives on their way to Paris—and when they got there, the killing would only continue.

"I'm not sure about this, Zimmerman," Fluse said.

They were standing in front of the door to the workshop. Fluse was shaking.

Emil had been worried about trusting Fluse, and he'd been right. Not because Fluse would sell him out to Wegener, but because he was falling apart before they started the mission.

Well, it wasn't like they had much choice. Emil couldn't operate the Panzer alone, and getting a better soldier into the compound overnight would be impossible. He'd have to deal with Fluse—after they were inside and out of earshot.

"Not sure?" Emil hissed. "You helped make these plans last night. You agreed, and they're counting on us. You can't back out now."

"But what if Grundig figures it out?" Fluse's eyes were welling with tears, and Emil noticed his unkempt hair for the first time. The man hadn't slept a wink last night.

"He will if we keep standing here arguing," Emil snapped. "Now shut up, and let's get inside and into the Panzer." He opened the door before Fluse could object.

Grundig was standing between two Panzers, talking to one of his Leutnants.

"Ah, Hauptmann Zimmerman," he wheezed. "Leutnant Fluse. It's so good to see you here early, and arriving together! Such a fine team!"

Emil nodded and smiled. Fluse frowned as if he'd swallowed a hand grenade.

Yes, a fine team. The best, assuming half of it didn't melt into a puddle on the floor.

"I've told the range to be ready for testing your heat ray today. I assume you'll have it finished soon?" Grundig broke into a fearful coughing fit then.

"Yes, sir," Emil said. "I'm hoping to power the ray up very soon."

Right around 9:45, if the plan held together. That was when Schmidt and Beckenbauer would start their mutiny. If Emil began too soon, the troops might be recalled to the compound. And if the rebellion started too soon, the Panzers might be dispatched to stop it.

"Outstanding," Grundig said. "Carry on, then."

Grundig expected Emil to power up the heat ray. So Emil would have no interruptions as he turned it on, ensured it was stable, and started firing on the other two Panzers.

Yesterday, Fluse had pointed out that Grundig was so focused on the heat rays that all the gunports were empty. Emil had thought they were empty because Grundig was waiting to arm them after the modifications were done, but it turned out they lacked ammunition for the guns. The other two Panzers would be harmless after Emil and Fluse disabled their heat rays.

The vehicles had originally been designed for large crews: six soldiers for the machine guns, two more to drive and navigate, and two more to use the 52-millimeter gun at the front. Grundig had redesigned the Panzers for a three-soldier crew: two for driving, one for the heat ray. But Emil and Fluse would have to operate their Panzer themselves.

They entered through the steel troop doors in the back. Emil fought the urge to close them behind him. He and Fluse needed to check everything out before starting, but there was no reason to attract undue attention by acting like they were hiding something. They would have made the same checks if they'd been preparing to test the ray, and the longer they acted normally, the better chance they had at pulling the plan off.

Emil set his coffee down on the floor and checked on Fluse. Putting him to work should settle his nerves.

"Let's verify everything," Emil said. "I'll check the wiring and the power supply. You take a look at the driving controls and make sure all of the gunports are closed."

Fluse stood there, frozen. So much for that idea.

Emil checked his watch. His heart was racing, and he started to sweat. He and Fluse had an hour before they needed to start the Panzer, but they still had a lot to do before then. He needed to help Fluse. The Leutnant had only ever directed combat from behind, and even that had gone badly. He had reason to be terrified, but he needed to overcome it—and quickly.

"I understand," Emil said. "You're scared. But the men are counting on us, and you hate Wegener as much as I do."

Fluse didn't move.

Emil crossed his arms and fought the urge to strike him. As satisfying as that would have been, it wouldn't help. Hitting Fluse, yelling at him, threatening him—none of that would help now.

"This is so easy for you, isn't it?" Fluse asked, a tear running down his cheek. "You've got no fear."

Emil recoiled at that. "Easy?" he asked, raising an eyebrow. Where was this going?

"Yes, easy. You were our best scout. How many attacks did you lead? Fifteen? Twenty? You never had to work at being a soldier. You strode into our unit, took over one of the most coveted spots, and did whatever you wanted." Fluse wiped his cheek with the back of his hand, looking more like an angry child than anything else.

"Coveted? You think I wanted to be a scout? You don't think I was afraid? Do you know what being a scout means? Do you think I enjoyed killing those . . ." Emil struggled for words. "Kids?" He thought of the gunner in no-man's-land.

Fluse shook his head and threw up his hands. "You took over my command, climbed higher than me in Wegener's ranks. And now you expect me to be like you." Tears welled in his eyes, and he was flushed from his neck to his cheeks. Was he . . . jealous?

Emil's heart was his throat. Fluse hadn't tried to court-martial and execute him because he was a bad soldier. Instead, Fluse saw him as a threat?

His head swimming, Emil took a deep breath and leaned against the wall. No time to worry about the past now. They had work to do.

"I don't know what you think happened in the trenches," Emil said. "None of that was easy for me. I was doing my best to survive—and in case you didn't notice, my best wasn't very good. You nearly got me killed on the battlefield and executed afterward." He smiled despite himself.

Fluse's mouth hung open. "You think that's funny?" The color receded in his face.

"Well . . . yeah. I do now. Back then, I only had to worry about you. There were no Martians and no Wegener. You were easy to manage."

The corners of Fluse's mouth turned up just a little.

"But I assure you, I hated killing every one of those men," Emil continued. "And I wanted nothing more than to go home every minute of every day. But good soldiers or not, we both have all of our soldiers and much of France counting on us right now. Please help me."

Fluse hugged himself, then let out a long sigh. "Yes. You're right. Let's get to work."

The wiring was solid. Emil disconnected the ray and checked each connection with a test light. It was ready.

Grundig had figured out how the Martian power supplies worked and set up simple voltage regulators with instrumentation for verifying the output level, load, and core temperature. Tesla had burned down a big piece of New York City presumably because he'd allowed his power supply to overheat. Grundig had avoided that so far. Emil would need to monitor the load when he used the ray and let the system cool before firing again.

Meanwhile, Fluse checked the cockpit. Driving and navigating alone wouldn't be easy, but if they disabled the other two Panzers quickly and left only small-arms fire to worry about, it should be okay.

Finally, they checked the intercom between fire control and the driver so they could talk to each other over the sound of the diesel engine, which sat only a few meters from them. The heat ray's armature covered the full 180 degrees at the front of the Panzer, but coordination would make it easier to swing in one direction or the other for aiming.

Emil closed the doors at 9:45 and verified that the hatch was locked. It was time. Fluse closed the gunports.

The next few minutes would decide their fate—and maybe the fate of all Europe. So many things could go wrong. Emil wiped his brow. What if the Panzer wouldn't move? They'd be sitting ducks for the other two. And what if the mutiny in Reims failed? They'd have to take on all of Wegener's officers with a single heat ray.

And, what if Fluse folded again? That was the most likely scenario.

"Are you ready?" Emil asked, looking the Leutnant straight in the eye.

"No," Fluse said. "But like you said, we have no choice."

"Good answer." And the only honest one.

They nodded to each other. Fluse started the diesel engine, and the steel chassis filled with an ungodly roaring. Emil put on his headset to drown out the racket and turned on the Martian power supply.

"I'm prepared to fire," Emil said into the intercom system. "Give me about forty-five degrees toward the other two Panzers."

"Understood," came the answer, sounding clear over the wood and ceramic headset.

The roar receded to a deep rumbling in the background. The Panzer's front swung toward the other two vehicles, providing a clear line of sight to both targets.

Grundig came running out onto the workshop floor, shouting and gesticulating.

"He wants to know why we didn't tell him to open the doors," Fluse said.

"Well, let me show him," Emil said.

He looked through the heat ray's sight, aimed at the armature on the closest Panzer, and opened fire. The eerie hum reverberated through the vehicle's steel walls as the device glowed orange, then red. Emil checked the power supply temperature out of the corner of his eye. It was climbing slowly, and he estimated he could engage the ray for about two minutes.

Grundig jumped up and down, alternating between gesticulating, screaming, and coughing as the other soldiers in the building pressed themselves against the walls in fear. At last, the target melted enough that it dropped to the floor, a desultory flame licking at its edges as it lay there.

Success. One of the two Panzers was little more than a troop carrier or a battering ram now, assuming that any of Grundig's men had the presence of mind to try to drive it. Emil's mouth went dry as the Panzer's engine and the excitement warmed him up.

Fluse cheered over the intercom. Emil turned and showed him a smile, then checked the temperature gauge. It read 75 percent. They needed to let it cool down. They were halfway finished in here, and things were going well.

Emil switched his headset to the public address system. "Attention," he said. "Leave this building now, and assemble near the general's headquarters for further instructions."

As he repeated the announcement two more times, a few soldiers fled out the door. But a small group went the other way —and piled into the third Panzer. The door closed, the engine started, and it moved to get around the disabled vehicle.

Emil swallowed and wiped his brow. Damn. Why did they have to make this difficult? Would he have to kill them?

"They're coming for us!" Fluse screamed. It was loud enough that Emil heard him through the headset, so Emil switched to the intercom.

There were four or five men in that Panzer, and Emil couldn't sight their heat ray from this angle. By the time he could, they'd be able to target him. Who would win? Would it be easier for a larger crew to fight, assuming they had experience with the vehicle? What would happen if both Panzers were destroyed? Would it turn into a melee? Five men versus two?

Emil could hit their fuel tank while they tried to maneuver their vehicle. That would disable the weapon and kill them. He swallowed again, picturing the men inside the Panzer bursting into flames the way Degenscheide had.

This was war, after all. But they had begun the war on the same side.

"Fire!" Fluse screamed into the intercom. "Fire! What are you waiting for?"

The mutiny would have started in Reims by now. If Emil didn't act, they'd have to face one of these monstrosities. The men in this workshop had switched allegiances to Wegener. To a madman. They were the enemy now.

Emil aimed for the fuel tank and fired.

The other Pazner shifted, and he tracked it with the armature, wondering if he'd need to melt steel to ignite the fuel. His answer came with a deafening explosion.

The soldiers inside were dead.

Coldness gripped Emil's stomach. There was no time for mourning, or for celebration.

"Drive!" he shouted into the intercom. "Drive! Head for the back doors!"

Fluse gunned the engine, spun the vehicle, and drove.

The Panzer tore through the steel doors like a well-kicked soccer ball through an unsuspecting bakery window. But instead of stopping, it headed directly for an oak tree that was tall and thick enough that Wotan might have planted it himself.

Emil ripped off the headset, ran to Fluse, and shook him out of his stupor.

The Panzer stopped less than a meter from the massive tree trunk.

"Which way?" Emil asked. He opened one of the gunports so he could look out—

And heard the unmistakable howl of a Martian Wanderer.

42

"What? What do you mean, *already?*" one of Captain Reynolds's marines asked.

"I'm getting a signal now," James said. "A strong one." He used a thumbscrew to set a new baseline on the tracker.

"Are you sure it's them?" Reynolds asked. "Is there a speaker so we can listen?"

"No sound," James answered. "No audio amplifier or discriminator. It would kill the battery faster and attract attention while we're sneaking around after curfew. Your operators are talking to them, so unlike the first time, they're broadcasting on a discrete frequency. I tuned the receiver to it."

"How far away do you think it is?" Susan asked.

James did some math in his head. "If I have to guess, less than three miles."

Reynolds whistled, then checked his watch. "It's not even nine p.m. yet. We should head out now. We might be able to find the transmitter before the cops start enforcing the curfew." He looked at Susan. "You'll stay here."

"No, I won't."

Reynolds looked at James, one eyebrow raised. Susan

frowned and crossed her arms. Deep down, James didn't want Susan to come, but he'd agreed to it back in Princeton and wasn't going to turn on her because Reynolds was questioning his decision. They'd stay out of the way. He'd make sure she was safe.

"She's coming with me," James said.

"Well, then she's—"

"I'm my own responsibility, Captain."

Reynolds shrugged, then turned and told his men to prepare. They claimed their weapons, and the group exited the pub through a back door.

James looked west. Nothing lay in that direction except the docks, warehouses, and a few ships. He considered the directional antenna but wasn't sure how well it would work if they were still a few miles away from the signal.

"I suppose they might be broadcasting from a ship?" he asked no one in particular.

"Doubtful," one of Reynolds's men said. "Anything docked for more than a week would attract attention."

It was as good as any reason to head east into Midtown. They started in that direction, with the men forming an irregular circle around James and Susan. The crowds on the streets had thinned while they were in the bar, and no one noticed or cared about a group of marines walking east on 45th Street. Uniformed soldiers were unremarkable.

The signal rose within a couple of blocks.

"Hold on a moment," James said. "I need to readjust the meter."

"We're going in the right direction, then?" Reynolds asked.

"Definitely."

"I wonder where it could be coming from?"

"Would the tallest building in the world work for you?" Susan asked, pointing southeast. The golden top of the Metropolitan Life Building scraped the skyline.

There were plenty of tall buildings in midtown, but this one had a huge cupola—an excellent spot for an antenna—and the structure had access to plenty of electric power. It was perfect. Why hadn't James thought of that? He considered kissing Susan, but she would have punched him in the nose in return.

"That seems like a decent direction to head in," Reynolds said.

They did, and the signal rose steadily as they approached the building. It was 9:45 p.m. when they reached Madison Square Park, directly across Madison Avenue from the skyscraper.

"The signal is nearly half as strong as it was in Coney Island," James said. "We're close."

"Nearly half?" Reynolds asked.

"They don't need to saturate the airwaves like when they were trying to *block* the radios. Remember, they're trying to pretend they're on the other side of the ocean. They just need to be stronger than the signal from there."

A pair of police officers approached as the group entered the park. "It's getting late, folks," one of the officers said. "Time to head home."

James took a step back, letting the marines block the officers' view of him and the pack on his back. Reynolds, already at the front, stepped up to address them. Their conversation was inaudible, but after a moment the cops nodded and walked away. Reynolds had been right about the uniforms.

James breathed a sigh of relief.

"What did you tell them?" Susan asked.

"That we're a special detachment of marines on a training mission," Reynolds said, "Fortunately, they weren't worried about you. Are we sure this is the building? I don't want to force our way into the wrong place."

It was time to test the directional antenna. James shrugged off the backpack and placed it on a nearby park bench. He disconnected the whip, unfolded his experimental aerial, and attached it so it was pointed at the cupola atop the Metropolitan Life Building across the avenue.

"What's this?" Reynolds asked.

"The best I can do," James said.

Using a directional to pinpoint a signal this close was a stretch, but it would have to do. James picked up the meter. It was reading near the limit, higher than it had with the other antenna. He swiveled the antenna a few degrees away from the building, and the meter dropped.

"It's working!" Susan said.

"What's working?" Reynolds asked.

"A directional antenna," James replied. "It can give us an idea of where the signal is coming from. I didn't trust it enough to use it to find the signal until we had a clear line of sight with a potential target. When I point this at the building, the signal jumps." He turned the antenna and showed Reynolds the meter. "When I turn it away, it drops." He turned the antenna and showed the meter to the captain again.

Reynolds nodded. "Makes sense to me. You think the transmitter is in the cupola?"

James stroked his chin as he looked up at the building, wishing he'd brought field glasses or a telescope instead of spending all that time playing with the new antenna. But they couldn't see much from the street anyway.

"The antenna is going to be high," he said. "But depending on how much free rein they have in the building, the broadcast equipment might be anywhere in the tower."

"All right, men," Reynolds said to his marines. "We're headed in there. Remember what we discussed. Our first and only priority is to knock them off the air so the real transmission can get through, not to question or detain anyone."

The men nodded.

Reynolds turned back to Susan and James. "Now, I can tell you to stay behind and out of sight so the police don't give you any trouble about the curfew," he said with a tight smile. "If you hear any shots, get the hell out of here before the SPs show up. We'll be back if it's the wrong building."

James swallowed. In his excitement over the antenna, he'd forgotten the other option. This could still be the wrong building.

He hefted the backpack and walked with Susan back into the park, taking refuge under a stand of trees well away from the arc lamps lining the park.

The city was always a little warmer than Princeton. But without the distraction of the marines, the chill settled in. Susan pulled her coat tight and huddled closer to James.

"What do you think they'll find?" she asked.

"Hopefully, a small group of surprised but peaceful radio operators," James said. The last time they'd found a trap, it had been a blocking signal. This transmitter was run by people pretending to be in legitimate operators. Would they be military? Spies?

Susan chuckled. "I'm proud of you, you know. I know it's tough for you to take a stand like this, but you're doing the right thing, James. You could be saving thousands of lives right now."

James hadn't given it much thought after deciding in that restaurant to do something. He'd done an admirable job of staying busy. Busy finding Urich right away. Busy coming here to see Reynolds. Busy building the tracker without Seward or Fleming getting wise. But it felt good to stop hiding and take action.

Soft popping noises interrupted his reverie. Flashes of light, followed by more popping noises, emanated from the gold cupola at the top of the tower.

It was a gunfight.

43

"Martians! Martians! They're here for us." Fluse's voice was inaudible over the rumbling diesel engine, but Emil didn't need to read lips to understand.

They needed to get to Wegener's cottage to see if the aliens were interfering with the plan. It was possible a Wanderer had strayed closer to the compound than usual, and there was nothing to be afraid of. But getting Fluse to settle down would take too long.

Emil gestured for Fluse to step aside. He put on the driver's headset and pointed to the fire controls. Fluse paused, then stepped over and prepared himself.

Emil slammed the Panzer into a spin and turned it toward the entry gate. He'd never driven one of these things before, but if Fluse had figured it out, he'd be damned if he couldn't.

His view was all but completely blocked from the driver's position. It was a miracle Fluse had driven as poorly as he had. But no Martians were visible from their vantage point, so he straightened the vehicle and angled it past the gate and the empty guard post.

"I see Grundig!" Fluse said over the intercom.

The ghoul was crouched over a tree stump, coughing his lungs out. One quick blast from the heat ray, and he'd never create another weapon again. The irony would be delicious, but Emil and Fluse needed to keep moving.

"He won't make it far," Emil said. "We need to stay on mission."

He gunned the engine. Panzers didn't move fast. Even with the throttle all the way open, the vehicle was going as quickly as a man in a hurry to help wash the dinner dishes.

The ride to the edge of the woods was short, bumpy, and frustrating. The rough forest path, combined with the slow Panzer, made the trip as bad as a one-wheeled carriage pulled by a three-legged horse, but its sheer mass meant it was nearly unstoppable. They lumbered over stones, holes, and a few small trees before breaking out of the hedgerow that separated Grundig's workshop from the rest of Wegener's compound.

Emil stared through the narrow slit in the driver's canopy, and his mouth fell open. The Martians were here. They'd finally attacked. Why had they ignored Wegener for so long?

Two Wanderers ranged over the tents. Emil slammed the Panzer into reverse and pulled back into the trees.

Fluse came close to bursting Emil's eardrums through the intercom with a high-pitched whine. Emil dropped far enough out of the driver's canopy to scowl at him, and the Leutnant cowered against the vehicle's front.

Another Martian howl—the first since they'd left the workshop—rose in the air. Had one of them seen the vehicle? Emil braced himself for the hum of a heat ray, but it didn't come. He turned the engine off, pulled off his headset, and peered through one of the gunports. They couldn't cross the open field with two Wanderers out there, and the view was too limited to pick out an alternate path. If only Emil had a pair of field glasses.

He looked back up toward the driver's canopy. There was a leather pouch next to one of the track controls. A dirty pair of field glasses sat inside. He cleaned them with the heel of his hand and use them to peer through the driver's slit.

One of the Wanderers was farther away, standing near the gate to Reims. Emil could make out the outlines of soldiers, but it was hard to tell what they were doing and impossible to discern who they were loyal to. The other Wanderer was positioned near the mess tents.

Emil couldn't find a safe path from inside the Panzer; his field of vision was too narrow. He stepped toward the troop doors at the back of the vehicle.

"What are you doing?" Fluse screamed.

"I need to see what's going on outside," Emil said. "If the Martians notice this Panzer, they're sure to open fire."

Fluse nodded, still shaking.

"You can stay in here, if you think it makes you any safer." Emil then thought about what he'd just done to the soldiers inside one of the Panzers and shivered.

He picked up his rifle and opened the troop doors. It was cold outside, but it was bracing after a half hour in the Panzer. Emil shifted his gaze toward the compound as he stepped out—

And nearly knocked Grundig over.

The Hauptmann was leaning forward, hands on his knees, gasping for air like a hooked trout. He raised his eyes from the ground, and his rheumy eyes expanded with shock.

"You . . . you . . ."

"Traitor?" Emil asked. "Thief? Murderer?" He stepped toward Grundig, grabbed him by the collar, and hefted him to his feet, surprised by how light he was. Their eyes met, but there was no one home. Grundig's shallow breath stank of rot and decay as he muttered to himself.

The stink eventually forced Emil to let him go. Grundig stumbled back and landed on the ground, wincing.

"What did you do?" The Hauptmann started to cry. "It's ruined. It's all ruined."

Emil didn't have time for this. It was tempting to leave

Grundig there and let him bawl like a child who hadn't gotten his treat, but he was still a dangerous man.

Emil grabbed him again and dragged him into the Panzer.

"He's a prisoner," Emil told Fluse. "Tie him up."

"With what?"

"Use the shoulder strap for your rifle. You're not using it."

Emil left the Panzer again and walked to the edge of the trees. The Wanderers were still standing in the same positions. He might be able to navigate the Panzer as far as the mess tents before they noticed him, but then what?

Another howl rose, followed by the hum of a Wanderer heat ray. It fired in the direction of Reims. Faraway screams emanated from out of sight. Small-arms fire and a couple of hand grenades followed the screams. Emil peered through the field glasses again and made out soldiers trying to stay under cover while firing on the closest Wanderer.

Fools! They would get themselves slaughtered. Were they Wegener's men? Or had Beckenbauer and Schmidt started the mutiny? Did it matter? Martians were here—and they were attacking.

Both Wanderers moved toward Reims then. Emil had to do something before there was no one left alive.

He ran back into the Panzer. Grundig was lying on the floor, still muttering to himself. His hands were secured behind his back. At least Fluse had gotten that right.

"Take the driver's controls," Emil shouted. "We have to help whoever the Martians are attacking."

"What?"

"You heard me," Emil said, locking eyes with Fluse.

"They'll kill us!"

"Maybe. Or they'll be distracted enough that we can take one of them down. If we wait here, they'll kill us after they're done with them."

Fluse's chin trembled.

"We're not going to sit here and do nothing," Emil concluded.

Fluse bit his lip and put on his headset. "Where are we going?"

"Wegener's headquarters. But we're going to fire on the move."

Emil went to the fire control station, put on his headset, and switched on the power supply. His throat was dry again; he hadn't had a drink since that cup of coffee this morning. He sighted the closest Wanderer, standing still and no longer firing on the troops. Hopefully, whoever was leading those men had them under good cover.

Emil fired the ray. It hit the Wanderer on the underside of its water tower chassis, where it met one of the spindly legs. If his attack on the first Panzer was any indication, the leg should overheat in less than a minute.

The Panzer sped over the clearing, and Emil struggled to keep the ray focused on one spot. Neither he nor Fluse spoke as the Panzer barreled toward the rows of mess tents standing between them and Wegener's cottage.

The Wanderer's leg burst into flames and fell to the ground. Its body followed. Emil let out a long breath while Fluse cheered into the intercom.

One down. They'd taken out a Wanderer! Had anyone ever done that before?

The other Wanderer spun on its spindly legs, its heat ray following the bottom in a wide arc. Emil's heart leaped into his throat. Facing a Wanderer that knew they were there was a different story.

"Take us behind that tent!" Emil shouted, hoping Fluse would understand.

Fluse did, and the Panzer drove behind one of the tents. The canvas and wood burst into flames a few seconds later.

But the Wanderer didn't move. What was it thinking? Was it not used to resistance?

"Now to the side that's burning," Emil barked into the intercom. "I need a shot!" He half expected Fluse to argue, but the Panzer moved forward to where Emil was just able to sight one side of the Wanderer.

"I'm going to fire, and he's probably going to shoot back," Emil said. "As soon as he does, start moving to the next tent."

He put the crosshairs on the closest leg and engaged the heat ray. The Wanderer returned fire seconds later but only struck the burning embers in front of them. Fluse moved the Panzer forward, and Emil was able to hold his shot a few seconds longer.

Emil let out his breath again. If he kept holding it, he'd pass out before they won or lost. Three or four more exchanges like that, and they might make it through alive.

Fluse spun the Panzer around, and Emil knew what he was thinking. The Panzer inched forward, and Emil fired as soon as he had a shot, hoping the Wanderer hadn't moved so much that he was hitting a different leg. The seam between the tentacle and the craft started to glow before it could return fire. Fluse dodged the Panzer back, and another tent burst into flames.

The Wanderer's leg was glowing. Emil had to hit it again before it cooled.

"Forward!" he screamed into his headset. "Now!"

Fluse complied.

Emil found the shot and took it. He closed his eyes and held the firing button with every inch of his strength.

The leg burst into flames. The Wanderer howled and fell to the ground.

Cheers rose over the sound of the Panzer's engine. Emil sprawled forward, leaning against the heat ray's controls, gasping for breath.

The familiar stink of rotting meat filled his nostrils. "That would have been easier with my other weapon," said Grundig from over Emil's shoulder. "But it would have destroyed the Panzer, too."

"What?" Emil spun around to look at Grundig, who was teetering to keep his balance with his hands and arms tied together.

"My other weapon could have taken out both Wanderers at once, but it would have taken the Panzer, and most of the compound with it." Grundig grinned. "Want to see it?"

44

James couldn't tear his eyes away from the skyscraper. Flashes, followed by the muffled sound of gunfire, continued for what seemed like forever. His heart raced, and even as the evening chill reached his bones, he wiped sweat from his forehead. He was back at Coney Island, but this time Reynolds had gone up with six marines instead of sending three and staying with James.

He held his breath, waiting for an explosion that never came.

"James, we need to go," Susan said, tugging on his sleeve.

James gasped for air as he snapped back to the present. Go? That was what Reynolds had said to do. Had he known he'd lead his men into a trap again? What would happen if James and Susan left? Had Reynolds stopped the transmission? What if he hadn't? This was the only way to stop the conspiracy.

James tore his eyes from the building and looked at Susan. Her eyes were pleading. She was right; they had to go before the New York City Police—or, worse, the SPs—arrived. The firefight might spread to the street at any moment. It was time to head to the Hudson and find an illicit ferry out of the city, or a place to hide until curfew was over—

The tracker! James could check it to see if the marines had disabled the broadcast.

"Wait," he said.

He turned the device on and trained the antenna on the building. The transmitter was still on the air. James's heart sank. At Coney Island, the transmission had only ended because it had been booby-trapped. Would Reynolds have to kill the conspirators this time? Or would the captain be killed himself? He'd sent another group of marines into a trap—and that had done nothing to stop the conspiracy.

"What are you doing?" Susan asked.

"They haven't stopped the broadcast," James said without taking his eyes off the meter. "It was all for nothing."

"That doesn't matter right now. We need to go, James."

"Of course it matters. If Reynolds and his men are captured before they stop it, what happens to them?" He stared at the meter, willing it to fall to zero.

"What can we do? Charge in front of a bullet? It's no good if you get yourself killed!"

James started to respond, but the meter fell to zero. They did it!

"Look!" he said, pointing at the meter.

"They did it?" Susan asked. "Or is it out of power?"

James's eyes fell to the power indicator, and he fought back tears. Susan was right. The battery had run out. The tracker had been running for nearly an hour. Even with James's new approach to the power supply, that was a lot to ask from it.

Without the battery, he had no way to be sure when Reynolds had succeeded, no matter how long he and Susan waited. He was blind without it. They could stand out there all night and never know if Reynolds had succeeded.

They were literally powerless.

Power. James had spotted a power supply in the wreckage from Coney Island. A power supply that let the conspirators saturate the airwaves all the way to Long Island. . . .

He looked at Susan and grinned. Power!

"What?" she asked.

"You're a genius, you know that?"

45

"Another weapon?" Emil asked as his stomach lurched. Grundig had built something that could destroy two Wanderers in one shot. Was it some kind of wide-angle heat ray? A super bomb?

"Yes, yes, it's fascinating!" Grundig said. "You see, it generates—"

"Hold it." Before Emil could listen to the ghoul, he wanted to learn if anyone else had survived the attack. Were his men alive? Were Wegener's loyalists still in charge? "Let's go outside and find the other men while you tell me about your wonderful toy,"

If he talked to Grundig outside, Emil could create some distance and relief from the Hauptmann's breath, too. That was reason enough to get out of the Panzer.

Emil wanted to learn about this weapon and decide if it should be destroyed or put to use against the Martians. He'd started the day wanting to make sure all three of Grundig's Panzers were destroyed forever. But after the encounter with the Martians, he was having second thoughts. The vehicle had proven to be a valuable weapon against the Martians.

Grundig stepped in front of Emil and held out his hands to be untied.

"After we find someone to put you under guard," Emil said, puttting one hand on Grundig's shoulder and leading him out of the Panzer. He beckoned for Fluse to follow.

They walked a few meters and were rounding one of the mess tents when Beckenbauer came running with Miller and a few other soldiers in tow. Emil heaved a sigh of relief. But where was Ludwig?

"That was you?" Beckenbauer asked, gasping for breath. "You destroyed the Wanderers?"

Emil nodded. "What happened in Reims? Did you have time to start the rebellion?"

"Yes. We'd already taken control of the troops and marched back to the compound, and the Martians were waiting for us here. We lost a lot of men." Beckenbauer set his mouth in a line.

Emil's stomach lurched again. More men were gone.

"Did the mutiny attract the Martians' attention?" he wondered out loud.

"I doubt we fired more than a dozen shots," Schmidt said as he approached.

So what brought the Martians now? Had Wegener summoned them somehow? No. That was ridiculous. He wouldn't collaborate with them, would he? And why would they work with humans? To Martians, humans were food, not allies.

"Did you see Ritter?" Emil asked.

"No," Beckenbauer said as Schmidt shook his head.

Had Ritter fled? Or was he with Wegener somewhere else? Emil scanned the perimeter as he wiped sweat from his brow.

"We should check those two Wanderers and make sure they're disabled," Beckenbauer said.

That was an excellent idea. Both had collapsed and burned. But what they were capable of withstanding?

Emil nodded. They set off for the closest Wanderer with Schmidt and a few other soldiers in tow.

The Wanderer's spindly legs formed a knot of tangled metal

underneath where it lay. A door was cracked open on one side, where the seams were so well-formed that they'd been invisible while the giant craft had been walking upright. Smoke was pouring out from the crack.

A tentacle not unlike the ones hanging off some of the Wanderers protruded from the hatch. But this tentacle was the color of underclothes that had been washed too many times. A sickly, unhealthy color.

Without a word, Schmidt approached the alien craft. Emil brought his weapon up to cover him.

With his rifle ready to fire like a sidearm in his right hand, Schmidt gingerly touched the door with his left to test the temperature. It must have been cool, because he opened the door—

And the Martian fell out. Or, rather, it poured out.

Beckenbauer retched. Emil started to heave, thankful he hadn't finished that mug of coffee.

"Looks like it tried to escape the fire," Schmidt said, unfazed.

There were no legs, only tentacles that seemed to be the inspiration for the snakelike tentacles on their Wanderers. If Emil had seen a drawing of the alien, he would have thought it too far-fetched. Set on either side of its misshapen soccer ball of a body were giant black saucers right out of a nightmare. Only a child who'd eaten too many sugar cookies before bedtime could have imagined them. Were they eyes? They were the size of cake plates, with no lenses or pupils.

"I still can't get over those ears," Grundig said from behind Emil.

"What?" Emil asked, unable to tear his eyes away from the creature.

"Those circles. Those are its ears." Grundig approached the Martian and touched one of the strange organs. The Hauptmann was smiling. He liked dead things nearly as much as he liked making the things that killed them.

"You've seen one before?" Emil asked. "You're familiar with their biology?"

Grundig shrugged as if to say, *Of course.* "Their eyes"—he pointed to black circles near the front of the body—"are tiny. I'm not even sure if they're useful for much more than sensing day or night. They seem to be more dependent on sound than sight. Although they seem to understand how much we rely on sight, since they've used the Smoke as a cover and to confuse our troops."

A group of soldiers formed around the Wanderer. Grundig stood up straight to address his audience. He seemed to be enjoying them as much as he enjoyed the dead body.

"An American—I think his name was Johnson? Jackson?—he noticed these organs during the first attack and deduced that their howls were more than simple signals. They're encoded with sounds we can't hear. Edison discovered him, and his work was the basis for their radio research."

"What's that?" asked one soldier, pointing to something near the bottom of the Martian's body, close to where the tentacles extended from it.

"That's its filter." Grundig pulled something away from the body and exposed a beak-like mouth.

"Filter?" Emil asked.

"Yes. Their weakness to Earth's microbes was what stopped the first invasion. They breathe through a filter now."

"That little thing keeps them from getting sick?" someone asked, laughing mockingly.

"Yes," Grundig answered. "Their filters protect them from the microbes. Some of them must have survived and figured out what happened."

Emil shivered. The Martians had learned from the first attack, and they'd adapted. While humans had figured out how to use Martian weapons on one another, the aliens had figured out how to defeat humans.

More soldiers trickled in, with Ludwig bringing up the rear.

Emil let out another sigh and embraced his friend, surprising himself with his lack of inhibition.

Fluse took custody of Grundig and stepped aside to speak to Miller.

"You made it," they both said, then laughed.

"So you're not content with being a Hauptmann," Ludwig said. "You've made yourself a Martian killer, too." He winked at Emil.

"Only out of necessity," Emil said. "But it does give one ideas, doesn't it?"

"You mean to take this Panzer home with us?"

Home? Ludwig was ready to go home?

"You want to take the battle to the aliens back home?" Emil asked, pointing at the Panzer. "With this?"

Ludwig shrugged.

Hearing the same idea from Ludwig was intriguing. But how much could a small group of rebels do? Did Emil want to be responsible for building more weapons? What would happen to the hardware if they won? Would it fall into the hands of another Wegener?

Something buzzed past Emil's head then. Less than a second later, he hit the ground face down like he'd been struck by the Panzer he'd been standing next to.

"Sniper!" Ludwig shouted, lying on top of Emil as if protecting him.

Within seconds, all of the soldiers were on the ground. Some of them were crawling toward one side of a mess tent for cover.

Emil's head swam. He was facing away from the Panzer, and his view was blocked. He tried to rise, but Ludwig held him down. Had that bullet been for him? He'd just started to think about facing the Martians, and now another man might be trying to kill him.

"Where did it come from?" Emil asked.

Ludwig only grunted in response.

Another shot rang out. Miller, who was lying behind Emil,

howled in pain. The shot was within hearing range that time. The sniper was approaching.

"Where?" Emil repeated, calmer this time. This wasn't the trenches, but it was close enough. Instinct kicked in.

"Back there." Ludwig flicked his head back and to his right. "Let's move behind that tent."

Emil crawled on elbows and knees, making for the tent as another shot struck the ground near his heels. He rolled to his side and unshouldered his weapon. Whoever it was seemed to like him. Two could play at this game.

Beckenbauer was working his way from the far side of the tent, with Schmidt and four other soldiers in tow. "Who's got a rifle with a scope?" Beckenbauer asked.

A rifle moved up the line and into his hands. Emil shifted so Beckenbauer could point the scope down where the shots seemed to be coming from.

He sighted downrange. Emil let out a long breath. Beckenbauer was a better shot; and with a scope, there was almost no way he'd miss.

"That Schwein," he whispered.

Emil tilted his head questioningly.

"It's Wegener," Beckenbauer said, still peering through the scope.

Emil gasped, then remembered what Schmidt had told him. Wegener had shot his previous rival. He'd shouldered his rifle, taken aim, and put one between the officer's eyes.

Emil was almost flattered. But how had Wegener known? There'd been so much confusion since Emil and Fluse had taken the Panzer. How had the general known Emil wasn't just using the Panzer to stop the Martians?

"Do you see Ritter?" Emil asked.

"No. He's alone."

"I want him alive. There are too many open questions."

"Hopefully, this scope is aligned," Beckenbauer said and

squeezed off a shot. "Verdammt. Tried for the shoulder, but I'm not sure if it was a little low."

Where was Ritter? There were close to fifty men gathered in and around the mess tents, but no sign of the Hauptmann or his cavalry. Had the Martians killed them? Had they fled? Or would Emil and his men face Ritter's mounted troops next?

Either way, Emil couldn't leave Wegener to bleed out. He needed to talk to him.

"Ludwig, send some men to flank him," Emil said, hoping he wasn't sending them to their deaths. "We'll keep watch from here."

Three men took the long way around and approached Wegener from behind as Emil held his breath. A few minutes later, they signaled for the rest of the soldiers to come over.

Wegener was spread out on the ground. Beckenbauer hadn't hit him in the shoulder, but in the chest and near his heart. The general was gasping for breath. He wouldn't last long, and Emil needed answers.

"Zimmerman," Wegener gasped.

Emil knelt beside him.

"You've doomed us," he rasped.

Emil swallowed.

"They were going to work with us."

They? No. Wegener couldn't have meant that.

Emil put a hand out to keep his balance as his mind raced through the past few weeks. Was that why they'd been able to pick up the scrap metal? Had the Martians been collecting it for them?

"The Martians?" Emil asked.

The men surrounding him and Wegener gasped.

"Would peace with the Martians really have been that bad?" Wegener managed a weak smile.

"What was your plan?" Emil asked, his voice rising as his mind raced through the possibilities. "What did you do?" Had

Wegener been helping the Martians? Helping them find cities and towns to destroy? Helping them find . . . food?

"I . . . tried to find a way . . . for some of us to live. They would have let the strong survive . . . eaten only the weak." Wegener groaned and tried to shift.

So, some humans would have lived, and others would have served as the Martians' food supply. How had Wegener made this deal? Who had he talked to? The aliens hadn't spoken to anyone the first time they'd come.

Or had they?

"But as soon as the mutiny started, I knew it was you," Wegener said. "I let you in, and you betrayed me."

"Did you call the Martians in today?" Emil asked.

"No. They must have been watching . . . decided that if we fought among ourselves, we were too much trouble." Wegener's face was turning gray.

"How did you talk to them? Who did you talk to?"

Wegener's head swayed back and forth on the ground. He groaned again. "Chu . . . Chu . . ."

And he died.

Emil rocked back on his heels, landed on the ground, and rested his forehead on his knees. They were doomed.

No one said a word.

"He wasn't lying, you know," Grundig finally wheezed.

Emil jumped to his feet. "You were in on this?"

"Of course I was. Why do you think I made my other weapon?"

His other weapon. The one that could have destroyed two Wanderers. Had Wegener been planning a double cross?

"Of course . . . ?" Emil asked, tilting his head.

"Yes, of course." Grundig pointed at Wegener's corpse. "He was a madman. He really thought he could make a deal with that Ausländer and his Martian allies. It was obvious they would eventually come for us. So I made sure I was ready. My Panzer did good against them, no?" He laughed, then broke into a coughing fit.

So Grundig accused Wegener of being a madman, and now he was cackling over his weapons like a boy with his toys.

Emil had to steady himself as the implications hit him. Martian sympathizers. Traitors. That was how they'd managed these new attacks.

Earth had seen them coming last time. No one had known the meteors hurling toward the planet were their craft, but they'd been aware that something was coming.

But there'd been no warning this time. Emil had assumed it was because they'd been in the trenches and no one had told them anything. But what if the Martians had never left? What if they'd been able to prepare this time, with the help of sympathizers?

What was coming next?

"What do you mean by 'that Ausländer and his Martian allies?'" Emil asked, stepping toward Grundig and grabbing the front of his uniform. "Do you know who he spoke to? Or what their plans are? Who else is working with them?"

Grundig whined as if he was in pain, then broke into another coughing fit. Emil let him go as the stench of his breath hit him. Grundig fell to his knees and coughed up black phlegm.

"Untie me," he moaned. "Please."

Emil nodded. Ludwig reached down and loosened the straps around Grundig's wrists, then helped him back to his feet.

"Now, talk," Emil said.

"After Wegener took over, he was approached by a brown-skinned man from the East. Turkey? Mongolia? Syria? Who can tell them apart? He said he had powerful 'friends' who could help." Grundig coughed into his hand and took a deep breath.

Ludwig, Schmidt, and Beckenbauer leaned in to listen.

"Wegener laughed at him, but Chuchan gave him this." Grundig reached into his back pocket, pulled out a leather pouch, and handed it to Emil.

Fluse walked up with Miller, who was leaning on his shoulder.

"Are you okay?" Emil asked. "Do we need to find a medic?"

Miller nodded. "We already did. It's fine."

Emil opened Grundig's pouch and found a carefully folded piece of paper. On it were schematics for a circuit that would draw power from a Martian power supply. Grundig hadn't figured out how to use it. He'd been given the instructions.

By a Martian sympathizer.

Ludwig peered over Emil's shoulder and stared at the paper, eyebrows furrowed.

"Instructions on how to use the Martian hardware," Emil said for the benefit of Ludwig and the other soldiers, then looked back at Grundig. "You used this to build the Panzers?"

He already knew the answer but hoped to gain some time to think. Time to sort it all out. Wegener was dead. Ritter seemed to be gone. But now there was a larger threat to worry about. A threat that should have ended the kaiser's silly war and unified all of Europe, if not the world. Instead, Wegener had been planning his own conquest.

"Of course I did," Grundig said. "Should I have refused? Should I have waited for them to come? Our weapons were toys compared to theirs. But I improved on those plans and built my other weapon. One that not even Wegener expected." He flashed a smile that would have curdled fresh milk.

What terror had this lunatic built?

"Can we contact this man?" Emil asked. "Can we figure out what the Martians are planning to do next?"

"You don't need to talk to them. They're going to come here tomorrow, destroy Reims, and then head to Paris. Wegener wanted to join them."

Emil's blood turned to ice water. It would all start tomorrow, and Reims would be first.

"They're coming here tomorrow," Emil repeated.

Grundig nodded.

Emil looked at the Panzer, then at the soldiers. How far could they run in the next eighteen hours? No. He couldn't leave Reims to be destroyed. Even if he did, it was only a matter of time before the Martians would catch them.

And they couldn't fight them with a single Panzer.

"This new weapon," Emil said. "It can help?"

"Yes, it can stop them," Grundig answered. "All of them. But at a cost,"

"What cost?" Emil sneered. Was Grundig going to blackmail him?

"It will permanently disable every Wanderer nearby. Everything electronic, really. Radios. Trucks. Panzers." Grundig looked at the Panzer they were standing next to.

"I'm fine with that," Emil said.

The men who were near enough to hear nodded, too. Ludwig pulled out a cigar and lit it.

"It'll also destroy everything within a few hundred meters of it," Grundig said.

"A few hundred meters?"

"At least."

"So it's a bomb?"

"Of sorts, yes."

Emil sighed and looked at Ludwig, who shrugged.

"We're going to save a city from the Martians with a bomb?" Emil asked.

"I just told you, it will disable their Wanderers," Grundig said. "It will disable anything electrical within a square kilometer or so. Then you can send in your troops and finish them off."

"But it won't destroy Reims?"

"Not if you position it far enough away. We need to find the right place to detonate it."

So, they had a Martian-killing Panzer, and Ludwig was finally ready to head home. But if they didn't act, Reims would be destroyed because of the attention Wegener had attracted to this area. Their only hope would destroy their most valuable weapon, and it was a single-use device.

Or they could flee. Head home and try to find a better place to face the Martians.

Emil looked up and found every eye in the compound on him. He didn't have to ask to know what they were thinking, and he agreed.

"We have less than a day to get a plan together, men. Let's get to work."

46

"The battery died!" James said with a big smile. "We have no power, so we can't do anything!"

Susan stared at him like he'd lost his mind.

"We can't go inside and turn off the transmitter, but *we can do the same thing to them*. We can kill their power." James held up one finger like a college professor making a point.

Susan looked up at the tower. "We can?"

"Sure. That's a New York Edison building. The power station is about four blocks east. We just need to go and convince them to shut it down."

New York Edison fell under the same umbrella as Edison Laboratories. There'd been talk of separating the companies, but Mr. Johnson had said that keeping it all together made dealing with the War Department easier for some reason. James chided himself for not thinking of doing this sooner, although getting a generator station to shut down wasn't as simple as asking a coworker for a favor.

Like many young boys, James had been fascinated with electricity. He'd also grown up with one of Edison's right-hand men as a surrogate father, so he'd seen maps of the New York City grid. Madison Square Park was a major landmark in this area, and its arc lamps had made the headlines when they'd been connected to a new Edison station that lit the entire neighborhood.

Where the stations were located wasn't a secret, but Edison didn't advertise it. The buildings didn't have signage and tended to have facades that made them look like nondescript brownstones or idle stores. In some neighborhoods, this was to preserve aesthetics. In others, it kept out the riffraff. Mr. Johnson had said the SPs were interested in protecting the stations, though James wasn't sure why anyone would try to sabotage lights and adding machines.

"How do you plan on getting inside to turn it off?" Susan asked.

James was an Edison employee and had his badge from the Princeton office with him. But Edison Electric was a different company. He might be able to bluff his way in—or he might grab a fire axe and threaten someone. He might even get arrested by the SPs at the power station instead of here. Would Fleming or his accomplices have been prescient enough to plant someone in an Edison generation station?

But running to the station and away from the shooting meant leading Susan away from danger. If the SPs caught them there, he'd tell them she hadn't known what she'd be getting into tonight.

"We need to go, James," Susan repeated.

But what would happen if the station stayed on the air, and Reynolds and his men went to prison—or were killed? James had come here because they'd planned to expose the conspiracy behind the fake broadcast. That hadn't changed.

He needed to cut their power.

"Tonight is our last chance, Susan. We go east and try to cut the power."

The shooting hadn't stopped, and a siren sounded from somewhere behind them.

Susan bit her lower lip. "You're right. We can't just go home. Let's go."

They took off at a trot, with James leading them east on 23rd Street. He wasn't a great runner, but the sounds of shooting continued and the thought of Captain Reynolds ending up like Christensen spurred him onward.

They turned left onto a deserted Park Avenue, and James led Susan on a diagonal directly to 24th Street. The power station was between 3rd and 2nd Avenues, so they had three more crosstown blocks to cover.

The first block was lined with pubs and restaurants. They probably made a good business feeding the Metropolitan Life Building employees. The newer, taller buildings created their own neighborhoods. Curfew or not, there wasn't much reason for these shops to be open on a weekend when the offices were closed.

Susan kept pace with James. She'd worn what she'd called "sensible shoes" on the way over the Hudson, and the run gave James an appreciation of what she'd meant.

The restaurants thinned out on the next block, giving way to tailors, dressmakers, and shoe stores. A dressmaker named Breitkopf had a new sign with gilt lettering, and the storefront next to it was under construction. The Tesla fire had reshaped most of Midtown; and this area was likely still in flux, even though it was more than a decade after the disaster.

James and Susan crossed Lexington Avenue. The storefronts gave way to apartment buildings and scattered garages. One more block.

James slowed as they crossed 3rd Avenue. If he remembered correctly, the station was about halfway down, on the north side of the street. He trotted to the middle of the block and found a storefront with darkened windows. Susan caught up with him as he tried the door. It was locked.

"Hello?" James shouted, pounding on the door.

Nothing.

He pounded harder, shouting louder. "Hello?"

Still nothing.

"FIRE!" Susan screamed, pushing past James and pounding on the door hard enough to rattle the blackened windows. "HELP! FIRE!"

Finally, the door opened.

"Fire? Where?" said a man wearing a gray uniform with the Edison Electric logo embroidered on his chest, his eyes wide. The deep thrum of the generators followed him through the door.

Of course. This man had been trained to react immediately to the possibility of fire. It was the most serious threat to any city, and always a risk with electricity.

"Over there!" James shouted, pointing at the Metropolitan Life Building. "There's a fire in the tower! You can see the sparks! Shut it down! Shut it down now!"

As if on cue, a pair of muzzle flashes sparked against the tower's backdrop.

The man spun around and ran back into the building.

"Mrs. Predrick always says the best thing a girl can do when she's in trouble is scream, 'Fire,'" Susan said, smiling.

A moment later, the hum of the generators slowed, and the tower went dark.

47

The view from the cathedral's top was spectacular. Emil could survey the entire city of Reims. The Vesle River ran to the south and east, with boats docked near the center and smaller homes on the far shore. Wegener's compound sat on the northern edge, with the closest buildings emptied in preparation for the explosion from Grundig's weapon.

Grundig's weapon was a small bomb fashioned from parts of a Martian power supply. According to him, a pair of French researchers had created controlled explosions using the material contained in the devices and had documented a "radioflash" that disabled electronics within a much wider range than the blast covered.

Emil brought the field glasses up to his eyes and peered out through the early morning light. No motion on Reims's eastern edge.

The soldiers hadn't had enough time to evacuate the city. It had been hit hard during the first Martian Attack, but Reims had rebounded to 90,000 inhabitants. With fifty men, it was nigh impossible to evacuate the area near the compound, let alone the whole city.

How many people would the Martians take this time? Would Grundig's weapon save them?

Emil moved to the cathedral's northeastern corner, taking a deep breath of cool air.

The explosion would level Wegener's compound, but buildings near the edge of Reims would be ruined, too. A necessary sacrifice so the electromagnetic effect from the blast would disable the Martian Wanderers throughout the city. Emil had struggled with that decision, but it came down to a few blocks of buildings or the fertile fields feeding the town.

The land to the west and south was dotted with farmers' fields and hedgerows that, even after dark, looked so much like Germany that they made Emil ache for home. The Panzer was working its way west, into the setting sun and out of range of the "radioflash" that would permanently disable it. The vehicle was piloted by Fluse and Grundig, with a complement of four men and all the electronics worth saving, including the Planetary Warning System radio.

The archbishop had balked at the idea of soldiers using the cathedral as a lookout. But after a patient translator helped Emil explain the stakes to him, he'd gone along with the idea of a few soldiers occupying the cathedral's two towers.

Emil suspected the Martians would attack from the east as soon as the glare from the morning sun would obscure their approach. Of course, he also assumed the Martians would anticipate resistance when they arrived in Reims.

He fingered the flare gun lying next to him on the floor. He or one of the other lookouts would fire the flare gun, but only when the attackers were within a kilometer of Grundig's weapon. One of Grundig's assistants was stationed in a basement with the trigger connected by a pair of redundant high-voltage cables. He would trigger the weapon when his lookout saw one of the red flares. Then, after the Wanderers collapsed, the men would approach and finish the occupants off.

Emil shivered as he thought about what they'd seen in the Wanderer yesterday.

They couldn't trigger the weapon until all of the Wanderers were in range, which meant they'd be in Reims wreaking havoc. Emil shivered again and checked the time. 17:15. Hours to go, and he was afraid he wouldn't be able to sleep.

"It's not time yet," Ludwig said, lighting his third cigar of the night.

"That doesn't mean you can't smoke those verdammt things in the other tower, where you belong," Emil said.

Ludwig smiled. "Miller can't stand them."

"Well, we can't subject him to the stench then, can we?"

"Of course not. You're the commanding officer, Emil. You make the sacrifice for your men."

Emil shot Ludwig a look that would have turned Perseus to stone.

"Speaking of command, Hauptmann Zimmerman, you think the Martians will attack from the east, yes?"

"Don't you?" Emil asked, raising an eyebrow. "It'll put the sun behind them."

"Oh, I agree. I also assume that's why you put yourself in this tower."

The Unteroffizier was a mind reader.

"You want to see the attack in case the one problem no one else thought of comes about," he continued, looking at the lit end of his cigar. He blew on it until it glowed like a hot coal.

"Problem?" Emil asked, bracing himself. Ludwig never missed a trick.

"Oh, come now, Emil. The Martians attack from the east. They stop to burn the houses on the other side of the Vesle before they cross. Then they work their way up to the cathedral." Ludwig paused to take a puff from the cigar.

Emil nodded as he thought about how they hadn't been able to evacuate the homes in Reims. They'd tried, and while a few residents had left, most had refused. Why should they accept the word of German soldiers while the French Army was fighting them on the other side of the country? Emil empathized, even as he agonized over what was about to happen.

"We'll detonate the weapon after all of them have crossed, but not before," Ludwig said. "We can't be sure that the 'radioflash' won't reach them all. We can't leave even one Wanderer standing."

"Yes, I'm aware of our plan," Emil said.

"But how will we know?"

"Know what?"

"When they've all crossed?" Ludwig outspread his hands to reinforce the question.

"We'll be watching."

"And they'll burn everything in sight. What happens if the smoke gets too thick?"

Verdammt mind reader.

"Someone will have to take a flare gun down to the river," Emil said, shrugging. The flare would be bright enough and reach high enough to be visible over the smoke.

"Someone."

"I'm the fastest runner we have," Emil said. It wasn't a lie.

"You were already planning on running down there." Ludwig shook his head and pointed the cigar at Emil. "You're the commanding officer."

"So I sit back while one of my men gets himself killed? Should I find a fancy uniform, too? Keep it clean for parades?" Ludwig expected Emil to act like a commanding officer, not the leader of a ragtag group trying to stop the Martians. Generalfeldmarschal Zimmerman! Would his statue be four meters tall? Or merely life-sized?

"That's not what I'm saying, Emil, and you know it," Ludwig said, fighting to keep his voice down. "Remember the day the Martians arrived? Back in Mametz?"

"How could I forget?" Emil replied. The only reason he and his platoon had gotten out was because they'd been in the command post. The image of Degenscheide being incinerated by a heat ray played in his mind for what must have been the thousandth time, each time clearer than the one before.

"Do you remember what was happening before they arrived?" Ludwig asked.

That had been two days after Fritz's death. Emil had attacked Fluse in the trench and tried to pick another fight with him the next day. Ludwig had stepped in and saved his life.

"Yes," Emil's face flushed, and he looked down. "I never thanked you for saving me from prison. Or worse."

"That's not why I'm bringing it up, but thank you for remembering." Ludwig smiled. "Tell me, how do you feel about that now? Not about how much of a brat you were, but about how you reacted to what happened to Seith."

Fritz had died because Fluse had sent the rest of the platoon early, before Fritz and Emil had cleared out the enemy gunners.

"Fluse got him killed," Emil said, sweating. This was not the time to be revisiting the past, not while they were still fighting for their lives.

"Did he?"

"He sent you in early, before we started taking out the gunners."

"Yes, that's true. Do you know why?"

"Because he couldn't wait. Because he wanted the credit for taking the trench. . . ." But who cared why? Fluse was the worst commanding officer they'd ever served with. He was so bad that Emil was in charge now. What was the point of this?

"No. That's not why. I'm not surprised he never told you, since you both were too busy acting like children, even when you were working together to steal that Panzer." Ludwig took a few puffs from his cigar, exhaling out a tower window.

"Well?" Emil asked.

"The Pioneers had arrived with their verdammt Smoke. Fluse saw them prepare it and sent us in to get us away from the deadly stuff. There wasn't any time to go over and ask them to move to a different location, and I doubt they would have listened."

Was this what Fluse had been referring to before the attack yesterday? And why he thought being a soldier was so easy for Emil? Because he could make the difficult decisions?

"So he made a bad decision because other commanders made worse ones? Wow. That's a great lesson about the military, Ludwig." A typical military mess, with one unit literally stepping on the other. Fluse had made a tough call he should never have had to make.

But this was different. Emil was the best man to run toward the Vesle if someone had to.

"You can take that lesson away from this, Emil. But you know better. 'The benefit of the many outweighs the benefit of the few' is one lesson. 'Don't jump to conclusions that might get you shot at dawn' is another."

Ludwig leaned against one of the tower's stone walls. His cigar smoke's musky perfume wafted over, evoking memories of home for Emil. His father had smoked cigars, often during a lecture over how Emil was wrong about the world.

Ludwig pushed himself off the wall and approached Emil, wielding his cigar like a bayonet on a rifle. "Fluse knew he was endangering you and Seith. But he had a whole company to worry about. He's a peacock. He's lazy. After he sent the men in, he hung back and hid from the Smoke. He's obsessed with the trappings of being an officer in the kaiser's army. He's also a child who led a company into combat because his commander was a reservist who couldn't."

"Degenscheide stepped up when it was time," Emil said.

"Yes, he did. But Fluse did the best he could with a no-win situation. What would you have done?"

Emil frowned and rocked back on his heels.

"I wasn't always supposed to be a military man, you know," Ludwig continued, taking another pull from his cigar, "I was in

Winden when the first attack came. There was a small theater school there, and my parents enrolled me in the program."

Emil looked at Ludwig and tried to picture a younger version of him on stage. He raised an eyebrow.

"Yes, theater. I wanted to be an actor and a singer. And a playwright. My father was a college professor in Berlin. My mother sang opera. I couldn't have strayed further from them when I became a career soldier." Ludwig took the cigar out of his mouth and spat out a piece of tobacco. "But while I was practicing my lines in Winden, a Martian spacecraft was flattening our home." His voice wavered a little.

"So I was sent to Euleheim to be raised by my mother's sister. She was too old to raise a young boy, especially a young boy with dreams of the theater. I never fit into your farming village, so I enlisted the day I finished school."

Emil didn't remember Ludwig back in Euleheim. The Unteroffizier was older than him, so they wouldn't have seen much of each other at school. He hadn't known Ludwig before he was drafted; and by then, the older man was all business. Being an outcast in Euleheim would have been tough. But to run away to the army? It must have been hell for Ludwig.

"You thought I was always destined to be a soldier, didn't you?" Ludwig asked, grinning. "Maybe I was born with a rifle in one hand and a cigar in the other?"

"Well, the thought did cross my mind," Emil said, chuckling.

"The Martians made a mess of all of our lives. I lost my family. You lost a sister. Fluse's father was killed leading a counterattack in Bayern."

Emil looked at Ludwig in shock.

"Yes. Fluse is a human being trying to live up to his father's sacrifice. Not a pleasant human being, but one of us nonetheless."

This is so easy for you, isn't it? Fluse had said. *You've got no fear.*

He'd lost a parent—a war hero—to the Martians, and Emil

had shown him up and treated him like an enemy. Emil grimaced.

"But you've managed to get past it, Emil. You stopped being angry at the world and yourself, and already made things better."

"Saving Reims will, too," Emil said. He was thinking about finishing the job. Why couldn't Ludwig see that?

"But you need to be here after Reims is safe for the next city. Maybe Karlsruhe? Paris? Stuttgart?"

Emil laughed. What was Ludwig talking about? "You want me to save the world?"

Ludwig wasn't smiling. "You liberated those men from Wegener. The men didn't follow me or Fluse. Many of them abandoned Wegener to fight for you. They'll follow you."

"It's not about me." Emil's chest constricted as he thought about the men looking up to him like Ludwig described. He didn't want that. He hadn't asked for it.

"You don't think it is, and that's what makes you a good leader. But they do. They need someone to follow. If you run down to the river and are killed, they'll lose that."

"I think you're overestimating my importance, Ludwig. They're fighting for their freedom. And their lives. Not for me. But fine. Who would go instead?"

"I'll pick some of the younger men and have them waiting at the foot of the tower. If we can't see what's happening, I'll give them my flare gun and send them down. . . ." Ludwig looked down at his cigar as his voice trailed off.

The cold settled into a weight in Emil's stomach. First Fritz, and now Ludwig? He'd started out wanting to hide from Ludwig and take the risk himself. Now the thought of Ludwig getting himself killed hurt.

"You were ready to sacrifice yourself, but you can't spare me?" Ludwig said.

"It's not the same."

"No, it isn't." Ludwig stepped forward and looked Emil in

the eye. He was serious. "You need someone you can trust to go to the river if need be. If you send someone who's too quick to send the signal, Reims will be destroyed with us inside it. If they wait too long, there will be no city to save."

Ludwig was right, of course.

"So maybe the best person is me. I just finished telling you how the army is all I have, Emil."

"But . . . I don't want to lose you," Emil said, surprising himself when he admitted it out loud.

"Ah, don't worry," Ludwig said. "My instinct for self-preservation was always better than yours."

Is this what being a leader felt like? Sacrificing your own safety was one thing, but sacrificing the safety of your soldiers was another. Now Emil had to send a man he cared for into danger, too. Was that a price every leader had to pay?

Who would lead them if Emil went and was killed? Beckenbauer might be up to it, but his first instinct was to find a leader, not lead. The men barely knew who Ludwig was. And Fluse? It would probably be Fluse—and who knew what he'd do with people like Miller and Grundig around to influence him.

"Okay," Emil said. "If someone needs to go, you can take the men. But only after we talk."

Ludwig nodded, and Emil turned to look out at the river again. If Ludwig stopped to find Emil, he could run to the river instead if it looked too dangerous. Emil would be in the tower. He'd know if the smoke got too thick, and he could beat Ludwig down the stairs.

48

The tables near the front of 'Wicks had a nice view. The pharmacy across Main Street was accepting a delivery, while a squad of high school kids were laughing and tossing a football back and forth as they strode past the restaurant. Down the block, a police officer was helping an elderly lady carry her groceries. It was a bright, sunny morning in West Orange.

"Good morning, Mr. Brogan," Penny asked. "What can I get you?"

"Good morning!" James replied. "I'd like just a cup of coffee, thanks."

The police officer. The pharmacist. The football players. They had no idea how close they'd come to disaster last night. Or how close they still were.

As soon as the lights in the Metropolitan Life Building had flickered out, James and Susan had fled the city. Leaving Captain Reynolds and his marines behind had been hard, but James wasn't willing to leave Susan alone, much less take her closer to danger.

They'd been walking toward the Hudson when a taxi stopped them and offered them a ride to the Hudson Terminal. It turned out the SPs were allowing outbound trains to New Jersey. They were home in a few hours.

Urich opened the restaurant door and flashed a broad grin. "James! And sitting right by the window! I guess the rumors are true, and I'll be sharing breakfast with the new head of Edison's radio team."

"Acting head," James said.

"Well, with Fleming in the wind and Ben Johnson . . . uh, still missing, who else can they appoint?" Urich took a seat across from James. "Especially when they've got a bona fide hero in their midst."

"You know what happened?" James asked.

He'd tossed and turned for the remainder of last night, consumed with fear over the fate of Captain Reynolds and whether the power had stayed off long enough for Sayville to regain contact with London or Germany.

Then Reynolds had arrived at James's door.

The mission had been a success, Reynolds told him. The marines had encountered armed guards on the floor immediately below the tower, where the rogue radio station had been located. They were still holding their own when the power had gone out and managed to overcome the guards shortly afterward.

But the bigger news was what had happened in Sayville. As soon as the rogue transmission ceased, they'd made contact with Planetary Warning. The Captain couldn't say anything more than the scheme had worked and the conspiracy had been revealed.

And the newspapers? They had a brief story the next morning about a fire at the Metropolitan Life Building.

"The usual, Mr. Urich?" Penny asked.

"Of course." Urich waited for Penny to step away before answering James. "Like I said, I have rumors. Did you really cut the power to an entire neighborhood?"

James gaped. The SPs had been waiting for James and Susan

at the office the next day, along with Senator Mather and Mr. Edison himself. After James was appointed acting head of the radio team, they'd all made it clear that what had happened in New York was classified and couldn't be discussed with anyone.

"Not even your darling mother," Mr. Edison had said.

"It's okay," Urich said now, with a faint smile. "You don't have to answer. I know what would happen to both of us if I tried to publish a story about it."

Fleming was long gone by then, either on a boat to Europe or looking for a place to hide in Central America. Mr. Johnson was presumed dead; he'd never made it to Washington after leaving the office the day after Coney Island.

James let out a long sigh of relief. Urich had requested to meet, and James thought he owed him at least that much, since it was Urich who had helped him connect with Captain Reynolds. But he didn't want to spend breakfast walking on eggshells.

"So what do you know about what's happening in Europe?" Urich asked after Penny brought him his breakfast and mandatory ketchup.

"Nothing yet," James said. "But I'm headed to Sayville tomorrow. I should learn something then. I doubt I'll be able to share it, though."

"I'm sure you've heard the rumors about the Martians being back?"

James scoffed. "They've been floating around for months. That's the kind of stuff the . . ."

"The *Spectator* would print?" Urich finished.

"Well, I didn't mean . . ."

"Careful, you're going to spill your coffee," Urich said before chuckling. "It's fine. I'm used to it."

"But the Martians died," James said. "They can't survive here. And if they were back, where are they?"

"Let's say they figured out how to survive our germs. Maybe the Martians didn't all come at once, and they warned the ones who stayed behind. How would they attack? Would they try to take the whole planet at once again? Do they need to?"

James tilted his head.

"What if the Martians wanted to take their time? And what if they wanted to take advantage of the confusion those anarchists created in Europe? Hell, what if the anarchists helped them?" Urich pointed a ketchup-coated fork at James.

"Helped?" James whispered. "They'd have to have sympathizers working with them!"

"And they'd need them to keep their return a secret over here, too."

James gaped again. "Are you saying Colonel Fleming . . . That's absurd!"

"Is it?" Urich asked.

49

Light broke over the river, casting a soft orange glow through the trees and tiny homes on the other side of the shore. Reims was quiet; and for a moment, it could have been a normal morning in a normal city on a normal planet.

Of course, normal or otherwise, Emil didn't belong in a city. Once upon a time, he'd dreamed of being a radio engineer in Aachen or Berlin, but he'd learned his lesson. He'd go back to the farm as soon as he had the chance, assuming he'd survive long enough to make the trip. If the smoke got too thick, he might have to run toward the attacking Martians instead of waiting up here in the cathedral.

Something moved in the distance. Emil's pulse quickened, and his mouth went dry.

"Schmidt, to the east," he said without lowering the field glasses.

Schmidt came over to the window on Emil's side of the tower.

"Wanderers," Emil said. "Four."

Four long shadows darkened the homes across the river. Emil counted spindly tentacles, legs, and water-tank-shaped bodies.

"Five," he corrected himself.

One howled as if in response. The faint, faraway hum of a heat ray reached the tower, and a home burst into flames. Emil swallowed, keeping his eyes on the near side of the river, and fingered the flare gun. Two of the alien craft crossed the water, revealing themselves in the ambient light of the main city. They strode across a barge and a few small boats as if they were a bridge.

Smoke rose, and Emil's greatest fear materialized. He squinted. Three more Martians were still on the far shore.

More buildings started to burn, creating more smoke to block his view.

"Six," Schmidt said.

"Six?" Emil asked.

"Yes. At least three are hanging back."

Grundig's weapon wouldn't reach them. If the soldiers left one Wanderer standing, it could kill thousands. Would some of them hang back and wait until all the homes on that side of the Vesle burned?

How long should Emil wait?

"We're not doing any good up here," he said.

Schmidt tilted his head.

"I need to head to the water and watch for when they cross there," Emil said.

"But Oberacker said—"

Emil hit the ladder before Schmidt could finish. He was the fastest runner, and that was all there was to it. He would go, not Ludwig.

He hit the bottom of the ladder and dashed to the stairs that would take him to the exit. Motion down on the street caught his eye as he angled his way across an exterior walkway.

Ludwig was setting off with three men. No! He couldn't go!

"Ludwig!" Emil shouted, his dry throat threatening to pinch closed in protest.

Ludwig said something to his men, then broke into a jog.

Emil hit the stairs, taking them two at a time, then three. Nothing else existed. Only the stairs stood in his way.

The streets around the cathedral were deserted when Emil arrived outside. His heart pounded in his chest.

Ludwig and his men were gone.

Emil could outrun them. He'd blow right past them, and they'd stop. There'd be no point in them continuing. He caught his breath and leaned into a sprinting stance.

"Hauptmann Zimmerman," said a heavily accented voice behind him.

Emil turned to face the archbishop of Reims.

"Excuse me, Your Grace. I need to—"

"You . . . go to . . . fight them?" The archbishop struggled with the German words, switching between French and Latin accents.

Emil exhaled, torn between a sense of urgency and an inability to explain why he was running toward the attack. Why was putting himself in danger alongside Ludwig better than just Ludwig?

"No, I . . ."

"You run away?" the archbishop asked. There was no surprise or anger in his tone or expression. He looked as if he was asking Emil whether he wanted cream in his coffee or butter to put on a dinner roll.

The question struck Emil, though. Was trying to beat Ludwig to the river running away? Was getting killed by the Martians better than seeing this defense all the way through? Who would take over if he died? Would Fluse lead the soldiers to their deaths? Or into the arms of another Wegener? Was Ritter looking to take the general's place? Would either of them continue to fight the Martians? Or just play power games?

"No," Emil said. "I'm not running away."

The army is all I have, Emil.

Ludwig had been right. Emil was the commander of this

operation. He needed to stay here, wait for the flare, and see this defense through.

"I'm staying here, Your Grace. We can watch for the flare."

The archbishop smiled and nodded.

Gradually, Emil became conscious of what was going on around him. Wanderers were visible to the south. They were firing on Reims but hadn't made their way to the cathedral yet.

Schmidt had arrived with a few more men behind him. "Ludwig went to the river to see?" he asked. "They'll fire the flare?"

"Yeah, he went," Emil said as the rest of the soldiers lined up. "We need to wait."

Five minutes passed. Where were Ludwig and his men? Had they made it to the river?

Ten minutes passed. Schmidt was holding a flare gun by then. He raised the barrel and made eye contact with Emil, but Emil shook his head. They had to wait.

A heat ray shot overhead, narrowly missing the cathedral.

Emil needed to move the soldiers. But before he could say a word, a flare arced into the air. His men cheered.

And then came the explosion.

The report from the weapon was overwhelming. Emil's ears throbbed, and he dropped to one knee for the longest second in his life. Was this what being struck by lightning sounded like? It shattered windows as it reverberated through Reims and in his mind. Would it leave the city standing? Would it work?

As Emil stepped forward to regain his balance, a creaking, rattling sound echoed off the vast cathedral facade. A Wanderer pitched to one side, then the other. It fell out of sight and landed with a crash, followed by two more. The sound of each impact ran together in one giant clattering mess.

Grundig's weapon had worked. Silence fell over the city, then cheers rose from every corner.

Emil and Schmidt embraced as they shouted. It was a

moment of victory against the invaders. Against impossible odds. Humans had defeated Martians. Soldiers were jumping into the air, clapping backs, shaking hands, and dancing with sheer joy.

Humans had prevailed over individual Wanderers before, but this was the first victory they'd ever had over the Martians. Nature, Earth herself, had ended the first attack. Humanity had had nothing to do with it. But now they had a weapon—a way to fight back—and it had been fashioned from one of the invader's weapons.

Civilians rushed into the crowd of soldiers and joined in the celebration. A group of Emil's men approached and took turns hugging him, shouting their congratulations. Beckenbauer approached, and Emil extended his arms to embrace him.

"Where's Ludwig?" Beckenbauer shouted.

Emil turned and looked toward the street. Ludwig was nowhere in sight. Was he still at the river? Had he started checking on the Wanderers to ensure the Martians were dead?

Emil raised his arms and shouted for attention. After a moment, the soldiers quieted down.

"Let's go," he bellowed to the group. "Let's make sure the bastards are dead. There were at least six of them. Groups of five men. Head out, find one Wanderer, and make sure whatever was in it is finished! Schmidt, Beckenbauer, with me. Let's find Ludwig."

Emil took off at a full run down the street Ludwig had taken earlier. Beckenbauer nearly kept up with him, but Schmidt fell behind within a couple of blocks.

Burning buildings lined Emil's path. Homes. Bakeries. Butchers. Bookstores. Not everyone had run to the cathedral to celebrate. Some residents were still emerging from wherever they'd hidden, carrying buckets of water or sand to fight the fires. Even with his focus on finding Ludwig, Emil ached for them. They were fighting to save their homes and livelihoods.

Ludwig should have been on his way back to the cathedral

by now. Where had he gone? Emil was sweating through his uniform despite the cool morning air.

He reached the river within moments, stopping to catch his breath before scanning the area for signs of soldiers. An inferno burned across the Vesle, making visibility poor.

Where was Ludwig?

Beckenbauer arrived, with Schmidt lagging about half a block behind.

Emil walked along the narrow road alongside the river. Fishing huts and boat launches were on his left, and wood-frame shops and homes burned on his right as residents tried to fight the fires or simply stood there in shock. Maybe Ludwig and his men were helping them?

"Here!" a woman called from an alley. A man in uniform was leaning on her shoulder. It was one of the soldiers who'd left with Ludwig. He'd been one of Wegener's followers but defected to Emil's side before the mutiny.

"Hauptmann Zimmerman," the soldier said.

"It's fine. Let's find a place for you to sit." Emil led him to a pile of crates near the alley opening. Burns spotted one side of the man's face, and his uniform was torn. In his right hand, he held a recently fired flare gun.

Emil took a deep breath, fighting the urge to interrogate him.

"I couldn't help them," the soldier muttered.

Emil's stomach churned. "What happened?"

"We got to the river, and three Wanderers were still there." The soldier pointed the flare gun across the Vesle. "We waited to see what they would do in the cover of an alley near the street. Then we heard screaming. A woman and her children in trouble." He started to cry.

"He ran over to there to help," the soldier went on, pointing again.

There was no house. Only a pile of ash.

50

The pushcarts of East New York were out in full force. The Ford had to stop a few times, but it gradually worked its way past the waterworks and made the turn into Queens. The ride was as silent as it had been when Christensen had driven it down the same road, but for different reasons.

"We're almost there, sir," the driver said. It was the longest sentence he'd spoken since picking James up at Edison earlier. They'd made the drive to the military terminal in Jersey City in total silence. The man was, in every way, the opposite of Christensen.

James's first act as the head of the radio team had been to ask Susan to return to work. He was going to need some time to get used to the idea of taking over, and he still hoped Mr. Johnson would resurface. But it was hard to believe he was still in hiding after days of turmoil and protests.

"Here we are, sir," the driver said as the Ford angled its way past the guard post and next to the building.

It'd only been a couple of weeks since James had been here last. The fence and guard station still made the place foreign, and

James couldn't help but notice there were even more marines milling about the place.

James pulled open the steel door, entered the station, and was greeted by the sight of Senator Mather, a pair of generals in full uniform, and Captain Reynolds.

"Mr. Brogan!" the senator said, offering his hand. "Good to see you again. Thanks for coming out."

James took it. Senator Mather had been Mr. Johnson's closest friend. They'd survived the Martian Attack together, and the senator took pains to mention that Mr. Johnson had saved his life whenever the subject came up. But he'd been pessimistic about Mr. Johnson's fate when James had spoken with him a few days ago.

"I still don't like the idea of bringing this . . . boy . . . into this, Senator," said one of the generals. He wore an army uniform festooned with enough medals that it was a miracle he could stand erect.

"Ben Johnson is missing, General, and no one misses him more than I do. But Edison said Brogan is our man," the senator said. "After what he and Captain Reynolds did for us, I agree."

He turned to James. "Mr. Brogan, what we're about to tell you can't leave this room. You've already signed a security release because of your work for the War Department. This conversation is covered under the same agreements, but it's the kind of briefing that used to be reserved for Ben Johnson."

James started to sweat. He reached for a nearby chair and then realized everyone else was standing.

"Yes, sir—er, Senator," he choked out.

"Captain Reynolds told you we've restored communications with Planetary, but he couldn't tell you more," the senator said.

James nodded.

"Well, there's good reason for that. As soon we were back on the air, we learned that the Martians have returned."

Even though Urich had warned him, the shock took James's

balance. He steered himself to the chair. "It's true," he whispered.

"Excuse me, son?" the general asked.

"I said I can't believe that's true."

"You think we're joking?" the general thundered.

"Yes, they're back," the senator said, holding up a hand to calm the general. "They showed up on the battlefields in Belgium and France, as well as inside Germany. We suspect they've moved on Russia, too."

James sat back in the chair and looked at the ceiling, trying to collect his thoughts. Martians. He'd been young when they'd attacked the first time, and the aliens hadn't made it into the city before succumbing—or at least appearing to succumb—to Earth's microbes.

But they were back. He'd been worried about the Germans, but things were worse. So much worse. And there was nowhere to run.

"Are they coming here?" James asked.

The general snorted. "They haven't exactly shared their plans with us."

The senator shot him a look.

"Well, that's where things get interesting, Brogan," said Captain Reynolds. "I know this is going to be hard to believe, but it appears that Colonel Fleming was involved in a conspiracy to help them."

"We don't know that for sure!" snapped the general.

"What more evidence do you want, Ross?" said the other general, speaking for the first time. He wore a dark brown marine uniform, decorated with fewer medals, which had the paradoxical effect of making him look more serious than his army counterpart. "The colonel was involved in an effort—a successful one, unfortunately—to get us to send troops out of the country and weaken our defenses."

So James and Susan had been right about what the

conspiracy was trying to do, but they'd been horribly wrong about why.

"We've sent word for the troops to come back, and the country owes you, Captain Reynolds, and his men our sincere thanks," the senator said. "Now, we need your help with something else."

What more could James do? Even though he was still seated, he reached out and put one hand on the nearby desk for balance.

"One of the nodes on Planetary Warning reached out to us," the senator continued. "It's currently occupied by a German military unit."

"I've already shared my misgivings about this!" General Ross said.

"They claim to have defeated six Martian Tripods with something called a radioflash, and are willing to send us plans. We need you to build a prototype."

All eyes fell on James.

51

"**B**eautiful morning, isn't it?" Beckenbauer said.

It was unseasonably warm. A field with freshly turned soil, worked by a farmer who was getting an early start, sat to the road's right side. Even with all the death and destruction surrounding Emil and his men, life went on.

"The weather will turn soon," Beckenbauer said, as if reading Emil's mind. "It's a beautiful Sunday."

"Sunday?" Emil asked. "I lost track. I guess there'll be a service at the cathedral in Reims today."

"Yes, because of you."

Emil winced. "Because of us. All of us." And because of Ludwig.

He climbed onto the lead cart. He and his soldiers were making good time and just might have a chance at saving Paris from the attack Wegener had thought he'd take part in. Either way, they were fighting back against the Martians. Finally, they were fighting the real enemy, instead of one another.

The soldiers had taken down the tents and were piling canvas bags and wooden crates onto fourteen more carts like the one Emil had just climbed onto. The horses were hitched, and the men were finding spots for themselves. It was time to get back on the road.

The carnage in Reims had been horrifying. Entire neighborhoods had burned to the ground or been flattened. Countless hundreds had been killed. But the damage had been confined to the area around the Vesle and only as far as a heat ray could reach from there. It could have been much worse if not for Ludwig's heroics and Grundig's weapon.

The thankful townspeople had supplied Emil and the other surviving soldiers with fifteen carts, thirty horses, and more than enough provisions. Five men from Reims had joined their cause, and more would have if Beckenbauer hadn't pointed out they'd already reached the breaking point carrying food and medical supplies.

That had been two days ago. They'd reach Paris in two more.

Emil squinted. He could just make out the heat ray armature where the Panzer sat behind the last cart. He'd worried about bringing the vehicle with them, since it needed refueling every few hours, but Grundig was taking care of that. Grundig took care of a lot of things, and Emil now saw why Wegener had tolerated the bizarre scientist and his unsteady loyalties.

Somehow, in the five days the soldiers spent preparing for their trip to Paris, Grundig had converted the Panzer to an electric motor from one of the pump stations near the Vesle. Then he'd outfitted five of the carts with heat rays of their own.

It had also been Grundig's idea to paint the top of the Panzer with mottled earth tones to make it harder for Wanderers to target it. But the front of the vehicle was decorated with a caricature of a man chewing on a cigar and the name of their international Martian-killing force.

Ludwig's Marauders.

Beckenbauer had recommended bringing the Planetary Warning System back online. Since then, they'd spoken to people in Germany, England, and the United States about sharing plans for Grundig's radioflash. As soon as they arrived in Paris, they'd transmit those plans via Planetary Warning's drafting servos.

The fight was far from over. They had a way to defeat the attackers, and Emil would make sure Ludwig's sacrifice was the beginning of something. Now it was time to take the battle to the Martians.

Emil stood and gave the hand signal to start. Beckenbauer smiled and hied the horses, forcing Emil to shift his weight to keep from falling back into the cart. The convoy started east, with a cheer rising behind Emil as he turned and sat.

They'd found Ludwig in the ashes of the burnt building, and the archbishop had arranged a service and burial without once asking if he'd been Katholisch or Evangelisch. Hundreds of residents—many times more than the few people who could have known or even seen Ludwig before the attack—had attended.

And, it seemed, every one of them had thanked Emil for saving Reims. He was tired of hearing it, and more tired of explaining that he couldn't have done it alone.

But they'd never stopped thanking him.

"He'd be proud, you know," Beckenbauer said. He didn't have to clarify who he meant.

Emil grunted, and was silent for the rest of the day.

"It's late," Beckenbauer said when the sun was low in the sky. "We should find somewhere to stay near this village." The convoy would have already stopped before then, but Emil preferred being near a village for easier access to water—and, if they were lucky, bath facilities.

"Yeah, you're—"

The howl of a Wanderer interrupted Emil. His throat went dry as he scanned the horizon. The Wanderer's outline protruded from near the steeple of the village church. The convoy stopped without needing a signal, but Emil stood and raised his left hand anyway.

This was it. Their first encounter. But it was late in the day, and everyone was tired and hungry. How many times had Emil been sent into battle while damning his officers for picking a lousy time?

No time for that. The enemy was right there, menacing another village.

Emil jumped off the cart and walked to meet Schmidt and another handful of soldiers.

"Should I call up the Panzer?" Schmidt asked, his expression twisted in a way that indicated he thought the answer was no.

The Wanderer was far enough away, and the setting sun was helping to keep the convoy out of sight. But sending the Panzer in would cause a stir, even with the quieter electric motor.

"No," Emil said. "We need scouts to run in and see where the Wanderer is standing. If it's on the other side of the village, we can try to race over there to take it out. If it's in the village, we may be able to lure it out—or at least figure out how to down it without burning their homes down."

"Are you sure?" Beckenbauer asked.

Wonderful. First mission, and Emil had to make all the decisions on his own. He hadn't missed Ludwig this dearly since the night he was lost.

"No. That might alert it to us, too." Emil stroked his chin. "Two scouts. Our fastest men. What I'd give for portable heat rays and radios."

"I'm working on it," Grundig said from the back of the group. "As soon as I can figure out how to make a smaller power supply without replicating Tesla's results in New York City," he added with a dry chuckle.

That didn't help.

Two young soldiers headed into the village. One of them, the boy carrying a flare gun, could have been the younger brother of the boy Emil had seen in the gunner's nest the day before the madness had started. The day Fritz had been killed by his own army.

"Get these carts spread out so the Martians will have to work a little to destroy the entire convoy and get our heat rays ready to fire," Emil said.

Then the waiting began. Five minutes turned into ten.

The Wanderer remained still. Then, a howl sounded.

Emil's stomach knotted.

Another Wanderer rose into the sky. This one was to the south, but it was closer, looming over the village. Where had it come from? Sweat trickled down Emil's brow, and he wiped it with the back of his hand. He heard someone exhale behind him and turned. Beckenbauer and Schmidt were staring straight ahead at the village. Fluse was walking up behind them. They all knew that two Wanderers would make this defense more complicated.

How were they moving around while staying out of sight? That would be another problem to deal with after Emil saved this village.

Another Wanderer rose into view. This village was doomed if Emil and his men didn't do something.

"We need to attack," Fluse said, shouting into Emil's ear from behind. "Now."

"If we open fire, that Wanderer"—Emil pointed toward the one still in the forest—"will realize we're here, open fire, and burn the village and our scouts. And if you keep screaming, he will before we turn our ray on."

"But if we don't act now, the village is doomed," Fluse said at a normal volume. "We can hit all three from here, and the tank can be there in minutes."

"But—"

"I know what you're struggling with Zimmerman," Fluse said, lowering his voice so no one else would hear. "But you know what you need to do."

Send his men out before his scouts were safe. Of course, Fluse knew what this was. For the second time in a few minutes, Emil was back in the trenches, scouting ahead of his unit and watching Fritz die.

Two scouts. An entire village. Was there a choice?

Emil's chest tightened. He wished again that Ludwig was there so he'd have someone other than Fluse to tell him it was the right choice.

"Call up the tank," Emil shouted to Schmidt. He nodded to Fluse, then turned to the carts. "As soon as the Panzer is past us, draw the Wanderer's fire," he said to the soldiers manning the heat rays. He stepped aside as the tank rumbled by, tilted to one side as it straddled the road and a shallow ravine on the far edge.

The Panzer reached the first cart, angled into the road, and accelerated, thundering toward the village at least twice as fast as it had moved when Emil had driven it.

As soon as the tank lumbered past the village border, its heat ray spoke. The Panzer now had two power cells for the drive and one for the heat ray. It was faster and deadlier than before, and Emil's only regret was that he'd let the other two be destroyed when Grundig's weapon had detonated. Maybe they could find another Panzer shell to retrofit before they reached Paris.

One heat ray targeted the furthest Wanderer. The cart behind Emil fired and aimed at the next one, while the Panzer focused on the closest. The battle was on.

The fight was mercifully short. All three Wanderers were down moments later, as if they were surprised to meet any resistance at all, let alone resistance that would hurt them.

"Send some men into the village with me, but stay back here in case there are any surprises," Emil said, looking at Schmidt and Beckenbauer. The Wanderer popping onto the horizon so quickly earlier had made him nervous.

Emil reached the village's main street in a few moments. Grundig and his men were already out of the Panzer and looking over one of the Wanderers, hoping to salvage another power supply.

"Have you seen the scouts?" Emil shouted.

Grundig shook his head and went back to giving orders.

Emil led his men in the direction of smoke rising from the far edge of the village. He found the younger scout helping a family lead their animals out of a burning barn.

The scout shook his head before Emil could ask about his comrade.

"You had no way of knowing," Beckenbauer said later, over dinner.

That didn't matter. Emil had sent the boy to his death. How could he continue? How could he lead a resistance if he lost men in every battle?

"Where would they be if you weren't here?" Beckenbauer asked.

"Huh?"

"If you weren't here. If you'd died in the trenches. Or never left Euleheim. Where would they be?"

"I—"

"Dead. Dead in the trenches. Dead in Wegener's compound. Dead in Reims." Beckenbauer set his jaw. "You gave them a chance, Emil. Without you, none of us would be here, facing the aliens."

Emil looked back at the convoy.

They had to continue. They had a war to win.

———

THE GREAT WAR OF THE WORLDS CONTINUES IN CLOUDS IN THE FUTURE!

What happened to the Marauders when they got to Paris? Where is Hauptmann Ritter? Get the new book in the series here.

And what's going on in New York? *Murder in Soft Words* will answer all your questions in October 2025! You'll learn what James is up to, why Susan isn't very happy with him, and what really happened to Fleming!

Pre-order *Murder in Soft Words* today so you get it the day it's published!

ABOUT THE AUTHOR

I'm Eric Goebelbecker. I write stuff.

I'm the author of *Shadows of the Past* and *Clouds in the Future* the first two books in an ongoing series about the aftermath of the Martin invasion in the War of the Worlds. The next book, *Murder in Soft Words*, is available for pre-order and will arrive in October 2025.

I was lucky enough to inherit an incurable curiosity about technology and a tremendous love of science fiction from his father. Both led to a career repairing radars in the U.S. Army, followed by another as a programmer on Wall Street. Now, I write about technology and train dogs, as well as work on my sci-fi and fantasy stories.

If you're not already a subscriber, you can find my email list here, get a free short story about Ben Johnson and James Brogan's father, and get the latest news on my next book and short stories.

Find me at my newsletter, on my website, and on the social links below.

And please consider leaving a review!

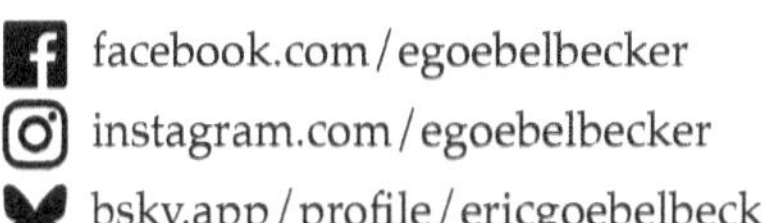

facebook.com/egoebelbecker

instagram.com/egoebelbecker

bsky.app/profile/ericgoebelbecker.com